RED
RABBIT

RED RABBIT

ALEX GRECIAN

NIGHTFIRE

TOR PUBLISHING GROUP
NEW YORK

For Christy

RED RABBIT

Copyright © 2023 by Alex Grecian

All rights reserved.

A Nightfire Book
Published by Tom Doherty Associates / Tor Publishing Group
120 Broadway
New York, NY 10271

www.tornightfire.com

Nightfire™ is a trademark of Macmillan Publishing Group, LLC.

The Library of Congress Cataloging-in-Publication Data is available upon request.

ISBN 978-1-250-87468-9 (hardcover)
ISBN 978-1-250-32372-9 (international, sold outside the U.S., subject to rights availability)
ISBN 978-1-250-87470-2 (ebook)

Our books may be purchased in bulk for promotional, educational, or business use. Please contact your local bookseller or the Macmillan Corporate and Premium Sales Department at 1-800-221-7945, extension 5442, or by email at MacmillanSpecialMarkets@macmillan.com.

First Edition: 2023

Printed in the United States of America

0 9 8 7 6 5 4 3 2 1

In this round world of many circles within circles, do we make a weary journey from the high grade to the low, to find at last that they lie close together, that the two extremes touch, and that our journey's end is but our starting-place?

—Charles Dickens, *Dombey and Son* (1848)

And so, with my inheritance in my purse and my uncle's parting words in my heart, I set out to hunt these fearsome creatures that walk the Earth as if they were men. The witch, the ghoul, the invisible devil. I knew not where my journey would take me, but I knew I must find their dwelling places and cast them out or else I would die in the effort.

—Ubel H. H. F. Crane,
The Call of the Nightfall King (1861)

They buried the girl next to her mother on the first warm day of spring.

The trapper, Cullen Stull, had come by the previous evening and volunteered to help. He spent the night in an old rocking chair by the hearth, and was already marking out a rectangular site in the yard when Andrew King stumbled out of the little house the next morning, pulling suspenders up over his narrow shoulders, the effects of drink still visible under his eyes. Cullen finished clearing the area of stones and Andrew handed him a hoe.

"It sure is a pretty day, though," Cullen said. "Listen to them birds chirp."

Andrew said nothing. He jabbed the tip of his shovel into the dirt and turned it, dislodging a clump of brown prairie grass.

"Yeah, sure is nice out here," Cullen agreed with himself. "And a good thing, since it looks like we'll be all day at this."

It had been a harsh winter, and the earth resisted their hoe and shovel, but they were determined to get the girl in the ground before nightfall. They worked silently for an hour, and had dug a shallow trench five feet long by four feet wide, when Andrew stopped and used his shirtsleeve to mop his forehead. He got Cullen's attention and pointed out a horse in the distance. They leaned on their tools and watched as the horse drew near, a gray roan with a black nose and a cropped tail. Cullen recognized the rider as Duff Duncan, a young hand from the Paradise Ranch.

When he reached them, Duff dismounted and tied the roan to a scrubby bush ten yards away. There was a wooden cross marking a fresh mound of dirt a few feet from where Andrew and Cullen were digging. Duff took off his hat and nodded toward the cross, paying his respects to Andrew's wife, Mary, who had passed away before the first real snowstorm of the winter. He put his hat back on and circled the grave. When he held out his hand, Andrew gave him a shovel.

With three of them the work went quickly, and by early afternoon they had dug down six feet. They stopped and Andrew brought a bucket of water from the house, along with some biscuits left over from the day before. They sat with their feet dangling in the hole, and ate. Andrew passed around a bottle of corn liquor and each of them took a pull or two.

When they had rested they went to the barn and carried Olivia's box to the grave site. None of them cared to view the body. Cullen had not been there for her last days, but he had heard rumors back in Riddle. Rumors about how Olivia's bones had broken and reknit themselves in bizarre configurations, how her flesh had run in rivulets across her wasted muscles, then solidified again in peaks and troughs, scales and horns. He hoped her face had resumed its human features in death. At least, he preferred to imagine that.

Andrew drove in the final few nails and they looped a rope around the box, lifted it over the hole, and lowered it in.

Andrew was not able to speak, and Duff pulled his hat down over his face, so it fell to Cullen to perform some sort of ritual. He had never learned to read, but he had attended many funerals and he had heard women speak from their good book. He did his best to remember their words.

"Earth to earth," he said, "and dust to dust. Lord, we commend this little girl to you and ask that you take her into your bosom and soothe her innocent spirit, set her to dancing in the fields of your bounteous afterlife, and reunite her with her sainted mother, Mary. And we also ask you to keep her there, nevermore to do herself or us no harm. It ain't ours to question your mysterious ways, nor why you took her the way you done, nor why you let bad things happen. But now we thank you for releasing Olivia from her pain and suffering, and we pray it was for the betterment of us all. Amen."

He shot the others a bashful glance and was pleased to see Andrew nod.

They passed the corn liquor around again and filled the grave. When they had finished, Andrew set up a wooden cross identical to the one he had fashioned for Mary's grave. He held it in place while Duff smacked it with the head of a shovel, driving it into the ground. They tramped over the site, packing down the earth, then the other two men followed Andrew up to the house. They sat on the porch and watched the sun move lower in the sky, and finished off the liquor.

"I ought to move along," Cullen said when he saw the bottle was empty.

"Ain't a good idea to travel alone after dark," Andrew said. "You could sleep in that chair again tonight."

"Well, I'd be grateful. That chair's a sight better'n a blanket under a tree."

Andrew nodded again and the matter was settled.

Duff looked away across the yard toward the new grave. "She woulda been old enough to marry in another month," he said. "She told me last fall at the dance she'd choose me when the time come."

"Way you was sniffing around here," Andrew said, "I figured you two, and maybe her mother, was up to something along those lines."

"Well, I loved her, Andy."

"I loved her, too," Andrew said. "She was always a good girl."

"She ruined everything."

For a confused moment Cullen thought he was still talking about poor Olivia, but then Duff went on.

"Sadie Grace did this," he said. "You know damn well she did this." He waved his hand at the horizon to show he was talking about more than Olivia's death. The others looked out at the stunted cornstalks that hadn't come up the previous spring, at the dead trees that marked the property line between Andrew's farm and the Paradise Ranch, at the two fresh graves.

Andrew shook his head and Cullen stood up and walked off from the porch a little ways. It was bad luck to mention Sadie's name. He stuck a hand in his pocket and touched the seven copper coins he kept there. Seven was a magic number and a good ward against witches.

"I know we ain't supposed to say it out loud," Duff said, "but we're all thinking it, and I just don't care anymore."

Andrew rose to his feet with a grunt and went inside the little house. He came back out with another bottle of corn liquor, and unstoppered it. He handed it to Duff, who took a long pull. Cullen ambled back toward the porch, his eye on the bottle.

"Ought to watch your tongue," Andrew said. "I guess I'm to blame. I got that witch riled at me and this was the price I paid."

"Hell of a price."

"I was too damn proud. If I'd given her some respect, that corn woulda come up and you mighta got the chance to marry my girl after all."

"Well, I'm gonna get her for this," Duff said. "I'm gonna kill her, Andy. I'll do it for Olivia, and for your Mary, too."

Cullen angled back away from the porch and walked farther out into the yard, putting some distance between himself and Duff, just in case. In town, they claimed Sadie Grace could hear her name spoken, even from a hundred miles away. It was also said that she'd lived in the same cabin outside Riddle for as long as there had been white people in Kansas. That she wouldn't ever die and she couldn't be killed.

Andrew nodded, and he kept on nodding, like he was thinking about something he found agreeable, but was maybe arguing with himself about it anyway. After a while, he stopped nodding and took the bottle away from Duff.

"I think she went too far this time," he said. "She went way too far, and it would be good if she was to bear some responsibility for this. She's got a little piece of herself in everything around here. Little hooks in me, in you, in the land. It's how she got inside Mary and little Olivia so easy." He closed his eyes and raised the bottle to his lips, but lowered it without taking a drink. "But Duff, there's not a damn thing you or me could do to her. Not on our own."

"But we—"

"We'd need some help," Andrew said.

"You been thinking on this already, haven't you? You talking about a bounty?"

"Cost us some money, I guess. Enough to tempt folks who ain't from here and got no ties to the land, no way for her to hook into them."

Duff said something in reply, but Cullen was already running away from them across the yard and he couldn't hear what Duff said. He hurried to the barn and got his mule and rode away from Andrew King's farm as fast as that mule could go.

Cullen Stull wasn't a stupid man and he didn't court trouble.

PART ONE

Kansas

CHAPTER 1

Word of the bounty on Sadie Grace spread quickly: one thousand dollars to any man who could kill the notorious witch of Burden County, Kansas. Ned Hemingway eventually heard about it all the way down in Oklahoma, below the Cherokee Strip.

Skeins of honking geese were returning north, and the black oaks and river birches had begun to turn green by the time Ned crossed the border into Kansas. He was riding with Moses Burke out of Texas and they were taking their time, not especially interested in finding fresh employment until their funds ran out. Moses was vaguely interested in visiting a cousin of his in Nicodemus, and Ned thought he might go along to satisfy his curiosity about the place. After that, they'd discussed the possibility of circling back south to Dodge City, but it was an idle thought and susceptible to change, depending on their whim.

They stopped over in Monmouth, to give their mounts a rest and to play a hand or two of poker. It was late in the day, and Moses was holding two aces and an eight when the saloon door opened and an old man limped into the makeshift saloon. He had a shock of white hair that stuck out in all directions from under his hat, and he was carrying a child's body over his shoulder.

He dumped the child on a table, then stepped back and addressed the room. By that time, everyone in the place had set down their drinks and their cards to gawk at the new arrival. The women stood up and moved toward the staircase in case the old man meant to stir up trouble.

"She got my boy," the man said. "The witch got my boy."

Moses stood and pushed his chair back, abandoning the excellent hand he'd been dealt. He brushed past the old man and bent low, putting his ear to the child's chest.

"Get away from him," the old man said. "You ain't fit to touch him."

"This child isn't dead," Moses said. "But his arm's out of the socket, and if he won't wake up there could be something wrong with his head, too."

"What do you know about it?" the old man said.

Moses grabbed the child's arm with both hands, braced his foot against the table, and pulled. There was a loud pop and the table shook beneath the tiny body. The old man started forward, but Ned put a hand on his shoulder and spun him around.

"My name's Hemingway, friend," Ned said. He let the old man go and rested a hand on his holster. "My partner here is Moses Burke. He learned some medicine in the war."

"Not on my side, he didn't," the man said. He glanced down at Ned's hand on the butt of his gun and up at Ned's eyes under the brim of his yellow cattleman, trying to size up his odds.

"I don't doubt that, sir," Ned said. "Moses is particular about the company he keeps."

In fact, Moses had served under Dr John DeGrasse in the 54th Regiment out of Massachusetts. Dr DeGrasse, the only black surgeon to have treated Union troops, had chosen Moses and four other volunteers to help him in the field. In the following months, Moses had learned enough medicine that Ned sometimes thought his friend should have stuck with it, if there were a hospital that would take him on.

"I think this child will be all right," Moses said. "That arm will hurt for a bit, but it should heal fine. I'm more worried about the head wound. And there's something else that doesn't sit right with me, but . . ."

Moses broke off and shook his head as if arguing with himself. He caught Ned's eye and motioned him over to the far end of the bar. Ned followed, but kept an eye on the stranger, who was now hovering over the small body on the table.

"Regardless of what this man claims," Moses said in a low voice, "that child is not a boy."

"You sure?"

"As sure as I can be."

"You think this fella's lying to us," Ned said.

"I can think of a few reasons for that," Moses said. "Not all of 'em sinister."

"Or it could be he's not lying." Ned liked to look at things from all angles.

"In which case he doesn't know that's a little girl he's slinging around like a bag of beans."

"Might be worthwhile to ask him some questions," Ned said.

One of the women had fetched a damp cloth from behind the bar. She folded it in half and laid it on the child's forehead, while another woman pushed the old man toward the bar where the saloonkeeper set out a shot of whiskey. The old man accepted the drink and swallowed it in one gulp.

"Next round's on me," Ned said. "What's your name, old-timer?"

"Tom Goggins," the old man said. "Of the Omaha Gogginses, if you're familiar."

"Well, I've never been there," Ned said. "But why don't you join us, Tom of the Omaha Gogginses, and tell us what this is all about."

"What it's about," Tom said. "is a witch."

CHAPTER 2

Rose Nettles found her husband, Joe Mullins, through a classified advertisement in the Philadelphia *Evening Telegraph*. The ad was pointed out to her by her mother one evening after they had washed the dinner dishes and put them away. After Rose had dried her hands her mother handed her the paper, opened to the classifieds page. An ad halfway down the right-hand column was circled in grease pencil. Rose found her glasses and read it aloud.

> **Wanted: A Wife.**
> **Hardworking man with 160 acres of tilled and seeded land seeking compatible woman to help with household and some farming duties. Would appreciate a comely face and pleasant voice, but not essential. Requires a good nature and willing companionship.**

Below the ad was an address in Kansas. Rose's mother had underlined the address twice with the grease pencil. Rose set the paper aside and took off her glasses, setting them on the table next to her while gathering her thoughts and choosing her words. But her mother spoke first.

"You ought to have a husband," she said. "I want to see you settled before I go."

Rose's mother had recently accepted a proposal of marriage from her banker, Giles Bradshaw, who had three grown daughters of his own with whom Rose did not get along. Rose was aware that her mother and Mr Bradshaw had discussed what was to become of Rose after the wedding, since she was unlikely to be welcomed into his home.

"You want me to marry a stranger who lives thousands of miles away?" Rose asked her mother. "I might never see you again."

Her mother turned away, and Rose knew she was hiding tears. She was glad to see that Giles Bradshaw hadn't entirely turned her mother against her.

"You're not getting younger, Rose, and nobody's come around asking after you in quite some time. I worry you've waited too long already. I know Charles Thurmond would have you, but you don't answer his letters."

Her mother reached out and squeezed Rose's hand, then hurried from the room.

There were several points—leaving aside the influence of Giles Bradshaw—that Rose felt she might object to if given the chance. In the first place, she wasn't certain she needed a husband. Her quiet life suited her: her books, her knitting, her work at the schoolhouse. Charles Thurmond was twenty years older than Rose, and smelled like spoiled milk. Rose had no desire to read Charles's letters, much less respond to them. And yet her perfectly comfortable life caused her mother distress. There was no arguing with that.

The following morning, with a deep sense of dread, Rose wrote a brief response and posted it to the paper.

My name is Rose Nettles. I am twenty-four years old. I am not too skinny, nor too tall, and I have been told my features and disposition are agreeable. I am in good health and strong, I can read and write, and my singing voice is untrained, but

**passable. I am willing to enter into an arrange-
ment with you and I await your response.**

Three tense weeks passed in which Rose and her mother barely spoke, then a letter arrived for Rose. It was brief and to the point.

Your particulars are acceptable. Please come.

The following day Rose handed Charles Thurmond her letter of resignation. The schoolmaster accepted it reluctantly and with a measure of kindness that surprised Rose. She went home that afternoon and packed her old leather valise with two long skirts, three white blouses, and several pairs of warm woolen stockings she had knitted for herself. She chose five novels from her shelves, but put one of them back when she judged the small stack to be too heavy, and replaced it with a selection of sheet music from the piano bench. She had saved one hundred seventeen dollars from her teaching salary, and she left twenty dollars on the kitchen table for her mother. A wedding gift. The remaining ninety-seven dollars she rolled up and hid in the toe of a stocking at the bottom of the valise. She left her best dress hanging in the closet—she did not think she would need it on a farm—and the only jewelry she took was a pocket watch and an old silver locket containing a sepia-stained photo of her mother in one side, and a miniature portrait from her parents' wedding day in the other. It was the only likeness she had of her father, whom she had never met.

She walked to the train station and bought a one-way ticket to Kansas City.

She had heard of Kansas, and she had the impression it was all dusty plains and howling winds. When she reached her compartment on the train, she locked the door and pulled the curtain before finally surrendering to despair. She set her watch on the seat beside her and cried for exactly fifteen minutes, then wiped her eyes, blew her nose, and unlocked the door.

She read intermittently from *The Woman in White,* and occasionally marked her page with a finger while she watched the countryside roll by outside her window. In the evening she bought a sandwich and a pint of milk from the porter and lit a lamp, reading until she could no longer keep her eyes open. She packed the book away and set her empty milk bottle in the passage outside her door, dressed for bed, and was rocked into a deep and dreamless sleep by the swaying carriage.

She breakfasted in the dining car, keeping to herself, smiling politely at other passengers as they entered and exited. When she had eaten, she asked for a pot of tea and took it back to her compartment, along with her book. The day passed uneventfully, and she dozed often enough that she lost track of time.

She was awake and had already repacked her bag when the train ground to a halt at the Kansas City station. A cluster of men stood on the platform, talking among themselves. One of them separated from the group and approached her when she stepped off the train.

He took the pipe from his mouth and wiped his lips with the back of his hand. "Would you be Miss Rose Nettles?" he said.

"I am," she said.

He looked her up and down, and nodded.

"You'll do," he said. "I'm Joe Mullins."

He took her valise and led her to a buckboard with two swaybacked mules hitched and grazing. He helped her up onto the seat, then set her bag in the back and clambered up beside her.

As the wagon rolled away from the station, Rose felt a dizzying sensation of separation from her past. Her life as she had known it was now far behind her, and her future was an alien thing, plain and unwanted, squatting somewhere on the path ahead. She took a deep breath and squared her shoulders, determined to make the best of whatever was to come.

The trip south to Monmouth took more than seven hours, but she was too nervous and uncomfortable to sleep. The landscape surprised her. Yes, there was flat prairie along the rutted muddy road, but there was also lush green woodland. Rippling brooks ran through fields of bright yellow flowers, and a small herd of deer ran alongside the wagon for a quarter of a mile, seemingly as curious about Rose as she was about them. She found herself smiling, but gasped when a deer turned abruptly and darted in front of them, causing Joe to pull up short. Rose bounced up and off the seat, but Joe caught her before she fell from the buckboard.

"Careful there," he said. The first words he had spoken since they left the station.

Rose sneezed and he handed her a handkerchief.

"Pollen," he said. "Bad this time of year."

He snapped the reins and the mules resumed their steady forward pace.

When they arrived that evening, she saw that her new house was a tidy thing of splintery planks that were slotted together without any sign of a nail or wood screw. There were two rooms, and a small kitchen in the back that was open on the sides and covered to keep off the weather. A tin bathtub occupied a corner of the kitchen, and Rose was touched to see that a cheerful yellow curtain was hung around it, the seams still pressed into its fabric where it had been folded and stored somewhere, awaiting her arrival.

The front room held a table and three homemade chairs, as well as a fireplace with a plain cross nailed to the wall above it. A doorway led to the bedroom, where Rose saw a second fireplace. Joe placed her valise on a small vanity next to the narrow bed.

He saw Rose's anxious expression and cleared his throat, looking away out the window.

"I got a bedroll and I don't mind sleeping in the other room until you get to know me," he said. "It's a new situation."

Joe Mullins was a small man with thinning hair and a droopy mustache. His arms and legs were thin, but roped with lean muscle, and he had a small potbelly that he seemed self-conscious about. He spoke rarely—in fact he had been alone on the farm so long that he seemed to have forgotten the art of polite conversation and sometimes went days without saying a word to her—but he was kind. Rose did not consider him to be physically attractive, but she grew accustomed to him as the weeks passed, and one night when a particularly chilly breeze had sprung up, she called him in from the front room and allowed him into their bed.

Ten weeks after arriving in Kansas, Rose received a letter from her mother. Joe brought it to her where she sat reading a Dickens novel, then went and pulled out a chair across from her, watching her, and she knew he was afraid the envelope contained a train ticket back to Philadelphia. Rose opened it, unfolding the single piece of paper inside.

"Dear Rose," the letter began. "The wedding was a small affair, and I am now Mrs Giles Bradshaw. I am selling the old house. Mr Bradshaw has asked after your health, and I would be glad to tell him that you . . ."

Rose stopped reading. She folded the letter back up and stuck it beneath the cover of *Dombey and Son*. She smiled at Joe, then returned to her place in the book and continued reading.

For seven years they lived as man and wife, Joe and Rose Mullins, though there was no formal wedding ceremony. Joe worked the land and brought in supplies, while Rose kept the house:

sweeping and washing, cooking their meager meals, and reading to Joe in the evenings as they sat by the fire.

They never spoke about it, but Rose knew that Joe wanted children—preferably sons to carry on both his blood and his name, and to help with the farm when they grew older—but the idea of bearing a child terrified Rose. What if she produced daughters, instead of the boys she was sure Joe wanted? Or—and this was an idea nearly as frightening to her as the prospect of raising a daughter on the prairie—what if she died while giving birth?

It had happened to an acquaintance of hers in Philadelphia, a girl named Marnie, sweet and energetic, with a spray of freckles across her nose that she refused to conceal with makeup. She and her baby had both died in childbirth, and her husband had remarried six months to the day after burying Marnie and her baby. As friends of the family, Rose and her mother were invited to the man's second wedding reception, but Rose had declined. It had all happened so quickly that Marnie seemed almost disposable, a broken ornament that had been tossed aside and forgotten. Of course, Rose knew this was nonsense. The poor man was incapable of living alone, and he had waited the proper amount of time after Marnie's death to remarry. Still, Rose knew she would be unable to look at him or to congratulate the new bride.

When Joe and Rose had sex, an act that was both infrequent and awkward, Rose would wait for Joe to begin snoring, then make herself a tea of boiled thistles and arsenic to keep his seed from taking root in her. If Joe was unhappy about her continued inability to conceive a child, he never said as much, but over breakfast one morning he slid a flyer across the table.

"Got this from the general store," he said. "I was thinking I might take the morning off, if you want, and we could go into town."

The headline read "Wanted: Homes for Orphan Children,"

and beneath that, in smaller type: "A company of homeless boys and girls from the East will arrive in Monmouth, KS, next Saturday. Ages six months to sixteen years. Come and meet your child. Distribution will begin at ten o'clock in the town square."

There was more, but Rose stopped reading. She set down her spoon and slid her chair back.

"The orphan train," she said.

"This could be a good home for a child," Joe said. "It's awful quiet here with just us two, and it'd be useful to have an extra hand on the farm when he comes of age."

"A boy?"

"Doesn't have to be. I'm open to your wishes, Rose. It's only an idea."

They arrived early. The train station was located at the town border, across from the stockade, nothing beyond it but farmland and grazing cattle. Joe hoped to get a look at the children before they were led to the square. Other couples had the same idea, and Joe elbowed his way through a small crowd to the platform. Rose stayed with the buckboard. The more she thought about bringing a child into their home, the more nervous she became.

An Indian man stood behind the tall wooden slats of the stockade, watching her. She moved so that her back was to him.

She had brought a book with her, a lurid gothic novel with a plain black cover, written by Ubel H. H. F. Crane. Joe had bought it because they'd enjoyed Mary Shelley's novel. Rose turned to the page where she had left off the previous evening.

The floor was formed of dirt and loose stones, and flickering torches lined the walls. At the far side of the room a purple curtain hung from the ceiling to the floor. Men and women were gathered there, around a long table heaped with platters of meat and cheese, decanters of wine, and a cornucopia of bread and ripe fruits. There was a hushed murmur that ran through the gathering like a wave, and a nude woman wearing a mask adorned with cat ears lifted a silver dome to reveal the severed head of an old man. The worshippers at the table leapt upon the head, gouging out its eyeballs and biting off its ears. I tried to look away, but my eyes were drawn against my will to the gruesome spectacle.

The masked woman lifted another dome and some sort of black sludge poured out over the table, glistening in the torchlight. The sludge broke apart, and I saw then that it was a mass of tiny black toads, wriggling and hopping about. The partygoers abandoned the severed head of the old man and leapt upon the toads, grabbing them up and stuffing them into their mouths. They unstoppered the decanters and gulped wine, washing the toads down their greedy throats.

The masked woman tore down the purple curtain, and the earth split open behind it, smoke billowing to the rafters above. An orange glow emanated from the pit.

The gathered throng pushed a young boy toward the pit, and the woman with the cat mask took the boy's hand and led him to the edge of the pit. I strained against my shackles and I heaved myself backward against the pillar, but it held fast. I screamed for it all to stop. I screamed until my throat was raw, but my efforts were for naught. The priestess pushed the boy and he fell from sight.

The train whistle startled Rose. She closed the book and watched the engine chug the last quarter mile to the station platform. She looked for Joe, but couldn't see him in the crowd. Behind her, she heard the Indian begin to sing, his voice deep and mournful, and Rose turned to listen.

The crowd around the platform broke up. Men and women

moved away down the street, but Rose didn't see any children with them. Joe rejoined her and leaned against the buckboard, waiting for the man in the stockade to end his song.

"His name's Traveling Horse," Joe said. "I talked to him when I come to get a new hammer last week. He took a rhubarb pie off a woman's porch while it was cooling, so the sheriff sentenced him to thirty days. Seems long to me. That woman can make another pie."

"What was he singing?" Rose said.

"Indian song about a great hunter they're scared of. Traveling Horse is worried 'cause the hunter's around here somewhere."

"Aren't there a lot of hunters around here?"

"I guess this one's sometimes a wolf, and sometimes he's a man, but you can tell him by his yellow eyes. Traveling Horse says he's been around as long as there's been white men in this country. Them Indians are a superstitious folk, that's for sure."

"Joe? What happened with the train?"

He stuck his hands in his pockets. "Some town up north of here claimed every last child they had on that train. They was all gone by the time it got here. No point in even making the trip to town, I guess."

Rose hoped her relief wasn't obvious. "Why don't you invite Traveling Horse to supper when his sentence is up?"

"To our home?"

"Well, he never got to eat that pie, did he?" Rose said. "And didn't you say the house was too quiet?"

One evening in late December as Rose read to him from *Lady Audley's Secret*, Joe clutched his stomach and cried out in pain. Rose set the book down and went to him, but he waved her away.

"It's nothing," he said. "A strained muscle, that's all."

But he retired early, and in the middle of the night had a seizure. She held him until his spasms subsided, but in the morning he was unable to rise from their bed. His forehead was hot to the touch, and he did not recognize her when she spoke his name. Rose rode into town, but by the time she returned with the doctor, Joe had fallen into a deep sleep from which he never awoke.

After he passed, Rose tore down the curtain from their bathtub and used it to wrap his body. She kept him cold behind the house, and covered him with stones from the creek to protect him from coyotes. When the snow and ice had melted away, and the ground was soft enough, she began the hard work of digging a grave. She buried him at the edge of the property, under the spreading branches of a sycamore tree. It took two full days to carve out a hole deep enough and long enough for his body, and she paused often for food and sleep. She left Joe wrapped in the yellow curtain, now faded and tattered at the ends, and rolled him into the hole.

Filling it back in was easier work.

The next day she pried the cross off the wall above the fireplace and hammered it into the ground over Joe's head.

She struggled that spring to till the soil, unused to handling the heavy plow or the two stubborn old mules. When one of them stumbled and fell, she left it in the field where it lay. Summer came and went, and she didn't touch the bags of seed Joe had left in the barn.

Over the years she had accumulated three new books through the mail. She read those, and the four books she had brought with her, over and over again, and sometimes she stepped outside on a cool evening to sing, thinking Joe might hear, wherever he was, and be pleased.

She knew that she could not stay on the farm forever. It would be impossible for her to plant and harvest one hundred sixty acres by herself. Joe had hired help in Monmouth each autumn to bring in the harvest, but Rose was worried about the kind of men who might come to the farm, and she didn't know if the ninety-seven dollars hidden in her old valise would be enough to pay them. She thought she might last another season or two in the little wooden house Joe had built for her, but she might not. She had few options, and none of them appealed to her. She began to contemplate her supply of arsenic.

As she was standing on the front porch one evening in early April, smoking Joe's pipe and looking out toward the crossroads, she saw three men and a child standing by Joe's grave under the sycamore tree.

CHAPTER 3

Ned Hemingway leaned in close to the tree where a crude straw doll was fastened to the trunk at eye level. A tenpenny nail had been driven through the middle of the doll's chest. Ned stepped back and tapped the head of the nail.

"Moses, you reckon that's where a witch's heart is?"

Moses shrugged. "Never met a witch."

Tom Goggins was irritated. "They keep their hearts at the same place as everybody else. They look just like a regular person," he said. "At least, when they want to. You wouldn't know if you met one or not, Mr Burke."

The sun was going down, casting long shadows behind the four of them. At the base of the tree was a thick branch, the size of a man's leg, jagged at one end. A wooden cross was pounded into the dirt a few feet away. Ned nudged Moses in the ribs and pointed.

"I saw it," Moses said. "Pretty sure we're disturbing somebody's grave here."

Ned took three steps away from the low mound he was standing on.

"Someone's coming," Moses said.

Ned looked up the grassy slope behind the tree and saw a woman marching toward them from a tiny house he'd assumed was abandoned. There were no lights in the windows, no smoke wafting from the chimney. It reminded Ned of the homesteads he had seen where people had given up or been driven out, their houses left to crumble away.

As the woman drew near, Ned walked out to meet her.

"I apologize if we're trespassing here," he said.

"You were standing on Joe's grave," she said, her voice low and guttural. She had a pipe clamped between her teeth and she held a Winchester rifle high across her chest.

"I assure you, ma'am," Ned said. "We meant no disrespect to you or to Joe. We was just admiring the little dolly stuck to your tree over there, and we had not the slightest idea Joe was underfoot."

"Dolly?"

The woman lowered the rifle and used the stem of her pipe to brush a strand of hair out of her eyes. The sleeves of her dress were pushed up and Ned noted her sinewy forearms, the dirt embedded under her short fingernails.

"Was Joe your husband or your boy?" he said.

"My husband," she said. "He took ill."

"I'm awful sorry. You're out here alone, are you?"

The woman's head snapped back and her eyes went wide as she raised the rifle again. Ned patted the air between them in a calming gesture.

"I keep stepping out on the wrong foot with you," he said.

"I know how to use this." The woman pointed the rifle at Ned's midsection.

"I'm sure you do, ma'am, but I was only asking about your situation in a neighborly way. We are not bandits, nor rapists, nor murderers, and I swear we mean you no harm. Well, at least Moses and me don't mean any harm. I ain't going to vouch for old Tom here, since we don't know him too well. If you want to shoot somebody, you might wanna start with him."

"Hey!" Tom shouted.

"He's Tom, then," the woman said, gesturing with the barrel of the rifle. "And you said that one's Moses. So who are you?"

"My name's Ned Hemingway." He tipped his yellow hat.

"What's this about my tree?"

Ned stepped to one side so she could pass. She kept the Winchester aimed in his general direction and squinted at the tree trunk, but the sun had fallen behind the horizon and the crude doll was just a dark shape against the bark. She might as well have been looking at a boll or the stump of a fallen branch. She lowered her rifle and touched the doll, squeezing it between her fingers.

"It was a real pleasure to meet you, ma'am," Ned said. "But I suppose we better go on our way now and let you get on with your evening."

"You can stop calling me ma'am. My name is Rose Nettles. It's getting chilly out here. You all might as well come up to the house and explain why there's a witch's hex on my husband's grave." She pointed in an offhand way at the silent child Tom had brought with them. "And I ought to take a look at that girl's head. She needs medical attention."

CHAPTER 4

Old Tom Goggins watched as Rose prepared a plaster with half an onion, a garlic clove, and a proprietary mixture of crushed spices from a small glass jar she kept on the mantel, heating it in a saucepan over the fire.

"That there's a boy," Tom said. "I guess you was mistaken 'cause it's dark outside."

Rose ignored him. She tore a sleeve from Joe's best Sunday shirt and told the girl to sit. The child sank to the floor without a word, and Rose knelt beside her, using her fingertips to comb through the girl's short hair, removing dirt and brown crumbs of dried blood. The wound wasn't deep and it didn't need stitching, which was a relief to Rose. She liked to knit, she was good at it, but sewing wasn't a skill she had mastered.

"I looked after her some," Moses said. "But I'm used to a rougher sort of patching up. Soldiers and cowboys."

"You did a fine job, Mr Burke. This child will heal nicely."

"Thank you, ma'am."

"What's your name?" Rose said to the girl.

"I call him Rabbit," Old Tom said. "Cause he give me a hell of a chase when I found him."

"And where did you find her?"

"Him," Tom said. "Rabbit was hiding out in the woods where his family's house got burnt down by the Pawnee. I found the bones of his ma and pa in the rubble, so I guess I'm all the family he's got now."

"Is that what you want me to call you?" Rose said to the child. "Rabbit?"

The girl looked up at her with wide brown eyes, and said nothing.

When the poultice had boiled down to a thick paste, Rose dragged the piece of shirtsleeve through the bubbling pan and applied it to the girl's scalp. Rabbit flinched and Rose gave her a comforting pat on the arm.

She rinsed out the pan and put water on for tea, then took a long-handled knife and cut down half a cured ham hock that Joe had hung up to dry. She set it on the table, along with a loaf of bread she had baked that morning, and eight bottles of beer that had chilled in the creek. The men helped themselves, and Rose put a hunk of bread on a plate for Rabbit, who devoured it greedily and held the plate out for another portion.

When everyone had eaten their fill, Rose settled into the rocking chair Joe had ordered from a Sears Roebuck catalog the previous Christmas. She clenched his pipe between her teeth and gathered her knitting in her lap. Rabbit squatted on the hearth, staring into the flames, and the men pulled chairs over from the table, so that the five of them formed a rough semicircle around the fireplace.

Rose cast a critical eye on her guests. Tom Goggins wore a threadbare beaver-skin coat, with sleeves that ended two inches above his wrists and a hem that stopped midway between his shins and his ankles. She guessed it was tailored for a much shorter man, and she wondered whether he had won it in a game or stolen it outright. On his head was a battered felt hat with a turkey feather stuck in the band. He had not removed the hat when he entered her home, and Rose silently gave him a demerit for behavior.

Moses Burke's shirt was frayed around the collar, but it looked clean enough and well cared for. His boots were similarly broken in, but had recently been polished, and he had taken off his faded brown derby when he stepped over her threshold, hanging it on the peg Joe had used when he came in from the fields. He got no demerits from Rose.

Ned Hemingway was uncommonly handsome, and the most dapper of the three men—the most dapper man she thought she had ever met. Every article of his clothing looked freshly laundered and pressed, even his mustard-colored Stetson, which he hung on a peg next to Moses's hat. When he unbuttoned his fringed vest after supper, Rose had seen a glint of metal in the firelight, a tin star pinned to the lining. She decided to reserve judgment about him.

"Thank you for the meal," Ned said. "Nothing hits the spot like a ham sandwich, a beer, and good company."

"Firstly," Rose said, "you're very welcome. And secondly, Mr Goggins, the Pawnee haven't caused any trouble around here. They're a peaceful people, and I don't believe they would burn down anyone's home."

Old Tom shook his head. "Did I say Pawnee?"

"That ham you just ate was got in barter from them," Rose said. "So you owe them some gratitude should you meet up with them on your travels. Now third of all, I want an explanation for why there's a hoodoo fetish nailed up over my husband's grave. I need to know what it's doing there before I remove it."

"I wouldn't take that doll down from there if I was you, ma'am," Tom said. "Putting it up nearly cost that boy his life."

They all looked at Rabbit, who was sitting close to the fire, rubbing her hands together and seemingly paying no attention to the adults' conversation.

"I don't like this one," Rose said, taking the pipe from her mouth and using it to point at Tom. "Would one of you other gentlemen please explain your situation to me?"

"Well, I do feel like it's Old Tom's story to tell," Ned said. "Although I can't say I like him any better than you do, Mrs Nettles."

"Go on then," Rose said to Tom. "Tell me."

"Well, I was about to tell you," Tom said, feeling mildly insulted, but also happy to tell the story again. He had been on the trail for quite some time with no one to talk to but Rabbit, and Rabbit didn't talk back. "This all started 'cause there's a sizable reward for the killing of a witch up north of here. It was put up by some farmers after the witch poisoned their crops and murdered their kin. I'm an experienced witch-master, and I've killed my share of those foul creatures, but I'm not as young as I was in my youth, and my thinking was I'd do the deed from a ways off, you see? Killing a witch can be a tricky prospect and you got to get at 'em from far off or else with a large amount of men, such that they can't curse everybody before they succumb to numbers. Now, the farmers who put the bounty on this witch . . . Well, my thinking is that, if they had the men in sufficient numbers, they wouldn't have put that bounty on her to begin with, so the best course of action was to kill her from afar. I didn't feel it was likely I'd get there and find myself equipped with an army."

Rose puffed on her cold pipe and narrowed her eyes, waiting for him to continue. He cleared his throat.

"So what I did," he said, "I used some straw and mushrooms and a few scraps of leather from a dead man's shoes, and I fashioned a likeness of the party in question—the witch, I mean— then I found a tree over a fresh grave and I drove a nail into the doll's heart. Soon's I did that, she likely took sick from iron in her blood. By tomorrow, or possibly the next day, she'll drop dead where she is. I've wired ahead to let them know what I done, and when I arrive up there to Burden County I'll collect what I'm owed without putting nobody in the path of danger or death."

He reached back to grab another bottle of beer from the table.

"Except the witch," Rose said. "You intended to put her 'in the path of danger or death,' as you say."

"Well, yes, her."

"And my husband."

"Beg pardon?"

"The purpose behind the grave and the tree," Rose said. "The principle is that you have chained the witch's soul to that of Joe Mullins, and it is now his responsibility to ferry her down the river of souls to perdition, is that correct?"

"Well, that's the general idea," Tom said. He was frowning, the firelight causing deep furrows in his brow to shift. "But I meant no harm to your husband. I never even met him."

"Tell her what happened to Rabbit," Moses said.

"Well, that's how we know it worked," Tom said. "Soon's I pounded that nail halfway into the witch's chest, a great heavy branch broke off from above and fell straight onto my boy's tender head. Knocked him to the ground and laid him out cold. I thought he was dead. Carried him to the nearest civilized place, and that's where I met these two gentlemen."

"Now you're caught up with where we all come into the story," Ned said.

"You say there's a reward for killing this witch?" Rose said.

Tom narrowed his eyes, worried he had given away too much information and the woman might try to horn in on his bounty. "It's not much," he said. "Hardly worth the trouble."

"You say she killed some farmers?"

"She done all manner of wickedness," Tom said. "Killed horses and cattle, too, and she dried up crops. She ate babies and smeared herself with the blood and offal of children, and—"

"Hush now," Rose said, with a sidelong glance at the child sitting by the fire. "There's no need for that kind of language."

Tom clamped his lips shut and appeared mollified.

"Anyway, your doll won't work," Rose said.

"That's where you're wrong," Tom said. "The trick's in using a nail that's pure iron. Most people don't know that."

"Maybe if you had pounded it directly into her," Rose said. "That doll I saw on my tree was just a mangled handful of straw and dirt. You'd need something of the witch's essence to weave into the doll, or you'd at least need to know what she looked like in order to make something that truly resembled her. That wouldn't work as well as a strand of her hair or some of her scat, but it might at least give her the vapors or an upset stomach."

"And what do you know about it?"

"Mostly what I've picked up from townsfolk and vagrants since I came to live here, some from the Pawnee and Sioux who've come to the house for shelter and to barter with my husband. But I've always been curious and I read a bit about this subject in my previous life."

"Your previous life?" Moses said. He sat forward. "What do you mean by that?"

"I was a schoolteacher. I had a great many books in my house. In my mother's house, I should say. And I had access to a library four streets over from my house. I have always loved to read."

"And you read about witches?"

"Some. What do you know about them, Mr Burke?"

Moses shook his head and looked away at the fire. "Nothing," he said. "And I don't want to know anything about them either."

"No, sir, you don't," Tom said. "What this woman says is fine for book learning, but I have many years of experience dealing with witches, haints, demons, and ghouls. Mrs Nettles, I thank you for the bacon and beer, and for your hospitality, but I must head out first thing in the morning. I'd like to be there before them farmers get a chance to bury her wrong. If that witch is facing the wrong direction in the ground she might come back and cause worse trouble."

Rose studied his face in the firelight, then looked around at Moses, who was watching the crackling fire, and Ned who had begun to lightly snore with his hands clasped across his chest, and finally at Rabbit, who was curled up on her side with her back to the fire, watching them without expression. Rose sniffed and stood up, tapping her pipe against the mantel. Ned started at the sound.

"There's extra bedding in the closet," Rose said. "Mr Goggins is correct. We should all get a good night's sleep and an early start in the morning."

"We?" Ned said.

"Yes," Rose said. "I've decided to accompany you."

That night, little Rabbit slept in the bed with Rose, while Tom Goggins laid claim to the rocking chair because he said his bones were too brittle for a night on the hard floor. Ned and Moses got their gear, and after they shoved the table to one side there was room for both of them to lay alongside the fire.

Moses began to snore almost as soon as he settled down, but Ned laid awake for a while, thinking. He had not intended to travel with Tom Goggins, and he didn't think Moses had either. They had only gone to the sycamore tree to see the hex Old Tom had put there. But allowing Rose Nettles and the girl to ride off with Tom seemed like a bad idea. He did not trust the self-proclaimed witch-master.

Ned had never seen a witch, but it seemed strange to him that he had never heard of a ghost-master or a devil-master or a ghoul-master. There were all manner of creatures that ought to be more dangerous than a witch, and if witches were so deadly as to require mastering, Tom Goggins didn't fit the bill, as far as Ned was concerned.

He knew Moses had seen things in the war, things beyond death and injury, things he couldn't explain and didn't like to talk about, but the worst Ned had encountered were bad men and rough weather. In his experience there was little mystery in the world. His mother had taught him a handful of basic wards to protect him from spirits and tricksters, but he had never used them, and when he tried to remember his childhood lessons the specifics escaped him.

He finally nodded off while trying to calculate the distance to Burden County, and wondering whether there might be a good card game to be had on the way. When he woke up the fire had gone out, and moonlight through the window lent the room a silvery sheen. A small man with a droopy mustache leaned against the mantel, smoking a pipe. His expression was curious, as if he, too, had just woken up and was surprised to see Ned.

Ned glanced at his gun belt, hung over the arm of a nearby chair, and when he looked back the man with the droopy mustache was gone. Ned watched the room for a long while after that until sleep eventually caught back up to him.

When he woke again, it was morning, and Rose had already put the rest of the ham out on the table, along with a pail of cool clear water. Ned decided he had dreamed about the man with the droopy mustache and he didn't mention him to the others; not even Moses.

But when they had finished their breakfast and were leaving the house, he waited until the others were gone and tipped his hat toward the spot where he had seen the man.

"I thank you for your hospitality, Joe Mullins," he said.

CHAPTER 5

Tom Goggins was not pleased with the recent turn of events. His plan had been simple: curse the witch from afar, then travel up to Burden County and collect the bounty on Sadie Grace. It had seemed foolproof to him. He knew the farmers might balk when it came time to pay up, but Tom's knowledge of curses wasn't limited to witches.

Finding poor little Rabbit had changed things, but not by a lot. With a child in tow, he had to travel more slowly than he'd have liked, but he appreciated the company. Rabbit was a very good listener. In fact, Tom couldn't be sure he hadn't told some of the same stories more than once.

Then Ned Hemingway and Moses Burke had latched on to them, coming out to the tree to see the thing nailed over Joe Mullins's grave. That was fine, Tom thought, and if they wanted to ride along with him to Riddle, he might find a use for them. He didn't understand why Ned treated the negro like his equal, but they looked like capable gunmen and they could help ensure the bounty was paid as promised. As soon as the money was in hand, Tom and Rabbit would give them the slip. It was only fair; Tom had done the actual work of killing the witch. It wasn't his fault if other people wanted to horn in on his success.

But now the woman had fastened onto him, too, and he felt like circumstances were spinning out of his control. There were suddenly five of them headed north across the state, and Tom couldn't quite get a handle on Rose Nettles. He didn't understand why she wanted to come along or what use he could put her to, and he had a vague feeling he might not be able to out-smart her, though he hadn't fully shaped that feeling into a solid thought.

He had immediately objected to the idea of her coming along, but was overruled by Ned and Moses. For the moment, it seemed he was stuck with the widow Mullins, and Tom was beginning to wonder if he was the leader of their expedition, after all.

It bothered Tom that he couldn't recall where he had learned the particular hex he had fixed above Joe Mullins's grave. He couldn't remember whether Rose was right about the doll needing specific ingredients to work. The truth about a thing sometimes got muddied over time by storytelling and embroidery. Still, he was certain he knew more about witchery than Rose Nettles could ever hope to learn.

On their way out, they stopped by the sycamore at the cross-roads, and Ned used his pocketknife to pry out the iron nail. He tossed it away into the long grass and handed the crude straw-filled doll to Rose. She produced a box of matches from some-where in her skirts and got her pipe going. With the last flicker at the end of the match, she lit a stray piece of straw under the bits of leather Tom had wrapped around the doll. She set it on a flat rock a few feet away, and they all stood silently, watching the doll burn. When it was gone, Rose crossed herself, took a puff from the pipe, and climbed up onto the buckboard next to the little girl.

"Let's get a move on," she said.

"What'll happen to your house?" Moses said.

"Perhaps the Pawnee will use it, if they decide they want it. Otherwise, I suppose the grass will claim it."

They turned their mounts and filed away down the trail, first Ned, then Tom, and Rose with Rabbit beside her on the high seat of the buckboard. Moses brought up the rear.

Old Tom turned in his saddle and saw Rose pass by her husband's grave without a single glance. She was a cold woman, he thought, and rough in ways he found displeasing. He didn't understand why Ned seemed to respect her right away, and he didn't like the way Rabbit had taken to the woman.

She was a guest, after all, on Tom's journey. They all were. He began to think about the various curses, spells, and hexes he knew. He thought he might need them sooner than anticipated.

CHAPTER 6

Moses held back, watching the other members of their little caravan swing out onto the trail and ride ahead. Old Tom had moved up front on his Choctaw, and Rose Nettles was behind him with the child. Her old swayback mule had refused to pull the ancient buckboard past the crossroads, so they had hitched Ned's two donkeys to the wagon and distributed their supplies evenly among the three horses. Rose had insisted Rabbit ride with her, rather than Tom, which Moses thought was a fine idea. He was glad to have someone along to care for the girl. No matter how well intentioned they were, he and Ned had no experience with children.

Ned fell back, pulling the little mule behind him and keeping pace with the buckboard. Ned was happy to have a concrete destination for a change, but he was bemused by the odd band of strangers he and Moses had accumulated. Tom Goggins was easy enough to figure out, but Rose was perplexing, and the child Rabbit was a complete cypher. He thought it might help if she would tell them why Old Tom thought she was a boy.

What confused him most of all was the purpose of their journey. Ned had seen men holler "witch" when they disagreed with a woman, but he had never known the accusation to hold any truth. He would talk with Moses; they would figure out what to do when they reached Burden County, bounty or no bounty. Meanwhile they had many days of riding ahead of them. The sky was clear, the air was warm, and his sorrel mare was content to follow the trail without prompting. Ned lowered his yellow hat and relaxed, his eyes half-closed, following the steady motion of Rose Nettles's swaying shoulders.

Rose struck another match and puffed on her husband's old pipe. She had kept the pipe, as well as a long pinewood crate of tools, and a few pairs of warm woolen stockings she had knitted for Joe, but those few things were all she had left of him. Still, she did not feel the slightest bit sad as she rode away from the house and the farm. She had done her duty as Joe's wife, but now he was buried and his name was buried with him. She would be Rose Nettles again for this third chapter of her life, and this time she would lead a life she chose for herself. She was no longer a schoolteacher who tiptoed around her mother's moods, nor a farmwife who tolerated her husband's silences. She was free.

The only responsibility she felt was for Rabbit. She thought she could trust Moses to care for the girl, but he and his friend Ned were wanderers. They would eventually leave Rabbit with a farmer or an innkeeper along the trail, and what would happen to her then?

Rose shook out the match at the exact instant it burned her fingertips, and blew out a puff of aromatic smoke. She dropped the match beside the buckboard on the rutted dirt trail. Beside her, Rabbit sat still and silent, staring at a dark line of trees on the horizon ahead of them.

CHAPTER 7

It had been a bad year. The summer was dry and dusty, with no sign of rain. The sky was flat and yellow all summer long, and a hard wind blew from the south, tearing the roofs off barns and breaking tender young stalks in the cornfields.

Every morning Sadie Grace found some new offering on her front stoop: seven fresh eggs wrapped in a clean cloth, a whole chicken, a cow liver on a slab of shagbark hickory that was still oozing sap. One day she found a letter of apology signed by the mayor of Riddle. She had long suspected that the mayor couldn't read or write, and she thought it likely his wife had written the note. She burned the letter in her potbellied stove and sprinkled the ashes in the well behind his house. The next day the mayor's wife took to her bed with stomach cramps.

On the first Sunday in September she had opened her front door and found a crying infant, swaddled in a blue blanket, his tiny fists balled up beside his round red head. This, she thought, was a bit much. She waited all day and well into the night, then stuffed the baby in the burlap bag she used to gather strawberries and carried him into town. She left him on the steps of the dry goods store, and she didn't need her scrying cup to predict what would happen. Hank Crenshaw would find the baby and take him home to Elizabeth. Elizabeth Crenshaw had raised six strong boys, without losing any of them to the cough or sleeping sickness. She would know what to do with a baby. Sadie certainly didn't.

It was possible she had once borne a child, but she did not

remember having done so, and she did not care to remember. She had woken one morning on the south bank of the Arkansas River, naked, cold, and muddy, with a deep gash in her throat just above her left collarbone. She had walked three miles to the nearest settlement. The local doctor stitched her wound and examined her, determining that she was somewhere between the ages of thirteen and sixteen, and that she had at some point probably given birth.

She recalled nothing of her life before waking up beside the river.

A farm couple had taken her in, but had soon grown fearful of her. Whenever she entered their kitchen, the pots and pans hanging above the stove began to shake and bang together. Three of the farmer's chickens disappeared one night, and a neighbor claimed to have seen Sadie squatting in the field under a full moon, howling and smearing herself with the birds' blood.

At the end of her first week with them, the terrified couple sent Sadie away with two dollars they had scraped together, as well as a secondhand gingham dress that fit her reasonably well, an old canteen with the words "Fifth Cavalry Regiment" stamped into the metal on one side, and a sack full of jam sandwiches.

"I'm sorry," the farmer's wife said. "We'll pray for you."

"Please," Sadie said. "There's no need for that."

Considering how the week had begun, her fortunes were vastly improved.

Since she had woken up south of the river and knew a little of what lay there, she decided to head north, crossing at a shallow spot where the current was gentle, pausing halfway across to fill her canteen. She walked all that first day across fields of wheat and barley, through dense green woods, and over wide stretches of prairie. She had no shoes, but the soles of her feet were tough as leather, and she felt no pain, even when she stepped on rocks and sharp twigs. She stopped only twice, to rest.

She slept that night in the branches of an oak tree, and woke feeling stiff and cramped when the sky was still purple along the horizon.

She walked more slowly the second day, and ate the last of the jam sandwiches early in the afternoon. Emerging from a field of tall corn, she found a dirt road and followed it until she saw a sign for a town called Riddle. She left the road and skirted the town, meeting back up with the trail on the far side. She didn't wish to encounter people yet. At the top of a hill overlooking a broad pasture was a lone house, white with bright green shutters. The front door stood open. She knocked, and when there was no answer she wiped her feet on a straw mat and entered.

Inside, the cabin's front room was neat and clean, with hand-made furniture and two lamps suspended from the ceiling. The air was heavy and smelled metallic, and bluebottle flies buzzed lazily about. Sadie opened a window before venturing farther into the house. There was a tiny kitchen with a potbellied stove and a pantry that was fully stocked with cured bacon, boiled eggs, and tins of flour and cornmeal.

Beyond the kitchen was a bedroom, and Sadie paused at the threshold, chewing her lower lip and looking around at the walls before finally settling her gaze on a bed in the center of the room. An elderly couple lay on top of the blankets. The woman's legs were black with gangrene, but her eyes had been closed and her hands placed across her chest. A pillow lay beside her head. Her husband—Sadie assumed it was her husband—lay next to her, the top of his head missing, a sticky brown stain on the wall behind him. His right hand hung limp over the side of the bed, one of the old man's fingers still caught in the trigger guard of a sawed-off shotgun.

"Well," Sadie said. "At least I won't have to sleep in a tree tonight."

CHAPTER 8

A thick tangle of trees and underbrush lay ahead of them, and behind them was a vast expanse of tall grass and wildflowers. Between the woods and the field was a tall wooden fence, sturdier than the common cattle fences they had encountered. Ned Hemingway was mildly annoyed. He thought it best to stick to the trail, but they had put it to a vote and he had bowed to the majority. Tom and Rose both wanted to take a straight line north and west to Riddle, in order to get there as quickly as possible. Moses had abstained from the vote, saying he had no preference either way. Rabbit, of course, had said nothing, which was fine with Ned. He didn't think a child ought to have an equal say in things, anyway.

He dismounted, climbed a fencepost, and scanned the length of the fence in both directions. He could see neither an end to the fence nor a gate that would allow them to pass through into the woods. He hopped down and rejoined the others.

"Way I see it," he said, "we either go back and find the trail again, or we follow this fence until we get past the trees. Either way, we just added a couple days to our trip."

He wanted them to know they had made the wrong choice in leaving the trail. Rabbit looked at him with her wide eyes, but seemed unconcerned. Old Tom had fallen asleep on his horse, and was softly snoring while the smoke-colored Choctaw nibbled clover.

Rose pointed past the fence. "There's a trail on the other side," she said.

Ned peered between two planks at a narrow weed-choked lane that pushed through the trees, disappearing into darkness a few yards beyond.

"I wouldn't call that a trail," he said. "It may be a footpath, at best, and we don't hardly know how far it goes."

"Let's find out."

"It's too narrow for your buckboard."

"It's not my buckboard," Rose said. "And I have no compunctions about leaving it behind. Besides, if you're right and we can't get through those woods, it will be waiting for us here, which will be one good thing about doubling back, should it come to that."

Ned looked to Moses, hoping for a word or two of support, but his friend only shrugged and looked up at the clear sky, as if avoiding Ned's eyes. Moses had been strangely quiet of late, and Ned wondered if he was unhappy about the company they had fallen in with. If so, Ned wouldn't argue with him. Old Tom was overbearing, and Rose was chilly. The only one of their bunch who wasn't a burden was Rabbit, and that was mostly because Ned kept forgetting she was there.

He recalled how easy it was to travel with Moses, and resolved to remember that feeling the next time they had an opportunity to throw in with a larger group. Their general tendency toward aimlessness had begun to bother him of late, but now he missed it terribly.

Moses stopped looking at the sky and looked at Ned. "I guess we'd have to leave the horses here, too," he said. "That fence is too high to jump 'em."

Ned was grateful to see Moses finally take his side.

"Why don't we disassemble the fence?" Rose said, as if that were the simplest thing in the world to do.

"Take it apart?" Ned said.

"Some farmer's likely to shoot us," Moses said.

"What farmer?" Old Tom said, scraping the sleep out of his eyes. The Choctaw, startled by the sound of his master's voice, stopped grazing and flicked his tail.

"What's he farming out here, anyway?" Tom added.

Ned took another look around. The old man had a point. Unless someone was harvesting sunflowers and arrowfeather, there was no farmer. The land looked as if it had always been wild, never tilled nor planted. This observation led Ned to wonder why anyone would go to the trouble of building such a long and sturdy fence. He turned and studied it again. It was rough-hewn and splintery, uneven where it followed the gentle slopes and gullies of the prairie, but every board looked solid and new, nailed neatly in place against posts that were sunk deep into the ground.

"Well, what the hell is it for?" he said.

While Ned pondered the meaning of the fence, Moses dug a shallow trench and crawled under it. He shimmied up a tall elm on the other side to get a higher vantage point than the fencepost Ned had stood on. Ten minutes later, he was standing beside them again on the pasture side of the fence.

"I can't see how far the trees go," he said. "But we aren't getting around this fence, not in any direction. At least, not today. And I'm not going back across this field either."

That seemed to settle the question. Rose climbed over the back of the wagon seat and opened the box of tools she had brought along. She selected a short-handled spade for herself, and Moses picked out one of Joe Mullins's skinning knives. They chose a length of fence and began prying out the long iron nails that held it together while Ned took a more direct route through the middle with a hatchet.

"I'll stick here and supervise," Old Tom said, and he moved his horse a little farther back from Ned's swinging hatchet.

Rabbit got down from the buckboard and sat in the grass, watching them.

It was warm for the season and Ned took off his vest. Rose noticed he folded it neatly, keeping the star she had seen tucked inside out of sight. She rolled up her sleeves, and Tom made a comment about how unladylike she was to work alongside the men, not to mention showing off so much of her arms, but Moses grumbled that she was at least making herself useful, which was more than he could say for someone else he knew. Tom frowned, but fell silent.

They made short work of it, clearing a way through for their horses—along with Ned's two donkeys and the swayback mule—in a little more than an hour. When they had moved the split lumber to one side and stacked it, and most of the tools were back in the box behind the wagon seat, Moses shaded his eyes and squinted up at the sun.

"Might be better to camp out in this field," he said, "instead of tramping around the woods after dark."

"We got a good couple hours before dark," Ned said. "And for all we know that tangle is barely ten trees deep. We could get across it before you have time to think up something else to worry about."

"For all we know, those trees go on and on, even longer than you stare at a hand of cards."

But he helped Rose unhitch the old mule from the buckboard and picked Rabbit up, setting her in the saddle.

"Shame to leave the wagon and all those tools behind," he said.

Aside from the box of tools and Rose's old leather valise, the only other thing in the back of the wagon was a small bundle of books tied together with a piece of twine, and Rose insisted on bringing them. Moses used a length of rope to lash Rose's books to the back of the mule. It didn't seem to mind the extra weight.

Rose's library had not grown much in her years with Joe Mullins, but she treasured the few volumes she did have. She thought she might read some of them aloud to Rabbit during their trip. The men might enjoy hearing her read, too. Joe had always enjoyed it when she read aloud after supper.

Ned rummaged through the toolbox and kept the skinning knife and a spade, sticking them in the top of his saddlebag. Moses took the hatchet for himself and a roll of old sailcloth.

"We might be in the woods for a time, and I would not care to see a woman or child sleep on the dirt," he said.

No one asked Old Tom if he'd like something from the box for himself, and he didn't dismount to take a look.

They left the buckboard in the pasture, and Rose could imagine it sitting there forever, grass growing up around it and small animals taking shelter beneath it. The idea pleased her.

She picked up her valise, then took the mule's reins and walked it past the ruined fence, following the others onto the narrow path under the trees. The sun was immediately lost from view, and she was surrounded by cool green darkness.

Rose had just noticed that the insects, so loud in the field, had gone silent, when somewhere ahead of her around a bend in the path, Moses began to shout.

CHAPTER 9

Moses had seen men hanged before—he had come close to being hanged himself in the closing days of the war, when three hungry deserters had stumbled into his camp—but it wasn't a thing he was used to seeing.

The young man's boots stirred gently in the cool breeze, his spurs jangling like faraway chimes. Moses got down from his horse and Ned did the same. Ned laid a hand on his friend's shoulder, but Moses shook it off. He was afraid Ned would tell him they should have stuck to the trail and avoided the woods. Moses wouldn't disagree, but he didn't want to hear it.

"Give me that rabbit-skinning knife you took," he said.

Ned rummaged in his saddlebag until he found Joe Mullins's old knife and handed it over. Moses clamped it between his teeth and sat on the ground. He pulled his boots off, then stood back up and went to the tree where the dead man dangled.

"He might've been a thief or a murderer, for all we know," Ned said.

"If he was a thief or a murderer, they would have taken his boots when they hung him. Those are good boots."

"They might've stuck a sign on him, too," Ned said. "If he was a thief or a murderer."

Moses wrapped his arms around the trunk of the tree and climbed. By the time Rose, Rabbit, and Old Tom arrived in the clearing, Moses was high above them.

"Oh, no," Rose said. She stared up at the dead man, then turned and covered Rabbit's eyes with her hand.

"Won't do no good to cut him down now," Tom hollered up at Moses. "Too late for that."

He turned to Ned and lowered his voice. "Did Moses know that dead negro?"

Ned ignored him. He fetched the length of sail canvas from Moses's pack and spread it out on the springy green moss beneath the tree.

Moses climbed higher, branch by branch, until he was directly above the dead man. He crawled out on a heavy limb and inched away from the trunk. When he was firmly situated, he took the knife from his teeth and peered down at Ned, far below him on the ground. Ned nodded, letting him know he was ready to break the body's fall whenever Moses was ready to start sawing the rope.

"Somebody might've had good cause to hang that boy," Tom said. "Could be we're interfering with a lawful act."

"He's hung too high up for that," Ned said. He didn't mention the boots in case Tom got a notion to steal them. "We figure he done this to hisself."

"Prairie madness," Rose said. "We lost a neighbor to it last year."

"It's a hard and lonely life out here for some," Ned said.

While Moses worked at the thick rope, Rose helped Rabbit down off the mule and took her by the hand, leading her along the path and back around the bend so she wouldn't see or hear the body when it fell. Tom dismounted and limped into the woods beside the path, muttering that he needed a leak anyway.

Moses wasn't fond of heights, and the rope was nearly as thick as one of Rabbit's arms, so it took him awhile to cut through it. The skinning knife was sharp, but he wished he had a blade with some tooth to it, like one of the bone saws he had used in the war. He closed his eyes, held tight to the branch with one hand, and kept at the rope until the weight of the young man's body finally snapped the remaining threads.

He heard the body hit the ground below him and, his eyes still shut tight, Moses backed along the branch until he could grab the trunk and stand up. From there, it was an easy climb back down with the knife clamped in his teeth.

By the time he reached the ground, Ned had already wrapped the body in sailcloth and had used the man's own noose to tie it up tight. He had done such a thorough job that Moses could hardly smell the rot.

"Wonder what his name was," Moses said.

"I took a quick look through his pockets, but didn't find nothing to lead us to his kin."

"A lot of roots here along the trail," Moses said. "Be hard to dig through them."

"Gonna have to pack him out of here. Bury him on the other side of these woods."

Old Tom chose that moment to stumble out of the underbrush, still fastening his belt, his eyes wide with shock.

"You fellas better come take a look," he said.

They left the body where it lay, and followed Tom off the path into the trees. Old growth choked off the sunlight, and whip-thin saplings had sprouted up around the roots of the ancient oaks, elms, and evergreens, tripping the three men and slowing their progress. Now Moses found himself wishing for a long machete like he had seen farmers use to clear their land. He wondered at the fact that Tom had gone so far off the path to do his business, and he was about to suggest they turn back when they pushed through a final knot of undergrowth and Tom led the other men into a dark glade. The breath went out of them in a rush.

Moses had looked up as they entered the clearing, hoping for a glimpse of sunlight, but instead he saw people in every direction, hanging from the trees by their necks, twisting and swaying in the brackish gloom of the deep woods. The dead occupied nearly every branch of every tree in the clearing. He took a breath and choked on an odor so thick that he could taste it on the back of his tongue. He swallowed hard to keep from retching, and turned in a slow circle, trying to count the bodies. He saw men, both young and old, and women, and more than one child. When he averted his eyes he saw more bodies laying on the ground, tangled in the roots and vines.

Moses looked at Ned. "I can't count 'em all," he said.

Ned shook his head as if he had forgotten how to talk, and they both looked at Old Tom. He was a witch-master, after all, and experienced in strange phenomena.

As if he had read their minds, he nodded. "This is the witch's doing," he said. "She done this to stop us coming to her, but it got to all these poor folks first."

"Some of these people been dead for years already," Ned said. "I didn't know I was coming this way until yesterday. How did she?"

"Anyway, you told us that witch was already dead," Moses said.

"So I did," Tom said. "It must have been some other witch then."

"No," Ned said. "It's like Rose told us. Prairie madness."

"All of them at once?"

"No, not all at once. Look at 'em." Ned pointed. "That one ain't much more than a skeleton. Some of these people have got so shriveled up they're as skinny as them ropes, and some of 'em on the ground look like they died right where they sat. Poison maybe."

"Or maybe they just gave up the will to go on," Moses said.

"You saying the trees killed these folks?" Tom said.

"Now how the hell would a tree kill somebody?"

"I think if you go mad, this is where you come to . . ." Ned paused. "Anyway this is where you come."

"The fence," Moses said.

It was clear to him now that the fence had been constructed to keep people afflicted with hopelessness out of the forest. But the fence that Moses had crawled under, and Rose had taken apart, and Ned had chopped through was powerless to stop a single man, woman, or child from taking their final journey.

Ned was quiet. He stared around them, at the silvery shadows between the trees, at the dead black leaves from the previous autumn fluttering across exposed roots and skeletal limbs, at the sparkling motes of dust floating through the gloom. His expression was a mixture of horror and confusion.

Moses himself felt a terrible wave of sorrow. After a moment, he grabbed Ned's elbow and the two of them made their way back through the trees to the path. Moses heard Tom crashing through the underbrush behind them, and he wished the old man had kept his gruesome discovery to himself.

It seemed to him that none of his many wishes and hopes had been answered lately.

CHAPTER 10

Rabbit sat with her back against a chinkapin oak and watched the body wrapped in sailcloth as if it might get up and walk away. The others stood a little way off so she wouldn't overhear them.

"All by their own hand?" Rose said. "You're certain?"

Ned nodded solemnly. "That's the way we figure it, ma'am."

"I think maybe this place is a big spiderweb," Moses said. "It pulls on a person's sadness and they get stuck to it."

"How awful."

"Their choice," Tom said. "I won't speak ill of the dead, but they dug their own graves, so to speak."

Ned continued to wonder why they were traveling with the old man. Virtually every word he spoke caused Moses and Rose to flinch. But Ned had traveled with less agreeable personalities than Tom, and he had learned long ago to shut them out when they talked, unless they had something useful to say.

"Moses," Ned said, "I know you're gonna want to bury all them folks proper, but I just don't see how we can do it."

"I know that," Moses said.

"It would take years off our lives, and in the meantime we might get stuck in that web of sadness you're talking about and end up in these woods forever."

"I said I know it. There's too many of 'em."

"But there must be something we can do for them," Rose said.

"We can burn the damn woods down," Tom said. "This is an evil place."

"I don't reckon we better burn it down with us still in here," Ned said.

"Why the hell not?" Moses said. "Might as well."

"Moses?" Rose said.

"Sorry, Miss Rose," Ned said. "Moses is especially liable to get caught in webs of sadness. He sometimes forgets there's others around who need him to keep his head on straight."

Moses shot him a look, but nodded. "We should move on from this wilderness and leave these bodies in peace," he said.

"What about that one over there?" Tom said. He pointed at the swaddled corpse under the tree.

"I rescued that one, didn't I? He can come with us."

None of them wanted to argue with him. Rose and Old Tom were confused, but Ned was accustomed to Moses's moods. His friend would snap out of it, he was sure, once he felt the sun on his face and a breeze at his back. Ned walked to the young man's body and bent, grabbing a double handful of sailcloth, and lifted one end. Rabbit dropped a locust she was playing with, scrambled to her feet, and grabbed the other end, but wasn't able to lift it off the ground. Moses smiled for the first time that day and went to help her. Together, the three of them draped their burden over the back of one of the donkeys. It brayed and kicked, but when the five of them saddled up and moved on, it followed without complaint.

Rose kept her eyes down, focused on the path ahead, and instructed Rabbit to do the same, afraid she might look up and see a swinging body. But her imagination wouldn't let go of the clearing the men had told her about, and part of her wished she had seen it, too, as if in seeing it she would suddenly be able to understand what had happened there.

They traveled in silence for more than an hour, the dank smell of the woods coating their nostrils and throats. The hems of the men's trousers and Rose's skirt caught on twigs and branches. Rose had begun to fear they would have to spend the night there when she heard Moses shout again.

"I see the sun!"

At that moment, the donkey tethered to Ned's horse squealed. Its hind legs buckled, and it fell forward. The corpse slid up on its neck, then toppled over and fell to the ground. The donkey squealed once more and dropped dead on the path, its solid body plonking into the dirt, stirring up a cloud of dust.

Ned had already dismounted, and after tying his sorrel to a nearby branch he kneeled next to the poor donkey. Rose took the reins of Rabbit's mule and led it past the donkey. Moses reappeared, riding back up the path. He passed Rose and Rabbit and stopped his horse behind Ned.

"What happened to it?"

"Old age, maybe," Ned said.

"Would've thought it had a couple good years left in it," Moses said.

"Well, I guess it didn't."

They moved the body of the hanged man to the other donkey, and distributed the dead pack animal's saddlebags among the other mounts. Old Tom was now at the front of the little convoy, with Rose and Rabbit behind him. Ned and Moses brought up the rear, leading the remaining donkey.

Tom was the first to leave the shadows of the forest, and he spurred his horse out into a sunlit field. When Rose joined him, she took a deep breath of clean air and smiled at Rabbit. The girl looked up at her without expression, but then turned her gaze to the blue sky that was laced with thin gray clouds. Rose heard crickets in the grass now, and the high-pitched call of prairie dogs, warning one another about the humans at the tree line. A moment later, Ned and Moses emerged from the gloom and stopped their horses alongside her. Ned smiled at Rose and she smiled back. Only Moses still seemed glum.

"Look," he said, pointing past them to the far edge of the field.

Another tall fence stretched as far as they could see in both directions.

PART TWO

Gone to Wichita

CHAPTER 1

Charlie Gamble was deputy of Aransas County, Texas, and his brother Jim was sheriff. Charlie had no designs on Jim's job, nor did he have the slightest desire to be more than a deputy. He had always been content to follow Jim's lead, even when the elder of the two brothers found a sheriff's job in Aransas and pulled up stakes, moving them both down to the tiny border town of Fulton.

Charlie hadn't slept well since his wife died, and he was irritable. To make matters worse, he had a rash on his legs and arms that had spread at an alarming rate and itched like a thousand chigger bites, but whenever he scratched it burned so badly he wanted to tear off his own skin. He thought there might be a salve he could rub on it, but he didn't know much about that kind of thing and Marie wasn't around anymore to mix one for him.

On top of the sleeplessness and the rash, Jim had brought in a horse thief the day before. A gallows was being built in the town square, but meanwhile the thief was locked up in the jailhouse, and it was Charlie's job to feed him.

Marie had been the cook in the family, and Charlie's rash was bothering him so much he could barely open a tin of beans anyway. He decided cold frijoles were all the horse thief deserved, and dumped them out on a plate without bothering to heat them. He slid two johnnycakes onto the plate, set it on the floor, and used his foot to shove it under the cell door. The thief, whose name was George Jorgensen, looked at the plate of beans on the floor, then rolled over in his bunk and farted.

"I swear," Charlie said. "You ought to have some manners, George."

"Why?" George said. His voice was muffled by the thin pillow. "You're gonna hang me anyway."

George Jorgensen was a hair over six and a half feet tall, and weighed more than three hundred pounds. Sheriff Jim Gamble had captured him when the horse George stole collapsed, pinning his leg. George was fine, but Jim had to shoot the horse.

"We're gonna hang you, sure," Charlie said, "but you could at least be civil until then."

He hiked up the left leg of his trousers and dug his fingernails into the flesh of his calf. He had an idea that if he only poked at his skin, but didn't actually scratch it, it wouldn't have cause to burn so badly. He kept the denim pulled up around his knee and hobbled closer to the cell. He poked his toe underneath the door, trying to edge the beans closer to George, but he couldn't quite reach the edge of the plate.

"If I were a mind," George said, without turning his face from the wall, "I could jump up off this cot and catch you by the toe of your boot and take them keys off you."

Charlie backed up.

"I swear, George, eat your damn beans. I don't got the time for this. And keep your voice down. Jim's asleep in the back room."

"What do I care? Pretty soon I'll be dangling at the end of a rope."

"Settle down," Charlie said. "You brought this on yourself. Anyways, don't you know I'm a widower now? You are causing me mental anguish when I'm trying to grieve the loss of my sainted wife."

George rolled back over and took another look at Charlie.

"Don't look to me like you're grieving anything at all. Looks to me like you been rolling around in some poison oak and you're anxious the rash is gonna get to your pecker."

It had not occurred to Charlie that the rash might spread to his pecker, and now he felt a surge of panic. He shook his head.

"No, sir, I know good and well what poison oak looks like," he said. "And I ain't fool enough to roll around in it."

George shrugged. "Them beans warm or cold?"

"You want warm beans, you shouldn't go stealing horses."

"When you gonna hang me, Charlie?"

"They're building the gallows. Ought to be tonight or tomorrow morning."

"Think there'll be a big turnout for it?"

Charlie leaned against the edge of Jim's desk and poked at his exposed calf with his thumbnail. His pistol was on the desk and he picked it up, rubbed the barrel against his shin. The metal was cool, and the friction eased the pain a bit.

"George, you know much about unguents and lotions, and the like?" he said.

"Lotions?"

"Like for poison oak. Except, like I say, this ain't poison oak."

"Come here and let me take a look at it."

Charlie hiked his trouser leg a little higher and hobbled closer to the cell, still rubbing his exposed skin with the pistol. George rolled off his bunk and approached the other side of the bars. He squatted and peered out at Charlie's inflamed leg.

"You was right, Charlie," he said. "That ain't poison oak, after all."

"Well, I told you that," Charlie said. "What is it?"

"That's hellfire, boy. Your skin's burning 'cause you got a demon in you, feeding on all the shame and anger you got bottled up inside."

"I got no such thing, you damn horse thief."

Charlie backed away from the bars and sat on the edge of the desk again. He rolled the leg of his trousers back down over his calf and winced when the fabric rasped against his tender skin. George was still staring at him, his eyes wide.

"You're the criminal," Charlie added. "Not me."

"Yeah," George said, "but it ain't no secret I'm a thief, and I'll suffer plenty of hellfire when I'm hanged. But you got to suffer it now, while you're alive, and then some more after you die, too. What did you do, Charlie, that's got your flesh set on fire from the inside?"

Charlie shook his head. He scratched his forehead with the butt of the pistol and bit his lower lip.

"Jim!" George shouted. "Jim, wake up and get out here!"

"Shut up, George." Charlie pointed the pistol at George for emphasis. "I told you Jim's sleeping."

"I know he's sleeping," George said. "Jim, there's a demon inside Charlie! Wake up!"

"I swear, George, you got to the count of three . . ."

"Jim!"

"One . . ."

"Jim, Charlie's fixing to shoot me! You better—"

Charlie pulled the trigger and George stopped shouting. He blinked at Charlie in surprise.

"You shot me," he said.

"Well, I said I was gonna shoot you."

"Yeah, but you really shot me. And you didn't give me a true three count, neither."

George staggered backward until he reached the cot and tried to sit on it, but missed and fell to the floor, smacking his head against the edge of the bunk on his way down. He raised himself on one elbow and reached up, as if he might find a handle somewhere to grab hold of, but his elbow gave out under his weight and he slumped over. He stared at Charlie and shook his head.

"You was supposed to hang me," he said. "Not shoot me."

The sheriff stumbled into the room, still pulling on his left boot. His hair was mussed and his shirttail was untucked, but his gun belt was buckled around his waist. He saw Charlie leaning against the desk, and stopped short.

"Sounded like gunfire," he said.

"I shot George," Charlie said.

Jim finally noticed George on the floor of the cell in a spreading pool of blood. He grabbed a ring of keys from the wall above a rack of rifles, and unlocked the cell door. He yanked on George's feet, sliding the horse thief's head out from under the bunk and pulling him halfway out of the cell. Jim had forgotten he was wearing only one boot, but after checking George's neck for a pulse, he smoothed his hair down against his scalp and tucked in his shirt.

"Well, I guess you killed him," Jim said. "Why'd you do it, though, Charlie? We were getting ready to hang him."

"He was making noise. I thought he was gonna wake you up."

Jim stared at his brother for a long moment, too bewildered to argue the point. Finally he walked around Charlie and sat at the desk.

"I guess I'm glad you didn't wake me up," he said.

"George said I got a demon eating me up on the inside."

Jim shook his head. "I don't think you got enough of anything inside you to bait a demon," he said.

"Well, he shouldn't have said it then."

"People around here have been looking forward to a hanging," Jim said. "Peggy Ann went and organized a potluck for after."

"People can still go to the potluck," Charlie said. He had begun to feel the way he did when he and Jim were kids, and Jim scolded him for some little thing, like skipping school to go fishing.

"Nobody's stopping them from going to a potluck," he added.

"I imagine they will go to the potluck, Charlie, but the whole time they're eating Peggy's fried chicken they'll be looking at that big old gallows they built, and thinking about what a waste it is to leave it sitting there empty. They might decide to put it to some use, after all."

"What do you mean, Jim? Nobody's gonna hang me for shooting a horse thief."

"Well, I don't really think so," Jim said. "But folks around here are feeling some disappointment in you these days, little brother. And you just keep on giving 'em reasons to be disappointed."

"Nobody's disappointed in me, Jim. Name one person who's disappointed in me."

He was afraid Jim would name himself, but Jim just tapped a finger on his desk and stared across the room at George's body.

"Alls I'm saying is you've got to think about your reputation," Jim said at last. "I can't do everything for you. You've got to figure out some right things to do on your own."

"What's this about my reputation? I don't have a reputation."

"Charlie, that Mexican kid . . . what was his name?"

"Cortez? You're talking about Benito Cortez?"

"That's right. That Cortez kid killed your wife and here you sit, like nothing happened."

"I know something happened," Charlie said. "But what am I supposed to do about it?"

"If somebody shot my wife . . . Well, hell, Charlie, I'd have him at the end of a rope by day's end. I wouldn't be sitting around the jailhouse, feeding beans to a horse thief."

"You *told* me to give George Jorgensen his beans. You said

'Charlie, you better feed George.' You said that to me right here in this room, and in those very words. You can't yell at me about feeding him beans after *telling* me to feed him the beans. That don't make sense, Jim. You have to see you ain't making sense."

Jim sighed and ran his fingers through his hair. He glanced again at the dead thief's body, George's torso in the cell and his feet sticking out into the room with them.

"Marie's been dead two weeks now, Charlie. I can't say I know how it feels to lose your wife, nor how I'd go about my business if it was my Laura who got shot, but there's people talking, and they're not saying kind things about you."

Charlie had been unaware anyone was talking about him behind his back, much less Peggy Ann, who had no right to talk about anyone after what had happened with her husband. Charlie had assumed all talk of Marie had simply stopped when she died. There was no reason, as far as he could see, to keep talking about anyone once they were dead and buried.

"Well, what are folks saying about me?"

"What I'm trying to tell you, Charlie, is some people think you don't care enough about what happened to your wife, and they think that maybe Marie made a mistake getting hitched to you in the first place, since you haven't even lifted a finger against the one who killed her. Dang it, a loving husband would do something about it!"

"But I called for the Marshals. They're gonna bring him in, or they'll bring in his body anyway. That's what you're supposed to do in a situation like this, ain't it? The law's very clear on it, Jim. I think the law's very clear."

"Well, there's the law and then there's justice. They ain't always the same thing."

"You're saying I'm supposed to find that Cortez kid all by myself? Without any help?"

Jim nodded and spread his hands out over the top of the desk. "I guess, yeah, I'm saying something like that."

"But the Marshals are gonna bring that boy back here any day now."

"I just don't know what to tell you, Charlie. You beat all."

"Just let me understand . . . You're saying I ought to go chase after that Cortez kid, even though the Marshals are already after him? You're saying I should waste maybe weeks or months, riding out after somebody who is about to get hisself caught and strung up, no matter what I do?"

"I am saying you ought to do something."

"Well, fine. I just wanted to understand what you meant," Charlie said. "I guess I'll take care of old George over there and then I'll be on my way."

He opened the cell door wider, and contemplated George Jorgensen's bulk. He realized he had committed himself to chasing down Benito Cortez, and he felt like kicking George. If the horse thief had waited to be hanged like he was supposed to, Charlie could be looking forward to a piece of Peggy Ann's fried chicken, instead of a month of cold nights on a lonesome trail. The rash had begun to bother him again, and he wondered if it was already making its way up his legs toward his pecker.

"I swear, I almost wish I could shoot George again," Charlie said.

"You shouldn't have shot him the one time," Jim said.

Charlie didn't have an argument for that. He bent and lifted George's feet and dragged him out of the cell.

CHAPTER 2

They had some experience getting through fences, and it took them less than an hour to create an opening wide enough to lead the animals through. This time, Tom dismounted and pitched in, using a small hatchet he produced from his bag. Early in the evening they rode through the hole they had made, and the only one of them who looked back at the dark woods was Rabbit.

Moses rode beside her. "It's to keep out the folks on this side," he said, thinking she was curious about the fence.

She looked at him, then looked away again and kicked her mule with her heels, pulling ahead of him.

Without the buckboard, they traveled faster, finding the small country lanes used by farmers to get from one field to another. They detoured around wooded areas, none of them willing to risk another horror like the last.

Rose watched farmhands leading plow horses over furrowed soil, and she wondered about the women toiling inside distant homes marked by smudges of chimney smoke against the sky. A small herd of four cows grazed in a meadow white with clover.

"Look," Rose said. "Stray cattle."

"No such thing as a stray cow, ma'am," Moses said. "Those beeves have wandered off a field somewhere nearby."

"We'll have to find shelter soon," Ned said. "Or make our own."

"Rabbit and me's used to sleeping out of doors," Tom said.

"Maybe," Moses said. "But the lady might not care to wake up covered with chiggers and ticks."

"Don't worry on my account," Rose said. "I've woken up with worse."

But Moses smiled in a way that indicated he would go on worrying anyway. "Maybe one of these farmers will put us up in exchange for a coin or two."

"There sure are a lot of us though," Ned said.

"But we're a presentable lot, aren't we?" Moses winked at Rabbit.

Rose saw the gesture and felt bad for him. Moses had been trying to befriend the child all day, but was making no headway. Rabbit continued to ignore him, but Rose didn't think the girl intended to be hurtful.

When he got no reaction from Rabbit, Moses slowed his horse to ride abreast of Rose. If he was bothered by Rabbit's discourtesy he gave no indication.

"I saw you watching those houses up on the hill," he said. "You pick out a likely one?"

"I'm sure one is the same as any other, Mr Burke. But I tend to agree with Mr Hemingway. I don't think there's anyone who'd want to take in five strangers for the night."

"Well, I guess we better try the biggest house first."

He spurred his Appaloosa and rode forward to talk to Ned, then they galloped away across a pasture full of blue sage and bright yellow dandelions. Rabbit kicked her mule again and followed.

"Stay where I can see you," Rose shouted.

"He's got his own mind," Tom said. "No point trying to argue with Rabbit or discipline it out of him, trust me on that."

Rose scowled at him and cut across the field after the others, leaving Tom to take up the rear. She let her horse pick his own pace. The old swayback mule wasn't capable of much more than a slow canter, and as long as Rabbit was within sight ahead of her, that was fine with Rose. It couldn't hurt to give the girl a little taste of freedom.

Rose caught up to the others at a snarl of barbed wire strung along a fence line. Ned had a spyglass held up to his eye, and Moses pointed at a distant hilltop where Rose could see another column of chimney smoke.

"Big ranch house up there," Moses said. "Probably has an out-building or two for the hands, and a barn. Whatever they've got, be it cattle or horses, the animals will be out grazing, now that it's warm, and the barn'll be empty. Or mostly empty. Might be shelter for the night."

"A stroke of luck," Rose said.

Ned collapsed the spyglass and stowed it in his saddlebag.

"Don't get ahead of yourself, Mrs Nettles," he said. "Luck ain't been on our side of late."

Tom caught up to them. "You can make your own luck," he said. "Or you can pay me to make it for you."

Ned ignored him. "Moses and I'll ride up there and get the lay of the land. Ma'am, if you could keep an eye on Old Tom for us and see he don't get in any trouble?"

"Hey, now," Tom said.

"Rabbit!" Rose said.

They all turned to see Rabbit's mule trotting across the sloping pasture away from them.

"How'd he get over that wire?" Tom said.

But Ned and Moses had already jumped their horses over the low fence and were galloping after the child. Rose wanted to fol-low, but she didn't know how to jump a horse. She could ride well enough; Joe had taught her. A steady clip was all that was required to pull a plow or go into town for supplies.

"Over there," Tom said. "That's how the boy got his mule through."

There was a break in the fence, ten yards from them and nearly invisible in the encroaching dusk. The wire had been cut and the ends trampled into the dirt.

"This must be how those cows escaped," Rose said.

"Damn clumsy to leave it open like this," Tom said.

Rose followed him through the gap and up the hill after the others. A cool breeze sprang up as the sun set, and insects sang out in the tall grass, reassuring Rose that the fence she had just passed through wasn't there to bar people from another atrocity like the one they had encountered in the woods. She could see the wrapped body bouncing on the back of Moses's horse and she shuddered.

The ranch house was huge and stately, as unlike the simple wooden shack Joe Mullins had built as it was possible to be, while still having four walls and a roof. White with bright red trim, it sat atop the hill, with a long white bunkhouse a few yards down the slope and a big red barn visible behind it. The dark bulk of an enormous carriage sat next to the barn, gold trim shining in the light of the setting sun.

Ned, Moses, Rose, Tom, and Rabbit had missed the road leading up to the ranch, and they approached the house along the side of the hill. Three pigs trotted out from the barn and down toward them, snorting and grunting at the strangers. A wraparound porch with four red steps and a painted white railing extended around the side of the house and across the front.

Two men sat in the yard on heavy wooden chairs. A small table was situated between them, and a bottle of whiskey sat on the table with two glasses next to it, both glasses half-full. The men were chewing tobacco, and they took turns spitting at the ground near their feet, occasionally taking aim at the pigs that had scurried back up to the house and were now running in and out of a crawl space beneath the porch.

Neither man stood as the riders approached. They were both thin, with long dark hair that curled out from under their hats. Their clothing was fine, but stained and dirty, and both of them wore matching silver stars pinned to their leather vests.

"Greetings," said the taller of the two as Ned and Moses approached.

"Salutations," said the other man. He raised his glass of whiskey.

Rose signaled to Rabbit that they should hang back a bit, and the child appeared to agree. She brought her mule around and let it graze next to Rose's horse out of sight of the porch. Tom edged past them, as if to prove he was on equal footing with the two cowboys, but then busied himself arranging the contents of his saddlebags, allowing Ned and Moses to do all the talking.

"Hello," Ned said. "Sorry to barge in on you like this, but your fence was broken, and we didn't see a gate."

"Gate's over yonder," the first man said. "At the end of the road."

"You follow the road back out and you'll see the gate," the other man said.

Ned ignored the invitation to leave. "Name's Hemingway," he said. "Ned Hemingway. This is Moses Burke, and over there's the other members of our company. We been traveling all day and we're looking for a place to bunk down tonight."

"I'm McDaniel," the first man said. His nose was badly sunburned, the skin blistered and peeling.

"I guess I'm Rigby," the other man said.

"You run this place?" Moses said.

"I look like a rancher?" McDaniel said. He spat tobacco into the dirt.

"We ain't ranchers," Rigby said.

"Wasn't any harm in the question," Moses said.

"What about the rancher, then?" Ned said. "He around here somewhere?"

"He left," McDaniel said.

"Gone to Wichita for supplies," Rigby said.

"Left us in charge."

"He'll be back in a day or two, if you want to wait for him."

"Could be three days, though," McDaniel said.

"Or even four," Rigby said. "You never know, he might not be in a hurry to get back."

Ned glanced at Moses. "What about the foreman?" he said. "He around?"

"He went with his boss."

"Most everybody's gone to Wichita."

"I guess you got to talk to us," McDaniel said. "Since there ain't nobody else to talk to."

"Not a soul," Rigby said. He giggled.

Ned and Moses looked at each other, then looked around at the other three. Ned sighed and tipped his yellow hat back on his head.

"Well, then," he said. "If you're the ones to talk to, we'd be grateful if we could spend the night in that bunkhouse, if there's room."

"That's a fine idea," McDaniel said. "But the foreman, he locked that bunkhouse door and he took the key with him."

"Damned inconvenient," Rigby said.

"What about the barn?" Moses said. "We'd be glad just to have a roof over our heads."

"Well, now, we can't have a pretty woman sleeping with the pigs," McDaniel said.

"Pigs sleep in the barn," Rigby said. "People sleep in the house."

"You're welcome to stay in the house," McDaniel said.

"Plenty of rooms in there," Rigby said.

"Well, that's kind of you," Ned said.

"Anybody'd do the same," McDaniel said.

"It's the neighborly thing to do," Rigby said. He winked at Rose. The donkey snorted and bucked, threatening to tip the body of the hanged man into the grass.

"Somebody ought to patch that fence back there," Ned said. "All your cattle are gonna run off. We'd be happy to do it in exchange for the rooms."

"Like we said, friend, they're not our cattle," McDaniel said.

"Not our fence, neither," Rigby said.

Ned squinted at them for a full minute while the two men sat chewing their wads and spitting. Neither of them seemed the least bit uncomfortable under Ned's scrutiny.

"Well, you two beat all," Ned finally said. "You mind we rest our horses in that barn?"

McDaniel shrugged, and a second later Rigby shrugged, too. Ned gathered the reins of his horse, while Moses helped Rabbit down off her mule and followed Ned, leading it and his own horse. The donkey was still tethered to the sorrel mare. Tom smacked his horse on the flank, and it trotted along behind the others without being led.

Inside the barn, a team of horses occupied six of the stalls. Ned and Moses led their mounts to the opposite side, where there were empty stalls. They fed and watered the animals and brushed them down. Moses walked around outside the stalls, taking note of the orderly bales of hay, the tools and rope that hung from nails in the walls, the lanterns on high hooks. In a back corner was a stack of five paint cans. The topmost can was streaked with bright red paint that matched the walls of the barn and the shutters on the house.

"Nice place," Moses said.

"I'd like to fix that fence," Ned said. "I hate to accept someone's hospitality without earning it."

Moses spread his hands wide and mimicked Rigby's high-pitched voice: "Not their fence, friend." He shrugged and dropped the imitation. "It's not their hospitality we're accepting," he said.

"It would be nice to know whose hospitality it is, then. 'Cause I'd be willing to bet twenty dollars and my left nut them two ain't US Marshals."

"I'm not taking that bet," Moses said.

CHAPTER 3

Joe Mullins stood under the sycamore tree for a long while, smoking his pipe and considering his options. Behind him was the farmhouse, but Rose was gone from there. It was nothing now, except an empty building without a wife or children to bring it to life.

Joe had always wanted children. Lots of them; boys and girls, both. A big family to gather around the table, to fill every room with sound and energy and life. But Rose had seemed skittish on the subject, and so he had left it alone. There would be plenty of time, he thought, to let her come around to the idea on her own. They had run out of time much sooner than he'd expected.

Ahead of him was the crossroads, little more than two dirt trails that overlapped each other at the southwest corner of his property. Buried where he was, he had more choices in death than he might have had in life. He could head out in any direction and leave the farm. But Rose had ridden north with the cowboys, and the old man with the turkey feather, and the strange child.

When he thought about Rose he heard a noise like a distant hornets' nest; the sound made him anxious. He decided he would follow her to make sure Rose didn't need anything from him. After all, he thought, she had uprooted her entire life to join him in Kansas. He would always feel an obligation toward her, and as far as he could see death had not parted them by more than a few miles.

The mule they called Brother had died out in front of the plow; what remained of him was visible from the crossroads. Joe thought that might mean the mule was still out in the field, the same way Joe was still under the sycamore. Catching up to Rose would be easier if he could ride Brother.

He left the shelter of the tree and walked up past the house and across the land Rose had tried to plow. He was dismayed to see how uneven the lines were, curving away in all directions, and for a brief moment he began to make plans to re-till it all, before he remembered he was dead.

It was actually a bit of a relief.

Joe found Brother's skeleton under a hedgerow at the northern end of the field. The old mule's body had been picked clean by buzzards; there was no sign of his spirit. Joe wondered if Brother had gone on to wherever mules went when they died or if his ghost had simply wandered away from the farm. Joe realized he didn't know if mules *had* spirits. He had a lot of questions about death, and he was peeved that no one had told him what to expect after he was rolled up in a yellow bath curtain and dumped in a hole.

He gave up on the mule and circled back around to the trail, following it on foot, north and west, skirting his neighbors' fields and watching for the tracks of the buckboard and the cowboys' horses.

At times it was night, and at times it was day, and sometimes it was neither or both at once. Time seemed flexible and confusing, but eventually he crossed a pasture thick with jumping bugs and tiny white daisies, and he stopped at a high wooden fence. It was a well-constructed fence, sturdy and solid, but someone had hacked through it with an axe, and pulled out the nails at the ends of the planks, and stacked the wood neatly to one side, leaving a hole wide enough for a horse to pass through. Beyond it was a thick stand of trees.

"Strange," he said. "Why not just go around?"

The sound of his own voice startled him so much he almost dropped his pipe.

"Best not talk to yourself, Joe," he said. "They're sure to lock you up."

He stepped through the opening and entered the woods.

The buzzing in his head was louder under the canopy of leaves, and his scalp tingled as if a storm were forming overhead. He heard voices, people talking in the shadows under the trees, and faces peered out at him from the dark.

"Who's there?" he said.

He heard a child giggle, and a pitter-patter of footsteps faded away into the underbrush. The darkness and loneliness of his surroundings might have been frightening under other circumstances—Joe had always been prone to feelings of loneliness and dread—but he reminded himself that he was already dead, and as far as he knew there wasn't much worse that could happen to him. Besides, the thought of a child wandering alone in the woods steeled his nerves, so he plunged through the tangle of leaves and vines and small branches. He was mildly surprised that the twigs and springy saplings didn't sting his face, and that he didn't slip on the rotten black leaves underfoot or trip over the long grasses. But then he remembered crossing the wide-open fields without growing tired or getting bitten by insects.

"There seem to be some advantages to all this," he said.

But he missed being able to taste the tobacco in his pipe and feel the breeze on his face. He missed the warmth of his wife's skin as she lay next to him in their narrow bed, and he even missed the smell of her terrible cooking.

He passed through the trunk of a mighty elm and entered a wide glade that wasn't touched by the sun. Around him, sitting on logs and standing between trees, were dozens of people: men, women, and children, all of them staring expectantly at him. He removed his hat.

"Hello," Joe said. "My name is Mullins. I hope I'm not intruding."

One of the men glanced around at the others, then stepped forward. He was wearing a light brown suit that had taken some wear in the elbows and knees, and a top hat that looked like it had been smashed and re-formed at some point in the distant past.

"My name is . . ." the man said. He stopped and looked around again as if embarrassed to have lost his place in an important speech. "Well, I guess I don't remember my name."

"It's James," a girl whispered. "Your name is James."

The man smiled at her. "Yes, thank you," he said. "It's been some time since I had cause to utter it."

"And my name is Hannah," the girl said. Joe thought she might have been the one giggling at him from behind the trees.

"Well met, Mr James," Joe said. "And hello to you, too, Hannah. I thought I heard a lost child, but there's all manner of people to look after each other here. I ought not to have worried after all."

"We are all beyond worry now," Mr James said. "But we are lonely. We so seldom receive visitors."

"You don't have a body here, Mr Mullins," Hannah said.

"No, miss," he said. "My body is feeding the worms back on my farm." Joe tried to point, but he had lost track of direction, and couldn't recall where his farm was in relation to the woods.

"I don't understand," Hannah said. "But how marvelous it must be to travel."

"It is not bad," Joe said. "I didn't used to like it, but now that my knees don't hurt and I don't get hungry or sleepy, I guess I don't mind it much. How did you all come to be here?"

Some of the people in the glade shook their heads and faded away into the shadow-patterns of the branches. Others turned their backs to him and spoke to one another in low voices.

"I apologize again," Mr James said with a grimace. "Some of us do not enjoy telling how we ended up here, and some of us have told it so many times we've grown tired of the telling. I don't mind talking about it with you, though. Please sit, if you care to."

Mr James gestured toward a rotting log at the edge of the grass and Joe lowered himself onto it. The girl came and sat next to him, and he plucked a match from his pocket so he could work at relighting his pipe.

"When I was alive I crushed my son's head with a heavy rock I found by the side of the river," Mr James said. "Then I chucked him in the water."

Joe dropped his pipe in his lap and fumbled to grab it before it fell to the ground.

"He was barely three years old, and he had a terrible earache. He screamed night and day, and his mama couldn't stop the noise. I took to spending my time out of doors, but even when I was some distance away from the house, I could still hear his cries. He wouldn't eat and he wouldn't sleep, and my wife and I couldn't sleep either."

"Wasn't there a doctor nearby?" Joe said.

"We couldn't afford a doctor, nor medicine. I caught seven mice and I burned them up, sprinkled the ashes in his ear. Supposed to be good magic, but it didn't work. We spent many sleepless nights, so that both of us were like as if asleep during the day, unable to do anything, barely able to move. It sometimes seemed like I could scarcely breathe. My wife began to chew on her fingertips. She chewed and she chewed until blood ran down her chin and dotted our floors wherever she walked. And still that boy screamed."

"So you took him to the river." Joe's voice was so quiet he could barely hear it himself.

Mr James nodded. "I did. Then I put on my hat and picked up a length of rope from the back of my wagon, and I walked to these woods and I sat down on this very log. By and by, the idea of what I had done sank into me like I was underwater with my boy, and I thought I wouldn't move again. But eventually I mustered enough strength to throw one end of my rope over a good stout branch and I tied the other end around my neck. And there I am."

Mr James pointed.

Joe got up from the log and looked above him. A few bones dressed in the tatters of a brown suit swayed gently in the whisper of a breeze. Mr James's leg bones had come loose at some point and fallen off. So had his old top hat.

"I wish you hadn't told me that story, Mr James. I don't feel as neighborly toward you now."

"I understand," Mr James said. "I can't explain why I did it, but I do hope it gave my wife some relief. And this place is where I pay penance for what I did. I sit and I think about it until I can't stand to think about it anymore. But there's nothing else to think about, so I keep at it anyway."

"Do you think you'll see them again?" Joe said. "Your wife and boy?"

"Heavens," Mr James said. "I certainly hope not."

Joe didn't know what to say after that, but Mr James didn't seem to expect a response. Hannah smiled at Joe, and he smiled back.

"I hope nobody drowned you in the river," he said to her.

"No," she said. "Nobody drowned me. The river was nothing but a trickle when I died," the girl said. "But I think that was a long time ago because I was here before Mr James arrived. My papa was a good man, but he had two children, and he couldn't afford food for us both. Nor was there enough water in the river for our crops, much less to drink. The water was down for more seasons than I can remember. But my brother loved me very much and I loved him, and I wanted him to have food to eat and water to drink. So one morning I gathered up the poison my papa put out for the rats in the barn. Then I walked out here and ate it all and fell asleep under one of these trees. I have lost track of which one it was."

"My gosh, girl, you ought not to have done that," Joe said. "I sure wish you hadn't done that."

He felt moisture come to his eyes, and he turned away from her so she wouldn't see. If the girl had walked away from the woods, she might have found the little farmhouse where he and Rose lived. Some years the crops were plentiful and some years the yield was bad, but Joe was certain there would have been enough food for another person. He reminded himself that Hannah must have died long before he had secured his hundred-sixty acres and brought Rose out to Kansas.

When he felt he had control over his emotions, he addressed her again.

"I will say that you were a good person when you were alive," he said. "A much better person than Mr James. I apologize for bringing it up in your presence, Mr James."

"Think nothing of it," Mr James said. "I am not proud of what I did."

"I am on my way to find my wife," Joe said. "We are childless, and I would be glad of it if you were to accompany me, Hannah."

"I would be honored," the girl said. "But I don't think I can. My body is here in these woods, and I have to stay here with it."

This made no sense to Joe. "My body is nowhere near here, and yet, as you say, I'm able to travel here and yon away from it."

"I guess I'm happy you can do it," Hannah said with a shrug. "I cannot."

He looked all around at the deep green of the forest, and his heart felt heavy at the notion that the girl would stay there forever. He hoped that someday, when her skeleton had crumbled to dirt, she might finally be free.

Joe tarried for a while, talking with Hannah and Mr James, and with a few of the others when they returned to the glade, either because they were curious or because it had been a long time since they had met someone new. Many of them had stories to tell, and some of those stories made Joe feel upset again, but he began to understand that his simple life had been a good one.

He tried to lift the spirits of the ghosts in the woods by telling them jokes he had overheard in Monmouth, at the general store and in the barbershop, but eventually he ran out of jokes and decided it was time to move on. He shook Mr James's hand, and he promised Hannah that he would visit her again someday.

When he left them and resumed his journey on the other side of the woods, he felt he had learned a great deal about unhappiness. Maybe, he thought, Rose had been more unhappy than he knew, though he had tried to make life good for her. Maybe that was why she had left her farm in the company of strangers. Maybe she didn't care about the danger and hardship that surely awaited her.

Joe heard the buzzing of hornets again, and he quickened his pace.

CHAPTER 4

Rigby got up from his chair and went into the house. Mc-Daniel sat, chewing a wad of tobacco and staring at Rose. Old Tom tried to make conversation, but McDaniel ignored him. Rose thought the old witch-master was used to being ignored, and she felt a touch of pity for him. She tried to bear up under McDaniel's scrutiny, but felt herself beginning to sweat under her cotton dress, despite the coolness of the evening. She felt vaguely nauseated, and would have liked to sit on the porch to fan herself, but she didn't want to walk past McDaniel.

Rabbit kept her back to the house and held on to Rose's skirt. She kicked at a tiny black toad wriggling through the grass.

Presently, Rigby returned, carrying two crystal drinking glasses.

"I didn't bring nothing for the kid," he said. "But there's a pump at the side of the house."

"The kid can drink water," McDaniel said. He frowned at Rabbit. "You ever talk?"

"Matter of fact, you look familiar to me, kid," Rigby said. "Damn familiar."

Rabbit ignored them. She watched the pigs snuffle in the dirt, smearing tobacco juice on their snouts.

"What are you, anyway, kid? With them duds you got on, I can't tell if you're a boy or a girl."

"He's a boy," Tom said quickly.

"Is that so?" McDaniel said.

"I can't tell," Rigby said.

"Take off them britches and let's have a look," McDaniel said.

"That oughta solve it," Rigby said.

Rose stepped forward, positioning herself between Rabbit and the two men. Old Tom put a hand on Rabbit's shoulder and pulled her back a step, farther away from the house.

"I'll have a drink of that whiskey," Rose said.

McDaniel chuckled and reached for the bottle. He poured two fingers of amber liquid into one of the empty glasses and held it out to Rose. She stepped forward and took it, then stepped back out of his reach.

"Is that your carriage?" she said. "There by the barn?"

Rigby turned to look, but McDaniel kept his gaze fixed on her. She hoped that mentioning the barn would remind the two men of the nearby presence of Ned and Moses. She felt they ought to have finished with the horses.

"Yeah," Rigby said. "That's our wagon."

"It's very nice," Rose said.

She took a small sip of the whiskey and felt it burn its way down her throat, warming her chest and flushing her skin. There was a nagging pain in her stomach, but it had been there for days. Whatever the cause, she didn't think the whiskey could hurt.

"I shall have to ask Mr Hemingway if this is a good brand," she said. She glanced again at the barn, wondering why the two cowboys hadn't returned.

Ned and Moses were also interested in the carriage parked beside the barn, which had provoked a mild argument between them. It started when Ned wanted to leave the body of the hanged man in the barn overnight.

"No," Moses said. "There's pigs."

"That fella's been dead long enough those pigs won't pay no attention to him."

"A pig'll eat anything that doesn't run from it."

"Well, I suppose that's so, but we can't take him in the house with us."

"It's getting late in the day to bury him, Ned, and we don't know that these people want a stranger buried on their land."

"McDaniel and Rigby won't care."

"They've been pretty clear about the fact this isn't their land."

"Well, dammit, Moses."

"It's not me," Moses said. "It's an inconvenient situation, is all." He hoped Ned wouldn't mention that Moses had brought the body. He didn't feel up to an argument.

"Well," Ned said, "if we can't take him inside and we can't leave him outside, it seems to me we don't have a lot of options left."

"There's always a third option," Moses said. It was a thing he often said, and sometimes it sparked an idea in Ned, who sometimes needed to be prodded in order to think of something new. It worked this time.

"We could put him *inside* a thing that's *outside*," Ned said.

"Like that carriage," Moses said.

"Of course, that ain't our carriage. It could belong to those so-called Marshals."

"They don't lay claim to much."

"We could ask them."

"Or we could do what we're thinking of doing, then leave in the morning before they even know we did it."

"True."

With that decided, they both felt better. Ned kept lookout from the barn's loft, watching out in the direction of the house in case the two men claiming to be Marshals decided to take a stroll. Moses hefted the dead man's body and carried it to the coach. He opened the door and set the body on one of the two long benches, sitting him upright as if he were a living passenger on the stagecoach. Moses was uncertain whether this looked dignified or silly, but it was better than being eaten by pigs in the night. He stepped back and looked at the carriage, seeing details of it for the first time since they had arrived at the ranch. After a moment, he waved at Ned to come down from the loft.

"Look at that," he said, when Ned had joined him.

He pointed up at a line of type stenciled in gold across the red trim under the roof of the carriage. Even in the semidark of dusk they could read the words: WELLS FARGO & COMPANY.

CHAPTER 5

They ate a simple meal with the two men claiming to be US Marshals: a few tins of beans that McDaniel and Rigby brought in from the pantry, and biscuits Ned made in his own cook pot over an open fire.

"Well, you finally did it," Moses said. "You made biscuits without burning them on the bottom."

Ned chuckled, but Rose took a second biscuit to reassure him that they were good.

"What direction was you two fellas headed?" Tom said between forkfuls of beans.

McDaniel fixed him with a steely glare, but Rigby answered.

"We come up from Texas," he said. "Not sure which way we're going from here."

"We're after a Mexican boy," McDaniel said. Whenever one of them spoke, it seemed the other felt a need to chime in.

"He killed a woman in Nacogdoches," Rigby said.

"It was Fulton," McDaniel said. "And he killed her right in front of her husband."

"We chased this bandit all the way up through Arkansas for the bounty," Rigby said. "Lost him somewhere around Oswego."

"Been trying to pick up his trail," McDaniel said. "Could be you ran across him in your travels."

"Name of Benito Cortez," Rigby said.

"You all meet any Mexican bandits called theyselves Benito Cortez?"

Ned shook his head and swallowed a mouthful of biscuit. "No, sir, I don't believe I've heard tell of him."

"Well, I suspect we'll catch up to him before too much longer," McDaniel said. "My gut says he's close by."

After supper, Rose expected to clean up, and intended to have Rabbit help her, but Ned suggested she sit by the fire and warm up.

"Saw you shaking a little before," he said. "I can do the cleaning."

Rose was grateful, and further grateful when Mr Burke stayed with her in the main room by the fire. She had seen Ned and Moses exchange a look, and she wondered if the two men had sensed the tension in the air when they returned from the barn. In any case, she was glad she had not been left alone again with the Marshals.

Moses examined Rabbit's scalp wound and smiled approvingly. "That's healing pretty good," he said. "Faster than I would've thought."

Rabbit stood and went to Tom's bag, which was draped over the back of a chair. She pulled out a sprig of aloe and showed it to Moses, and he nodded.

"That's right," he said. "That stuff speeds things up." He turned to Rose and winked. "Your teacher's doing a good job."

Rose frowned. Rabbit had not learned the medicinal properties of aloe from her, but she didn't care to admit it.

McDaniel and Rigby sat next to each other a few feet from the fire, passing a flask back and forth. When he had finished with the chores, Ned rejoined them. He had found a guitar in a room near the kitchen, and he played it while Moses sang a sad song that reminded Rose of Joe and of lonely nights on the farm. Ned joined Moses on the refrain, and together they sounded better than Rose had expected.

Come along boys and listen to my tale,
I'll tell you of my troubles on the old Chisholm trail.

> *Come a ti yi yippee, come a ti yi yea,*
> *Come a ti yi yippee, come a ti yi yea.*

Oh, a ten-dollar hoss and a forty-dollar saddle,
And I'm goin' to punchin' Texas cattle.

> *Come a ti yi yippee, come a ti yi yea,*
> *Come a ti yi yippee, come a ti yi yea.*

I wake in the mornin' afore daylight,
And afore I sleep the moon shines bright.

> *Come a ti yi yippee, come a ti yi yea,*
> *Come a ti yi yippee, come a ti yi yea.*

It's cloudy in the north, a-lookin' like rain,
And my durned old slicker's in the wagon again.

Rose got out her needles and a skein of red yarn and began knitting a scarf while she listened. After four songs, Ned's voice began to crack and he put the guitar away. Old Tom got up and performed a few magic tricks, primarily for the child's amusement. Rabbit remained stony-faced, but Rigby laughed when Tom caught his shirtsleeve in the fire. Ned grabbed a sheep hide from the back of his chair and threw it over the witch-master's arm, patting him down. Tom appeared unhurt, but he was deeply embarrassed, and refused to finish the trick he had been performing. His accident changed the mood in the room, and they all decided to turn in.

McDaniel and Rigby told the others they were welcome to any of the rooms along the west hallway upstairs, but to leave the east hall alone. Tom elected to stay in the front room where he could sulk and stir the embers in the fireplace.

"Try not to catch yourself on fire again," Rigby said.

Rose brought a pitcher of water upstairs. As before, she insisted that Rabbit share a room with her, and Ned and Moses chose the next room along the hallway. Before they had settled in, Ned rapped his knuckles lightly on the jamb and Rose stepped out into the hall where the two cowboys were waiting for her. Ned tipped his hat and cleared his throat.

"Moses and me thought we should apprise you of our discovery," he said.

"I see." Rose leaned back into her room. "Rabbit, why don't you dress for bed. I'll be right in." She closed the door and folded her hands in front of her. "What did you find, Mr Hemingway?"

Ned glanced at Moses who nodded that he should go ahead. "Well, you know that wagon you can see from the porch, the one parked by the barn?"

"Yes," Rose said. "It belongs to Mr McDaniel and Mr Rigby."

"That's the thing of it," Moses said. "That wagon doesn't belong to either of those men, nor to the US Marshals."

"It's a Wells Fargo coach," Ned said.

"What does that mean?"

"It means them two fellas robbed a bank. Or, rather, they held up a coach, probably for the payroll it was carrying, and then they rode off with the whole damn thing."

"At least, that's what seems likely to us," Moses said. "And if so, they're bandits."

"But they're *chasing* a bandit," Rose said. "Someone named Benito Cortez."

"Don't mean they ain't bandits themselves. Some men'll do anything for money, and a bounty ain't as quick as a coach full of cash."

"We think it's possible the coach had already run into some Indians when these two came across it," Moses said.

"Or maybe other bandits," Ned said.

"Maybe the driver and the guards were injured or dead already."

"Some of them, at least."

"Would make it easier to take. Those coaches are well guarded."

"If those men stole money," Rose said, "it must be nearby."

"Our thoughts exactly," Moses said.

"We already searched the barn, but the house is hard to explore with them two fellas always around."

"Well," Rose said, "if we did find the money, we would be obligated to return it to the bank, wouldn't we?"

Another look passed between Ned and Moses, and Moses reluctantly nodded again. "Yes, ma'am, I suppose that would be the right thing to do."

"Perhaps we should discuss this in the morning," Rose said. "A good night's sleep will give us a better perspective."

Ned sighed. "It might not be worth the trouble to tangle with them so-called Marshals."

"And we do have a child to consider," Moses said.

"We have a lot to consider," Rose said. "I thank you for including me in your deliberations."

She said good night and locked the bedroom door, then helped Rabbit get ready for bed. She made the girl wash her face in the basin and hang her clothes on the valet stand to air out.

When she woke it was dark in the room, and stuffy. She laid still, trying to figure out what had disturbed her sleep. Beside her on the bed, Rabbit was curled in a ball. Over the sound of the girl's heavy breathing, Rose heard a rasping noise. She got up and struck a match, lighting the lamp on the bedside table, then tiptoed to the door. She watched as the knob turned a quarter inch, first one way, then the other, and someone grunted in the hallway outside.

"Who's there?" Rose whispered.

"It's me, Ned Hemingway."

"I am not fooled, Mr Rigby," Rose said. "You sound nothing like Mr Hemingway."

"I could sound like him if you want me to. I could look like him, too."

"Mr Rigby, if you do not move on, I will shoot you through the door. I have a pistol in my hand."

"No, you don't, Mrs Nettles."

"Then I will scream. My companions are in the next room."

There was a moment's silence, then Rigby moved quietly away down the hall. It sounded to Rose like he wasn't alone.

She got back into bed, but left the lamp burning and laid awake for a long time, staring at the ceiling and listening.

When she woke again, pale morning light was streaming through the window and Rabbit's small warm presence was gone from the bed. It took Rose a few drowsy seconds to notice the bedroom window was open and a warm wind was blowing through the room. She leaped out of bed and pulled the billowing curtains aside. Directly below was the sloping roof of the wraparound porch. Rose looked out across the yard to the fields beyond, but she saw no trace of the child.

She dressed quickly, and splashed water on her face, then unlocked the bedroom door and opened it a crack. The hallway was deserted, and she hurried to the room next to hers. She knocked softly on the door, and after a long moment it opened. Ned peered out at her through a narrow crack. He was behind the door, but she could see that he was shirtless. Rose was too preoccupied to care.

"Rabbit's missing," she said. "I don't know how long she's been gone."

"Moses went out to check the horses," Ned said. "Maybe she

went with him. Give me a minute to get dressed and I'll take you over there."

He shut the door without waiting for an answer, and Rose stood in the hall, unwilling to venture farther into the house for fear of running into one of the false Marshals.

Ned was quick. He joined Rose in the hall within five minutes, and together they went downstairs. There was a fire blazing in the fireplace, and Tom was limping around the big room, clanking coffee mugs together. McDaniel and Rigby were playing cards at a small table in the corner.

"Got coffee made," Tom said. "Working on some bacon."

The Marshals glared at Ned and ignored Rose. Neither of them said a word.

"Be right back, Tom," Ned said.

He and Rose rushed out the front door without waiting for a response, and Ned led the way down the hillside to the barn. As they drew near, Moses appeared in the open doorway.

"Is Rabbit with you?" Rose said.

"I was just coming to ask the same of you. Her mule's missing."

"Where would she go?"

Moses frowned. "You don't think those two Marshals—"

"They're inside," Rose said. She decided not to mention the late night visit from the two men. It would only complicate matters; locating Rabbit was the priority. "I locked the bedroom door last night. It was still locked when I woke up, but the window was open. I think she crawled out onto the porch and ran away."

"Where would she go?" Ned said.

They looked out over the unending plains. Cows grazed and birds wheeled through the air, but there was no other sign of movement.

"Why would she run away?" Moses said.

"I hate to say it, but she ain't our kid," Ned said. "None of us have got a right to hem her in if she don't wanna be hemmed."

"She's a child," Rose said.

"Yes, ma'am. I was only thinking about how I was when I was her age, and I come out all right in the end."

"That's debatable," Moses said. "And we're wasting daylight. I'll look to the west," he pointed.

"I'll go north, then," Rose said.

"Should we get Tom to help?" Ned said.

"Leave him be," Rose said. "He's too slow. We can ride in circles if we keep the house in the middle, and cover the ranch ourselves."

The horses were well rested and lively. Ned helped Rose onto Tom's horse since it was bigger and faster than her donkey. They rode out from the barn and away from one another, all of them scanning the tall grass and hillocks for any sign of the little girl.

CHAPTER 6

I know that child," Rigby said. "That's a girl child."

Old Tom had eaten his fill of bacon and leftover biscuits and was dozing in a chair, snoring softly into the same sheepskin that had saved him the previous night. The two men pretending to be US Marshals ignored him.

"I like the big one," McDaniel said. "The one named for a flower."

"Ah," Rigby said. "Daisy."

"Rose," McDaniel said, "she said her name was Rose."

Rigby belched and held out his hand and a small toad jumped from his mouth to his palm.

"I wish you wouldn't do that," McDaniel said.

Rigby lowered his hand to the floor and the toad hopped away under the chair.

"If wishes were fishes, horses would ride," Rigby said.

"I don't think that's how the saying goes," McDaniel said.

"That's how I always heard it."

"Them two cowboys ain't gonna let you nowhere near the girl. Nor the woman, neither."

"The white cowboy poses no problem, so far as I can tell," Rigby said. "But I believe the slave fancies himself a man of science."

McDaniel winced. He had told Mr Rigby on more than one occasion that there weren't any more slaves. The president had declared it so. But Rigby kept pretending he didn't know it, and

McDaniel had begun to think Rigby was trying to get under his skin.

"It amuses me when you squirm," Rigby said.

McDaniel jumped as if he'd been jabbed with a hot poker. Sometimes Rigby seemed to read his mind. He had encountered the smaller man on a path along the Rio Grand and had struck up a conversation. Rigby had accompanied McDaniel when they broke camp, agreeing with him on nearly every subject, even repeating the things he said back to him in a companionable way that McDaniel found pleasing. Presently they had come across an old Indian tracker McDaniel had hired once or twice before. The Indian, named Traveling Horse, rode with them a short way, but eventually expressed a profound dislike for Rigby.

"You have fallen in with the Devil," Traveling Horse said to McDaniel, without realizing that Rigby had ridden up beside him.

Rigby smacked the Indian over the head with the butt of his pistol, knocked him off his mount, and tied a rope around his neck, then spurred his horse and galloped along the riverbed, over rocks and old tree stumps, through weeds and prickly pears, dragging the old man behind him and far out of sight. When McDaniel caught up to him at sunset, Rigby had a campfire going. A hunk of meat was roasting on a spit. Fat dripped into the flames and spattered the river rocks lining the fire. Rigby tore off a piece and offered it to McDaniel, who burned his fingers on the charred meat. When he bit into it, grease dripped from his chin, staining his favorite leather vest.

"Don't taste much like horse, do he?" Rigby said.

Every time McDaniel remembered that first taste of human flesh he began to sweat. His skin tingled and his stomach turned. And yet he had taken a second portion of thigh meat that evening.

Over the course of the days and nights that followed, they had devoured all of Traveling Horse, down to the old man's bones. Later, McDaniel wondered why he had been so willing to ingest the flesh of another human being and, though he did not ask the question out loud, Rigby answered him.

"For the same reason you encountered me on the trail," he said. "There are no coincidences in life, Mr McDaniel."

This wasn't as clear an answer as McDaniel wanted, but he didn't pursue the question. In fact, he avoided thinking about most things, and from that point on he followed Rigby's lead in all matters.

A week after murdering Traveling Horse, Rigby barricaded a schoolteacher and eight students in a Texas schoolhouse and burned it down. McDaniel pitched in with enthusiasm, and when he woke later that night screaming, he rolled over and went back to sleep. By morning the incident was a hazy memory.

He wondered aloud about the lack of consequences for their actions. He had been raised to think bad acts were followed by punishment.

"Oh, they will be," Rigby said. He winked. "You'll just have to wait awhile."

The next day Rigby said he was tired of being on a horse all the time. He wasn't used to riding so much.

"My nethers are sore," he said. "I want to ride in a coach."

They waited behind an outcropping of shale on the road between Liberty and Smithfield. They ignored the horsemen that passed by, but when a Wells Fargo coach came along at half past noon, the two men jumped out and pointed their shotguns at the driver. He snapped the reins, intending to trample the bandits, but Rigby spat on the ground between them. The horses bucked and whinnied and came to a halt, nearly tipping the wagon into a ditch. Meanwhile, McDaniel fired on the shotgun messenger, hitting him in the shoulder before he could bring his Winchester to bear. Rigby motioned the driver down off the wagon and made the two Wells Fargo men stand side by side.

"They'll hang you boys," the shotgun messenger said. "The US Marshals will come after you for this."

"Texas Rangers, too," the driver said.

"They'll come after us all right," Rigby said. "I'm looking forward to it."

McDaniel went to the coach and looked inside.

"They got mail in here, and a strongbox," he said. "Hell, Rigby, there must be a thousand dollars here."

"Take the money," Rigby said.

"This safe is heavy," McDaniel said.

"Always, always, always," Rigby sang. "Always take the money."

Rigby pointed to the Wells Fargo driver. "You, draw your pistol," he said. "And I want you to shoot your friend in the heart."

"I won't," the driver said. But his body shook and his bones cracked, and he drew his revolver and pointed it at the messenger anyway. "I ain't doing this, Frank. I swear I'm not the one doing this."

Frank had no chance to respond. The driver pulled his trigger and Frank toppled over. He rolled down the side of the road, coming to rest beside the withered corpse of a squirrel.

"I didn't do that," the driver said. "I swear I didn't do it."

Rigby grinned at him, his mouth so wide and his teeth so large and yellow that McDaniel had to look away. When he glanced back, it seemed to him that the driver was hovering a few inches off the ground.

It might be a trick of the light, McDaniel thought. *Or it might be that I'm tired and seeing things wrong.*

The driver gurgled and gasped, and Rigby went on grinning.

"I'm gonna kill you real slow now," Rigby said. "So slow it might take a whole day to get it done. I'll give you just enough air in your lungs so you don't pass out and miss all the fun. Or if you've got a preference on the matter, you could take that pistola in your hand and shoot yourself like you shot your friend. I guess that'd be the only way this goes quick for you, mister."

McDaniel dumped the mail from one of the satchels and transferred the money from the strongbox. The satchel was much easier to heft. He laid it on the floor inside the coach and sat down on the steps. He thought perhaps a half an hour had passed when he heard a gunshot echo down the little canyon. The sun was setting and McDaniel's eyelids had begun to feel heavy, but he heaved himself up and walked to where the driver lay in the road.

"I guess we should bury them before it gets too dark," he said. "Unless you plan to eat them."

A trickle of blood flowed from Rigby's right eye. "No," he said. "White men taste like dirt. Let the critters have 'em. I want to get going before someone else comes along."

He climbed into the wagon and shut the door. McDaniel stood for a short while and thought about how far he could get if he started running, but then he climbed up onto the driver's seat and snapped the reins.

They took the coach down little-used roads and up overgrown trails, and they saw few fellow travelers, but the US Marshals eventually found them. Two Marshals were hunting a Mexican murderer named Benito Cortez when they got the news about the dead Wells Fargo men and the stolen coach. They recovered most of the mail being transported, but the empty strongbox was found in a ditch. The Marshals temporarily set aside their pursuit of Cortez.

They caught up to McDaniel and Rigby in Travis County, and Rigby kept the Marshals alive for a day and a half, inventing new ways to make them suffer. Then he took their badges and handed one to McDaniel.

"Where should we go next?" McDaniel said.

"Them two were looking for a fella named Cortez," Rigby said. "Let's go ahead and find him. Show how good we are."

"But we ain't lawmen."

Rigby looked momentarily confused and McDaniel understood that it was only the idea of hunting a man that appealed to his companion. He further understood that Rigby might decide to hunt *him* if he failed to help divert the demon's attention. He resolved to look for interesting places to take Rigby as they looked for the bandit. He didn't think he'd want Rigby to get bored.

When Cortez's trail led them to the sprawling ranch, McDaniel felt a profound sense of relief, having come upon a sufficient distraction for his master. He was glad, too, when new people arrived at the ranch two days later, and even happier to see a woman with them. And a child.

"You'll never get near that kid," he said to Rigby.

"I think I will," Rigby said. "I didn't see the girl this morning, and the woman just went out riding by herself."

Rigby used a long fingernail to pick his nose.

McDaniel looked away. "The cowboys must be with her."

"She has gone off alone, riding northward. It was her own idea. The other two have gone to the west and to the south. Shall we saddle our horses and ride north?"

"I imagine they'll be coming back soon enough."

"I say we go," Rigby said.

McDaniel sighed and stood up. He had learned long ago he could only argue with Rigby so much before the other man grew impatient and caused his skin to blister or his hair to fall out in clumps.

Old Tom Goggins raised his eyelids a fraction of an inch and watched the two Marshals leave. When the door closed behind them he sat up, ran a hand through his unkempt hair, and thought hard about what he had just heard. The small one, Rigby, was clearly possessed by a demon, and the other one, McDaniel, was no doubt the demon's familiar. Tom believed he was an expert in dealing with witches and haunts, but demons were outside his purview. Still, he had picked up a bit of knowledge here and there in his travels.

He went to the window and watched the two men amble away toward the barn, and when he was certain they weren't coming back he got painfully down on his hands and knees, wincing with each pop and creak of his old bones. He peered under the chair Rigby had occupied all morning.

"Here, toady, toady, toad," he called.

CHAPTER 7

It took Sadie four hours to drag the old couple's bodies from their house and across the yard to the base of a cottonwood tree. Then she went back and took apart the bed they had died on. She carried the planks of the bed, and the mattress, along with the soiled sheets and blankets outside and piled them on the stony ground. She burned them, making sure the wind carried the smoke and ash away from the house toward the cornfield. With a bucket of lye soap and water, and a wire brush from the pantry, she scrubbed the old man's blood and brains from the bedroom wall.

By the time she finished, night was coming and Sadie was exhausted, but she donned the aspect of a bear and circled the little house, urinating in the dirt at each of its four corners. She used her bear claws to cut her leg, and painted a bloody sigil on the doorframe. When she was satisfied the house was properly claimed, she went inside and fell asleep on the hearth.

She slept for two days. While she was asleep, coyotes came from the cornfield and dragged the bodies of the old people away. The coyotes smelled her bear scent and kept a safe distance from Sadie's new home.

She woke refreshed on the morning of the third day and searched the house. At the bottom of a flour tin full of weevils she found thirty-four dollars and fifty cents, the old couple's life savings. With the money in her pocket, she walked a mile down the trail to Riddle. At the Burden General Supply she paid for a few staples: eggs, cornmeal, candle wax, and a salt lick, to be delivered to her new house.

The shopkeeper, whose name was Grover Riddle, raised an eyebrow. "That's the Vilander place," he said.

"No," Sadie said. "It's mine."

"Since when is it yours?"

"Since three days ago."

"Well, I'll be damned."

"Yes," Sadie said. "I believe you will."

CHAPTER 8

Neither Ned nor Moses was much of a tracker. They knew how to follow a white man's horse in dry weather, if he wasn't too far ahead of them, but in general their abilities were as poor as their eyesight. Moses had once joked that Ned couldn't see an elephant if it was right in front of him, but since neither of them knew exactly what an elephant looked like Ned didn't consider it one of Moses's wittier comments.

In tall grass Ned's tracking skills were virtually nonexistent, so he didn't even try to look for Rabbit's trail. Instead, he followed his gut, which told him the girl would be headed back the way they had come, maybe on her way to where Old Tom had originally found her.

Ordinarily, he would have let her go. He believed there was no point holding someone back if they didn't want to stay. In fact, the idea of hanging on to someone against their will went against Ned's strongest principles. But there were two factors that made him override his convictions: he didn't want to disappoint Rose, and the girl was probably too young to be on her own. He decided it was in Rabbit's best interest that someone bring her back.

He rode out south, down the hill and back along the crude path they had taken to the ranch house. He used his spyglass to watch ahead for anything bigger than a squirrel or a bird.

What he saw were small groups of cattle, not nearly enough to make up an entire herd, and a handful of horses. One of the horses had a saddle on her back.

"If those are wild horses, I'll eat my hat," he said to himself. "Hell, I'll eat Old Tom's hat, turkey feather and all."

Ned collapsed the spyglass and changed course to intercept the horse with the saddle. She was spotted, gray on white, with a black mane and nose. As Ned approached, three other horses noticed him and galloped away in different directions. One of them had a bridle. The spotted horse held her ground, watching him. Ned got down from his sorrel and led her, talking softly to the spotted horse. When he was still a few yards away, she trotted over and nuzzled his hand, looking for a treat.

"Now, who do you belong to, girl?"

McDaniel and Rigby had told them the rancheros were in Wichita with their employer. It had made little sense to Ned at the time, since someone surely had to stay behind to watch the herd. But, after all, the two Marshals were there, and the rancheros were not, so it was barely possible the day-to-day responsibilities of the place had been left to McDaniel and Rigby. Aside from the team of six, there were no other horses in the barn, which had subconsciously reinforced the Marshals' story. Ned realized he had now found one of the rancheros' horses.

"What happened to you, girl? And what happened to the fella was riding you?"

He stroked the horse's nose and brushed her mane with his fingertips. She nickered and stamped her feet and rolled her head. He tethered her to his sorrel and led them both across the pasture toward the distant fence.

Reedy-looking grasshoppers and tiny brown crickets hopped away as he walked; white butterflies fluttered up from the weeds, and dragonflies zipped past his nose. In the distance he saw a hawk wheeling across the sky, chased by two loud crows.

When he reached the fence, he walked along the wire until he found the place where it was broken. He pulled the separate ends up out of the dirt and examined them.

"I don't think these were cut," he said to his horse. "Or broken, neither. This bit right here don't fit with this bit over here. I think somebody shot at the wires on this fence."

The sorrel looked up at him, then lowered her nose and began to graze. She was used to hearing him talk to himself when Moses wasn't nearby. The spotted horse nuzzled his neck and nibbled playfully at his hair. He took off his hat so she wouldn't chew the brim.

"You're a friendly gal, ain't you? Somebody took good care of you. Bet he'd be ticked off to see you wandering around like a mustang. I sure wish you could tell me what's going on around here."

But the evidence, however scant, that the fence had been shot apart, coupled with the riderless horses, painted a picture. Someone had come from the bizarre woods and had encountered the fence. They'd shot it apart and ridden through. The sound of gunfire would have brought cowboys from the ranch, but they had been outdrawn or outgunned.

"Problem is," he said to the friendly horse, "I don't see no bodies."

But then he did see somebody. Walking across the field, following the same path Ned and his company had used the previous day, was a small man with a potbelly and a droopy mustache. He was still some distance away and he walked slowly, as if through water. The man was smoking, and when he saw Ned he took the pipe from his mouth and waved with it.

"I know you," Ned said, hollering because of the distance between them. "I saw you a couple nights ago, didn't I?"

The man simply stared at him.

"Unless I miss my guess," Ned said, "your name is Joe Mullins."

The man's eyes went wide and he smiled. He mouthed a few

words, but Ned couldn't hear anything except the chirping of crickets and the cawing of angry crows.

"You can't talk to me, can you?"

Joe Mullins shrugged, evidently able to hear Ned, even if he couldn't make himself heard.

"Come on back with me, sir. Your wife's around here somewheres and I bet she'd be awful glad to see you."

Joe smiled and took a step forward. Then a beam of sunlight slanted through him and he was gone as suddenly as he'd appeared. Where Joe had been standing, Ned saw the long morning shadows cast by a clump of buckthorn bushes. He rubbed his eyes and looked around, his gaze settling on the new horse.

"Did you see that, girl? Or did I finally go crazy?"

The horse bit his earlobe.

CHAPTER 9

The ranch house sat atop a high hill, where the rancher and his wife could relax on the porch in nice weather, watching their cattle graze and their rancheros ride across the valley below. It seemed to Moses, as he rode away down the hill, that he was giving up a good vantage point. He had no way of knowing when Rabbit had taken the mule out, nor in which direction she had gone.

He started out riding west, but as he descended into the valley, and the grassy hills rose higher around him, he began to doubt the wisdom of his choice. He pulled up hard on the reins and turned his Appaloosa around, returning to higher ground.

He circled the barn and looked out over a wide swath of the ranch below. He could see Ned down near the broken fence, and Rose far off to the north, but there was no sign of Rabbit. It occurred to him that she might be playing a game. He had no children of his own, but he was one of four boys. He and his brothers had sometimes played hide-and-seek in the evenings when their chores were done. Rabbit was an unusual child, but it was barely possible she had decided to hide from the adults and wait to see if they sought her out. She was a quiet girl—or boy, if Old Tom was to be believed—and it was hard for Moses to work out what she might do.

He tied his horse to a post behind the barn and began to search. First he looked inside the Wells Fargo wagon, but the hanged man was alone in the carriage. The sailcloth wrapping had come loose around the torso, and Moses made a mental note to wrap the body tighter before they buried it.

"You keep resting up, sir," Moses said. "Soon's we find this missing girl, we'll get you in the ground."

He scanned the fields again, noting the relative absence of cattle, just a few small groupings that dotted the pasture below. By the time the rancher returned with supplies his stock was all likely to have wandered off through the broken fence. In better circumstances, he and Ned might have stayed and helped round the cattle up, but they had other responsibilities. A woman and child depended on them to get safely north. Not for the first time, he wondered why they were taking this strange journey, and why they had so easily given up their aimless wandering.

Maybe, he thought, they were simply tired of being aimless.

Aside from the house, the barn, and the outhouse, the only other structure Rabbit might have hidden in was the bunkhouse. Moses knew it was a long shot, but he didn't want to ride off again without being thorough. After another long look around at the surrounding fields, he walked down the hill to the bunkhouse and circled it, watching for broken windows, crawl spaces, or loose boards. It was well built and maintained, the corners tight, the paint fresh, and the roof in good repair. There was no space or opening large enough for a mouse to sneak through, much less a girl.

A high window spanned the length of the back wall, with plantation-style shutters to let in the breeze that came off the hilltop. Moses stood on tiptoe to get a look inside, but the shutters were latched and the interior of the building was dark.

He walked around the far corner, closest to the house, pausing at the front door of the bunkhouse to try the knob. To his surprise it turned and the door swung open. The Marshals had apparently been mistaken about the bunkhouse being locked, but Moses was glad. Otherwise, he might not have spent a comfortable night in the main house.

He took a step inside and the smell hit him with a nearly physical force. He gagged and pulled his bandanna up over his nose, then shuffled across the room to the window and unlatched it, throwing open the shutters. Fresh air and sunlight rushed in past him, and when Moses turned back around he screamed. His bandanna fell down around his neck and he accidentally took a deep gulp of air, then bent over and vomited on his boots.

Moses had seen the bodies of many dead men. In the war he had held men's hands as they breathed their last. He had buried so many men he had lost count, and only the day before he had cut a dead man down from a tree. But the bodies of the rancheros in the bunkhouse were damaged in ways Moses couldn't comprehend. Men had been pulled apart and put back together, limbs had been torn off, internal organs had been squeezed out across the floor. The walls were painted with blood and viscera, and the expressions on the rancheros' faces indicated they were alive through much of their ordeal.

Panting and retching, Moses hurried from the bunkhouse and collapsed in the yard, his eyes closed tight, his cheek resting on the cool dirt. He reached out and grabbed a reassuring handful of grass, anchoring himself to the world as he understood it.

"Well, well," someone said. "Look what we have here."

"Will you look at this," said another voice.

Moses rolled over and opened his eyes. McDaniel and Rigby leaned against the outside wall of the bunkhouse, watching him. McDaniel's pistol was aimed at Moses's head. Rigby giggled.

"I could swear we told you not to go in there," McDaniel said.

"Can't tell a slave nothing," Rigby said. "You got to show him."

CHAPTER 10

In the months after Joe's death, Rose had grown accustomed to being alone, but the vastness of the empty ranch made her feel insignificant. As she rode farther away from the house, the lush green grass thinned and gave way to clumps of bluestem and dandelions. She let Tom's horse find his own way and he uncovered an old bridal path that looked like it hadn't been used in years. The trail followed a rocky hillside, circling boulders and fallen trees. Shumard oaks and river birches cast long, irregular shadows, and Rose slowed often to look for signs of Rabbit. It seemed impossible to her that a child on a mule could make it so far without turning back, and Rose began to think about turning back herself until she heard a rasping sound, like a dry water pump.

The path curved around an outcropping of limestone and Tom's horse stopped abruptly, nearly throwing Rose from the saddle. The old mule, Sister, lay across the trail, her belly split open and her intestines spread out around her. Sister's corpse was surrounded by turkey buzzards, hissing and yanking at her flesh.

Rose shouted at them, and one of the vultures flapped a short distance away, a strip of mule skin dangling from its beak. The others ignored Rose and continued their fight over Sister's carcass. Rose blinked away tears. She knew the buzzards were only the first wave of scavengers; coyotes would come in the night.

She steered Tom's horse off the trail and farther around the bend, averting her eyes until they reached a thicket of sand hill plums at the bottom of a high hill. She dismounted and looped the reins over a springy green branch that she hoped would hold the skittish horse.

She cupped her hands around her mouth and shouted. "Rabbit!"

Given the state of the mule, Rose held out little hope that the child was still alive. She wished once again that she knew the girl's real name. At the very least, she would want to have it etched on a proper tombstone.

She pulled her skirt up around her knees and climbed the hill, clinging to the yellow rocks around her. She was used to physical exertion on the farmstead, and she had built up stamina over the years, but not the sort of strength it took to climb over rocks. Not for the first time, she cursed Joe for bringing her to Kansas, and her mother for sending her. She wanted to sit and catch her breath, but the possibility that Rabbit might still be alive, alone in the middle of nowhere, spurred her on. By the time she reached the top of the hill she was filthy, her legs scratched and bleeding.

A sudden stabbing pain in her abdomen made her gasp. It was followed by a rolling wave of nausea. Rose closed her eyes and dug her fingernails into the dirt until the pain subsided. When she was able to breathe normally, she stood and turned in a slow circle, watching the landscape for any sign of movement. Another vulture appeared overhead, wheeling slowly down toward the dead mule below, but nothing else drew Rose's eye. She found a flat rock, sat, and put her chin on her hands and thought. If she were young and scared, and her mount had been killed, what would she do?

Rose decided she needed help. She had narrowed the search for Rabbit, but there was too much ground to cover alone. Her best course of action, she thought, was to return to the ranch and get the others.

She slipped and slid down the hill and back to the stand of sand hill plums where Tom's horse waited for her, grazing on thistles. Rose ran her hand through his mane and leaned her cheek against him, gathering her strength.

A rustling in the brush startled her, and she almost dropped the horse's reins. She wrapped them around her wrist and pushed through the branches of the plum trees. At the center of the little copse, nestled in the dirt and roots, was a small brown rabbit.

CHAPTER 11

Ned eventually reached the same conclusion Moses had, that the ranch house on the high hill provided the best vantage point from which to survey the valley. Leading the new friendly horse, he rode back along the trail and climbed the hill toward the house. When he reached the bunkhouse he stopped the horses and dismounted, staring in disbelief.

Moses floated three feet off the ground, twitching like a scarecrow in a strong wind.

It crossed Ned's mind that he was seeing one of Old Tom's magic tricks. He blinked and looked past Moses at the two false US Marshals. Rigby waved his arms and giggled. His eyes rolled wildly in separate directions and his mouth split into a grin so wide that the corners of his mouth cracked and bled. Beside him, McDaniel stood still and quiet, aiming a pistol at Ned. Ned drew his own revolver and aimed it at Rigby.

"Moses?" Ned said. "You come on down from there."

Moses had the muzzle of his pistol pressed against his head. The fingers of his free hand clawed at his throat and he gasped for air.

"Mr Rigby is giving Mr Burke a choice," McDaniel said. "This could go on quite awhile, but if he wants to go quicker Mr Burke can shoot hisself."

"Moses ain't gonna shoot hisself," Ned said. "And he usually likes his feet on the ground. You better let my partner down."

McDaniel shook his head. "I can't talk to Mr Rigby when he

gets like this," he said. "It's best just to wait. After a while he'll get back to his normal self."

"My friend will most likely be dead by then," Ned said.

"Yeah." McDaniel sounded tired. "I'm sometimes sorry I fell in with Mr Rigby. I would appreciate it, Mr Hemingway, if you would holster your pistol."

Moses rolled his bloodshot eyes at Ned, and Ned could see his friend had run out of time. Ned would have to shoot Rigby, but then McDaniel would shoot Ned. He hoped McDaniel's bullet wouldn't hit anything vital. Ned had just made up his mind, and his finger was tensed on the revolver's trigger when he saw Tom Goggins approach from the direction of the main house.

McDaniel heard the old man and took his eyes off Ned for a moment, but his gun hand didn't waver.

"You made a mistake," Old Tom shouted. "You left something of yourself behind, and the greatest witch-master in five states got hold of it."

His hands were clasped and he opened them to reveal a black hop toad, much like the toads Ned had caught by the river when he was a boy. He tried not to let his disappointment show.

Rigby continued to cackle, oblivious to Tom, and McDaniel turned his gaze back to Ned. Neither of them seemed the least bit concerned.

"I'll deal with you in a minute, old man," McDaniel said. "Mr Hemingway, this is the last chance I'm gonna give you. I hate to shoot you, but it might be better for you anyway than if Mr Rigby gets hold of you."

"If you got something up your sleeve, Tom, you better do it now," Ned said. "Moses is about dead, and this fella's gonna shoot me no matter what he says."

"I most definitely have something up my sleeve," Tom said. "In the past I have hexed presidents, and opera singers, and outlaws. I can sure as hell hex a demon."

He pinned the toad to the palm of his hand with his thumb and pushed down on its back. Ned heard a loud crack, and Rigby's head suddenly snapped sideways onto his shoulder, his spine pressing up against the flesh of his throat so that Ned could clearly see the outline of each vertebrae. Rigby's eyes widened and his grin disappeared, the torn corners of his lips healing instantly.

Moses dropped to the ground. His hand opened and the pistol fell into the dirt beside him.

McDaniel lowered his pistol and reached out, as if he thought he might put Rigby's head back where it belonged. Ned fired a single shot and ran to his friend's side, loosened the bandanna around Moses's throat, and unbuttoned the collar of his shirt.

"That was as close as I like to come." Moses's voice was a whisper and Ned had to lean in to hear him.

McDaniel slid down the front wall of the bunkhouse, a hole in place of his right eye. Rigby pivoted so he was facing the witchmaster, his head flopping about in a way that made Ned feel sick to his stomach.

"You've made a bad mistake, old man," Rigby said.

"I don't think so," Tom said.

He pushed down again with his thumb and Rigby's chest collapsed as his rib cage broke. Rigby staggered toward Tom, but the old witch-master smashed his hands together, crushing the toad. Rigby seemed to smear across the air, his limbs stretching and breaking apart, his skin cracking and blistering. He collapsed in the dust, and Ned was hard-pressed to identify his remains as a human body.

Tom walked around the thing that had called itself Rigby and stopped in front of Ned and Moses. He opened his hands and showed them the sticky black residue spread across his palm.

"I think we should probably burn what's left of this," he said.

CHAPTER 12

The sun was directly overhead when Rose returned to the ranch house with Rabbit on the back of Old Tom's horse. The day was warm, but Rose had wrapped the child in two heavy horse blankets.

Out in front of the bunkhouse a fire was going, and thick black smoke rolled across the pasture. Old Tom poked at the flames with a long stick. McDaniel was laid out on the ground, his right eye missing, his face streaked with blood. Ned and Moses were busy digging a grave next to the body, but they stopped when they saw Rose coming. Ned pushed his hat back and brushed the hair out of his eyes.

"I see Mr McDaniel," Rose said. "But where is Mr Rigby?"

Ned pointed at the fire and Tom looked up, his sweaty face smudged with ashes. He smiled and saluted Rose with the stick he was holding, then went back to stirring the fire.

"Turns out Old Tom knows a thing or two, after all," Ned said.

"You found the girl," Moses said, leaning on the handle of his shovel. "Good work."

"Thank you," Rose said. "Let me put Rabbit down for a nap in the house, then perhaps you'll tell me what's happened here?"

"We've kept ourselves occupied," Ned said.

By the time Rose got the girl to eat a biscuit and laid her down in the bedroom, the cowboys had buried McDaniel and were tamping down the grave. The fire had died, and Tom used a shovel to scoop dirt over the embers, piling it high.

"Is the girl okay?" Moses said.

"She'll be fine," Rose said. "She just needs some sleep."

Tom joined them, and Rose noticed that Ned and Moses were friendlier toward the old witch-master. The three men took turns telling their story.

"Don't look in the bunkhouse," Moses said. "What those two did . . . Well, just don't look."

"We ought to bury the folks that are in there," Ned said.

Moses shook his head. "We'd have to figure out which parts went with which people," he said. "I don't have the stomach for it, Ned, and I know you don't either. I say we let them rest on their own land here, knowing the villains are dead and gone. Hopefully that's enough."

After hearing the story of Mr Rigby's end, Rose needed to sit down, and they all went to the barn so they wouldn't wake Rabbit. Ned pushed three bales of hay together to form a crude bench and they sat in silence for a time. After a while, Moses looked around at the stalls.

"What happened to your mule?" he said.

Rose shook her head. "She's gone."

"That leaves us short a mount," Ned said.

"Not by my count," Moses said. "It looks to me like we just inherited a whole team of horses, plus that friendly one you brought in."

"Oh," Tom said. "I guess them Marshals won't need their horses, will they?"

"They never will," Ned said.

"Nor that wagon, neither."

"There's a problem with that, though," Moses said. "Any lawman finds us driving a stolen Wells Fargo coach is liable to hang us first and ask questions later."

"Should we look for the money they stole?" Rose said.

"Where?" Ned said. "This is a big chunk of land. It could take us weeks, and I'd like to get clear of this place as quick as we can." His reasoning was helped along by the idea that Rose would probably make them return the money to the bank, which made searching for it seem pointless to him.

"It would be nice if the lady and the girl could ride in that wagon, though," Moses said. "I might have an idea about that."

He stood and went to a corner of the barn, and came back carrying two cans of red paint. Ned raised his eyebrows and shrugged.

"Wouldn't be too much work," he said.

All four of them pitched in, painting the stolen coach bright red and covering over the Wells Fargo logo along the top trim. As they worked, Ned occasionally looked in through the wagon's windows and shot pointed glances at Moses, who ignored him. Finally, Ned set down his brush and pulled his friend to one side.

"We should bury that boy now," he said. "The one you cut down off the tree."

"Not here," Moses said. "This is an evil place."

Tom overheard Moses's remark and approached, wiping red paint down the front of his brown shirt.

"I was thinking," he said. "It's possible Rigby burped up more of them toads. If so, there could be bits of him hopping around."

"You think so?"

"I don't know."

"Can't you whip up a spell to kill all the frogs?"

"I maybe could, but I'd need at least a dozen maggots."

They all looked at the floor of the barn, but it was clean.

"There's the bunkhouse," Tom said. "Bound to be maggots there."

"No," Moses said. "Leave it shut."

"Anyway, I don't see no toads about," Tom said. "Seemed like I killed him pretty thorough."

"Even so, I'm not gonna bury that young man here. I want to take him farther north from here, farther from those woods, and farther from this place."

Ned nodded. "It's your body," he said. "You brung it along. I was just thinking since we already dug one grave today, we might as well dig another."

"No," Moses said again. And that settled the matter.

It was late, and the paint was tacky. The four of them decided to stay another night at the ranch. Rose and Ned found a treasure trove of tinned goods and potted meat in the pantry, and spent an hour carting them out to the carriage and stacking them around the body of the hanged man.

"He don't hardly smell at all," Ned said.

They ate well that night and went to the rooms they had chosen the night before. Rabbit was still sleeping, and Rose locked the window, then undressed and slipped in beside her. She fell asleep immediately and was not disturbed by unwanted visitors in the night.

In the morning, they ate again and piled their bags on top of the carriage. They hitched up the team of horses that McDaniel and Rigby had lodged in the barn. Rose saddled the new friendly horse that Ned had named Betty, but Rabbit climbed into the carriage and sat across from the body wrapped in sailcloth.

"Oh, no," Rose said. "We are not sharing the carriage with a corpse."

But Rabbit didn't budge, and after hesitating a moment, Rose climbed in after her. Ned took the driver's seat up top, after ponying his sorrel and Betty behind the carriage. Moses and Tom rode their own horses out; the remaining donkey was set free, but followed along behind them. Ned was touched by its loyalty and felt a pang of regret that he had never given it a name.

They had gone perhaps five miles north along the trail, when the man wrapped in canvas sneezed.

Rose jumped, then leaned forward and poked the man's body. He wiggled and squirmed and loosened enough of the sailcloth to pull it away from his face. He took a deep breath and blew it out, then grinned at her.

"Hello," he said. "What direction are we going?"

He was young, perhaps seventeen or eighteen, Rose thought. Dark skinned, with long curly hair that hung in front of his eyes.

"You're not the man we took from the woods," she said. "Who are you?"

"My apologies," he said. "My name is Benito Cortez, and I hope you are taking me away from Texas."

CHAPTER 13

Some time after seeing the cowboy with the yellow hat, Joe Mullins came upon a big house with a red barn and a matching bunkhouse. There were many rancheros milling around outside the bunkhouse, along with an old woman and a tall thin man who was missing an eye. Every once in a while one of the cowboys would take a swing at the one-eyed fellow. They were none of Joe's business, though, so he kept walking along the trail until he came to a stump where a young man sat watching the rancheros. The man was dark skinned, and his clothes were old and patched in many places. He nodded politely at Joe and scooted over on the stump to make room for him. Joe, being a neighborly sort, sat and offered him a puff on his pipe.

"My name's Mullins," he said. "Joe Mullins."

"I'm Isaiah Foster," the young man said. "Glad you come along, Joe. Them boys over there are angry all the time, and unpleasant to chat with."

"They seem it."

Joe and Isaiah sat for a while, sharing the pipe and watching the men quarrel. The men did not seem to notice anybody else, and their disagreement never ended. Joe wondered about the passage of time, and how ever since he died it had felt like a river that ran every which way. The ranch hands were caught in some kind of whirlpool, Joe thought, and they might stick like that forever unless they could reach an accord with the one-eyed man.

A butterfly passed through the smoke from Joe's pipe, and for the briefest moment it stopped in midair, like a painting of a butterfly, then the smoke floated away and the butterfly flapped its delicate yellow wings and continued on its way. Joe wondered if the insect had perceived being stuck in time or if that split second was lost to it.

"I reckon you're dead," Joe eventually said to Isaiah.

"I am," Isaiah said. "And you are, too, if I guess rightly."

"You do guess rightly," Joe said. "Mind my asking how it happened?"

"I don't mind. I had a farm up beyond them woods, a nice little place, and I married a pretty gal and we had ourselves a baby boy. It was all about as good as I could expect, but one year—and I don't know if it was last year or fifty years ago . . . You notice time works kind of different when you're dead?"

"I was just thinking on that," Joe said.

"Well, one summer it was hotter than usual and dusty all the time so's you couldn't hardly see in front of you, and the river dried up, and our crops never come in. I took some work on the railroad up by the Nebraska border, just to make ends meet, give us enough to get through the winter and plant again. But when I come back, my wife was gone, and my boy. I don't know what happened to 'em, whether they run off or was taken."

"Damn it," Joe said.

"I was in a state. I looked for them in every direction, all down past Monmouth and into Oklahoma past the Cherokee Strip and up again. And just when I was despairing of ever seeing them again, I rode up on them woods over yonder."

"You went in there?"

"I did," Isaiah said. "All that worry and sadness I was carrying around sort of fell on me like a rock and it crushed me. So I took a coil of rope and I climbed up the tallest tree and . . . Well, I'm not proud of it."

"I been in them woods," Joe said. "They have an effect on a man."

"They do."

"You still hanging up in there?"

"Nope," Isaiah said. "A while later—and I don't know how long it was—a couple men come along and cut me down. One of them men could climb a tree like it was a ladder, and the other had a yellow hat."

"A yellow hat? I don't suppose they had a woman with 'em, and maybe a child, all traveling together?"

"Why, yes," Isaiah said. "Those are the ones who cut down my body and carried it out of the woods."

"Well, I suppose it's good to know I'm headed in the right direction," Joe said. "But I'm sorry to hear how it happened to you. I hope you find your wife and son pretty soon."

"I don't think I will," Isaiah said. "My body's been passed around quite a bit lately. A Mexican kid buried me in a shallow hole and I've been feeling tired, like I ought to stop and rest awhile."

"I felt like that myself," Joe said. "But then somebody nailed a hex over my grave and woke me back up in time to see my wife run off with some men who come to the house."

"How did you die? Was it the hex?"

Joe puffed on his pipe thoughtfully.

"I found a jar of arsenic in the cupboard a few months before it happened," he said. "I suppose it might have ended up in something I ate or drank."

"Your wife hated you enough to kill you?"

"No," Joe said. "I don't think she hated me."

"But she run off with another man?"

"Several of 'em. It was them two cowboys and an old fella with a turkey feather in his hat."

"Why, I don't even know what to say about that," Isaiah said. "I can't imagine a woman running off with any man had a turkey feather in his hat."

"Takes all kinds."

"I suppose you're pretty angry about it all."

Joe shrugged. "Not especially. It was my own fault for marrying a fancy lady from up north. I should've found me a farmer's daughter or a good Pawnee squaw for a wife. My Rose wasn't meant for the kind of life I could provide. No, it was my own damn fault for marrying above my station."

"What will you do now?"

"I'm gonna keep following along until I catch up to her. I got a bad feeling my wife's put herself in the path of some danger, and I ought to see she don't need my help. When that's done, I might lay down and rest for a spell."

"That seems most natural."

"I could use the company. I'd be grateful if you'd walk with me for a bit and give me someone to talk to. Being dead is a lonesome business most of the time."

"I guess not," Isaiah said. "I thank you for the offer, but my body's over there behind the barn, so I think this stump is as far as I'm going."

"Suit yourself," Joe said. "If I see your wife or your boy I'll let 'em know you was thinking of 'em."

"I appreciate that," Isaiah said.

Joe tapped his pipe against the stump, then stood and tipped his hat to the young man, and walked away up the trail, following the tracks of the horses, and the donkey whose tracks ran back and forth behind the others. He noticed there was now a double rut in the road, and he smiled at the idea that his fine educated wife had found herself a carriage to ride in.

PART THREE

Burden County

CHAPTER 1

It didn't take long for Sadie Grace to find out about the bounty. Despite the recent troubles in Burden County, there were those who still felt indebted to her.

Sarah Cookson, for one, was barren until Sadie gave her a simple fertilization totem. Sarah and her husband now had seven boys and four girls, and Sarah sometimes thought the totem was more of a curse than a blessing. Still, she didn't blame Sadie for her husband's lustfulness.

And when Reggie Dwyer's son Bobby was struck blind in a lightning storm, Sadie mixed a plaster that gave the boy his sight back. Bobby died the following month when a calf he was branding kicked him in the head, but these things sometimes happened, and Reggie didn't hold Sadie responsible for the actions of a frightened calf.

Sarah and Reggie visited Sadie at different times on the same day, a Thursday, to tell her about the rumors they had heard in Riddle. Sadie was grateful to them. She was glad the whole of Burden County hadn't turned against her.

She waited until both of them had come and gone from her little house with the green shutters before turning her inner eye across the county and beyond it in every direction. There were a few parties who had taken up the farmers' cause, and she thought one of them might make it to Riddle the following day if he moved quickly enough up the trail. Most of the other men who had heard of the bounty were too frightened, or lazy, or simpleminded to cause her much trouble.

But there was a small group of people far to the south that gave her pause, and she focused her vision on them. Two cowboys rode up front, but cowboys were rarely a cause for concern. There was a witch-master with them, but he was old and wore a turkey feather in his hat. There was a Mexican boy and there was a Yankee woman. The woman was interesting, but Sadie decided she was more of a curiosity than a threat. What concerned her most was the other member of the group. At least, she thought there was someone else with them, but she couldn't be sure. Whoever it was, Sadie's eye could only make out a vague presence, a red glow at the edge of her sight. No matter how hard she tried to focus, her vision sputtered and seized when she tried to look at the sixth member of the company. Sadie's eye had never failed her before, and a kernel of dread began to grow in her like a kidney stone.

As she drew back her eye, she noticed someone coming up behind the group, someone who flickered in and out of reality.

She decided to do something about the people coming from the south, preferably before they crossed the Burden County line. She had been tired lately, and it would be wise to keep danger as far from her doorstep as possible.

She knew she would also have to do something about Andrew King and Duff Duncan, her neighbors who had put the bounty on her. She was especially unhappy with Andrew, but it was not the first time he had disappointed her.

First, though, she would deal with the lone traveler who was due to arrive the following day.

CHAPTER 2

Late Friday afternoon a stranger walked into Riddle and stood in the middle of Main Street for a long time, examining a map. He was short and plump, with a fringe of brown hair around the back of his head and a pair of rimless spectacles perched on the bridge of his nose. He stood in the road long enough that half the town came out of their homes and businesses to watch him. Eventually he put his map away, clapped his hands together, and strode confidently into the saloon. He tossed a silver coin on the bar and asked for a small beer. The barkeep, One-Finger Finlay—so named because he had lost one finger chopping firewood—scowled at the stranger and shook his head.

"One-Finger's only got a single kind of beer back there, plus one kind of whiskey," Andrew King said. "And one shotgun, if you ask for something he don't got. I guess he's being nice since you ain't from here."

With no crops to worry about, and his wife and daughter in the ground, Andrew had spent nearly every day for a month in One-Finger's saloon. He was sitting three stools down from the stranger, but didn't bother to shake the man's hand when it was offered. Andrew had grown more irritable with every passing day, and he often bothered the other clientele, but One-Finger appreciated the regular business.

"My name is Ubel Crane," the stranger said. "But you might have heard me referred to as Noble Crane. I don't suppose you could tell me where to find either Andrew King or Duff Duncan?"

Andrew frowned. "Why you looking for them?"

The man straightened his shoulders and puffed out his chest.

"You haven't heard of me, then? No? Well, I am the premier witch-master of the entire eastern seaboard, sir. I am responsible for killing more witches than any man alive, and when I learned of the problem you people have, I boarded the first locomotive out of Boston. I am here to pledge my services to your benighted settlement."

Andrew burped and poured a finger of whiskey into his glass. He drank it and poured another while Ubel Crane stood stiff and uncomfortable, waiting for a response. He glanced at the only other person in the bar, Big Bill Cookson, and shrugged.

Big Bill finished his beer in two swallows and left without a word. He went straight home and told his wife Sarah about the witch-master who drank small beer.

"You'd better fetch Duff off the Paradise Ranch," Sarah said. "Knowing Andy King, he's already too far in his cups to make much sense."

Bill Cookson did as he was told, and saddled up his fastest horse. Sarah watched him ride out of sight, then went to her writing desk and got a piece of her best stationery. After a moment's consideration, she wrote out a note and folded it in half. She handed the piece of paper to her youngest son, along with a penny.

"Take this to Miss Grace's house. When you get close enough to see her chimney, put this penny under your tongue. And don't choke on it."

The boy, named Willie after both his father and his older brother William Jr, grabbed the piece of paper and the coin, and ran as fast as he could. Once he was sure his mother couldn't see him, he slowed down and caught his breath. The road ended after a quarter of a mile, at the edge of town, and narrowed to a dirt trail, barely wide enough for a single wagon. On the rare occasion someone entered Riddle at the same time someone else was leaving, one driver had to pull his coach off into the weeds so the other could pass. That Friday afternoon, no one was entering or leaving the town, and Willie Cookson had the trail all to himself. Willie had not enjoyed an afternoon by himself in many weeks. He was amazed by his sudden luck and unexpected freedom. He hadn't taken the time to put on his shoes, for fear his mother would change her mind about the errand, and now he veered off the trail so he could feel the new spring grass between his toes.

He shoved his mother's note into the pocket of his overalls, along with the copper penny, in order to have both hands free to catch a grasshopper. He chased it through the grass on his hands and knees, and when he grabbed it, it pushed its strong legs against his fingers and spat brown goo on his knuckles. He stroked its head with the tip of his index finger, and admired its bulging black eyes, then set it down and watched it spring away.

"Be more careful next time," he hollered after it. "The next boy might squish ya!"

Not for the first time, Willie wished he had a dog. He would throw sticks and the dog would bring them back; they would wrestle in the soft grass, and when they were tired Willie would lay his head on the dog's warm body and take a nap. But his father said dogs were for herding or guarding, not for playing.

Willie lay down under a sweet-smelling spruce and grabbed a pinecone from the ground, picking off its hard woody petals and chewing them. With the sun on his face and a cool breeze in his hair, he fell asleep and dreamed he was chasing his own puppy around the field.

When he woke the sun was lower in the sky and there was a woman sitting across from him, her legs crossed Indian style. He recognized the woman, who smiled at him when she saw he was awake. Sometimes she came into town for supplies, and if he was with his mother or father they always made him cross to the other side of the street. He realized he was supposed to have gone to her house instead of falling asleep under a tree.

"You have something for me, don't you?" she said.

She seemed nice enough, but his parents were afraid of her, and Willie thought he probably should be, too. He belatedly remembered the penny his mother had given him and groped for it in his pocket. He got his fist around it and the piece of paper, and pulled them both out at once. He popped the penny in his mouth and handed her the note.

"Thank you," she said.

She smoothed out the crumpled paper and read what his mother had written, then nodded to herself and tucked the note away in the pocket of her trousers.

"I didn't know your mother could read and write," she said.

"She's teaching me." With the penny under his tongue, it came out: *Teeth teething nee.*

"Good," she said. "Well, I already knew about Ubel Crane, but I appreciate your mother's warning just the same. Please thank her for me."

Willie nodded.

"How old are you?"

Willie held up all the fingers of one hand and two fingers on the other. His mother had already taught him to count to ten on his fingers, and to write his own name.

"That penny isn't much of a hedge against me, if I had reason to be cross with you."

Willie's eyes widened and he felt tears coming on.

"But I have no reason to be cross with you. In fact, I think you're a very good boy. I saw you set the grasshopper free when you caught it. Another boy might have squished it."

Willie spat the penny out onto the palm of his hand. If what she said was true, it wasn't helping him anyway, and it tasted bad.

"I told it that same thing," he said. "I said it should be careful about the next boy who come along."

"Very good," Sadie said. "I hope it takes your advice to heart. Now, the man your mother warned me about is riding up the road toward us at this very moment, and your father is out looking for you. I think it would be best if you crossed the field that way." She pointed. "Then I want you to circle back to the road behind Mr Crane so he doesn't see you. And if you go in the back door of your house very quietly and tell your mother you got back an hour ago and were doing your chores, I think she'll believe you. I wouldn't want you to be punished for trying to help me, Willie."

The thought of punishment galvanized the boy. He jumped to his feet and had taken several steps from the tree when he turned around and ran back. He held the damp penny out to the witch and she took it from him, then he sprinted away in the direction she had suggested.

When he got home, he followed Sadie Grace's instructions and snuck in the back door. He was already peeling a bucket of potatoes when he heard the front door open and his father's heavy footsteps.

"I'm in here," Willie shouted. "I been doing my chores all afternoon."

His father entered the kitchen with his hands behind his back, and Willie worried that the witch had been wrong. But Big Bill was smiling. His eyes glinted the way they did when he had a surprise.

"I thought you was out," Big Bill said. "There's gonna be trouble and I was worried."

"Honest, Pa, I been right here."

"Well, I found something while I was looking for you," Big Bill said.

He pulled his hands from behind his back and held out a brown puppy with white spots. The puppy wiggled and wagged its tail. Willie took it gently into his own hands and buried his face in its warm fur. The puppy licked Willie's nose.

"It was wandering out in the road," Big Bill said. "Might've been stomped by a horse if I didn't see it there."

"Can we keep him?"

"Long as nobody comes along and claims it," Bill said. "But it's your responsibility, you hear? Over top of your regular chores. You got to feed that thing and take care of it. I ain't gonna do it for you."

Willie nodded and held the puppy up to the lamplight so he could examine it from every angle.

It was, he thought, the best penny he had ever spent.

CHAPTER 3

"Witches are a blight upon the land, Mr Duncan," Ubel Crane said. "And they always have been." He took a sip of water and absently scratched his cheek.

They were sitting across from each other in the saloon. Andrew King was dozing in a chair next to Duff, and Ubel Crane had given up trying to explain what a small beer was. He had settled for a glass of well water that swirled with motes when he lifted it to his lips.

"No, sir," he said. "Yours is not the first township to be victimized by those vile creatures. Not even the first within this barren territory. I have dealt with my fair share of them across this great country, and my father battled them in Europe before me. His father did the same before him. We Cranes have always fought the good fight."

"Well," Duff said, "I guess we got ghouls and ghosts and shape-shifters around here, too, and I've heard tell of invisible things that can take your body and live in it like a turtle in a shell, but witches are probably the worst."

"Oh, very much so, Mr Duncan. Ghouls are not generally uncanny in nature. They're as human as you or I, except they have abandoned their inhibitions and feast on the flesh of their fellow men. They are common and can be killed as readily as anyone else, while ghosts are simply people who became confused after their death. They don't understand they belong somewhere else, but they can be persuaded to move on. As for the invisible things you mention . . ."

"Like a turtle without a shell."

"Not precisely like that, no. They are something like a spirit, but with powers like a witch. They take possession of weak people and force them from their own bodies. I wrote a book about them: *The Call of the Nightfall King*. I don't suppose you've read it?"

"Sorry," Duff said.

"It's just as well. My editor had a heavy hand and the end product was less informative than I would have liked. Rather a potboiler, I'm afraid. As for shape-shifters . . . well, I'm afraid there's no such thing."

"I've heard there are such things," Duff said. "Cullen Stull told me he run across a—"

"Superstitious poppycock. Be afraid of real things, Mr Duncan. Real things can kill you. And they can *be* killed, if one happens to have the skills and knowledge to do so."

"How do you know so much about 'em?" Duff said, embarrassed that the portly witch hunter had put him in his place.

"Rigorous training and an exceptional education. Tell me, have you heard of the *Malleus Maleficarum*?"

"That another strange critter?"

"I call it *The Hammer of Witches*." Ubel chuckled and reached into the bag that was slung over the back of his chair. He pulled out a leather-bound book and thumped it down on the table, hard enough to make their drinks slosh about.

"It's another book," Duff said.

"It's the authority on witches, Mr Duncan, and I am translating it into English for use in this country. Everything you might wish to know about killing a witch is written down here."

"Well, how many witches have you killed, then?"

Ubel chuckled again. "That's hard to say. But I've killed a good many, that's certain."

"I heard a bullet won't kill 'em, nor a knife."

"You heard right, sir."

"Believe me," Duff said, "if I could've done it myself, I sure would have. That witch took my fiancée from me."

"Witches are a lonely and vindictive lot. If they see any sign of romantic happiness in another, they are sure to stamp it out. Is it possible this particular witch wanted you for herself? Might you have been ensorcelled at some point?"

"I guess not." Duff was confused by the question.

"What I mean," Ubel said. He cleared his throat and started over. "Have you engaged in relations with this witch?"

Duff pushed his chair back and stood. "I was always true to Olivia King, and that's a damn fact, mister."

Ubel held up his hands and smiled. "Please sit back down, Mr Duncan. I assure you, had it happened it would not have been your fault, and you might not even remember it."

Duff sat, but didn't bother to pull his chair back up to the table. "I think I'd remember a thing like that."

He had long since decided to save himself for marriage to Olivia. He still considered himself to be in mourning, but had begun to think his abstinence might now be pointless. One-Finger Finlay had recruited a young whore—"no older than fourteen, so she claims"—who was due to arrive in Riddle within the month. Judged solely on One-Finger's second-hand description, Duff felt she might be a good woman for him, though Olivia would always hold a special place in his heart.

"Witches have potions," Ubel said, "and powders, and candles with aromas that can cloud a man's mind."

"I never smelled a candle that could make me forget I smelled it."

"Well, you wouldn't know, would you?"

Duff nodded and pulled his chair closer. It was a good point.

"We men aren't devious like those wicked women. They like to take advantage of our inherent nobility."

"With candles?"

"With everything at their disposal. And as you mentioned, there are very few methods of killing a witch. I know of only four." Ubel counted them off on his fingers. "We can press a witch, we can drown her, we can hang her, or we can burn her."

Duff leaned forward. "You done those things?"

"Many times," Ubel said. "I must say, hanging and drowning are not as satisfying to witness as, say, a pressing or a burning."

Duff felt his stomach turn at the thought. He didn't have much of an imagination, but his mind conjured images of women swaying at the ends of ropes, or screaming as their flesh melted.

"What's pressing mean?" he said.

Ubel took another sip of dirty water and wiped his lips. He smiled. "A witch is tied to a flat surface, and I stack heavy rocks on her; on her chest and shoulders and legs and arms. More and more over time. But slowly. The rocks push the breath out of them and crush their limbs, cause their joints to crack and their eyeballs to pop out of their skulls. Once it took so long for a witch to die that I finally took mercy on her and added my own weight to the pile of rocks atop her torso. The air went out of her lungs, even as I perched upon her and watched."

"You did that to somebody?"

"It was sadly necessary, I assure you."

"And you figure you'll do that to Sadie?"

"This very evening, if you'll direct me to her dwelling."

Duff put his hands on the table and examined his fingernails. There was dirt under them. Much as he hated Sadie Grace, the idea of watching her eyes pop out of her head didn't appeal to him. He had thought there might be something quicker and cleaner.

"Maybe you could just drown this one," he said. "Don't seem necessary to squash her like a bug."

"I can't make any promises," Ubel said. "I must do what I determine to be necessary once I've interrogated the woman."

"Meaning you'll talk to her first."

"Yes, Mr Duncan. I'll talk to her first. I may spend a great deal of time talking to her."

This seemed a little better to Duff. He had done what he thought he had to, in putting up half the reward and bringing a witch-master to Riddle. The matter was now out of his hands, and it would be up to Sadie Grace to plead her case. Maybe she could persuade Ubel Crane to drown her, after all. Drowning didn't seem so bad to Duff.

"All right," he said. "I'll tell you where she lives."

"Will you take me there?"

Duff shook his head. "I better leave the witch-mastering to the expert, sir," he said.

He knew how to deal with horses and cows, but witches were beyond him. He worried that if he accompanied the witch-master he would embarrass himself. Duff wanted nothing to do with killing Sadie, but he was already thinking about claiming some of the glory after Ubel Crane left town. The fourteen-year-old whore coming up from Mexico might be impressed if she heard he had helped kill a witch.

Ubel Crane took another sip of murky well water and wiped his lips with the back of his hand. He smiled.

"Well, then point me in the right direction," he said.

CHAPTER 4

It was late in the day when Ubel Crane found the road to the witch's house and set out, hoping to finish his preparations before the sun set. Ubel knew the witch might sense him in the area at any moment, and he wanted to strike while he might still have the element of surprise.

He could feel magic energy all around him, like an itch under his scalp, and he understood why the witch had chosen Burden County for her home.

He held a flat iron disk under his tongue—better magic than a penny—and had sprinkled himself with dog urine to hide his scent from the witch. He was on foot, which he felt was stealthier than riding up on a horse. Besides, he didn't like horses and had never learned the knack of riding them.

When the road turned into a trail, he set off across a nearby pasture. The land was flat and grassy, dotted with stubby evergreens. It seemed odd to him that so much acreage was untilled, that no farmer or rancher or homesteader had made use of it, and he wondered if the witch had claimed the land for herself. It wouldn't have surprised him. Witches were impractical creatures, and overly fond of wild growing things. He sniffed the fresh air and stood for a moment, listening to cicadas sing and squirrels chirp.

Ubel had once met an Indian tracker from Texas who was traveling through Boston with a group of cowboys. Ubel purchased an afternoon of Traveling Horse's time in order to learn native ways in case his travels ever took him to Indian territory.

Traveling Horse's English was excellent, but he misunderstood Ubel's name and called him Noble Crane. Ubel had not corrected him. He liked the idea that the Indian might tell people all across the countryside about the famous witch-master from Massachusetts named Noble Crane.

Traveling Horse had taught Ubel how to catch small animals—field mice, squirrels, possums, and frogs—and read the future in their entrails. Ubel had kept in practice. The previous week he had caught a bat in the attic of a neighbor's house and cut it open, squeezing its intestines out onto a table. The pattern they made revealed that he would soon come to Kansas and encounter the most fearsome witch he had ever met. Ubel immediately packed a bag and bought a ticket for Kansas, excited for the opportunity to prove himself in a new land, and finally put Traveling Horse's teachings to good use.

When the train stopped in Nebraska, he heard about the bounty on a fearsome old witch named Shady Grave who lived in Burden County, and his pulse quickened.

But now that he had arrived in Kansas, he thought it wise not to barge in on the old witch without more information. He found a spot under an old ash with soft roots and dug a hole one foot across and three feet deep. It was hard work, and Ubel was sweating by the time he made the hole deep enough and wide enough to suit his purpose. He had not thought to bring a proper shovel with him, so was forced to use an old tin trowel he had discovered alongside the road. He scouted around and found a flat heavy rock that was big enough to cover the hole. He snipped a thin branch from the ash and cut it into three pieces, then pounded the longest piece into the dirt next to the hole. Using a length of twine from his bag, he tied the two shorter pieces of wood together to fashion a crude swing, which he balanced between the stick and an edge of the rock, so that anything touching the swing would pull it loose and fall into the hole as the rock slammed down to trap it. Ubel covered the base of the swing with grass and carefully placed a handful of dried corn atop the grass.

By the time he finished he was exhausted. He leaned against the tree to catch his breath and closed his eyes for a moment, pondering whether he should camp in the pasture or return to Riddle and take a room for the night.

"What do you plan to catch with that thing?"

Startled, Ubel sat up straight. His chest tightened and he could feel his pulse in his temples. He scanned the field around the tree and the surrounding meadow, but there was nothing to see. The witch was invisible. His books hadn't taught him about invisible witches.

"Up here," the voice said.

He looked up and saw a lovely young woman sitting on a wide branch, her back resting against the ash's knobby trunk. Her arms were folded across her chest and she looked quite comfortable. He realized she must have been watching him since he left the road, waiting while he dug the hole and set the bait.

"I asked you what you plan to catch," she said.

"Two things," Ubel said. His heart had stopped racing quite so hard and his breath was easing back to its normal pace. "First, a squirrel or two. The squirrel will help me find an old witch named either Shady Grave or Sadie Grace. I have heard it pronounced both ways. When I find her, I will catch her, too."

"With dried corn and a hole?"

"Not at all," Ubel said. "Allow me to introduce myself, young lady. My name is Noble Crane."

She smiled and arched an eyebrow. It occurred to Ubel that the coming night might not be so cold or lonely after all, and his pulse quickened again.

"Why don't you come on down from there?" he said. "So I don't have to holler up at you."

"I'm fine where I am," the woman said.

"Aren't you old to be climbing trees?" He had rarely seen a woman wear trousers, and he wasn't at all sure it was proper attire.

"Aren't you old to be catching squirrels?" she said.

Ubel waved his hands about for dramatic affect. "The squirrels speak to me," he said. "I have the power to make them talk."

"You mean you squeeze out their guts and poke around in 'em, right?"

Ubel cleared his throat and frowned. The woman was undoubtedly scaring away all the squirrels with her chatter, and she wasn't making any moves to descend from her high perch. He had begun to feel disoriented and found it hard to form a coherent thought.

"Where's your home, girl? I might like to purchase a bed for the night?"

The woman laughed and covered her mouth, as if she felt embarrassed for him. "Ubel Crane," she said, "if you had harmed a single creature in my meadow, be it squirrel or bird or grasshopper, I would have squeezed *your* guts out and I wouldn't bother to read them."

He felt his chest tighten again. "You're the witch," he said. "But you're not old at all."

"Stop it. You flatter me."

"Which is it, then? Is your name Shady Grave or Sadie Grace?"

"Well, I don't think I want to tell you that. If you'd paid better attention to what Duff Duncan said, you'd know my name for sure, but you were too busy trying to impress him."

"The townsfolk fear you, witch, but I do not." His vision blurred and the ground seemed to wobble under his feet. He felt a trickle of sweat under his collar. "I'm their only hope against you."

"Mr Crane, I'm going to give you a chance to walk away. I know you don't have a horse, but if you head back up that road very fast and pay Reggie Dwyer handsomely for a night in his spare room, I'll let you leave Burden County on the first train tomorrow. That's the best I can do, since you came here to kill me, and I think it's a generous offer."

"No, ma'am," Ubel said. "You are a blight on these people and an evil influence on their children. You kill livestock, you ruin crops, and you destroy good people's lives. You must go, not me."

"Well, I gave you a chance," Sadie said.

She unfolded her arms and leaned forward on her branch. Ubel took a step back from the tree—ready for the battle of witchcraft he had spent his entire adult life preparing for—and his foot knocked over the delicate twig and twine swing he had set up. He stepped into the squirrel trap and the heavy flat rock came down hard on his shin. He heard something snap, and his upper leg moved forward while his lower leg stayed where it was. He shrieked and fell to his hands and knees. The iron disk popped out of his mouth and rolled away into the grass.

"That trap would have worked pretty good on a squirrel," Sadie said.

But Ubel didn't hear her over the sound of his own screams.

Sadie took her time climbing down from the tree. She descended on the other side of the trunk, so Ubel couldn't reach out and grab her, but he was too busy twisting about and hollering to even notice her. She lifted the big rock off his leg and held it.

"Oh, thank God," he said. "Oh, thank you!"

"Do you know what they do to horses that break their legs?"

"No," he said. "Help me!"

She smiled and took three steps and dropped the rock on his

head, then picked it up and dropped it again. Ubel Crane made a noise far back in his throat that sounded like a new calf being born. He looked at her and smiled, his teeth smeared with blood.

"Whore," he said.

She bent and picked up the rock again.

CHAPTER 5

Duff Duncan stood on the porch of One-Finger Finlay's saloon and watched the sky change as dusk settled in. Andrew King lay at the bottom of the porch steps, softly snoring. They had spent less than an hour talking to the witchmaster from Boston before he'd hurried away, reassuring them the witch would be dead by morning.

Duff was cautiously optimistic. It was the first response they'd had to the bounty offer, and the man certainly seemed knowledgeable. Noble Crane—which sounded more like an Indian name to Duff than the name of some Yankee swell—had told them about twin girls in New York who had been accused of witchcraft. Noble was called in by their parents, concerned that the girls' ability to summon spirits would get them in trouble with the law. A local alderman claimed the girls were frauds, but the city's elite, desperate to for any chance to contact their dead loved ones, sought their favor. They were invited to the most exclusive parties and showered with expensive gifts. Noble Crane wasted no time in determining the girls were indeed witches, and recommended they be hung by the neck until dead. He insisted their mother be hanged, too, for having birthed them.

His hatred of witches impressed Duff tremendously.

Duff helped Andy King up out of the mud. He took some of Andrew's weight and together they staggered to the tether post, where Duff got Andrew draped over the back of his horse. He mounted his gray roan and led Andrew's horse around the back of the saloon and up the hill three miles to the farm. Andrew's home was dark and empty, and once again Duff felt a pang of grief for the loss of his fiancée, Olivia. The distinction between a fiancée and a promise to one day become a fiancée had vanished in his memory.

He dumped Andrew onto his bed and pulled off his boots, then covered him with a blanket that stank of sweat and urine. There was no longer anyone in Andrew's life who cared to wash a blanket or even open a window. Duff considered tidying up after his friend, but the task seemed overwhelming. He left the house and pulled the door shut behind him, and he tried not to think about what had become of the man who would have been his father-in-law had things gone a different way.

Andrew's land had fallen into neglect. Husks of abandoned corn hunched against the horizon like an accusing army. Duff covered his mouth and choked back a sob. Everything had gone wrong; the witch had ruined their lives. He felt a sudden flash of anger and stalked out across the yard, punching the air and kicking clods of dirt. He wanted to destroy something, but everything was already dead. He picked up a rock and hurled it at Andrew's dead crops. He grabbed a handful of brown crunchy leaves and flung them as hard as he could. When they fluttered back to the ground, Duff stomped his foot and glowered at the useless field.

Strange patterns created by the broken stalks of black corn laid across the crooked shadow of a scarecrow, an easy target for Duff's frustration. He started toward it, but slowed as he drew near, some ancient instinct sounding an alarm. He approached the dark shape, a feeling of dread forming in his stomach. The moon crested the roofline of the house behind him, throwing the scarecrow into stark relief. Duff gasped in recognition.

The man's skull was crushed, but his fringe of dyed brown hair was enough to identify him as the witch-master. The man who had called himself Noble Crane was tied by his wrists and ankles to a crisscross of spruce branches. He had been sliced open, from his throat to his groin, and his entrails lay steaming at his feet.

Duff turned and threw up his whiskey.

He didn't look back, nor did it occur to him to cut Ubel Crane down off the latticework. As he ran across the dark field to his horse, the anger built within him. Andrew King was wrong. They didn't need outsiders to solve their problem. What was needed was someone fierce, someone motivated. Not a dandy from Boston, but a prospective bridegroom from Riddle, Kansas, who had been wronged by Sadie Grace. All Duff needed, he thought, was a posse behind him.

He mounted his roan and pointed her toward the Paradise Ranch.

CHAPTER 6

Her bedroom was still dark when Sadie woke up, and there was a lump in her throat. She turned her head and coughed, and spat a stone into her hand. It was the size of her thumbnail, chalky white and light as a feather. Its dimpled surface was covered all around with tiny holes, and when she held it up to her ear she could hear wind in the treetops of a faraway forest.

She mixed a resin and coated the stone several times, until it was as hard and shiny as a nut, then took it outside where the morning sky had begun to turn pink along the horizon. She set the stone in the middle of the long trail that ran south from her house, through ruined cornfields, and over the Arkansas River.

She left the stone there and went inside, laid back down in her bed, and went to sleep.

CHAPTER 7

Ubel Crane's squirrel trap had been filled back in and the flat rock rested against the trunk of the tall ash. Three squirrels chased each other around the tree, ignoring Ubel's dried blood on the low-hanging leaves. One of the squirrels was especially bothered by fleas, and she stopped frequently to scratch herself with a hind foot. The fleas burrowed deeper into her fur and continued to bite, and the squirrel twitched and shivered and tore at her ears, but nothing helped. After a particularly vigorous bout of scratching, she looked up and noticed her companions bounding away across the field. Within seconds, she forgot about them entirely and scampered toward the trail where travelers sometimes dropped crumbs of food from their wagons.

There was a shiny thing in the middle of the trail. It looked like a nut, but the squirrel sniffed at it and determined it wasn't a nut. She went off a little ways and scratched herself for a while, then noticed the shiny thing again, and ran back to it. It still wasn't a nut, but she picked it up and stuffed it in her cheek. She paused to scratch her left ear, then she began to run.

She had a nest in a fork of an evergreen tree in the field. The nest was made of dead leaves and bits of corn husks and twigs. It was full of fleas, but it was warm and safe from predators, and it was reasonably dry, as long as it didn't rain too hard. The squirrel ran past the tree with her nest, and she felt a pang of worry when she realized she was abandoning it, but she continued to run along the side of the road until she had left the field behind.

She ran on, through tall green grass, and over shallow mud puddles, and around piles of hot black cornstalks. She found a small worm-eaten apple under a tree and sniffed it curiously, but didn't stop. She had to keep going.

The squirrel was seven months old and had spent most of her life in the same field with her warm nest. She had lived through a mild autumn and a harsh winter, but barely remembered either season. She had seen other squirrels taken by predators, and run over by wagons, and shot by humans, but she always ran faster than the others, and there was safety in the trees where dogs and wagons and humans never came. She had survived longer than her nest-mates by being cautious, but as she sped along the side of the road with the shiny thing in her cheek, she forgot to check the shadows under the corn where snakes sometimes coiled, or the cloudless sky where hawks sometimes circled.

She scampered over a tangle of brittle branches from an old elm that had toppled the previous winter when the ice was thick, and she didn't hear the hawk's wings above her. She didn't feel its talons in her abdomen until it was too late to escape. She twitched and screeched as her tiny body was lifted high into the air. When the hawk clamped down harder, she went limp. The fleas stopped bothering her and her black eyes glazed over, but the shiny thing that was not a nut remained firmly planted in her cheek.

The hawk wheeled away to the south and kept flying.

He flew for more than two hours, finally stopping to rest on the highest bough of an old bur oak. He draped the squirrel's limp body over the branch beside him. The hawk was tired, and his wings trembled from exertion. He wanted to eat the squirrel, but he waited. He watched the surrounding grasslands until a fox, creeping along the near bank of a low stream, caught his attention. The fox was thin and mangy, but still too large for the hawk to catch, so he stayed where he was, high in the oak, and watched the fox come.

The fox had not eaten in three days, being too sick and weak to catch anything larger than a grasshopper, but the scent of the squirrel's blood excited her. She crept as close to the tree as she dared, wary of the hawk's keen beak and sharp talons, and sat. The fox watched and waited as the sun moved slowly across the sky.

The hawk's wings were tired, and he wanted to rest a bit longer before resuming his journey, but the fox made him nervous. He shifted his weight and spread his wings, hoping to scare the fox away, but his sudden movement shook the bough. The squirrel's body slipped loose and fell, tumbling through the branches and careening off the knurly tree trunk until it landed with a soft thud directly in front of the fox.

The hawk circled above the fox, screeched once, and flew away in search of fresh prey. Within moments he had forgotten about his lost meal.

The fox scooped the body of the squirrel into her mouth and trotted away along the bank of the stream, following the trickle of water south. She was weak and slow, but she was crafty, and she hid whenever she saw predators, intent on keeping the squirrel until she could find a secluded place to eat it.

She finally stopped at a crossroads and dropped the squirrel's carcass at the foot of a sycamore tree. She didn't pause a moment before ripping the tiny body open and beginning to eat. The squirrel had cooled, and the blood was thick, but the fox was hungry.

She bit off the bushy tail and let the wind blow it away, then gnawed through the squirrel's midsection and gobbled up the guts. Her powerful teeth crunched the squirrel's skull and she lapped up the brains, then licked out the soft black eyes and chewed the meat off the cheeks. There was something hard and round in the squirrel's mouth, and the fox swallowed it whole before moving on from the head and getting to work on the squirrel's tougher hindquarters.

A sharp pain in her hind leg startled the fox. She yelped and the remains of her meal fell from her mouth. She sprang up and limped in a frantic circle, dragging her useless leg, but a second arrow pierced her throat and pinned her to the sycamore tree.

The last thing she saw before her sight faded was a man with a long gray beard, standing at the center of the crossroads. The man lowered his bow and removed a wicked-looking knife from his belt.

CHAPTER 8

The Huntsman had lived for a very long time, so long that he had forgotten the name he was born with. On the rare occasion he visited a settlement and was asked his name, he would sometimes claim to be Jacob Skinner. Other times he called himself Joshua Strawne or Jack Starkey. But most of the time he didn't need a name, or even need to speak. He avoided people whenever possible. He preferred the dark woods and boundless grasslands where he could stalk and kill what he needed to stay alive.

He retrieved his arrows from the fox's corpse, then cut its throat and let it bleed out. He stripped the mangy orange fur from the meat and bones, and split open the fox's belly, scooping out the contents of its stomach. The handful of undigested meat looked and smelled like squirrel, and the Huntsman tossed it in a small iron pot he carried on his back. He turned the fox's stomach inside out and scraped the lining, then draped it over a flat stone to dry in the sun.

There was a smudge on the stone's surface where something had been burned. The ashes had drifted away, but there was a chalky residue. The Huntsman dragged his finger across it and tasted the powder. Someone had destroyed a witch's hex. He searched the grass under the tree and found a bent iron nail, which he put in his pocket. He straightened up and grunted, and looked across the field at a plain square house, its windows dark and its chimney cold. He decided he had time to investigate it before nightfall.

Meanwhile, it was the work of mere minutes to strip the

stringy meat from the fox's bones. He wrapped the meat in oil-skin for later, and added the bones to his pot. He poured in a pint of water from his canteen, and gathered enough kindling from the sycamore to start a small fire.

The field across from him was partially and unskillfully tilled, the furrows overlapping and petering out after a few yards. While his stew simmered, the Huntsman walked across the field to the plain little house and peered through the windows. When he saw no sign of movement, he knocked on the front door. There was no answer, and the knob turned freely under his hand. He entered and looked around.

A table was pushed up against the far wall, and three chairs were positioned in a semicircle in front of the fireplace. He found a scattering of pipe ash on the hearth. On the vanity in the bedroom was a clear spot in the dust where a tobacco tin had been removed. An unfamiliar scent puzzled him, and he kneeled to sniff the mattress. A man had died in the bed, and more recently a woman had slept there. The Huntsman struggled to place a third scent, but finally gave up. He stood and walked back through the house to an open-air kitchen. A tin bathtub sat at one end of the long porch. In the yard he found a set of wagon tracks, plus the traces of three horses, two donkeys, and a mule.

A woman had lived there by herself for a time, and had left with passing travelers. She had taken all the food in the house, along with her tin of tobacco. The Huntsman thought it probable she had left voluntarily. In any case, he decided, she would not be back and there was no reason to sleep under the sycamore tree when there was an empty bed available.

He walked back across the field to where his stew bubbled in the pot. It was a warm day. The grass rippled in a gentle breeze, locusts chirped in the sycamore, and the grave under the tree was undisturbed by spirits. A fine day to eat outside.

The Huntsman, whose name was not Jacob Skinner, Joshua Strawne, nor Jack Starkey, sat and dipped a spoon beneath the layer of grease at the top of the pot. He dredged up a bite of squirrel meat and blew on it to cool it off, then popped the spoon into his mouth. A moment later he bit down on something hard and chipped one of his few remaining teeth. He cursed and spat the foreign object into his hand.

It was smooth and round, and shiny with spit and grease. He wiped it on his trousers and saw it was coated with resin. Someone had sent it to him, and he thought ruefully that he might have spared his aching tooth if he had known to expect a delivery that day.

He chipped off the resin with his knife to reveal a white stone, riddled with tiny holes. He held the stone to his ear and listened to the faraway voice of Sadie Grace.

PART FOUR

Quivira Falls

CHAPTER 1

They had slathered the Wells Fargo stagecoach with two coats of red barn paint, covering up the straw yellow trim, the sunshine-bright wheel rims, and the company's famous gold leaf trademark. But the carriage still stood out against the landscape, tall and wide and crimson, as it bounced along the rutted trails beside fields of corn and barley and rye. Farmers—with buckboards, and mud wagons, and canvas-topped hacks with steel spring suspensions—pulled over into the grass to let them pass, then sat and watched them go by, the great coach rocking on its leather cradle made from the hides of a dozen oxen.

After they discovered Benito Cortez under the sailcloth, Ned stopped long enough to let Rose and Rabbit out by the side of the road, then he drove the coach to the middle of a meadow, where he and Moses could keep the boy under their control while they decided what to do with him. But Benito made no move to escape or cause them trouble. He grinned and spread his arms wide, as if soaking up the sunlight.

"Thank you, my friends," he said. "My legs were beginning to cramp, and that canvas smelled like death itself."

Benito's eyes seemed too large for his face, dark and lively, and his curly hair sprang up on top around a cowlick. His clothes were hard-worn and dirty; his cotton vest was ripped down the side.

"Why were you hiding in there, boy?" Tom said. He poked Benito's chest with his shotgun.

"I saw you put the body of your friend in the carriage and

I knew that you would steal it," he said. "I thought to myself, 'Benito, you must be a passenger when they leave or you will never escape the bad men who are chasing you.' And I was right! You *did* steal the carriage, and you took me with you!"

Ned holstered his gun and scratched his head.

"I wouldn't say we stole it," he said. "Wasn't nobody laying claim to it at the time."

"What happened to the body that was in there?" Moses said. "What did you do with it?"

Benito lowered his gaze and dropped his arms to his sides. "I am truly sorry about the dead man," he said. "I buried him. I know it was not my place to do so, but I thought the needs of the living must come before the needs of the dead. And since I am the living, my decision was not difficult to make."

"You buried him?"

"Please don't worry. I did it properly so his spirit will not wander or become angry."

"I didn't want him buried there," Moses said. "That ranch was an evil place."

"Were you at the ranch that whole time we was there?" Ned said.

"At one point I was merely an arm's length away from you in the barn loft," Benito said, pointing at Ned. "I am very good at hiding. There were many times on the trail when the bad men passed by me as I hid, and I thought I had escaped them, but always they caught back up. When they arrived at the ranch I nearly despaired. But then you came."

Seeing there was no apparent danger, and feeling left out of the conversation, Rose brought Rabbit across the meadow. The girl plucked a clover blossom and leaned against the coach, but she watched Benito carefully.

Rose made Tom put his shotgun away in its scabbard, then

introduced each of the men to Benito by name. He bowed and smiled at them all, and turned in a slow circle to show them he was not armed.

"I have only a small knife," he said. "But I have no gun, and sadly I have no hat. I had to leave my hat behind or you would have known the man under the cloth was not the dead man you put in the wagon. I don't suppose you have an extra hat with you?"

He eyed Ned's mustard-colored hat.

"Nobody's got extras of nothing," Tom said. "Including food, so you might as well get on your way."

"But you have a wagon full of food. It was piled all around me on the seat."

"That's ours."

"Oh, hush, Tom," Rose said. "We can share the tins we took. They were easily come by."

"Thank you, dear lady," Benito said. "All I have besides my knife is this little fellow I found, but I think he would not taste very good."

He produced a small black toad from his vest pocket. He cupped it in his hands and held it out for Rabbit to see. She squinted at it, then looked away and held the clover blossom up to her nose.

"This is my friend Mr Frog," Benito said. "He kept me company all night while I waited for you. He doesn't talk much."

Tom grabbed Benito's wrists.

"You are strong for an old man," Benito said. "But I think you should let go of me."

"You say this was in the coach last night?"

"I found him under the seat as I was moving the dead man."

Tom snatched the toad away and dropped it in the grass, then stomped down hard, grinding it under his foot.

"Mr Frog never bothered you, or anybody else," Benito said. His eyes flashed with anger.

"What you don't know would fill a bucket," Tom said.

"I know I do not like you, sir."

"Benito," Rose said, "was there really a bounty on you, or did those men at the ranch lie to us about that?"

"I am afraid it was no lie," Benito said. "But it was a great misunderstanding. There was a woman . . ."

"There's always a woman," Old Tom said. He caught the look that flitted across Rose's face. "No offense meant, Mrs Mullins."

"What about the offense to me?" Benito said. "You squished my frog."

"Tell us about the woman," Rose said.

"Ah," Benito said. "Marie was more beautiful than any other woman who ever walked the earth. It is not an exaggeration to say so. I loved her, and I know she loved me in return."

"That doesn't sound like a reason to involve the Marshals," Moses said.

"Ah, but she was a white woman."

"Oh," Ned said.

"And her husband didn't care for me, personally."

"Her husband?" Moses said.

"His name is Charlie Gamble, and someday I will find him and avenge my sweet Marie."

"Then she's dead?" Rose said.

"Sí," Benito said. "When she died, my spirit died with her."

"You killed her?" Tom said.

"Her husband killed her," Rose said. "Is that right?"

"He shot her through the heart with my own pistol," Benito said. "I foolishly left it on the far side of the room and he reached it before I could. It is why I am unarmed now. I escaped with my life, but her killer fixed the blame upon me. And he told the sheriff that I raped her." He blushed and spoke to Rose without looking at her. "I should not speak of such things in front of a lady."

"I am aware of the existence of rape," Rose said. "But if you were innocent, why didn't you stand up for yourself and pursue justice for Marie?"

"Because Charlie Gamble is the deputy of Fulton, Texas, and the brother of the sheriff."

"So they set the Marshals after you," Moses said. "If you killed my . . . If it was someone I cared about, I believe I'd come after you myself."

"I'd come with you," Ned said.

"Charlie Gamble is not brave. He knew I would kill him if he faced me like a man. His cowardice was one of the many reasons his wife didn't love him."

"So you ran," Tom said. "That don't sound like bravery to me."

"Be careful, old man." Benito shook a finger at Tom. "I am still angry with you about my friend Mr Frog. I left because I was greatly outnumbered. Sheriff Jim Gamble is a great believer in hanging a man first and determining his innocence later."

"Better to live and fight another day," Moses said.

"Yes, but the Marshals chased me, including those two gentlemen you helped me escape."

"Them two wasn't much of a gentleman," Ned said. "Nor a Marshal. And they're dead now, besides."

"By your hand?"

"Well, Old Tom did it."

"Then I thank you for that, Old Tom, and I forgive you. Those men were relentless. When I tried to fight them, one of them caused the breath to leave my lungs. If I hadn't fallen into the river, I would have choked to death. As it is, my clothes were torn on the rocks."

"You were lucky, I guess," Moses said.

"Lucky in life, perhaps," Benito said. "But unlucky in love. If you are satisfied with my answers, would you please tell me now why you killed Mr Frog?"

CHAPTER 2

They left the meadow and continued northward, with Rose and Rabbit in the big red coach, and Benito riding the horse that Ned had named Betty. Moses was quiet, and Ned left him alone, knowing his friend was thinking about the hanged man they had left behind at the cursed ranch. Moses had intended to bring the man north and bury him far from the place where his life had come to an end. Ned sometimes thought Moses chose too large a burden for himself, as if he could take responsibility for everyone who needed it. Ned believed life was hard enough that responsibility ought to be a personal issue. Or at least confined to a very small circle of one's choosing.

But if Moses had turned inward, their new companion, Benito, seemed to have no inner life at all. He was open and garrulous, pulling his horse up and slapping the side of the coach, imploring Rose and Rabbit to look out the window at every little thing that caught his eye.

"See the geese in the sky?" he said. "How do they know to fly like that, Mrs Nettles?"

Rose felt strangely wistful watching him, while also enjoying Benito's undisguised delight. The idea that he was a wanted criminal seemed utterly ridiculous to her.

Tom Goggins rode beside the coach and commented on the things the others said. "That goose at the front is ensorcelled," he said. "It's a child in a goose feather coat and it's trying to find its way back to its human parents up north. Them birds behind it are just dumb enough to follow along."

Benito smiled. "I don't know if you are making a joke, Old Tom, but one way or another I think they are indeed magical creatures."

"Quit calling me Old Tom. I'm not that old."

"You seem very old to me."

Tom scoffed and spurred his horse, galloping past Moses who slowed and waited for Benito to catch up to him.

"Looks like you riled Tom up," he said.

"He is easy to rile, but I will apologize for not believing his goose story."

"I wouldn't worry about that," Moses said. "He'll get over it soon enough. I wanted to talk to you, though. The two men who were chasing you weren't US Marshals, but if you killed a deputy's wife the real Marshals might be on your trail."

"I told you I didn't kill Marie."

"I misspoke, but my point stands. You've got a target on you, son, and I'm wondering how long you plan to travel with us. We have a woman and child to think about."

"That child . . . There is something strange about her."

"We can give you some of the foodstuffs we took from the ranch, if you wanted to ride off on your own."

"I would not like that at all," Benito said. "When I was on my own I became very lonely and wished for the company of friends. I had to settle for the company of Mr Frog. But now that I have met you, my new friends, I should not care to go back to the loneliness and fear I felt before. Look, here come more of the geese. Watch how they stay together in a shape!"

"I've seen geese before."

"So have I. I never tire of it."

"Benito—"

"Moses, if we encounter an actual Marshal I promise I will

ride away and take my chances. If I think there is any danger to you or the others I will turn myself in, but I would like to continue on with you, if you will allow it. I won't cause you trouble."

"Son, we might be riding into trouble ourselves. We're going up near the Nebraska border to see about a witch who's been killing farmers and burning their land. It's possible she's already dead. Old Tom claims she is, but he's been wrong about things before."

"He said the birds were children in disguise."

"He says things like that." Moses shook his head. "But sometimes he's right."

"He was not right to squish Mr Frog without asking me first. And if he is wrong about this witch's death, I will help you face her. I have met witches before, some good and some not so good. They are not to be taken lightly."

Moses scratched his chin where his beard had begun to grow out. He hoped they would come across a town soon so he could buy a bath and a shave. There was entirely too much gray appearing in his beard and he wanted to be rid of it.

"I've told you about the danger, to you and to us, if you stick around," he said. "If you want to ride with us a while, I guess you're welcome to."

"Thank you, Moses," Benito said.

"That makes five of us now," Moses said. "Quite an army we're gathering."

"If you count the child, we are six," Benito said. "But there would be better magic in seven."

"We're not there yet," Moses said. "Could be we'll find another bandit pretending to be a dead man."

CHAPTER 3

It was midday when the big red coach rolled down the main road of Quivira Falls. Ned pulled up in front of a rooming house with a white picket fence and a sign out front advertising vacancies. The branches of a shade tree spread over the small front yard, and a porch swing swayed lazily in the breeze. A woman stopped sweeping the front walk long enough to wave at them, then turned and went inside the house. From his high perch on the driver's seat, Ned saw a hulking figure watching them from inside.

Moses, Benito, and Tom rallied their horses around the rear of the coach, and when Ned hopped down to join them, Rose opened the door next to her so she could hear the men talk.

"What a lovely town," Benito said. "Do you think there's a waterfall?"

"This is Kansas," Ned said. "Ain't no waterfalls in Kansas."

"Nor much of anything else, to tell the truth," Moses said.

"Then why is it called Quivira Falls?"

Ned and Moses both shrugged.

"How long we staying here?" Tom said. "Overnight?"

"I could use a bath," Moses said. "For that matter, so could one or two of you fellas."

Ned raised an arm and sniffed. "I guess I wouldn't turn down a soak," he said.

"That's if they take negroes here," Tom said. "Better ask before you get too worked up about that bath."

Ned started toward Tom's horse, but Moses moved his own horse between them.

"If they don't have a room for me I'll sleep in the coach," Moses said. "It's better than some places I've stayed."

"Well, if they don't, we'll move on," Ned said.

"I was only saying some places don't take negroes," Tom said. "I'll move on with you fellas, if it comes to that."

"Lucky us," Moses said.

"But if we was to be here awhile I might send a telegram to them folks in Riddle and wait for a response," Tom said. "Might be good to have an idea what we're heading into up there."

Rose motioned to Ned and he stepped closer to the coach's open door.

"I worry we aren't thinking clearly," she said.

"What do you mean?"

"We are going to meet a witch."

"Tom is," Ned said. "Moses and me's riding north 'cause we don't have any other thing to do right now. I think of it as kind of a long Sunday outing, ma'am."

"We are going to see a witch," Rose said again. "And she may already know we're coming."

"How would she know that? And so what if she does?"

"Because she's a witch. Or is said to be one. And I believe it's possible she's been setting obstacles in our path. How else do you explain every step of our journey so far? We have been through a haunted forest and a cursed ranch. Our donkey died, we lost our wagon, and Moses was nearly killed by some sort of a devil. We have encountered a great many unsettling things in a very short span of time."

"Well, heck, anything's a coincidence if you look at it right."

But he had not told the others in the company about seeing Joe

Mullins's ghost, and now he mentally added that to Rose's list of strange occurrences. Rose watched his face, sensing he wanted to tell her something, but when he didn't she went on.

"Given our recent history, Mr Hemingway, I am already frightened of this town, simply because it lays between us and the witch."

"Well, what do you want us to do?"

"I don't know. Can we keep going?"

"I don't know. The horses are tired. We keep pushing 'em, they're liable to quit somewhere without a bed."

Ned stepped back and tilted his hat so he could look up and down the street. He rubbed his chin and looked over at the others, then stepped close to the coach again and leaned his arm against it.

"I'm torn between two ideas, Mrs Nettles. So how 'bout if Moses and I do the asking here, and try to get a feel for things, while you keep young Rabbit with you in the coach? We can make a decision easier if we know more about the place."

"Give me your gun."

"Well, no, ma'am, but another thought occurs to me. Our new friend Benito is a wanted man. It might not be a good idea for him to show his face until we know if anyone's looking for him here."

"Another reason to keep moving."

"Well, what do you think about me setting him to guard you two, while Moses and I ask about rooms for the night? I don't reckon Benito's especially dangerous, but he might scare off the locals if they get a mind to steal this fancy red coach of ours."

"That would be fine," Rose said. "I don't think Benito is dangerous either."

"Good," Ned said.

Moses and Benito dismounted and tied their horses to the back of the coach. After speaking with Ned, Benito climbed inside and sat next to Rabbit on one of the long leather cushioned seats.

Ned patted the back of the coach, then followed Moses through the gate in the picket fence and they walked together up the front path. The woman who had been sweeping came out onto the porch wiping her hands on her apron. She was small and stoop-shouldered with pale hair pulled back behind her ears, and although her face was unlined, it was impossible to guess her age. She had the air of someone who was neither old nor young. Ned thought she might be in her sixties, while Moses had the impression she was in her thirties. She peered at them over a pair of spectacles set low on her nose.

"Would you boys be looking for rooms?"

"We might be," Moses said.

"That'd be fine. We've plenty of vacancies just now."

"It's just some places don't take the likes of Moses," Ned said. "We was concerned this might be one of them places."

"The meat's the same under the skin," the woman said. "It's not just the two of you, is it?"

"No, ma'am," Ned said. "We got a woman and a child, and two other men with us. You got that many rooms to let?"

"Who does the woman belong to?"

"Ma'am?"

"Is she your wife or is she his wife?" She pointed at Moses. "Or the wife of one of them other men?"

"None of those," Moses said. "She doesn't belong to anybody."

"And yet, by my count, she's traveling with four men?"

"Yes, ma'am."

The woman shook her head at the ground and clicked her tongue. "What is this world coming to? Well, it does complicate things, since she'll want a room of her own. She will be in her own room?"

"Yes, ma'am," Ned said. "She'll be wanting her own room."

"And the girl will stay with her," Moses said. "And we'll all want a bath and a shave."

"That'll be fine," she said again. "Some of you others will have to bunk up together, but we can accommodate you."

"We could use some help getting the horses stabled," Ned said. "I could swear I saw a big fella around."

"That's my son, John Junior. He's busy right now, but you'll meet him later. Move your coach around the back, so the children don't get ideas about it. How long you staying for?"

"Just tonight," Moses said.

"Well, then, I guess we'll have to work quick," the woman said.

"Ma'am?"

"To get you settled in."

The woman turned and went back into the house, and the screen door slammed shut behind her.

"She seems nice," Ned said.

"Only the slightest bit peculiar," Moses said.

CHAPTER 4

The train station was on the other side of town, across the street from the biggest church Tom had ever seen. He tethered his horse and climbed the steps of the station's platform. A girl sat at the edge of it, dangling her legs and sucking on a hard candy. A patch over her left eye matched her jet-black hair. When she saw Tom coming, she jumped to her feet and spat her candy out into the dirt.

"You're fat," she said.

"You ought to mind your manners," Tom said.

"You walk funny, too."

"For your information, I was in the war and I come by this bum leg honestly. Why don't you go on home and stay there for the rest of your life?"

The girl poked his belly and laughed, then ran away, clomping across the planks of the platform in her red leather shoes.

"People ought to raise their children better," Tom muttered.

He pushed open the door of the station and looked around at the low ceiling and the single row of dusty benches. A man with one leg sat at the end of the bench farthest from the door. A man with one arm stood talking to him. They both looked up when Tom entered.

"Well, hello," said the man with one arm.

"Welcome, stranger," said the man with one leg.

"I want to send a cable," Tom said. "One of you fellas in charge of that?"

"Why, certainly," said the man with one arm.

"We can do that for you," said the man with one leg. He grabbed a pair of crutches leaning against the wall behind him. "Will you be waiting for a response?"

"I guess I'll come back," Tom said.

"Excellent," said the man with one arm. "I'm Peter."

"Tom."

"Well met, Tom. This is Hiram."

They led Tom to a small room at the back of the station where a telegraph machine sat by itself on a table.

"Train come through here pretty often?" Tom said, to make conversation.

"Oh, hardly ever," Hiram said. "I think it's been six months or more since we saw one."

"Where are we sending this?" Peter said. "Your telegram, I mean."

"Riddle, Kansas. Care of Andrew King, or Duff Duncan. Or the county sheriff, if one of them others ain't around to read it."

"The county sheriff? That sounds serious."

"It is," Tom said. He puffed out his chest. "It's official business. I aim to collect what's owed me by them two men. Or collect from somebody, at least."

The two men exchanged a look, and Peter chuckled. "Well, then, let's get you a pencil and write this down," he said. "I'll send it off straight away."

"So you'll be staying overnight, at least," Hiram said. "Over to Mrs Bender's place, I suppose?"

"Is that the lady runs the rooming house?"

"That's her, all right. Is it just you or could there be more in your party?"

"We got . . ." Tom paused and silently counted. "Well, I guess we got six of us by now."

"Six?" Peter said.

"Wow," Hiram said. "What a boon for Mrs Bender!"

"She keeps a nice clean house," Peter said. "You won't want to leave."

CHAPTER 5

There were cowboys on the Paradise Ranch who were itching to do something about the witch, and as soon as Duff broached the subject they eagerly signed on to the posse he was forming. He went to the twins first: Walt and Wayne Traeger. Walt was a gentle sort, but Wayne was known for his fiery temper and his willingness to do violence. Duff had barely uttered the word *posse* when Wayne stopped him.

"No need to even ask," he said.

"I guess I'll go along," Walt said.

"Damn witch has got it coming to her," Wayne said.

Johnny Barth was urinating against the side of the bunkhouse, and he overheard them. He buttoned his trousers and ambled over to where the three of them, Duff and the twins, were discussing the matter.

"You fellas need some company when you ride against that witch?" he said.

"Be glad to have you," Duff said.

He was amazed by how easy it was to recruit riders, and wondered why he hadn't done so before mustering up the bounty with Andrew King. Direct action always felt more satisfying, and he regretted not taking it sooner.

But Duff knew there was magic in the number seven, and he would need three more ranch hands to join them.

Jim Garber was practicing a rope trick down by the horse corral. When he saw Duff coming, he swirled his lariat over his head and cast it at Duff's feet, trying to trip him. Duff easily side-stepped the rope.

"Jim, you got a minute to talk?"

"This about the posse you're getting up?"

Duff rocked back on his heels and raised his eyebrows.

"Now, how'd you know about that?"

"Johnny Barth's been telling about it."

"But I only just left Johnny out by the bunkhouse."

Jim shrugged and twirled his lariat over the ground, stirring up dust devils at his feet.

"You know how Johnny is," he said. "Soon's he knows something, well that's as soon's everybody else knows it."

"I swear, they should close down Western Union and use Johnny to send messages."

"Well, anyway, I ain't so sure about joining up with you. That witch can do things to people. I heard she can kill you with a nasty look."

"Sadie Grace don't scare me," Duff said.

Jim stopped twirling his rope and took a little backward hop away from Duff.

"I sure wish you wouldn't say her name," he said. "You say her name and she can hear what you're talking about. She can strike you dead on the spot with lightning from the sky, even on a clear day."

"Sadie Grace," Duff said again.

Jim flinched.

"See," Duff said. "There's no lightning. It's just superstition, same as everything else they say about her. She can be killed as dead as anybody else."

Jim watched the sky, which was cloudless and blue. A hawk banked and wheeled overhead, then flapped its wings and flew away toward the creek.

"Well," Jim said. "I reckon if Mr Paradis says it's okay, I'll go with you."

Teddy Paradis sat on his wide front porch, with a blanket draped over his shoulders and a tumbler full of rum in his hand. The old man spent his days sipping rum and watching his men work.

Duff climbed the porch steps and stood in front of the old man. He took off his hat and cleared his throat.

"Mr Paradis, I wondered if I could take a minute of your time, sir."

Teddy took a sip of rum and motioned for Duff to sit beside him in a rocking chair that matched his own. When he spoke, his voice was a low rasp that Duff had to strain to hear.

"I know what you're doing," Paradis said. "Heard it from Johnny Barth. How many you got so far, willing to brace the witch?"

"Well, sir, I've got Johnny, of course, and there's Walt and Wayne, too. Jim Garber says he'll come along with us if you say so. Counting me, that makes five, sir."

"Seven's a better number," Paradis said.

"I had the same thought, sir."

"Especially if you're going against a witch."

"Yes, sir."

"Then take Matt Hawke with you, and the new fella, Bill Cassidy. That'll round out your number."

"Yes, sir."

"And, Duff, don't you come back here until that bitch is dead and in the ground."

CHAPTER 6

Deputy Charlie Gamble thought the Mexican boy was likely to have fled south and west, over the Texas border and away from white settlements, so he rode the opposite way, straight north out of Fulton. He had no desire to encounter Benito Cortez. He had missed his one shot at Cortez when the boy tumbled out the bedroom window, and Charlie still dreamed about that moment; he always woke up feeling frightened and sad. The idea that he should confront Cortez again, when the Mexican might be fully armed—and fully dressed—terrified him.

He scratched at his wrists and knees as he rode, unable to ignore the fiery rash spreading over his skin. He didn't think the horse thief George Jorgensen was right about a demon eating him up from the inside, but he had begun to wonder if he'd earned the rash, one way or another.

He resented his brother Jim for forcing him out on the road. The weather was warm and pleasant, but Charlie missed his cozy home in Fulton. When he thought of his two-story house with the wraparound porch, his memories always included Marie, and it was troubling to think she was no longer there. Her absence was the reason Charlie was supposed to chase Benito Cortez, and yet he was unable to muster much hatred for the Mexican.

His relationship with Marie had been strained for many months before Cortez rode into Fulton, with his charming ways and his quick smile. Now when Charlie thought about the day he found Marie in bed with Cortez, he felt shame rather than anger.

He wasn't actually looking for Cortez, and he couldn't return home until the US Marshals captured the boy, so he took his time on the journey, stopping off in every town along the way. He wasn't good at cards, but he enjoyed sitting at the table and watching other men play in San Antonio, Fort Worth, and Dallas.

A young woman offered herself to him in a Plano saloon. She had dark hair and dark eyes, and she fidgeted with a ribbon in her hair while trying to get his attention. He asked her name, but before she could answer he burst into tears and fled the saloon, embarrassed.

He preferred a room and a bath when he could get them, but he had no way of knowing how long he might be on the trail, nor how long his money would have to last, so he slept outside more often than he liked. He was frightened of coyotes and of scorpions, and he kept his pistol under him at night, but the uncomfortable gunmetal bulk of it against his ribs kept him awake.

An Indian woman who was camped under a tree by the road somewhere below the Oklahoma line mixed a poultice for him, which he spread on the rash that now covered his legs and arms. His burning skin cooled immediately, and he felt such relief he hugged her. She seemed amused, but wagged a finger at him. He paid her more than she asked him for and he went away up the trail. His shirtsleeves and trouser legs stuck to him where the poultice was smeared on his skin.

He passed through Choctaw Country and the Cherokee Strip without seeing another traveler on the road, but he heard animal calls from the hillsides around him, and the distant beat of horses' hooves, and he assumed he was being observed. He overpaid at supply depots along the way, and didn't light fires, and crossed the border into Kansas feeling as lonely as he had ever been.

"This ought to be far enough," he told his horse.

He had put most of two states behind him, and was far enough from Fulton, and his brother, Jim, that he felt certain he wouldn't be recognized. He decided he would rest awhile and wait for word of Benito Cortez's capture.

He paid for a room above the saloon in Monmouth, Kansas, and stabled his horse, then sat and watched three men play cards at a round table that would have accommodated at least twice as many customers.

"Business is slow, huh?" he said to the saloonkeeper, but the man scowled at him and Charlie felt foolish.

He bought a shot of whiskey and watched one of the men beat the other two with a pair of sixes. The man pushed his chair back and tossed a coin to the saloonkeeper, who caught it in the air.

"Shot of whiskey here, and another for my good-luck charm," the man said, pointing at Charlie with his thumb. "I lost four hands in a row before you sat down here, brother."

Charlie smiled at the other men to show he wasn't playing favorites with whatever good luck he had brought to the room, but he accepted the whiskey and drank it in a single gulp.

"What brings you to Monmouth, brother?"

The cardplayer had a blond mustache that tended to disappear in the low light of the saloon, and shaggy hair that fell over his ears. There were ground-in mud stains on the knees and elbows of his clothing, and he reeked as if he slept with hogs. Maybe he did, Charlie thought; it wasn't his place to judge. He had, after all, shot his own wife to death while trying to kill her lover. Sleeping with hogs wasn't worse than that.

"I guess I'm waiting for the US Marshals," Charlie said.

"Marshals? Two fellas? One's got a sunburnt nose?"

Charlie shrugged, but he felt an icy tingle spreading across his scalp. He reminded himself that the Marshals had business all over the country. There was no reason to think their presence in Monmouth had anything to do with Benito Cortez.

"Well, them two come through here a few days ago," the man with the wispy mustache said. "They was looking for somebody name of Cortez." He turned to the saloonkeeper. "Name was Cortez, ain't that right?"

"Bandito," the saloonkeeper said. "Bandito Cortez."

"I swear," Charlie said. "You don't mean to say 'Benito,' do you?"

"I don't think so," the saloonkeeper said.

"Yeah, that's what it was, all right," the cardplayer said. "It was Benito Cortez they was looking for, but none of us seen him round here, and anyway them Marshals was queer. Nobody much wanted to give 'em the time of day."

"What you're saying," Charlie said. "You're saying two US Marshals come through here a few days ago, and they was looking for Benito Cortez?"

"Yeah, that's pretty much exactly what I said," the cardplayer said.

He looked to the other men for confirmation, but they only shrugged and one of them dealt out another round of cards. The cardplayer who had bought Charlie a shot of whiskey lost interest in him and scooted his chair up to the table.

Charlie's scalp continued to tingle as he tried to think. If the Marshals had chased Cortez to Kansas, it meant Charlie had ridden in the wrong direction, and not only was Cortez somewhere in the area, but Charlie, being the wronged party, might be expected to join in the hunt for him.

"Do you know where they went when they left here?" he said to the saloonkeeper. "The US Marshals? Where'd they go?"

The man shrugged again and picked up Charlie's empty whiskey glass. He walked away, wiping the glass.

Charlie stood on trembling legs and went upstairs to his room.

He packed his bag and went to the livery, got his horse, and rode north out of town. North was the direction he had kept to, and there was no sense changing course when he didn't know where anyone else was.

"I'm sorry, old girl," he said to the horse. "I guess we'll have to go a little farther, after all."

The moon was three-quarters full and the road was brightly lit. The horse kept a brisk pace, having recently been fed and brushed. They passed a crossroad beside a big old sycamore, and presently they came to a fork in the road. Ahead of Charlie was a broad field of wildflowers and waving grass, and across the field, like a smudge against the sky, was a tall wooden fence and a dark tangle of woods.

"I don't think we want to cross through that without a trail," he said to the horse.

He turned the horse west and kept going, looking for a path that might take him directly through the dark forest, but he never saw one. For the rest of that night and all the next day he rode on the narrow trails that skirted the woods.

Near dusk he came to a ranch house on a high hill. It was painted white, but it reflected the pink and orange hues of the setting sun, and its red trim made it look to Charlie like the doll-house his brother Jim had built for Charlie's niece the previous Christmas. A white bunkhouse was nestled into the hillside below the house, alongside an enormous red barn. Charlie rode past them up the hill to the house and knocked on the door. When he got no response, he went inside. The place was neat and clean, but there was no sign of habitation and the pantry was nearly bare.

Charlie left the house and rode back down to the bunkhouse, but the door was locked and it was too dark inside to see anything through the high window at the back. He took the horse to the barn and put her in a stall, fetched oats and water, and left her there. He went back up to the house, admiring the sunset as he walked, and he paused on the porch long enough to wonder at the lack of people, horses, and cattle. Then he went inside the house and locked the front door behind him. If the homeowner returned, Charlie reckoned he had done nothing worse than trespass. He didn't think anyone would take great offense at such a minor transgression.

Meanwhile, the big ranch house was a good place to hide until he heard news about the Mexican.

CHAPTER 7

When Tom returned to Mrs Bender's rooming house, the others were gathered in the parlor, with the exception of Rabbit. When he inquired after the boy, whom he still thought of as his ward, Rose informed him that the child was asleep in a bedroom on the second floor. Ned once again corrected Tom's language, insisting that Rabbit was a girl.

Annoying as Ned was, Tom had begun to doubt himself on that point. But he was too stubborn to give in. He had, after all, known Rabbit longer than the others had.

Mrs Bender had three rooms to let, and the five adults quickly divided them up among themselves, with Ned and Moses sharing a room again, and Rose claiming Rabbit's company for the night. This left Tom to room with Benito, which didn't overly please him since they hardly knew the young man and Tom wasn't sure he trusted him. The Mexican was, after all, a wanted criminal.

But Benito seemed delighted by the arrangement.

"We will get to know each other better, Old Tom," he said.

"I don't need to know you better," Tom said. "I just need a place to lay my head for the night."

"Ah, we will be up all night talking. There is much you can tell me about magic and witchcraft. I am looking forward to it."

Tom stifled a yawn. He doubted any of them would be awake past sunset. Moses in particular seemed ready to nod off while sitting upright on the sofa.

Mrs Bender entered with a tray of glasses and a plate of watercress sandwiches. She had put her hair up and wore a clean white apron over her dress. While Ned went to a sideboard stocked with bottles, Tom took off his hat and quickly combed his fingers through his beard.

"Well, ain't you a sight, ma'am," he said to the landlady.

"Can I mix you something, Mrs Bender?" Ned said.

"Thank you," she said. "I don't drink. I keep alcohol for my guests, but it interferes with my digestion."

"It aids mine," Benito said, accepting a glass of bourbon from Ned.

"Your waistcoat is torn, young man," Mrs Bender said. "Give it to me and I'll mend it."

Benito took off his ripped vest and handed it over. Mrs Bender sat on the edge of an upholstered chair and produced a spool of thread from her apron pocket. She licked the end of the thread and poked it through the eye of a needle.

"May I ask about your husband?" Rose said.

"Mr Bender passed away six months ago," Mrs Bender said. She didn't look up from her work. She pushed the needle through the fabric in her lap and pulled each stitch tight.

"Oh, I'm so sorry."

"Don't be. It was his turn. The time comes for all of us."

"Six months is pretty long to be alone," Tom said. "I imagine every man in town's come courting."

"What happened to your husband?" Moses said, ignoring Tom. "If you don't mind the question."

"As I say," Mrs Bender said, "it was his turn."

"And you've had to look after this place on your own?" Rose said.

"Here you are," she said. She held the vest out to Benito and he made a show of gratitude. The rip was so neatly mended that it was nearly invisible.

"I have my son, John Junior, to help," Mrs Bender said. "We are perfectly capable, and we have all our limbs. Mr Bender saw to that. He left us in fine shape to soldier on here, and we will always be grateful to him." She stuck the needle in a card and returned it to her pocket, along with the spool of thread, then stood with a sigh and smoothed her apron. "I'd better tidy up the kitchen and ready things for our evening meal. I hope you'll make yourselves at home here. There are games in the cupboard, and supper will be served promptly at five o'clock. If you decide to take a walk around the town, please be back before then."

"You need some help in the kitchen?" Tom said.

"Suit yourself," she said.

With a surreptitious wink at Ned, Tom followed Mrs Bender from the room.

"Moses and I might go ahead and take a gander around town," Ned said to Rose. He glanced at Moses. "Unless you want that shave and a soak first?"

"I'll come along," Moses said. "I don't suppose my beard'll grow a whole lot more in the next hour."

"I would like to come with you," Benito said. He stomped his foot on the parlor floor like a show pony.

"Well, we ain't stopping you," Ned said. "What about you, Mrs Nettles?"

"I'd better check on Rabbit," Rose said. The idea of leaving the child alone in a strange place filled her with dread, and she wondered at how quickly she had accepted responsibility for Rabbit's welfare.

"Benito, maybe we can find you a new hat," Moses said. "Something with a wide brim we can hide your face under."

"What is wrong with my face?" Benito flashed a wide grin.

The rooming house was at one end of town, and Tom had mentioned the train station was at the other, so the three men decided to walk along in that general direction. Mrs Bender's warning that they should return by supper allowed them more than enough time to explore the small town.

As they exited the rooming house, Moses saw an enormous figure hurry around the corner away from them. He got only a brief glimpse, but the man was at least a head taller than Moses, and outweighed him by fifty pounds or more. He was wearing a stained leather apron, and his features, before he turned away, were disturbing. His neck was as thick as his head, and his eyes were too close together. One of his ears seemed to sit higher on his skull than the other, and Moses wondered if that was a trick of the light.

"I think we almost met John Junior," he said.

"I guess we'll see him at supper," Ned said.

They closed the little gate behind them and set out. A tangled line of trees bordered the town to the west, backing up against the Bender home and the other buildings on that side of the town's single street. Railroad tracks cut through the prairie to the east, running parallel to Quivira Falls before angling toward the station at the north end of town.

The main street was long and perfectly straight, with no twists or bumps or holes. It was clear to Moses that the town had been carefully planned in advance, unlike most of the places he and Ned had visited, where homes and businesses grew up haphazardly around a saloon or bordello, and roads were merely afterthoughts, always too narrow or too wide.

"If the Marshals did come to shoot me," Benito said, "you would protect me?"

Moses smiled. "I guess you better stick close to us. Don't go running off on your own."

"I had to shoot a so-called Marshal the other day," Ned said. "I'd rather not do it again, if I don't have to."

"Do you think we will find a good hat here?" Benito said.

Ned shrugged. "Whether we do or we don't, I just want to

scout around a bit. Something Rose said has got me thinking too much."

"Never think too much," Benito said. "It leads to wrinkles and bad breath."

"Tell it to Moses. He's the king of thinkers."

"I'm no such thing," Moses said. "Tell me what she said that got you to worrying?"

Ned quickly filled them in on his conversation with Rose. Benito had not heard the story of the suicide wood, and Moses went silent again at the mention of it, so Ned had to explain that, too.

"I say we wait until we see a new bad thing before we begin to worry," Benito said.

As they passed by, people stepped out of their homes and businesses to watch the three men. Benito waved at the children, as if he were leading a parade, but Ned noticed that everyone they saw seemed to be missing a limb, or an eye. Moses noticed it, too, and caught Ned's attention. Ned shook his head. It was strange, but the war had left its mark on many people.

Before they came to the train station, they passed a blacksmith's forge, a funeral parlor, and a general store, all in a row, set above the street along a low boardwalk across from a massive church. When they reached the general store Benito took the three steps up onto the boardwalk in a single bound, but Ned walked in the opposite direction, out into the middle of the street. It ended ahead of them, just past the station at the train tracks. Weeds and small trees had grown up between the ties, and a handcar with one wheel lay on its side.

A dreamy look came into Ned's eyes as he stared at the tracks.

"Ned?" Moses said.

"You fellas go on in and size up the hat situation," he said. "I think I'll take a stroll down by the tracks, but I'll catch up to you in two shakes, okay?"

Without waiting for an answer, he walked away up the street. Moses stood in the shadow cast by the Quivira Falls Mercantile, watching Ned go and wondering if he ought to follow.

"What is it?" Benito said. "Is he still thinking of the bad things you have seen?"

"I don't know," Moses said. "Ned's been acting queer since we crossed into Kansas." He turned and flashed a reassuring smile at Benito. "But he's not one to keep secrets. He'll tell us about it when he's ready."

"You and Ned have been friends for a long time?"

"Since the war," Moses said. "Found him half dead on the battlefield and patched him up. He stuck with me after that."

"I once came upon a prospector," Benito said. "An unpleasant old man, who was bleeding from his leg. He was shot with two arrows, and I took off my belt to tie the man's leg up high, so he would stop spilling his blood on the ground."

"A tourniquet," Moses said.

"Perhaps," Benito shrugged. "I didn't ask where he was from. But he drew his revolver and pointed it at me, spat on the ground, and called me a dirty Mexican. I had bathed only that morning. So I left him there, too weak to climb back on his horse. I think he must have died, rather than accept my help."

Moses paused a moment before responding. "I guess there's plenty of men like that," he said. "But Ned Hemingway isn't one."

He glanced at the dwindling figure of his friend, then shook his head and climbed the three steps to the mercantile's door.

"Let's see if we can't find you a hat."

CHAPTER 8

At last the priestess took off her mask and dropped it to the floor beside her. She picked her way around her dead and dying worshippers, went to the door and out, shutting it softly behind her.

Something began to rise from the depths. A massive gnarled hand clutched at the dirt beyond the pit, and an enormous creature with burned and peeling skin pulled itself up and into the room.

I gasped and the beast turned its baleful eye in my direction.

The demon's hair had burned away, and the flesh was blackened and cracked around a single horn that grew from its forehead. It looked at me with bloodred eyes, and took a tentative step toward me on its new legs. There were cat's paws where its feet should have been. As God is my witness, it walked on paws!

I knew in that moment that the beast had lived in many bodies over many centuries; it had occupied the space beneath men's skin after obliterating their minds. This evil thing had taken many lives, and I had but a few breaths left in me before it would take mine. It would wear my body and it would go to my home. It would call itself by my name and be welcomed by my unsuspecting family.

I screamed again, but there was no one left to hear me. The demon smiled in a most charming way and took another step.

Rose stopped reading and closed the book. She ran her hand over its plain black cover. Rabbit was gently snoring next to her. Rose wondered, not for the first time, whether she should leave their party and take the girl with her. Rabbit ought to be in school somewhere, not on the trail with a witch hunter.

The child slept a lot, in Rose's opinion, but her experience with children was limited to the classroom, so she wasn't sure what was healthy or normal. Rose felt like curling up next to the girl and taking a long nap. She smoothed Rabbit's short hair away from her forehead and laid the back of her hand on the girl's forehead, then sighed and stood up from the bed.

A sharp pain in her abdomen doubled her over, and she clamped her teeth together to keep from crying out. The pain passed, and after a moment she was able to shake off the lingering nausea and stand up straight.

She looked around the little bedroom and contemplated the few remaining artifacts of her life: the warm woolen socks, the books, the knitting needles, and the handful of Joe's tools that were small enough to fit in her bag. She had packed less than Ned Hemingway, for instance, but still more than she thought she ought to. The tools and the socks were useful, and she felt justified in bringing them along, but the books gave her a wistful feeling. She had thought she might read aloud to the men in the evenings, and to Rabbit as a part of the child's education. But the men had shown little interest in being read to, and Rose was unable to tell how much Rabbit understood or appreciated the stories she read. It was impossible to know what thoughts passed behind the girl's dark eyes.

Rose set *The Call of the Nightfall King* atop *The Farmer's Grimoire* on her small stack of books, and ran her fingers over their spines, their textured leather covers firm to the touch, promising wonder within. She picked up *Dombey and Son* and flipped past the frontispiece of a fat man with a hook for a hand, who was directing a young boy's studies. For perhaps the hundredth time, she read the first sentence:

> *Dombey sat in the corner of the darkened room in the great armchair by the bedside, and Son lay tucked up warm in a little basket bedstead, carefully disposed on a low settee immediately in front of the fire and close to it, as if his constitution were analogous to that of a muffin, and it was essential to toast him brown while he was very new.*

"It was essential to toast him brown," she read aloud, and chuckled.

No, she decided, the books were useful, too. They, more than anything else, reminded her of who she really was. She was not just the widow, or the traveling companion, or the ward of a strange child whom she barely knew. She was Rose Nettles, and no other label was enough.

A folded piece of paper slipped out of the book and fluttered to her feet. Puzzled, she bent and picked it up, unfolded it, and read: "Dear Rose, the wedding was a small affair . . ."

And she suddenly remembered Joe bringing the letter to her at the table in their little house. It was early in their marriage. She remembered how he had perched on a chair across from her, anxious to see if the letter was a summons home; or perhaps he was only anxious to be near her. She had never read her mother's letter. She had folded it back up as soon as she realized what it was, and she had promptly forgotten about it.

But Joe wasn't there, waiting to know about their future together. They had no future together. Nor did she have a future in her mother's home; there was little chance she would ever return to Philadelphia. What would she do there? Who would still know her? She was a different person now. The letter meant nothing, and, therefore, it could no longer hurt her to read it.

Dear Rose,

The wedding was a small affair, and I am now Mrs Giles Bradshaw. I am selling the old house. Mr Bradshaw has asked after your health, and I would be glad to tell him that you are well and also that you think well of him.

I am in a state, what with my new duties as the wife of a banker. Can you imagine? At my age! When I think of it, I feel as giddy as one of your schoolgirls.

Mr Bradshaw has recently been called to settle an estate in London, an important client, and I am left to my own devices to appoint the new house and hire the help.

It is quite lonely here, to be honest. I miss the clack of your knitting needles, and I miss our interesting conversations. I do wonder how you are doing in your own new home, with your own new husband, and I only hope he is as accommodating and kind as Mr Bradshaw.

I hope you will write back. I plan to check the post constantly until I hear from you.

Your Loving Mother.

There was a tiny scrawl of a postscript at the bottom of the page, and Rose had to squint to read it.

PS: As I am posting this, I have received news from London that Mr Bradshaw met with a terrible accident and will not be returning. Please come immediately if you can possibly get away, Rose. I simply can't bear it.

Rose laid the letter down atop the books and backed away from it. She sat on the bed and gazed at the sleeping child without really seeing her.

How many years had passed? If only she had read the letter when it came. And why had her mother never written again?

Rose wiped her eyes with the sleeve of her dress and stood back up. She went to the desk, found a pencil, and despite her fear that any response would arrive years too late to comfort her mother, she began to compose a telegram.

CHAPTER 9

Ned's pace slowed as he reached the end of the street, and he stopped in front of the tipped-over handcart. He reached out and spun its remaining wheel. It creaked and wobbled, grinding rust. Ned squinted at the sun, then tipped his yellow hat to a small boy who stood on the other side of the tracks.

The boy smiled at him. With his fingers still on the brim of his hat, Ned swiveled his head back and forth, taking in the long line of children. Ned counted perhaps sixty or seventy of them, all nicely dressed, their hair slicked down against their scalps, each of them clasping a bible. The boy stepped up onto the tracks, and reached his hand out to Ned. He moved the way Ned had seen Joe Mullins move, as if underwater, floating forward and pushed back by some unseen wave. Ned reached out to take the boy's hand, but his fingers glanced away as if he and the boy were magnets of opposite polarity. He reached out again, but the harder he tried to make contact, the more resistance he met. He put his hand down and shrugged. The boy shook his head and mouthed words at him.

"I can't hear you," Ned said. "To be honest, and I don't mean to be hurtful when I say this, but I ain't so sure you're real. I think you might be a figment."

The boy motioned to the other children and they stepped forward in twos and threes, climbing the gentle slope to the train tracks, then down the other side, moving around Ned until he found himself at the center of a ring of children, their small bodies undulating in a breeze that Ned could neither see nor feel.

A girl, taller than the others, with long straight hair and a serious expression, got his attention and moved her lips slowly.

"I'm sorry," Ned said. "I met a man like you a couple times, and I couldn't hear him either. I don't know why. I wished I did, so I could maybe figure out how to talk with you."

The girl shook her head and mouthed words at him again. He thought they were the same words, and he leaned in closer.

"Again," he said. "Say it again, girl."

She did.

"You're saying even if I can't hear you, you can hear me," Ned said. "That right?"

The girl nodded, and the boy smiled at him again.

"Can you hear everybody?"

She nodded again.

"But nobody can hear you," he said.

The boy shook his head.

"I reckon you young ones are dead, huh?"

The girl took a step back; some of the smaller children broke away from the circle and began to silently cry. The girl knelt and wiped the eyes of a smaller girl, whom Ned guessed was only two or three years old. He noticed that a few of the children at the outer edge of the semicircle were holding babies in their arms. One of the boys who was carrying a baby looked over his shoulder, then moved to one side. The girl next to him moved over, too, and a woman approached Ned, drifting slowly through the sea of children as they stepped back, one by one, to let her pass.

She was pretty, perhaps twenty-five or thirty years old, her eyes wide and colorless, and her hair tucked up under a spring bonnet decorated with a spray of pink and blue flowers. Ned removed his hat as she approached.

"Ma'am," he said. "I apologize if I've upset your children."

She patted the air in front of her, reassuring him, and offered a small sad smile. When she spoke, he thought he could hear something in the distance like leaves blowing in the wind, and he concentrated on the shapes of the words as she mouthed them. It was easier than trying to understand the children. He motioned that she should repeat herself, and felt a tingle of excitement when he finally parsed her meaning.

"No, ma'am, I don't believe the train is coming through here today," he said. "I don't believe the train comes through here at all anymore."

He thought this should be evident from the state of the rusty tracks and the upended handcart, but he didn't know what she could see, or how long she had been waiting.

"Something pretty bad happened here," he said. "I'm glad these children have you to look after them, though. That might be a hardship for you, but I bet they're right grateful."

Many of the children nodded in agreement, some of them mouthing words to him or to the woman. The little boy he had first interacted with took the woman's hand in his, and she smiled down at him. Ned noticed she was the only one of them who wasn't carrying a bible. Something nagged at the back of his mind, a story he had heard years before. His skin prickled and he stumbled sideways as he came close to a boy who was standing behind him, and the magnetic repulsion they generated pushed Ned away.

"The Orphan Train," he said.

The woman nodded.

"Was there an accident?" Ned said. "With the train, I mean."

The woman shook her head, and pointed at Ned, then pointed away down the tracks. She seemed frustrated with him, and repeated the series of motions with more emphasis.

"You want me to find a train for you?"

She shook her head.

"You want me to go away?"

She nodded.

"You want me to leave Quivira Falls," he said.

She nodded again, and Ned glanced back in the direction of the rooming house. Once again, he was reminded of the unease Rose had felt upon entering the town.

"Are we in some kind of danger here?" Ned said.

But when he turned back to the woman, she was gone. Where she had stood, a scattering of dead leaves swirled across the tracks. One by one, the children in the circle blew away like puffs of smoke, until finally only the first boy was left. The boy held out his bible as if offering it to Ned, then he, too, was gone.

Ned stood for a long moment, waiting to see if the orphans would return. At last, he gave the wheel of the broken handcart another spin, and stepped away from the train tracks.

"I wished I knew for sure if I was going crazy," he said. "That might be a comfort."

CHAPTER 10

Rose heard Tom Goggins's familiar uneven gait on the landing, and opened her door a crack, wide enough to peek out and see him enter the room across the hall from her own. He was carrying his hat and he looked flushed.

Rabbit was still sleeping, her knees against her chest and one hand under her head. Rose slipped out of the room and closed the door behind her, then crossed the hall and tapped on Tom's door with her fingernails. A moment later he opened it and stepped back, allowing her to enter. He left the door open and gestured toward the bed.

"Sorry, the Mexican and me don't got a chair in our room, but if you wanna sit on the bed, I won't think nothing about it."

"I'll stand," Rose said.

"Something the matter with our little Rabbit?"

"She's fine."

"I hope you got them windows locked in your room," Tom said. "That child tends to run off when you ain't looking directly at him."

"I wondered if you might look after her while I run to the station," Rose said. "I have a cable I'd like to send."

"Mrs Bender's waiting downstairs. Told her I'd be just a minute while I freshen up. That poor woman's been without a man for half a year already. Don't wanna keep her waiting too long."

Rose suppressed a shudder and looked around. Aside from Benito's bedroll on the floor beneath the window, the room was identical to her own: a single narrow bed with brass posts, a writing desk, and a pine wardrobe against the opposite wall, standing open and empty. None of them had much to hang up, and Rose felt a flicker of nostalgia for her old room at her mother's home, its fragrant cedar wardrobe filled with pretty dresses and skirts. She closed her eyes a moment and banished the memory. When she opened her eyes, Tom was sitting on the bed, his hat on his lap, watching her.

"Well, I suppose if it's all that important I'll stick with Rabbit for a bit," he said. "But I was just over to the telegraph office. I sure wish you'd gave me your cable to take along."

"I didn't think to send it until a few minutes ago. Perhaps I'll ask Mrs Bender to show me the way. I could put in a kind word with her on your behalf."

She wasn't sure what a kind word about Tom would be, but he perked up at the suggestion.

"You'd do that?"

"I would be happy to. And thank you, Mr Goggins."

He waved his hand dismissively. "Aw, that child was my responsibility before you ever come along. I kinda miss having that for myself."

Rose took a step toward the door, but turned back.

"I've been wondering something," she said. "And I'm not sure how to . . . Well, you claim to have experience with the black arts and—"

"Claim nothing. I am a master of the arts. You'll see when we get to Burden County and I collect my bounty. I wired 'em this morning to expect us, so they ought to be getting that witch's body up on display for us right about now."

"You told them to expect all of us?"

"Well, Ned and Moses, at least. No need to mention you or the child. Nor the Mexican, I guess. But if they know I got some cowboys along, they're more likely to pay up without a fuss."

"Then you'll share the bounty with Ned and Moses?"

Tom's face turned red and he fiddled with the turkey feather in the brim of his hat. "I swear, I was feeling good about you a minute ago. 'Course I'll cut 'em in on it. What you must think of me, I swear."

"I apologize. I occasionally think quite highly of you."

"I ain't cutting the Mexican in on nothing, no matter what you say. He's a stowaway and he don't deserve consideration in the matter."

"I have apologized, Mr Goggins," Rose said. "There's no need to be petty."

"I ain't petty. I am being clear about certain things." He adjusted the feather, smoothing it against the crown of his hat in an effort to make it stand up straighter. "Anyhow, I guess you got something to say about witchcraft?"

"I had a question for you, but now it seems foolish."

"Foolish or not, go on and ask it."

Rose took a breath and braced herself for the eventuality that Tom might laugh at her.

"Mr Goggins, have you ever heard of a person who could change shape?"

"I knew a fat man once who took ill when he got hold of some bad pork. In a fortnight he turned hisself into a skinny man."

"That isn't . . . Mr Goggins, do you know of a human who is able to change into an animal, or vice versa."

Tom's eyes narrowed. Rose returned his gaze without flinching, until he finally blinked and resumed fiddling with his hat.

"There's different kinds of critters can do what you're talking about, Mrs Mullins. There's witches, of course, who can make it like they's inside the skin of an animal if they're of a mind. And there's lycanthropes and vampires, though personally I ain't never seen a specimen of that sort, only heard rumors in low places frequented by men who's got nowhere else to go of an evening."

Rose imagined Tom Goggins often found himself in such places.

"What are those things you mentioned? I've heard of vampires, but . . ."

"They say one kind can turn hisself into a wolf, and the other can turn hisself into a bat," Tom said. "Or maybe they already are such things and they only look like human beings sometimes. There are animals can make theyselves look like people. I learned that from an Indian fella name of Traveling Horse."

"That name sounds familiar," Rose said. "I believe I've met him."

"Well, Traveling Horse gets around. He told me that looking like a human person helps a critter move amongst us without being ate. I ain't seen it myself, but the Indian says his people know about such things. They say it's because us white men come along and filled up the land, so the animals had to get thoughtful about how to keep on living here. Traveling Horse said the critters gotta hide theyselves in the skin of white folks 'cause we eat up everything we see and don't leave nothing for nobody else."

"And those are the only examples you can think of?"

"I'd say so, off the top of my head. Why do you ask?"

"Oh, no reason," Rose said. "I had read of such things in a book once, and I wondered if they were real."

"Well, aside from witches, I can't say for sure. I'd wait to believe in such things until you see 'em for yourself. Book writers tend to make things up."

"Thank you, Mr Goggins."

"Any time," he said. "Now you best skedaddle and send your cable. Don't forget to put in a word for me with the landlady."

CHAPTER 11

There was a company traveling northward from the Oklahoma border on a meandering course that would eventually take them to Burden County. Sadie Grace was unclear about the number. There were five of them, she said, or possibly six, and there was an outlier, someone or something coming up behind them, but perhaps not traveling with them.

Examining the tracks outside the farmhouse, the Huntsman initially determined the number of the company to be five.

There was an ailing woman, and the sharp trace of her scent, arsenic and silver, stung his nose. There were three men, one of whom carried a large amount of iron and a bizarre mixture of powders that the Huntsman found disagreeable. There was a fifth member of the group whose scent was difficult to detect and frequently changed. The Huntsman was excited by the prospect of meeting this person.

But he didn't understand why Sadie thought there was an outlier. So far, he could detect no trace of anyone following the company of five. The Huntsman had never met an invisible man, woman, or creature who left no spoor. He could not conceive of such a thing. Still, he kept his guard up and moved carefully.

He left the farmhouse after a single night and followed the scent of the five travelers. They had made no attempt to cover their tracks or throw off pursuers, and the Huntsman was confident he would catch up to them well before they reached Burden County.

The company had crossed a wide field of bluebells and dandelions and broom sedge. The Huntsman got down on his hands and knees and crawled through the tall grass, his nose close to the dirt, sniffing at the traces of arsenic and iron. After a time, he came to a wooden fence, both tall and wide, and he stood back up. The travelers had demolished a section of the fence, and beyond it were shadowy woods, dank with the smell of decay. The Huntsman stood and listened to the strange music that came from the trees. It was pitched too high for human ears, but the Huntsman could hear it. The music made him nostalgic for his littermates and for the touch of a woman he had known more than a century before. A sense of melancholy settled in his chest. He had heard of such places, where sadness had leeched into the soil and evil had sprouted from it.

The travelers had stuck to a narrow path, for the most part, but the three men had veered off, and the Huntsman chose to follow their tracks. One of the men had left a pile of scat, covered with leaves, and all three had entered a small clearing.

The music was strongest in the clearing, and the Huntsman found himself thinking about the woman again: her scent, ripe and earthy, and the fine downy hair on her arms and legs. He growled at the trees, but the music continued.

He set his bag down next to a rotting log, and took out his patch box. He dug a hole in the soft bark with his knife, poured gunpowder into it, and struck a spark, blowing on it to keep it alive until it found the gunpowder. He watched as a vein of orange fire spread beneath the thin black bark, and when the log collapsed on itself in a shower of sparks, the Huntsman picked up his bag. He hurried back to the path and out of the woods. He crossed another field at a trot, and stopped when he came to a second tall fence. The travelers had cut a hole through this fence, too, but the Huntsman climbed it and sat on a crossbeam.

He dug an apple from the bottom of his pack and watched flames consume the cursed woods. When he began to feel the warmth of the fire on his skin he swung his legs over the beam and jumped down on the other side of the fence.

Burning the woods was not part of the job Sadie had set for him, but he was glad he had done it. His feelings of sorrow and regret were already fading.

He found the scent of his quarry again and bounded across the pasture, heading north, closing in on the company of five.

CHAPTER 12

Joe Mullins decided there were some good things about being dead. Since leaving his grave beneath the sycamore tree, he noticed he was more attuned to the unseen things happening around him. He could feel worms burrowing through the soil beneath his feet, and sense a nest of squirrels curled in a hollow tree.

But there were some things he didn't like as much. He could see the grass blowing in a gentle breeze, but he couldn't feel it. He stopped and watched a boy eat an apple beside a brook, and he tried to remember what apples tasted like. He didn't think he would probably ever eat an apple again.

He kept walking, driven onward by the buzzing in his head that he somehow knew would lead him to Rose.

The trail was sometimes narrow, choked with grass, and sometimes it was wide enough for two wagons to pass each other. Joe delighted in the birds and horses along the path, and even the occasional bear, all of them going about their business with no awareness of him. He watched farmers working their fields, and herds of cattle grazing behind barbed wire fences.

He stopped to watch a rancher build a fence. The man was driving posts into the ground, parallel to the trail, and there were great spools of wire laid out ahead of him. Joe could see the long neat row of holes, waiting to hold fenceposts. Though he knew it was hard work digging postholes and stringing wire, Joe felt a wave of yearning wash over him. He missed his hundred-sixty acres and the little house he had built there, and he wondered if he would see them again. He walked up and down the fence line, admiring the rancher's handiwork. He wanted to congratulate the man, wanted to sit under a tree and share a sack lunch and discuss the weather. But, of course, the rancher couldn't see him or hear him.

Joe reached out and touched the man's sledgehammer as it came down on the end of a post, knowing it would pass through his hand without harming him. To his surprise, the hammer stopped in midair, vibrating furiously against Joe's hand. Then it freed itself and continued its downward swing, smashing the post into the ground. The rancher didn't appear to notice the interruption.

Joe remembered the butterfly that had stuck in midair for a moment, and he thought about the strange timelessness he had experienced since his death, the sun moving erratically through the sky, the seasons changing on a whim.

Curious, he reached out again and touched the rancher's shoulder. The man stopped what he was doing, seemed to freeze for a second or two, and let the sledgehammer drop to his side. Then he looked around and scratched his chin, confused, shook his head, and picked up the hammer again.

Joe thought back on all the times he had entered a room and forgotten why he was there. As if his memory had skipped a beat. He wondered how many spirits had touched him, and how many he had walked through, oblivious to their presence.

"I apologize, sir," he said to the man. "I meant no harm or insult."

Joe walked back up to the trail and continued on his way, pondering his encounter with the rancher, and the new thing he had learned.

Time, it seemed, was not a straight line.

CHAPTER 13

The owner of the Quivira Falls general store had fashioned a saddle for the stump of his missing leg with a wheel that Moses guessed had been taken from a handcart. The man pushed himself along with his right foot and rolled around the shop faster than Benito and Moses could follow.

"I didn't catch your name, mister," Moses said.

"It's Clyde. And I don't need to know yours. A name only complicates matters. You're here for a hat, and that's all I need to know."

Moses fished a coin from his pocket. "I'd take a nickel's worth of jerky, too," he said.

"Don't got jerky," Clyde said. "Nor other meat, but I've got taters and corn and carrots. You can make a good vegetable stew with all that, if you've a mind."

"Never mind," Moses said.

"Hats, though? I think I might have one or two of them."

Clyde whizzed past them to a display counter piled with items. There seemed to be no rhyme or reason to the layout of the store. Clothes, and toiletries, and potatoes were all jumbled together in baskets and bins, but Clyde seemed to have some internal map of the place.

"Would this hat be for a boy or for a girl?"

"It would be for me," Benito said.

Clyde peered up at Benito, then clamped the Mexican's forehead between his hands. Benito jumped, nearly knocking the shopkeeper off his wheeled contraption.

"I'd say you was a seven and five-eights," Clyde said, unperturbed. "That about right?"

"If you say it is," Benito said.

"Be right back."

Clyde zoomed away through a curtain at the back of the shop. Benito rubbed his temples and leaned against a shelf stacked with books.

"That man is strange," he said.

"This whole town is strange," Moses said. "But we're not so normal ourselves."

"I was not judging. Only saying what I think."

"That's judging."

"Well, then, what is so wrong with judging?"

Moses plunked his unused nickel on the countertop. "There's five cents if you keep your thoughts to yourself until we're out of this place."

Benito scooped up the coin and stuck it in his pocket.

"I have no thoughts," he said.

Clyde wheeled back in carrying two hats. He held out a newsboy cap that was clearly too small, frowned and shook his head, then tossed it atop a basket of freshly shucked corn. He offered the other hat, a derby, for Benito's scrutiny.

"It's missing a piece of the brim, but that's not too noticeable."

"Thank you," Benito said, "but this is not the sort of hat I wanted. Besides, these hats have been used. Do you have anything that has not been worn by someone else?"

"Worn by someone else," Clyde repeated, rubbing his chin.

He tossed the derby aside, knocking a book onto the floor behind the counter, then wheeled out again through the curtain.

"Moses, I am very happy I became your friend," Benito said.

"I have a horse now, and a coin in my pocket, and it is all thanks to you and Ned. You are both very generous."

"It's only a nickel," Moses said.

"Yes, but with a coin in my pocket, I feel I can go anywhere."

"Where you plan to go, then?"

"Wherever you and Ned go."

"I might want that nickel back," Moses said. "You were supposed to hush up long enough for me to think." He glanced out the front window overlooking the boardwalk. "Looks like Ned's done wandering."

The bell above the front door tinkled and Ned entered, his face pale and his eyes wide.

"You okay, Ned?"

"I just don't know," Ned said. "I really don't."

Clyde rolled back in with an armful of hats of various sizes and styles.

"Well, well," he said. "Another new customer?"

"What the hell?" Ned said. He gawked at the homemade contraption at the end of Clyde's left leg, then wiped his mouth on the back of his hand and took a deep breath. "Sorry, mister. I never saw a fella roll around while he was standing up."

"It's my own invention," Clyde said. "People around here are so used to seeing me, I forget I might take a stranger by surprise." He swiveled to face Benito. "Now, young man, let's take a look at what I got for you here."

He held up a huge cattleman hat with a wide brim and set it on Benito's head. It immediately sank down over his ears, and Moses chuckled.

"Better grow out your hair some more," he said.

"Nope," Clyde said. "Didn't think that one would do, but decided it might be worth a try. Next!"

He pulled the hat off Benito's head and tossed the cattleman onto the counter. More books slid off onto the floor and Ned bent to pick them up. Clyde plucked another hat from under his elbow and held it out, but Benito shook his head.

"That is not a hat for a man," he said.

"Well, maybe it is, if you was to take off the lace and the flowers," Clyde said. He plucked at the spray of tiny blossoms. "It'd fit you, at least."

"Moses," Ned said.

Moses had covered his mouth, stifling a bout of laughter, but a glance at Ned sobered him. He had seen that particular look in Ned's eyes once before, in a Texas saloon where Ned had beaten a cardsharp nearly to death.

"What's the matter with you, Ned?" he said.

Ned was staring at the hat in Clyde's hands. He was still holding one of the books he had picked up, and now he thrust it at Moses.

"It's a bible," Moses said.

"They're all bibles," Ned said. "Every last one of these books are bibles. Must be a hundred of 'em here."

"Of course they are," Clyde said. "We're God-fearing people in Quivira Falls. What other book would you have us read?"

"We won't be needing anything from you, sir," Ned said. "C'mon, Moses. You too, kid."

"But my hat," Benito said.

"Forget the hat."

Ned stalked out of the store, and Moses and Benito followed him. The little bell above the door tinkled behind them.

When they reached the street Moses grabbed Ned's elbow and turned him around.

"What the hell's going on, Ned? You gonna tell me or what?"

"I seen that hat before, Moses. The one with all the pink and blue flowers on it, I seen it just a little bit ago."

"We all saw it."

"No, I mean I seen it before I went into that shop. And all those bibles . . . Moses, every bit of that stuff was took off of dead children."

CHAPTER 14

There were at least two dozen potatoes in a bucket, and bunches of carrots on a cutting board, but when Rose asked Mrs Bender about the telegraph office, the older woman offered to accompany her.

"Thank you, ma'am," Rose said.

"Please call me Elvira. But what about the child? Will she be all right if she wakes up?"

"Mr Goggins will be nearby, should Rabbit need anything," Rose said.

"Give me a minute to let John Junior know I'm going out."

In fact, it was nearly ten minutes later that Elvira Bender bustled back into the kitchen, with her hair up and her apron folded over her arm. In that time, Rose had made a dent in the pile of vegetables, having peeled a quarter of the potatoes and chopped half the carrots. As tired as she was, she felt a need to contribute.

"You're quick," Elvira said. "Thank you, dear."

The two women left the rooming house and Elvira closed the gate behind them before taking Rose's arm and steering her up the street.

"I hope you and your companions are enjoying your stay so far," Elvira said.

"We are. I wish we could stay longer, but we're expected up north soon."

"Well, what would happen if you did stay longer? Don't tell me they'd send out a search party?" Elvira chuckled.

"No, I don't suppose anybody would do that."

"I'm afraid there's not much to occupy your menfolk here in Quivira Falls," Elvira said. "Saloons and brothels are outlawed, and puppetry is strictly prohibited in our charter."

"Puppetry?"

"A disgusting habit."

"About the town, Mrs . . . excuse me . . . Elvira, some of us wondered why you call it Quivira Falls when there are no falls nearby."

Elvira waved at a little girl with an eyepatch. The girl waved back, then lifted the patch as if to see Rose better with the empty socket.

"Tell me," Elvira said, "have you ever heard of original sin? The idea of it, I mean. Most people think it means we're all born bad, but that's not quite it."

"I believe it means we are born into the concept of sin itself," Rose said, "and are therefore tainted by it, despite maintaining free will."

"You've heard of the angel Lucifer?"

"The fallen angel," Rose said.

"We in this town believe we are fallen, too. We may once have been good or pure, or our ancestors may have been, but we were born here, and are descended from the fallen, so we are fallen ourselves. And we continue to fall. In another life, perhaps we will be lifted up once more, but while we are on this earth, and in this town, we fall as if into a deep dark well, without ever touching the bottom of it."

"I'm sorry, Elvira, but that sounds like a dreadful burden."

"We carry it willingly," Elvira said. "This place was founded quite by accident. My parents were part of a wagon train from the East that was forced to stop in this spot during a devastating blizzard. The snow was as high as their horses' knees, and their leader could not see more than three feet in front of him. He sent a man named Nestor Quivira forward to scout out a better place. Nestor returned on foot three days later, his hands and feet black with frostbite, and declared there was nothing ahead of them. Nothing at all, and no purpose in going forward. With his dying breath he screamed that we were in Hell." Elvira shrugged. "If that is so, we have tried to make the best of it."

"But why stay here?"

"After a time, when the weather changed, other people passed through and we received news from outside. We discovered there were settlements to the west, but by then we had begun to build all that you see here. We had planned it. By the time the railroad came to Quivira Falls our roots were here and we had no desire to go anywhere else."

"Not even the young people?"

"One or two, I suppose," Elvira said. "But they quickly saw the error of their ways. No one has ever left the Falls. No one."

Rose had more questions, but they had already walked nearly the entire length of the street and the station was in sight. There were shops beside it, and Ned was standing in the street talking to Moses. It looked to Rose like they were arguing. Benito was there, too, standing on the porch in front of the general store.

When Ned saw Rose, he left Moses and stalked toward the two women.

"I ain't staying one single night in this town," he said. "And I ain't leaving none of you behind, neither. Get your things together. I want this place well behind us by nightfall."

"Mr Hemingway, you are being impolite to Mrs Bender," Rose said.

"You're overtired from your travels," Elvira said. "A rest will do you good."

"Besides," Rose said. "I have a cable to send."

"Then send it quick," Ned said. "In one hour I'm heading out of this town, and if you're not ready to go I'll carry you." He pointed a finger at Elvira. "I don't care if I'm impolite. Shame on you people."

He marched away in the direction of the rooming house, and Rose turned to apologize to Elvira, but the older woman was smiling at Ned's retreating back.

"He'll come around," she said. "Like I say, he just needs some rest."

CHAPTER 15

Charlie Gamble sat on the front porch of the ranch house, sipping from a bottle of rum and watching the horses in the pasture below. The door was open behind him, and he could smell the stew he was cooking in the fireplace. There was a beam of sunlight that slanted in under the porch's roof, and his chair was angled so the light covered him like a blanket. He was warm, inside and out, and was looking forward to his supper.

The horses also seemed to enjoy the afternoon. Three of them cantered about in big circles, taking turns chasing one another and stopping frequently to graze, their long tails swishing at flies.

One of the mares raised her head from a patch of clover and stared at the nearby trees. She whinnied and shook her mane, then galloped away. The others followed, and a moment later a big black dog loped into the pasture. It was the size of a wolf, and it watched the horses as it came up the hill. It stopped a few yards from the house, sat, and fixed its gaze on Charlie. The dog's chin was gray, and it had yellow eyes.

Charlie put down his bottle of rum and grabbed the shotgun that leaned against the wall behind him. "Scoot!" he yelled. "Get on out of here, dog!"

The dog yawned and stretched its long front legs, one at a time, then it advanced toward the house.

Charlie fired, blasting a divot of grass far to the left of the dog, who continued toward the porch. Charlie shot again, and a clod of dirt exploded to the right of the dog. The dog kept coming.

Charlie cracked the shotgun open and fumbled a pair of shells from his pocket. He dropped one and it rolled away across the porch. The dog was up the steps before Charlie could reload; it passed him and bounded through the open door into the house. Charlie belatedly snapped a shell into place and followed the dog inside, but after the bright sunlight, the interior of the ranch house was so dim he couldn't see. Charlie stood at the threshold for a moment waiting for his eyes to adjust.

The dog was nearly invisible in the flickering shadows. It sniffed the stewpot, and glanced at Charlie with its yellow eyes, then padded past him, disappearing through a doorway that led to the back of the house.

The dog had been unfazed by the shotgun, but it hadn't threatened Charlie. It didn't act rabid or mean, so Charlie leaned the shotgun against the wall and left it there. Curious, he followed after the dog.

The kitchen was empty, but Charlie heard movement farther back in the house, and he peered around the corner. A strange man was standing in the pantry, holding the last strips of jerky that Charlie had stockpiled. The man was old, with a long gray beard and weathered skin, and a lumpy burlap sack slung across his back. Charlie got the feeling he was a very capable old man who ought to be treated with respect, even if he was rummaging about in Charlie's pantry.

"Excuse me," Charlie said. "Can I help you, sir?"

The stranger turned and took Charlie in with his yellow eyes, then grunted once and began poking at the jars of tomatoes on a low shelf.

"Are you a man, sir, or are you a dog?" Charlie said.

The stranger looked at him again and frowned.

"Why should I pick one over the other?" he said.

Charlie nodded. It was a fair question. "I believe I would like to be a dog sometimes, if I could," he said. "Is that something a person can learn?"

The stranger picked up a jar of tomatoes and contemplated it, as if the answer to Charlie's question might be found somewhere in the red pulp.

"I don't reckon so," he said at last. "Leastwise, it's not something I ever learned. It's just how I was made."

"That's too bad," Charlie said. "I wish I was made that way, too." He pointed at the tomatoes. "If you're hungry, I've got a stew going," he said. "You're welcome to share."

The stranger grunted again. "I smelt it."

Charlie hadn't realized how alone he felt, and he was suddenly grateful to have someone to talk to, even if the man didn't seem inclined toward conversation.

He glanced at the ceiling. The previous day he had found a satchel of money under the floorboards in an upstairs bedroom. The cash was bundled and wrapped with bands that read WELLS FARGO CO. Charlie hadn't counted the money yet. If this man— who was possibly also a dog—wanted the money for himself, Charlie did not think he should stand in his way.

Charlie returned to the front room, and the stranger followed. The simmering stew had reduced, leaving a greasy orange residue around the inside of the pot. Charlie stuck his finger in and tasted it.

"I'd say that's just about edible," he said.

"Good," the stranger said. "I'm hungry."

"I've got bowls in a cupboard there," Charlie said.

"I've got a bowl," the stranger said.

He rummaged in his sack and produced a spoon and a battered tin dish that was too deep to be a plate and too shallow to be a proper bowl. Nevertheless, he held it out and Charlie scooped stew into it. The stranger sat on the floor and began to eat while Charlie went to the kitchen and got a bowl for himself. When he returned, the stranger was helping himself to a second portion of the stew.

By the time Charlie got his bowl under the pot, there wasn't a lot left, but he scraped the orange grease off the insides, and sat on a wooden chair across from the stranger.

A bit of doggerel popped into his head, something his grandfather had said when they were fishing at the old creek. He hadn't heard the old rhyme in many years, and was surprised to find he still remembered the words.

> If in the wood and by surprise you meet a creature in disguise,
> Man or beast or otherwise, you'll know him by his yellow eyes.
> > Hush!
> > Make not a sound when the Huntsman's around.
> He tracks his quarry anywhere: the deepest cave, the village square . . .
> Listen, do you hear him there? His footstep on the darkened stair?
> > Hush!
> > Children, watch out when the Huntsman's about.

Charlie had always wondered if there was a different version of the rhyme that mothers told to their daughters. He watched the stranger scoop up the stew, a trickle of tomato juice dribbling from his chin back into the tin dish. Charlie's stomach rumbled.

"Sorry," Charlie said. "There wasn't a whole lot of meat in the house, but I put in a little of the jerky."

"S'alright," the stranger said.

"You know," Charlie said, contemplating the orange goo in his bowl, "I've only heard tell of one person could change back and forth into a dog or a wolf or what-have-you, without it being some type of moon up above. You ever hear of the Huntsman?"

The stranger grunted and spooned more stew into his mouth.

Charlie took a bite and burned his tongue. He sucked in some air and swallowed, then set his bowl on the floor beside the chair to let it cool.

"Our Grandpa Gamble told my brother Jim and me about him, when we was little, so I guess the Huntsman would have to be about . . ." He tried to do the math in his head, but lost his place when he tried to carry the three. "Anyway, he'd be dead by now, if he ever did exist. Grandpa Gamble tended to make shit up, so we never knew whether a thing was real or a story."

"A thing don't have to be one or the other."

"The way Grandpa Gamble told it, there was a woodsman living way up in the mountains somewheres, maybe Kentucky, and one day an old witch knocked on his door and told him that one of his dogs was gonna have a litter of pups, and when it happened she wanted one of them pups for herself. And the woodsman knew about this witch, and he knew she was fearsome and not to be crossed, so he agreed. And, sure enough, some time later one of his bitches crawls under the cabin and gives birth to seven pups. Only, when the woodsman checks under there to see everything's all right, one of the pups is a human baby. It's a little boy, and it's nursing at the teat with the other pups, and the woodsman knows in his heart he's been cursed for some reason, and this is a pure abomination, so he casts about hisself for a rock, and he brings it down on the bitch's head and crushes her skull. And then he takes that rock to each of the pups, one after another, and knocks their brains out in the dirt, and then he comes to the last one, which is the little human baby, and he raises the rock to kill it, but just as he's about to do the deed something grabs him by the ankle and yanks him out from under his cabin. It's the old witch, and she says, 'You was about to break your promise to me, mister. That pup is mine.' Well, the woodsman is so afraid he drops the rock and begs for his life. The witch tells him he will live one more day for each of the pups he kilt, and the seventh day will be his last, and she takes that human baby, the last of the litter, and she leaves him there. And, sure enough, the woodsman didn't live past another week. A pack of wolves come and tore him to bits just seven days later, and the witch raised that human pup like it was her own baby, and taught him mastery over the land and the animals, and now he roams the country, hunting men and doing the bidding of any witch that asks him."

It was the most Charlie had ever spoken at once, and he was breathing hard. The stranger licked out his tin dish, watching Charlie over the rim. When the bowl was clean, he put it back in his sack.

"I shouldn't wish to call your granddad a liar," he said. "But that ain't the way I heard it. You gonna finish your stew?"

"No," Charlie said. "I guess I'm not very hungry after all."

"I'll eat it then."

The Huntsman—Charlie was certain now that it was indeed the Huntsman—crawled over and snatched up the bowl before Charlie could blink. A second later, the stranger had returned to his spot on the floor and was slurping up the last of the stew. A terrible thought entered Charlie's mind.

"Mister, if you was the Huntsman, would you be hunting somebody right at this moment, or is it maybe that you're in-between hunts?"

The Huntsman set the empty dish down and crossed his legs in front of him. He reached into his sack and produced a tin of tobacco, then pinched a wad and stuck it behind his lower lip.

"I am," he said.

"You mean, you are hunting somebody?"

"I am," he said again.

"Well, hell, mister, you ain't hunting me, are you?"

"No," the Huntsman said. "I'm after two white men, a colored man, a lady, and a Mexican who joined them when they passed through here. Also another thing or two that's traveling with 'em, but I'm not after you."

The relief Charlie felt was profound, and he wished he hadn't given away his bowl of stew. He was suddenly hungry again.

The Huntsman crawled over to the fire and curled up on the hearth with the lumpy sack under his head.

"I'll stay the night here," he said. "I'll be on my way in the morning."

"There's plenty of rooms upstairs," Charlie said. "Plenty of beds."

"This'll do fine."

"The Mexican you said you was hunting . . ."

"I said I was hunting two white men, a colored man, a lady, and a Mexican. And another thing or two that's traveling with 'em."

"But one of those you're hunting is a Mexican," Charlie said. "I don't suppose you would tell me his name, would you?"

"Don't know his name, but I know his scent."

"Well, is he old or young, do you know?"

"He's young, and he puts something in his hair that smells of mint. Now be quiet so I can sleep."

Charlie stood and picked up his bowl. He crept to the pantry and opened a jar of tomatoes and dumped them out in the bowl, salted them, and ate them with his fingers while he stood at the counter and considered.

The country was full of Mexicans, and Benito Cortez was only one of them. The odds that the Huntsman was after Cortez were steep. And yet the boy who seduced Marie had put something in his hair that smelled of mint. Charlie had smelled it on his pillow. He thought it possible that all Mexicans put mint in their hair, but he had a gut feeling it was Cortez the Huntsman was after. If the Marshals and Charlie—at least, in theory—were already chasing Cortez, wasn't it possible the boy had run afoul of a witch who put the Huntsman on his trail, too? Cortez seemed to be a magnet for trouble.

If, as Charlie had already convinced himself, the Huntsman was sniffing after Cortez, the Mexican's days were numbered. Charlie could go home to Fulton, Texas, secure in the knowledge that justice would be done, one way or another. He could take the satchel of money from under the floorboards and buy a new porch for his house; and he could get himself a comfortable chair, and sit outside in the evenings, say hello to the pretty ladies, and enjoy the sunset with a bottle of rum.

But what if Jim asked him how it had happened? And what if word got back to Fulton that the Huntsman had done the thing Charlie was supposed to do?

"I've got to see it happen with my own eyes," Charlie said to the empty kitchen.

He chased a stewed tomato around the inside of his bowl with trembling fingers, and tried not to think about that old children's rhyme.

"You'll know him by his yellow eyes," he said.

The sound of his own voice startled him and he dropped the bowl on the floor where it shattered. He got to work finding a broom.

CHAPTER 16

When Charlie went outside the next morning the Huntsman was standing in front of the bunkhouse. The door stood ajar and the Huntsman sniffed the air.

"I was gonna fix something to eat," Charlie said. "You want me to rustle you up something?"

The Huntsman fixed Charlie with a stare that made him squirm. He did his best to return the Huntsman's gaze, even looking him in the eye for a full second, and at last the Huntsman nodded.

"I could eat," he said.

"Well, I'll see what's left in the house. No promises, though. I'm Charlie, by the way."

The Huntsman nodded again.

"You got a name?" Charlie said.

The Huntsman appeared to think about it for a moment. "You could call me Jack Starkey."

"Well, I'll go see what I can rustle up in the kitchen, Jack."

"Hurry up. I'll be leaving this place within the hour."

"Oh," Charlie said. "I thought . . . I was thinking maybe you'd let me ride along with you a ways."

"Why?"

"That Mexican you said you was tracking. I might have some history with him."

"I told you I'm tracking two white men, a colored man, a lady,

and a Mexican. Also another thing or two that's traveling with
'em. The Mexican is not a great concern."

"Well, I'd say he's my biggest concern at the moment, and I
might possibly be of some use to you along the way."

The Huntsman smiled, and it was the most frightening thing
Charlie had ever seen. He took a step back, but forced himself
not to run.

"How would you be of use to me?" the Huntsman said.

"Well, sir, it seems like you enjoyed my cooking. I could cook
for you on the trail. And I can clean and set up camp. I'm good
at a lot of things."

"I don't set up camps."

"I noticed some holes in your trousers. I can sew pretty good.
I used to sew my brother Jim's clothes for him before he went and
got married."

The Huntsman scratched his ear and ran his fingers through
his long gray beard. At last he nodded again. He pointed at the
bunkhouse.

"You haven't been curious about this building?"

"No, sir, I mostly stuck around the house, in case somebody
come along with news. I didn't wanna be surprised."

"There are men . . ." He sniffed. "Men and one woman in this
building, and they should be buried. Something happened here
that's outside the natural order of things, and the bodies should
be under the dirt or there will be restless spirits about."

"Spirits?"

"Bury them. After that, if you can catch up with me, I'll let
you cook and sew for me."

The Huntsman walked away across the pasture without another word. Two stray horses were grazing on clover. They pawed
the ground and galloped away from the Huntsman, but he didn't

appear to notice. He continued in a straight line until he was over the hill and out of sight.

Charlie opened the bunkhouse door and was immediately overwhelmed. The putrid air was thick with buzzing black flies, a fog so dense that Charlie couldn't see what he was supposed to bury.

He leaned forward, put his hands on his knees, and vomited up the handful of stewed tomatoes he had eaten the night before. He wiped his watering eyes with his knuckles.

A small black toad hopped out of the swarm of flies and stopped short of the puddle of half-digested tomatoes. Charlie picked the toad up and held it in the palm of his hand. It sat and looked at him with clear green eyes.

"Hello," he said to the toad. "You're a friendly fella. Are you looking for company?"

He waited a moment, and thought he heard something, as if a voice were calling to him from the cloud of flies.

"Well, I guess I'm looking for a friend, too," Charlie said. "I think I'll call you Mr Frog, if that's all right with you."

He carefully slid the toad into his shirt pocket and walked down to the barn to find a shovel.

CHAPTER 17

Mrs Giles Bradshaw
1911 Rittenhouse Square Philadelphia PA
SORRY FOR LATE RESPONSE STOP WILL RE-
TURN HOME BY RAIL ASAP STOP TRAVELING
WITH CHILD AND WILL BRING HER WHEN I
COME STOP PLEASE RESPOND CARE OF RID-
DLE KANSAS STOP
YOUR DAUGHTER ROSE

CHAPTER 18

When they returned to Mrs Bender's house, Moses excused himself and went upstairs. He could feel his eyelids growing heavier, and the thought of saddling up again when there was a comfortable bed waiting for him made him weary.

He had been unable to make Ned see reason, and had finally agreed to move on from Quivira Falls before sundown. But he was concerned about his friend. He had coaxed from Ned the entire story about the children on the railroad tracks, and their guardian with the spring bonnet. But Ned had also admitted to seeing Rose Nettles's husband on the trail behind them. It was not like Ned to keep secrets from him, and Moses worried that the strain of the journey, and the added responsibility of caring for a woman and child, were weighing on him.

Moses didn't doubt Ned's sanity, but he was afraid the others might if they heard what Ned had seen. Moses had walked to the train tracks and seen nothing. He doubted the others would see the children either. And how would Rose feel if she heard that her dead husband was following them?

Moses wondered where he and Ned would be if Tom Goggins and little Rabbit had never interrupted their card game in Monmouth, if they had never heard of Sadie Grace or Burden County.

He decided to take ten minutes to give himself a proper shave. Ten minutes, he told himself, would make no difference in the long run. While there was little prospect of a decent night's sleep ahead of them, a shave might leave him feeling at least somewhat refreshed. He didn't know when they would encounter civilization again, and unlike Ned he couldn't tolerate a dry shave.

He sharpened his razor on a leather strop hanging above the basin in his room, then built a lather in his tin cup and soaped up his cheeks and chin. He was exhausted and the simple act of working the lather into his stubble made his arms feel like jelly. He set his razor down on the table and leaned forward, resting his forehead against the mirror on the wall. The dingy green wallpaper, decorated with dusty flowers, made Moses feel old.

"Why'm I so damn tired today?" he said aloud. "I haven't done a single blessed thing except shop for hats."

The mirror shifted, and when he reached up to steady it his hand brushed against the razor. It twirled away, hit the wall, and fell behind the table.

Cursing under his breath, Moses pulled the table away from the wall, careful not to slosh water from the basin, and knelt to pick up the razor. The wallpaper was bright and clean behind the table, where sunlight had not touched it in years. The painted flowers were spattered with tiny brown dots, and a trickle of rust stretched to the bottom of the baseboard. A brown puddle had dried on the floor beneath the table, and Moses stared at the stain for a long time.

The sun moved, and light through the open window shifted, stretching Moses's shadow up the wall beside him, and startling him into action. He stood quickly and folded his razor, slipped it into his pocket. He wiped the shaving cream off his stubbled cheeks with a clean towel, and left the room.

He met Ned on the stairs. Ned had waited with Rose while she sent her cable, then escorted her back to the rooming house, casting baleful glares at Elvira Bender along the way. When they arrived, Elvira had gone to the kitchen, and after scowling at Ned, Rose followed her. Ned knew he had upset them both, and he realized he should have waited until the company was alone before voicing his suspicions. When he saw Moses waiting for him on the landing he braced himself for a scolding.

"I need you to come take a look at this," Moses said. "My eyes are tired and my mind is muddled, and I think I might be jumping to conclusions."

Benito stepped out of the room across the hall and stood with his hands on his hips.

"All of Old Tom's things are here, but he is not."

"Probably looking for Mrs Bender," Ned said. "He seemed kinda sweet on her."

"Ned," Moses said, with more urgency in his voice.

Ned snapped to attention. He and Benito followed Moses back to the bedroom, where the table was still pulled out from the wall. Moses pointed and Ned squatted to get a better look at the stains on the wallpaper. He ran his finger across the brown residue and scraped it with his fingernail.

"That's blood," Ned said.

"I thought so, too," Moses said.

"Somebody was shaving," Benito said. "Somebody cut himself."

"And didn't clean it up?"

"People are lazy," Ned said. "But I should've thought Mrs Bender would scrub it away. She runs a pretty clean house, far as I can tell."

"Maybe she was in a hurry," Benito said.

Moses sighed. It was true, people cut themselves shaving all the time. It was foolish to fuss over a stain on the floor. He cast a longing glance at the bed. Night was coming and he didn't want to sleep in a bedroll under a tree; he wanted to stay and sleep.

"You fellas feel especially tired since we got here?" he said.

"I have been thinking of nothing but a nap," Benito said. "No, that's not true. I have been thinking of a nap and a new hat."

Ned took a deep breath and held it while he slowly nodded, staring at the dried trickle of blood that marred the wallpaper. The others watched him. Finally, he blew out the air in his cheeks and turned around.

"My bad feeling ain't getting better," he said.

"I, too, have a bad feeling," Benito said. "I will pack my things, and Old Tom's."

"Rose is downstairs," Ned said. "I'll pack up and fetch her."

"I'll get Rabbit," Moses said.

Ned gathered Moses's shaving kit and pushed the table back against the wall. Their bags were still packed at the end of the bed. He yawned. It might be good to get a few minutes' sleep, he thought. They didn't know where the next town was or how long they would have to ride. He didn't actually make the decision to take a nap, and was startled to find himself in bed when Moses rushed back into the room.

"She's gone," Moses said. "The window's open, and that child is missing again."

CHAPTER 19

At the precise moment Ned Hemingway jumped out of bed, Joe Mullins stood outside Quivira Falls, weighing his options. He had followed the road, drawn along by a vague feeling that his wife needed him. As always, the sun had moved forward and backward through the sky as he walked, and sometimes snow had blown across his path, though the winter's snow had all melted before he died.

The town ahead of him exerted a strange repulsion that was the opposite of the pull he felt toward Rose, as if he were unwelcome there. The thought of walking down the main street made his skin crawl. Or it would have if he still had skin.

He hoped Rose had passed through the town without lingering.

The landscape was thick with brush, which didn't matter much to Joe. He could pass through it without getting tangled. But he could see train tracks far off to his right that paralleled the road into town. He walked to the tracks and followed them. A deer crossed his path, running backward, and vanished at the tree line. By now he was used to seeing such things, and didn't give the deer a second thought.

The tracks curved away from Quivira Falls, then back, circling the squat buildings at a distance, which was fine with Joe. Proximity to the town made him slightly nauseated, which was odd because he hadn't eaten anything in months.

After a time, he saw the train station, where the tracks crossed the road and continued west. Dozens of children were gathered there, watching him approach. One of them, a little boy of perhaps eight or nine, waved at him and smiled. The pleasure Joe felt at being seen was like an electric shock running through his body. Joe waved back at the boy.

The crowd of children parted to allow a woman through. She waited for him beside the tracks, and he picked up his pace to get to her. When he got close enough, Joe cupped his hands around his mouth and shouted.

"Hello!"

The woman smiled, and the boy shouted back at Joe.

"Hello yourself, mister!"

They had heard him.

Joe had not realized how isolated he felt until that moment. He had spoken with the spirits in the dark woods, and with the dead man Isaiah at the cursed ranch, but those encounters with unhappy people had left him feeling bereft. Here, outside a town that gave him a stomachache, was a whole crowd of cheerful people lined up to greet him.

Two of the children ran forward, grabbed his hands, and led him the rest of the way. The woman bowed her head slightly as if she were shy, or unaccustomed to meeting strange men outside train stations. She wore a spring bonnet with a delicate spray of flowers, and Joe took off his own hat, holding it awkwardly out of the way of the children who clung to his arms.

"Good afternoon, sir," the woman said.

"Is it?" Joe said, surprised. "Afternoon, I mean? I should have thought it was early morning with the sun down over there."

He pointed east, and the woman turned to look, then turned back and pointed overhead.

"I believe the sun is right there, sir."

"Well, I'll be," Joe said. "That old sun sure is a rascal, 'cause it's fooling one of us."

"My name is Madelyne Russell," she said.

"And I'm Joe Mullins. Pleased to make your acquaintance. And these children, too." He looked up and down the tracks, and back at Madelyne Russell. "Are you all waiting for something?"

"We're waiting for the train," said one of the children.

"Well, it don't look to me like the train's been through here in a bit and a half. There's weeds growing up through these ties, and that handcart's surely seen better days."

A low murmur passed among the children, and one of the girls stepped forward and scowled at Madelyne Russell. The girl, like all the children, was holding a bible, and she tucked it under her arm so she could clasp her hands in front of her.

"Miss Russell, you said the train would come back for us some-day," she said.

"Yes, I did," Madelyne said. "Perhaps Mr Mullins is mistaken."

He caught a look in her eye and hurried to contradict himself. "Maybe I am mistaken," he said. "You don't hardly know about trains these days, and my eyesight has been playing funny tricks on me."

The girl still seemed suspicious, but Madelyne smiled at him.

"I cannot tell you how good it is to converse like this," Joe said, to change the subject. "I been traveling for quite a while—not really sure how long, what with the sun jumping all round in the sky—but a man gets lonely for someone to hear him speak."

"Yes," the woman said. Her expression had softened. "The children have each other, but most other people don't hear us at all."

"Well, there was a cowboy I met once or twice who seemed like he could almost hear me," Joe said. "He was trying, at least. Funny fella, wore a yellow hat."

"That's the man we saw, Miss Russell," the girl said.

"I would not be surprised," Joe said. "He was headed this way with my wife. I don't suppose you saw her?"

"Oh, you're married, Mr Mullins?" Madelyne said.

Joe blushed. "I don't suppose I am married," he said. "Not anymore."

"But you're following her?"

"I got a funny feeling I ought to. It's not by way of winning her back or nothing. I just want to make sure she's settled proper, then I guess I'll go my own way after that."

"I see," Madelyne said. But the way she said it made Joe's heart beat a little faster.

"I don't suppose it's any use asking how far behind her I am," he said.

"I guess you're in front of them," the girl said.

"Your wife is still in Quivira Falls," Madelyne said. "She and her companions are staying at Mrs Bender's rooming house."

"There's a fat old man traveling with your wife," the girl said. "And the yellow-hat man, plus a black man, and a very handsome Mexican boy. There's a little girl, too. If you wait here with us, I imagine they'll be along soon."

"Well, that sounds agreeable to me," Joe said.

"Now, Katie," Madelyne said, "there's no reason to think they'll come here to the train station when they pass over. They may very well linger at the rooming house, or go to the church where the others are. They might even move on from this earth, as some of you children did."

"What do you mean 'when they pass over'?" Joe said. "They ain't gonna die, Miss Russell. Rose is still a young woman."

"Of course they'll die," Katie said. "John Junior's been getting things ready to butcher them all day. They'll be along pretty soon now."

"Now hold on, girl. Somebody's fixing to butcher my wife?"

"That's what happens when people come to Quivira Falls. It's why they let John Junior keep all his legs and arms in lean times, instead of sharing his meaty parts with the rest of the town. His mom uses sleeping hexes on people so they'll stay a night or two, and then Junior chops 'em up."

"Now, Katie," Madelyne said again.

The buzzing in Joe's ears grew louder. "Well, that ain't right," he said.

"No, Mr Mullins, but it's what they do here. Ever since they had that big blizzard so many years ago. They ate each other from necessity, starting with a man named Nestor, but I think now they've got a taste for it."

"I better do something about this," Joe said.

The thought of entering the town made his stomach churn again, and he had no idea what he could do to help Rose if nobody could see or hear him, but Joe thought perhaps this was why he had followed his wife in the first place.

"I better do something," he said again, and with a quick farewell to Madelyne and the children he turned and crossed the border into town.

CHAPTER 20

When they found Tom Goggins he was hanging upside down in a shed behind the rooming house. His feet were lashed to a meat hook, and his hands were tied behind his back. An empty tin bucket had been placed on the floor beneath his head.

"Get me the fuck down from here!" he bellowed when he saw Ned, Moses, and Benito in the doorway.

"Old Tom!" Benito said.

"Where's Rose?" Ned said.

"And where's Rabbit?" Moses said.

They drew their pistols while Benito went to work untying Tom's hands. Tom swung back and forth as Benito wrestled with the thick twine.

"You're making me dizzy," Tom said. "I don't know where them two are. I just laid down for a second, and I woke up here with some monster grinning at me."

The shed was roughly fifteen feet wide and twenty-five feet long, with a sloped stone floor and a trough at one end. There were no windows, but there was a second door at the back of the shed. The walls were polished oak, and the roof was reinforced with heavy oaken beams. Six hooks dangled from the ceiling, one of them occupied by Tom. A solid block of a table, ancient and stained, sat along one wall of the otherwise bare room.

"I need a knife," Benito said. "My fingers are too tired to untangle this."

Ned produced Joe Mullins's skinning knife and tossed it to

Benito, who deftly caught it and began to saw at the twine. In a moment, Tom's hands were free and Benito went to work on his feet.

"Hurry up and get me down before that giant comes back," Tom said. He windmilled his arms uselessly.

"You must mean John Junior," Ned said.

"Why did he leave you here?" Moses said.

Tired as he was, he knew the answer before he had finished asking the question.

"Ned, Ben, we need to go right now," he said.

"Don't leave me here," Tom said. "Get me down!"

"I am trying," Benito said. "Hold still."

"Ned," Moses said.

The back door of the shed opened and an enormous man stepped into the day's last beam of sunlight. He held the biggest cleaver Moses had ever seen, a tool for butchering buffalo. Moses whirled at a sound behind him, and saw Elvira Bender enter through the shed's front door, leading Rose by her elbow. She had a pistol pressed to Rose's ribs. Elvira kicked the door shut behind her.

"Please point your revolver elsewhere, Mr Burke," Elvira said. "I will not hesitate to shoot your lady friend."

Rose clutched her stomach and grimaced in pain. "They're ghouls," she said. "The entire town."

Moses and Ned had traveled together long enough that they could coordinate their actions without words. Since Moses was already facing Elvira Bender, Ned aimed his pistol at her giant son.

Benito lifted the skinning knife and pointed it at John Junior, who was almost close enough to touch. Benito could feel the nickel Moses had given him, its slight weight pressed against his hip through the thin fabric of his pocket. He wondered if he would have a chance to spend it, and he wished once again for a hat and a gun, so he might die like a man if this was to be his last day on earth.

"This could all have been painless," Elvira said. "We have a spell over the house that puts our guests to sleep before we do anything to them. We're good people."

"You killed a trainload of children," Ned said.

"More than one trainload," Elvira said. "We had a steady supply until they stopped running the trains through here. Meat's scarce now, which is why, much as I might like you folks, I must ask you to holster your weapons and surrender yourselves to my son."

"Ben, get me offa this hook, right fucking now," Tom hissed.

"You're fine where you are, Mr Goggins," Elvira said. "Boy, why don't you hand your blade to John Junior?"

"Your son already has a blade, ma'am," Benito said. "A big one, too."

"We got us a stalemate," Ned said, watching the enormous man with the cleaver.

"No, Mr Hemingway, we don't," Elvira said. She raised her pistol and pointed it at him. "You see, Mr Burke has fallen asleep."

At the sound of his name, Moses snapped his eyes open and realized he had, indeed, dozed off and, though he still clutched his pistol, his hand had fallen to his side.

Three things happened then, all at once. Ned turned his head to look at Moses, taking his eyes off John Junior, while Elvira Bender fired her pistol, and Joe Mullins entered the shed through the north wall.

Elvira's bullet entered Joe's chest and hung there for three seconds, shivering in midair. At the sound of the gunshot, Ned dove to one side while Benito lunged at John Junior, slashing at him with the skinning knife. The giant grabbed Benito's face and threw him at Tom, who banged into the wall and swung back into arm's reach. John Junior grabbed Tom's hair and brought his cleaver down at the witch-master's throat as Rose pushed out against Elvira Bender. Elvira fired her revolver a second time, but the bullet lodged itself harmlessly in a leg of the big table.

Moses brought his own revolver back up just as the bullet suspended in Joe Mullins's body came unglued in time and continued on its way, traveling through Ned Hemingway's abdomen and shattering John Junior's left kneecap. Moses finally fired, his bullet entering Elvira Bender's right eye and exiting through the back of her head.

Her monstrous son crumpled silently to the stone floor, and Benito seized the opportunity, leaping on John Junior's back and stabbing repeatedly at the soft tissue of the giant's neck and shoulders.

Rose pushed Elvira Bender's body away and hurried across the shed to Tom. Behind her, the door opened and two men entered, drawn by the sound of gunfire. One of them was missing an arm, the other a leg. Rose recognized them from the train station. Both of them had guns, but Moses was now fully awake and Ned had regained his feet.

"Drop 'em and back out," Ned said.

Both men tossed their pistols on the stone floor and smiled at the assemblage.

"I can't back up very quick," Hiram said. "Sorry."

"I'll be happy to help him do it, sir," Peter said.

John Junior had stopped struggling, and Benito stepped back from the body, still gripping his knife. Rose beckoned to him, and he bolted the back door of the shed before going to her.

"Mr Burke," Rose said. "We need your medical knowledge."

"You two stay where you are," Moses said to the telegraph men.

"Gladly," Hiram said.

"We can see things haven't gone our way," Peter said. "We'll make no trouble for you."

"Mr Burke," Rose said again.

Moses scooped up Elvira Bender's revolver, along with the weapons dropped by the telegraph men, then stepped over John Junior's body, leaving Ned to guard the door.

The buzzing in Joe's head had receded, and he reached out to Rose, brushing his fingers through her hair and into her skull, but his touch only slowed her movements as she tried to stanch the blood pouring from Tom Goggins's throat into the pail beneath him. John Junior had missed Tom's jugular with the enormous cleaver, but had sliced the flesh away from his shoulder bone, exposing Tom's clavicle.

Benito finished sawing through the cord around Tom's ankles, and Rose helped him catch Tom's body when he dropped. Together, they carried him to the table and laid him down.

Moses gave the guns to Benito, and pressed his handkerchief against Tom's wound. Mercifully, Tom had already passed out.

"It's too much blood," Moses said. "I don't know if we can stop it." He had seen worse injuries on the battlefield, but he had not seen a man survive a wound as bad as Tom's.

Joe backed away from Rose and reached out to Tom. He touched the old witch-master and the flow of blood stopped. Moses gasped and snapped his fingers at the others.

"I need a needle and some thread or some fishing line," he said. "I have to close this wound right now."

He was fully awake now, and although he didn't know why Tom's bleeding had slowed, he was anxious to seize the window of opportunity.

"Mrs Bender's apron pocket," Rose said.

Benito was across the shed in three bounds. He flipped the

landlady's body over and lifted the apron over her head, bringing the entire thing back to Moses.

"Can you save Old Tom?" he said.

"It would take a miracle," Moses said. "But we're due for some good luck, aren't we?"

"Moses," Ned said from the doorway. "When you finish up with him, I might need a pair of eyes on this bullet wound."

With that, he slumped against the wall, and slid to the floor.

CHAPTER 21

A sizable crowd was gathered outside the shed when they came out. To Benito it looked like the entire town was there. He wasn't familiar with the gun Moses had given him, and had little experience with guns to begin with, but he stood outside the door and spread his legs to make himself look bigger and pointed the pistol.

"There's no need for that," Hiram said.

"We're feeders," Peter said. "Not butchers."

"John Junior was our butcher," Hiram said.

"We'll have to find a replacement now," Peter said.

Benito waved the gun at them, and kept his mouth shut, afraid anything he said would give away how confused and frightened he was.

Behind him, Moses and Rose carried Tom outside. They laid him on the ground beside the great red coach, and Rose climbed in. She threw out tins of food, jars of potted meat, and sacks of oats, making room to lay their wounded across the seats.

When she had emptied it out, Moses helped her lift Tom into the coach. They laid him across one of the long leather seats, left him there, and returned to the shed. A few minutes later, they brought Ned out and laid him next to Tom.

"We'd better find Rabbit quick," Moses said.

"She and I had a discussion after the last time she went missing," Rose said. "She won't go far from us again. She runs when she senses danger. I think that's why she . . . why Tom named her Rabbit."

"How does she sense danger?" Moses said. "Couldn't she tell us, so we can run, too?"

As Rose was backing out of the coach, Ned woke up and grabbed her wrist.

"It was your husband," he said. "Joe Mullins saved us."

Rose pulled her arm away. "You just rest," she said.

A little girl with red shoes pushed her way through the crowd and pointed at Benito.

"Leave the fat man here," she said. "I saw how bad off he was and he's gonna die. You'll waste the meat if you take him."

Benito shuddered and accidentally fired a round into the dirt at the girl's feet. Hiram and Peter closed ranks, pushing the girl behind them.

"You would shoot a child?" Hiram said.

"That's uncalled for," Peter said.

"You've killed us, you know," Hiram said.

"The whole town," Peter said. "We'll die without meat."

"Here," Moses said. He picked up a potted ham from the stack beside the coach and tossed it at the crowd. It bounced in the grass and rolled to a stop against Hiram's foot. "You want meat?"

"That will not do, sir," Hiram said.

"What is wrong with you people?" Benito said. He wanted to fire the pistol again, but he was afraid he might hit someone.

"Our fathers did this to us," Peter said.

"Elvira Bender's husband made a pact with the Devil to keep us alive through our first winter here," Hiram said.

"The first sacrifice—" Peter said.

"Nestor Quivira," Hiram said.

Benito heard a murmur pass through the crowd, and several people bowed their heads.

"He gave his life so we might live."

"And we were cursed for it."

"I don't care," Moses said. "You better move back, 'cause this coach is coming through in a second, and I'm not gonna stop if I run some people over."

"Rabbit," he whispered to Rose.

She put her fingers in her mouth and whistled.

A moment later, the child emerged from the woods behind the rooming house. She walked to the coach and climbed in, and Rose climbed in after her.

Moses hauled himself up onto the driver's seat. Benito made a last threatening gesture with the pistol, then ran to the coach and clambered up onto the seat next to him. Moses snapped the reins, and the horses moved out.

The sea of townspeople parted for the red coach. It bumped down off the grass onto the packed dirt of the road, and rolled away from the Bender house. Benito turned to watch, but no one chased them. Moses kept the horses moving as they passed the funeral parlor, the mercantile, and the train station. Clyde rolled out onto the porch of the general store and watched them go.

When the coach reached the railroad tracks, Ned opened his eyes and struggled to sit up.

"Just lie still," Rose said. "We're all right now."

"Help me up," he said, and she did.

He leaned his shoulder against the cushioned wall and gazed out the window. The coach rocked from side to side as it bounced over the tracks, and Ned smiled and waved, but when Rose looked out the window, she saw nobody. She put a hand on his forehead.

CHAPTER 22

The Huntsman reached Quivira Falls an hour after sunset. Not a soul was about, but he smelled desperation and fear in the air.

The company he was tracking had already gone from the town, he knew, but he also knew he was not far behind them. The woman with arsenic in her veins was easiest to follow, despite the team of horses muddying her scent. The tracks of the coach ran off the road, and were deepest where it had sat for some time behind a rooming house. The Huntsman surveyed the piles of tinned beans and vegetables, the potted meat, and the bags of grain that were left in the dirt. He could make no sense of it, but he gathered a few items and stuffed them in his sack.

The Huntsman could smell blood. He opened the door of a long shed. Inside he saw a sloped stone floor built for drainage, a butcher's block, and a number of meat hooks hanging from the ceiling. A large man and an old woman hung from two of the hooks, their throats slit, their blood collecting in pails beneath them. The woman was missing an arm. The man's rib cage was split open; his liver, heart, and both kidneys were gone. Blood had splashed from the pails and pooled on the floor. The Huntsman smelled gunpowder in the air, and he dropped to all fours to explore the room thoroughly. The company had been ambushed in the shed. There had been a gun battle, and two of their attackers had been killed.

But the hanging bodies puzzled the Huntsman.

Curious, he left the shed and circled the rooming house. The front door was open, so he stood and entered as a man would. He heard voices at the back of the house, and he sniffed the air, then drew his bow and nocked an arrow.

He walked through an arched doorway into a kitchen, and surprised two men working at a low counter. An enormous pot bubbled on the stove, and the Huntsman could smell carrots and potatoes. One of the men was leaning on a crutch and trying to work a meat grinder fastened to the end of the counter. The other man was using a huge cleaver to split a human arm at the elbow. The Huntsman was confused for a moment because the man was missing an arm himself. It looked for all the world as if he were butchering his own appendage. But he turned when the Huntsman entered the room, and the Huntsman could see that the man's wound had long since healed over with new skin.

"Well, hello," said the man with one arm. "Hiram, we have company."

The man turning the crank of the meat grinder looked up and smiled at the Huntsman.

"Well met, stranger," he said. "I'm afraid you've caught us at an inopportune moment."

"If you're looking for a room for the night, I'm sure we can accommodate you," said the man with one arm.

The Huntsman shot him through the throat and nocked another arrow before Hiram could react. He shot Hiram in the chest, and both men fell at the same time. The Huntsman circled the counter and checked to be sure both men were dead before retrieving his arrows.

He looked around the rest of the house, and determined that his quarry had spent some time in three of the rooms upstairs. They had left nothing behind.

He exited the house, closed the door behind him, and walked north up the street, sticking to the long shadows cast by starlight.

Curtains moved in windows as he passed. A door halfway down the street opened and a little girl stepped outside. She wore red leather shoes and a patch over one eye. He ignored her.

At the end of the street was a general store, and the Huntsman went inside. A small man with a wheel strapped to his leg rolled out from a back room, saw the bow and the nocked arrow, and quietly reversed direction.

There was no rhyme or reason to the store's displays. There was a stack of bibles, and a pile of assorted hats, and another pile of used boots and children's shoes. The Huntsman found a quiver of arrows, and took them. There was an assortment of knives, and he chose two that were sharp and well weighted. He left a coin on the counter.

The little girl was waiting for him outside.

"You're too skinny," she said.

He passed her and crossed the street to the church. The girl followed him.

"What are you doing?" she said.

"Go away, girl."

"Are you looking for something?"

"There's a pile of bibles in the general store, but the church is across the road. It makes no sense."

"Why do you care?"

"I told you to go away."

But her question bothered him. Why *did* he care? He was supposed to be following the people in the coach and ending their journey. He knew he was wasting valuable time, but he had grown increasingly curious. His quarry had escaped the ghouls in the shed, and the atrocities at the ranch. They had not tarried in the wood of sadness, with its strange music designed to ensnare travelers. They were either very fortunate or they were possessed of powerful magic.

"The church isn't for outsiders," the girl said.

The Huntsman ignored her.

The church was the largest and most elaborate structure he had seen in Quivira Falls. It was gleaming white, with a steep roof and stained-glass windows on either side of a massive front door that must have been imported from the East. The Huntsman took a moment to examine the windows. One of them portrayed a black goat sitting at a table. Laughing men sat arrayed on either side of the goat, and a large platter was being placed in front of it by a nude woman with the head of a cat. On the platter was a selection of red objects that the Huntsman took to be cuts of meat. The colored glass in the other window depicted a man with his arms stretched wide as several pairs of hands reached out to him from both sides. The man's skin had been peeled away and pinned back, but he smiled at them.

The Huntsman looked for the little girl, but she was already halfway down the street. He pulled the heavy door open and entered the church.

There was a font at the entrance and choir lofts hung under a high ceiling. A dark red rug was laid down the center aisle to an altar at the opposite wall. The Huntsman could smell old blood and could guess what had been used to dye the rug. He realized he was thirsty after the long morning. He lapped from the font, then walked down the aisle to the altar. A human skull sat atop a cross made of bones. The Huntsman lifted the skull and sniffed it, but there was no scent left. It was hollow and meaningless.

In his past, he had done many things in service of others. He had tracked a poacher who stole beavers from a trapper's snares. He had guarded a senator traveling through the Midwest on a tour, and killed six men in an assassination attempt. He had rescued a Sioux woman's daughter from a river mermaid.

Once he accepted a task, he carried it through without regret or a backwards look. But he believed this job for Sadie Grace to be the strangest of them all. He reflected on his journey since she had asked him to follow the coach. He had burned the woods, and he didn't regret that. He had not burned the bunkhouse, and he *did* regret that. In his experience, a lack of action usually led to future complications. The only thing that killed a scent was fire.

The Huntsman, whose name was not Jacob Skinner, nor Joshua Strawne, nor Jack Starkey, set his bag on the altar and rummaged through it. He found his tinderbox and stuffed his handkerchief in the hollowed-out skull of Nestor Quivira. He struck the flint and got a spark, then fanned it into a fire. He nocked an arrow and stuck it through the skull, then turned and shot at the ceiling above the choir box.

He loped back up the center aisle and turned and watched as the fire took shape above him, crawling like a spider down the curtains and across the carpet, then he pushed the door open and exited into the night.

A crowd awaited him, men and women carrying guns and knives and pitchforks. He shot the man in front of him with an arrow, nocked another, and shot the next man. He slung the bow over his shoulder and drew the two knives he had taken from the general store. He slashed a woman's throat, and kept moving, stabbing the man with a wheel for a leg and a man brandishing a fireplace poker.

When he reached the other side of the crowd he glanced back. Some of the remaining townsfolk were already running back and forth with buckets of water. The roof of the church was aflame, sparks spiraling off into the night sky.

The Huntsman believed he had left enough of the townspeople alive to bury their dead. Or maybe they would eat the bodies.

He didn't care. He walked on, past the train station, past a ruined and rusty handcart, over the tracks to where the road ended.

He looked in the grass for the wheel ruts of a coach and followed them away.

CHAPTER 23

They made camp on wet grassland a few yards from the tree line, and Moses built a fire. The woods that bordered Quivira Falls extended onward for miles. The sky was cloudless and black, and the moon was three-quarters full. A column of smoke wavered above the horizon, far to the south.

"I ain't going through no more woods. And I ain't staying in towns, neither," Ned said before passing out.

Ned's bullet wound had begun to scab over, but it looked ugly, black with faint spiderwebs that arced through his skin. Moses heated his knife in the fire and cut the wound open, then sewed it again, more carefully. He held the knife in the fire again and pressed it against Ned's abdomen, turned him on his side and flattened the blade against his back where the bullet had exited. The flesh sizzled and smoked. Ned woke and screamed, then fainted again.

Joe Mullins sat by Ned's side with his hand on the cowboy's chest, slowing his heart rate. The other man, the old one, was too far gone. Joe wasn't sure how he knew it, but he knew he couldn't help him.

"Tom doesn't look good," Rose said.

"No," Moses said.

He removed the bandages from Tom's throat and shoulder—the fabric soaked through and crusted with blood—and dressed the wounds with fresh bandages. He glanced across the fire, where Rabbit was curled up on the ground with her head resting on Rose's right foot. Rose was reading to her from a slim book of poetry.

"You're good with that child," Moses said. "Even got her trained to come when you whistle. You ever have children of your own?"

"No," Rose said, startled. She closed the book and set it aside. "I don't think I would be a good mother. There's a balance I fear I would lack. Too much affection, or too little; too much discipline or too little. I worry I would err to one side or another."

"Well, I think you might be a little hard on yourself," Moses said.

He felt mildly embarrassed to have asked such a personal question, and he was reminded that he had only known his traveling companions a few days. Rose was virtually a stranger to him, or he would already know she didn't have children.

Rose stared at the fire and stroked Rabbit's short hair. It was, she thought, only the fact that Rabbit was not hers that allowed her to care for the feral child. Wherever Rabbit had come from, and whatever had happened to her, Rose bore no responsibility. There was no part of her that was also in Rabbit, and she could look at the child without seeing herself reflected back. She was able to instruct and protect Rabbit without feeling a trace of shame or guilt or anger. It was why she had enjoyed being a schoolteacher.

It was a hard thing to understand about herself, and she knew she would never find the words to convey her feelings to Moses, or to anyone else. She thought Moses might make a good parent someday, if he ever ceased his endless travels and settled down.

Joe watched his wife's face. He wanted her to see him and hear him, so he could say goodbye, so he could ask for her forgiveness and tell her he forgave her. Of course, it was too late. From a practical and legal standpoint, their marriage had ended when she wrapped him in a curtain and buried him under a sycamore.

"Too much unfinished business," he said.

Ned opened his eyes and frowned up at Joe, then closed them again.

"Ben," Moses said. "This fire isn't gonna last all night, and I should probably stick here to keep an eye on our injured."

"I will gladly fetch wood," Benito said. "I wish I had thought to do it before you asked."

"There's a hatchet in Ned's saddlebag," Moses said.

Benito found the hatchet and considered borrowing Ned's yellow hat, too, but thought better of it. His head was cold, but a hat was a personal thing. He walked away from camp, toward the black trees, swinging the hatchet through the air like a sword. Moonlight gave the grass around him a silvery sheen. It was good to be part of a group, he thought, and to have found such decent people to travel with. He had been running for weeks, hiding from Marshals and bounty hunters, afraid to talk to anyone, and unsure if he would ever again find someone to trust.

He was worried about Ned and Old Tom, and worried, too, that once they arrived at their destination the company would break up and go their separate ways. He didn't care to be alone again. When the time came, perhaps he would ride on with Ned and Moses, if they would have him. Or he might apprentice himself to Old Tom and learn to be a witch-master. Maybe Rose would buy a farm or a ranch, and remain in Burden County with Rabbit, and maybe they would hire him on as a hand. He had some experience at ranching, not much, but what he didn't know, he would learn.

There was also the possibility he might meet a beautiful young woman at the end of the trail and make a home of his own. The thought brought a smile to his face, and banished his worries for the moment.

Benito plunged into a thicket and the moon disappeared behind a dense tangle of branches above. He moved forward carefully, peering into the shadows for young saplings or dead timber he could hack apart with the small hatchet. He found a clump of sumac and began chopping low to the ground. The hatchet easily bit through the sumac's thin stems, and he gathered them with his free hand.

When he judged he had cut enough for the night, he pushed the handle of the hatchet into his belt and wrapped his arms around the bundle of kindling. He had misjudged its girth, and he staggered forward, bouncing his shoulders against trees to keep his balance.

Before he had taken a dozen steps he saw a dog. It was large and black, well back in the trees, a hunched shape with yellow eyes. If not for the eyes, Benito thought, he might have mistaken it for a collection of stumps and branches, an optical illusion. But the dog blinked at him, the glint of yellow vanishing and reappearing.

"Hi, puppy," he said.

There had been dogs on his family's farm in Mexico, and he had gone hunting a time or two with a favorite uncle, who used dogs to chase down foxes and raccoons, but Benito had no knowledge of wild dogs. He thought about the pistol he had left behind in camp, and he thought about the hatchet on his belt.

"I am sorry if I disturbed your rest, sir," he said to the dog. "I wish you no harm."

The dog didn't move, so Benito took a step toward the pasture, which he could now see through the trees, a silver shimmer in the moonlight. The dog rose from a sitting position and Benito saw it was much larger than he had originally thought.

"No need to get up," Benito said. "I will be on my way now."

He quickened his pace, glancing first at his feet to make sure he wasn't going to trip over a root, then at the dog, his head moving frantically back and forth. The dog kept pace with him, moving easily through the shadows, never coming closer, but never falling back.

Benito reached the tree line and stepped out onto the grass. He walked across the field, forcing himself to keep a steady pace. He knew it would be a mistake to run or show fear. The fire was ahead of him, only a few yards away, but he could hear the dog at his heels. He could almost feel its breath on his neck.

And then Rabbit appeared from the darkness. He hadn't seen her approach, but she was suddenly by his side. She reached up and put her small hand on his elbow. Frightened that she would share his fate if the dog attacked, Benito dropped his armload of sumac and whirled, pulling the hatchet from his belt.

But the dog was already loping away, already nearly invisible against the wall of dark trees.

Benito stood for a long minute, gripping the hatchet so tightly that his knuckles hurt, but the dog did not return. At last, Benito stuck the hatchet back in his belt, and bent, hefting the sumac onto his shoulder. He took Rabbit's hand, and together they walked back to the campsite.

CHAPTER 24

Tom Goggins watched Benito and the child return to camp. Benito had a massive load of thin branches slung across his shoulder.

"That's sumac he's got," Tom said. "Damn fool Mexican. That kinda wood's gonna spark like crazy in the fire."

He turned to his companion, and realized he didn't know the fellow. The man sitting beside him at the fireside was slightly built, with a droopy mustache and a pipe clenched between his teeth.

"Where'd you come from?" Tom said.

The stranger took the pipe from his mouth and looked away at the column of smoke on the southern horizon.

"Name's Joe Mullins," he said.

"Mullins? You wouldn't be related to Rose, would you?"

Across from him, Benito had dropped the pile of wood and was talking to Moses in hushed tones. Benito seemed upset. He stamped his foot and threw his hands in the air.

"That boy looks like he just lost his best friend," Tom said.

"Were you two awful close?" Joe said.

"If you can be close with a Mexican." He noticed his wounds no longer pained him. "That negro is a damn fine medic," he said. "I haven't felt this good in a year or two, I guess."

"Well, there's some upsides to it. I suppose it's on me to break it to you, since you ain't figured it out yet."

Tom took the news of his death poorly. He argued at first, and tried to punch Joe. He got up and stalked off into the darkness, but didn't get far. A few yards beyond the campsite he found he was making no further progress and when he stopped thinking about walking away he was suddenly back at the fire, staring down at his own body, stiff and still on the grass.

"I guess it's true," he said. "I'm deceased."

He walked over to where Moses was pulling a short-handled shovel from his bag. Moses's horse whinnied and shied away from Tom, but Moses stroked the Appaloosa's mane, quieting her.

"Moses, you got to try harder," Tom said. "Don't let me go like this."

He felt a flush of embarrassment. He could imagine how his reputation would suffer, now that he had been killed by ghouls in a Kansas rooming house. He had expected to die in a terrible fight with a powerful witch. Then he remembered he had the necessary thing in one of his bags. He had bought a miraculous powder from an old woman in Missouri, a powder that was said to slow the progress of death. Not for long, but it might buy Moses time to save him with proper medicine.

But when Tom tried to open his bag, his hand slipped through the canvas. It felt like his fingers had fallen asleep. They tingled in a fairly pleasant way, but he wasn't able to get a grip on the bag, let alone pull it open.

He thought for a minute, then went back to where Joe Mullins sat. Joe was watching Ned Hemingway and occasionally reaching out to rest his hand near Ned's chest. Whenever he touched Ned, the cowboy's labored breathing slowed.

"Is Ned about dead, too?" Tom said.

"I don't know," Joe said. "I think if he makes it through tonight, he might live."

"Well, that ain't fair," Tom said. "I wanna live, too. I got people waiting on me up north."

"I'm sorry about that," Joe said.

"I don't mean I want Ned to die, though," Tom said. "That ain't what I meant at all."

"We'll see if he does," Joe said. "I tried to help you, too, but you was too far gone."

"I appreciate the effort and I'm sorry I tried to hit you just then. I guess you're dead, too?"

"Have been for a while, but I guess it takes a minute to get used to the idea."

"What am I supposed to do now?" Tom said.

Joe shrugged. "Every spirit I've met so far has just sort of stayed put and waited."

"Waited for what?"

"I don't know."

"Well, I ain't got time to wait. Like I say, I got people in Burden County expecting me."

"I reckon they'll deal with the disappointment." Joe found the witch-master abrasive, but seeing the expression on Tom's face, he softened. "I guess these others will go ahead and collect that bounty for you."

They had gathered around the campfire, quietly avoiding one another's eyes. Benito tossed a piece of kindling on the flames, and as Tom had predicted the sumac popped and spat, sparking so furiously that Rose moved Rabbit away from the fire. After a moment, Benito took the shovel from Moses and stalked away from the circle of firelight. Tom heard the shovel biting into dirt.

Then it was morning, gray clouds overhead, and Tom was alone with Joe. The fire had died and the great red coach was gone.

"What happened?" Tom said. "Where'd they go?"

"They moved on at first light," Joe said. "You'll have to practice how you see things now. Sometimes the world seems like it's spinning fast, and sometimes it goes slow. Sometimes you'll see a person, then they're all of a sudden gone, and sometimes it's the other way around. It takes some getting used to, but you'll get the hang of it."

Joe tipped his hat. "I wish you well," he added.

"Where you off to?"

"I'm following along until I see Rose don't need me no more," Joe said. "I don't know what I'll do after that, but I guess I'll figure it out."

"Well, I'll come with you," Tom said.

Joe sighed and pointed to a nearby mound of fresh dirt. In the ground at one end of the mound was a crude cross fashioned from sumac branches. A turkey feather was pinned to the top of the cross.

"That's my grave?"

"It is," Joe said. "Since they buried you out here in the middle of nothing, I guess this is where you'll stay. I'd keep you company awhile, but my Rose is headed north, and so am I."

"I can't leave?"

"I ain't seen another spirit could do it."

"But you did it."

Joe shrugged again. "That's true," he said. "I think maybe it's 'cause my grave was hexed. In fact, I think you was the one that hexed it for me."

"I did no such thing."

"Someone nailed a little doll to a tree right over my body."

"That was a witch hex," Tom said. "I didn't hex you. I hexed the witch."

"Well, then maybe it wasn't that. I don't pretend to know about such things. But whether it was the hex or something else, I left my body back there. I hope you'll have similar luck someday."

With that, Joe Mullins turned his back to Tom Goggins and walked away north, following the tracks of the coach.

CHAPTER 25

Charlie Gamble came upon Quivira Falls early in the morning, when the sun was just a thought in the dark eastern sky.

It had taken him ten hours to bury the bodies in the bunkhouse. He had paused several times and gone to the barn, laid on a bale of hay, and cried. When he left the ranch he had propped the bunkhouse door open, though he didn't think any amount of fresh air would help with the stench.

He thought he might never be the same again.

Now he was in a hurry to catch up with the Huntsman. There was a rooming house by the side of the road, and it had a vacancy sign posted in the front yard, but Charlie had no intention of stopping. As much as he wanted to return to Fulton, Texas, he needed some proof that Benito Cortez was dead.

He spurred his horse forward. Far ahead at the end of the road he could see the smoldering remains of a building, with people milling about in front of it. Wisps of smoke wafted in the morning breeze, darker than the purple sky. As he drew close, he saw that the building was burned nearly to the ground. The roof had collapsed, leaving charred support beams standing useless in the smoking rubble.

People crossed the street in twos and threes, carrying bodies into a train station. Some of them looked up at Charlie as he rode past, their faces ashen and fearful, their clothing bloodstained and covered with soot. He was curious about what had happened, but hesitant to ask anyone. Nobody looked particularly friendly.

A little girl stood on the platform in front of the station. Her hair was black and her shoes were bright red. She had a patch over one eye, and Charlie wondered if she had lost the eye in the fire. She pointed at him as he drew near, and shouted something unintelligible.

Charlie smiled at her, pitying her lack of an eye, and he was surprised when she leaped off the platform at him. She grabbed his leg and Charlie lost his balance, sliding sideways on his saddle. The satchel of Wells Fargo banknotes came loose, and Charlie caught it with one hand, scared to let go of the horse's reins. He instinctively kicked out at the girl, striking her in the face with his boot. She dropped a knife he hadn't seen, and fell away from him, her nose gushing blood.

He righted himself in the saddle and looked back. The girl picked up the knife from where it lay in the middle of the road. Ignoring the blood that flowed freely from her smashed nose, she ran after Charlie.

He snapped the reins, and the horse broke into a fast trot, carrying him over a set of weed-choked train tracks, far into a pasture, and the little girl was lost to sight behind him.

He reined in his horse and dismounted, watching in case the girl suddenly reappeared. He could imagine her bounding through the grass, brandishing her knife, and he shuddered at the thought. He checked his saddle and tightened it, then made sure the satchel of money was properly secured. He opened his shirt pocket and looked inside.

"How are you, Mr Frog?" he said. "That was strange and scary, wasn't it?"

He had worried the small black toad might have been squished during the girl's frenzied attack. Charlie had done much flapping and windmilling of his arms, but the toad seemed fine. Charlie crouched down and caught a cricket, and held it above his open pocket, but the toad didn't seem interested. Charlie let the cricket go and climbed back up on the horse.

To the north the sky was fiery orange and red where it reflected morning sunlight. Charlie felt as if he had fallen into a deep hole and the light was unreachable. He could see the faint marks of wagon wheels and bent stalks of grass that led in a straight line north.

With a last backward glance at the town, he snapped the reins again and rode on.

PART FIVE

Riddle

CHAPTER 1

Andrew King woke from a dream in which a black bear circled his home, sniffing at windows and looking for a way in. Andrew's mouth was dry and his head throbbed. He was on the floor, and he couldn't remember if he had started the evening in a chair. He maneuvered himself up on one elbow and reached for the whiskey bottle next to him, but it was empty.

"I could give you something for your head," said Sadie Grace.

She was sitting on a chair by the cold fireplace, her face half in shadow. Andrew blinked and pushed up off the floor to sit with his back against the wall. He tried to speak, but his tongue was thick; he took a moment to muster some saliva and clear his throat.

"What are you doing here?" he managed when his mouth was somewhat moistened.

Sadie got up and went to a table under the window. It was late in the day and the sun was behind the barn. Andrew had to blink and focus in order to see his uninvited guest. She examined a pitcher and poured water into a glass, brought it to him, then went and sat back down in the chair.

"Drink," she said. "That water has dust in it, but it'll help."

He did as he was told.

"You know, you have caused me some trouble, Andrew."

He spat a mouthful of dirty water at her. The spray fell short and spattered across the floor. Sadie shrugged.

"Feel better?"

"You killed my daughter," he said.

"Did I?"

"Olivia was to be married soon."

"Did she know that? Or is that something you and your friend Tuck Tumbleweed cooked up between you, like you cooked up the bounty on my head?"

"It's Duff," Andrew said. "His name's Duff."

"Either way, it's a ridiculous name. Were you aware he's putting together a posse?"

Andrew squinted at her, confused. His head was pounding so hard he thought his skull might crack.

"Ah," Sadie said. "He didn't include you in his plans, did he? He thinks he has seven men with him, and he thinks that's enough magic to bring against me."

"What do you mean 'he thinks'?"

"One of his men is loyal to me. Duff should have been more careful in his choices."

"One man don't matter much," Andrew said. "Duff will have your scalp, witch."

Sadie sighed. "Why are you so angry with me, Andrew? What did I ever do except help you?"

"I just told you!" His own voice hammered through his head, and he shut his eyes.

"When Mary got the pox, what did we talk about?"

"We didn't talk about my daughter dying in front of me. She died horrible, Sadie."

With no warning, Andrew burst into tears, surprising even himself. He sobbed and shook, and pounded the floor. Sadie averted her eyes. The sun had nearly set. The sky was streaked with pink and orange and a shade of deep blue that she only saw at dusk. She imagined the posse would arrive at her house soon.

When she thought Andrew could hear her over his labored breathing, she went on. "When Mary died," she said, "you came to my house and asked me—no, you *begged* me to help you. If you got the pox from her, you wouldn't be able to work and you'd lose the farm. Do you remember telling me that?"

"Yes," Andrew said. His voice was barely audible, and there was a gob of snot on his upper lip.

"Do you remember what I did?" she said.

"You gave me a powder, and I put it in my coffee, like you said."

"And did you get the pox?"

"No, but Olivia—"

"Did you ask me to protect Olivia from the pox?"

"No."

"Did you share the powder with her?"

"No," he said again.

"You could have," Sadie said. "You had options, and you had chances, Andrew, so how am I responsible for your daughter's death?"

"You didn't save her."

Sadie shook her head and rose from the chair. She regarded Andrew in the fading light.

"Are you going to kill me?" he said.

"I saved you once," she said. "It would be a waste to kill you now. The worst thing I can do to you is leave you to wallow in your misery." She reached out and took a bottle down from the mantel. "Here, I even brought you a parting gift."

She stepped forward and set the bottle on the floor within his reach. He grabbed for her ankle, but she skipped backward.

"Oh, Andrew. You don't make it easy to forgive you, dear."

She left him then, walked out onto the porch in the gloom, and closed the door behind her.

He listened to her footsteps on the porch stairs, and when he was sure she was gone he picked up the bottle. He unstoppered it and sniffed at the brown liquid inside, then tipped it up and swallowed a mouthful.

CHAPTER 2

Sadie had wasted an hour waiting for Andrew King to wake up, and now she was running late. The talk itself had revealed nothing new to her, but she wanted him to understand that he was wrong. In the end, it was why she had left him alive. She thought he should see the consequences of his actions.

"Pridefulness," she said to herself. "That was nothing but pridefulness, Sadie Grace, and you ought to be ashamed of yourself."

She, more than most, knew that the world operated by an unwavering set of rules. Fairness and justice had no place in the system of cogs and levers that kept the moon in the sky and the fish in the sea. What bothered her most was that Andrew King really believed she had been unfair. He had deluded himself into thinking he was the wronged party. Still, she thought, it was sheer hubris to want him to see it. She only hoped she had time to get home before the show began.

She heard hoofbeats behind her, and ran to her favorite tree in the field beside her house. She had barely got herself situated in the uppermost branches of the ash when she saw the silhouettes of men on horseback coming down the road in a cloud of dust that glittered in the moonlight. The lead rider carried a torch, and flickering shadows danced across his features. She had never met Duff Duncan—the boy with the ridiculous name—but she knew it was him. The rest of the men fanned out behind him. Seven of them were coming for her, just as she had predicted.

The little white house with green shutters was shut up tight, but she had left a candle in the window and a fire in the potbellied stove. A plume of smoke curled away from her chimney, making it look for all the world like she was settled in for the night.

The posse rode past her tree without slowing, and she wished she had a heavy weight, another big rock she could drop on their heads. When they were still several yards out from her house, the men reined in their horses. Duff paraded his mount around in a little circle, as if sizing up his army, then urged the gray roan closer to the front porch.

"Sadie Grace," he hollered. "We seven representatives of the county have come to pass judgment upon you!"

He waited, and when there was no answer from the house, he turned in another little circle and held the torch up high.

"Judgment for the crimes you have committed against us!"

He was making the horse dance now, its black nose in the air, its cropped tail swishing. Duff was edging ever closer to the house, and Sadie began to worry that he planned to burn her out. The house would not burn easily, but it would cause her some irritation if she had to reset her wards and protections.

She snapped her fingers and the gray roan bucked, throwing Duff to the ground. The torch flew from his hand and smashed into the road, showering sparks across the hard dirt. The other horses whinnied and pawed at the ground. Sadie snapped her fingers again and two of them spun around and raced back down the road, ignoring the protests of their riders, who pulled uselessly at the reins.

One of the remaining men dismounted and ran to Duff. He turned him over and felt for a pulse in his throat, then looked up at the three still on their horses.

"He's dead," the young ranch hand said. "Our boy Duff is dead."

Sadie spat at the branch below her. She hadn't meant to kill the boy, only dissuade him from taking a torch to her house. The entire evening was going wrong because she'd been in a hurry. Once again she scolded herself for taking the time to visit Andrew King. But of course the boy with the silly name was too reckless and headstrong to have lived much longer anyway.

The young ranch hand scrambled to his feet and snatched up Duff's torch. He spun on his heels and raced toward the house, waving the torch over his head.

"She killed Duff, boys! Duff's dead!"

"Wayne," one of the others called out. "Wayne, I gotta ask you to stop!"

The younger man turned, and when he saw the pistol in his friend's hand he did indeed stop. Another of the ranch hands wheeled his horse around, working to free a shotgun from the scabbard on his saddle, but the one with the gun waved it at him.

"You stand down, too, Walt. I ain't gonna shoot your brother, but he needs to listen."

The other men seemed confused. Their horses sidled toward one another, as if herding together for safety. Wayne waved his torch again and took a step toward the one with the gun.

"Johnny, don't you point that at me!"

"Don't wanna see you make a mistake," Johnny said. "You say Duff's dead? I got to wonder what he died for."

"Gosh, Johnny, he's the one put this posse together. Don't we gotta carry out his dying wish? Don't that mean something to you?"

"It might if we was doing something meaningful in the first place. But enough people died around here already. What's gonna happen, you take a torch to her house?"

"Walt?" Wayne said. "Walt, tell me what to do."

Walt shook his head. "I think Johnny's right. I think maybe this wasn't such a good idea. You know how Duff was always saying the witch's name out loud, even though he knew better. I don't know, Wayne. Maybe Duff didn't think things through."

"Well, hell, boys," Wayne said. "What do we do?"

Johnny holstered his pistol.

"What about we just go on home?" he said.

Sadie watched the boy, Wayne, as he struggled to make a decision. She was rooting for him to make the right one.

Finally, he let the torch slip from his hand. He walked to where Duff's body lay on its side, his face in the weeds by the side of the road. Walt slid down off his horse and went to his brother. The others dismounted and, together with the twins, they picked Duff up and draped him over his gray roan. They tied him down, and the four of them got back up on their mounts, then the sad remains of the posse turned back toward the Paradise Ranch. They rode more slowly now, their shoulders slumped, their dead friend bouncing on the back of his beautiful horse.

Duff Duncan's abandoned torch guttered and died. When she was certain the cowboys weren't coming back, Sadie climbed down from her tree. There was a hollow ache in her chest.

The only positive thing to come of the entire evening was the fact that her agent at the Paradise Ranch hadn't needed to reveal himself.

CHAPTER 3

The day after Duff Duncan's death, Sadie walked into Riddle. Townsfolk peeked at her from behind their curtains, but no one came outside to greet her. She walked past the hotel and the bank, and entered the General Supply.

A little bell above the door tinkled and John Riddle stuck his head out through a curtain at the back. He saw who it was and smiled.

"I'll be right with you, Miss Grace."

When he emerged from the tiny back room—where he was unpacking a shipment of rat poison, dried oats, and women's shoes—Sadie was sitting at the piano bench, lightly plunking the keys. The tune sounded familiar to John, but he couldn't place it.

"I didn't know you played," he said.

"I didn't either," she said.

"What's the song?"

"I have no idea."

"If I didn't have a crate to unpack, I'd sit and play with you." John scratched his nose and frowned at the piano, then he smiled again and rubbed his hands together. "But I'm sure that's not why you stopped in. What can I do for you today?"

Sadie stood and smoothed the crease in her trousers, then looked around the cluttered store. She usually had her purchases sent up to the little house with green shutters. In person, the variety of goods on display was impressive.

"I'd like to settle my bill, John," she said. "And I'll need a new bag."

"A handbag? I have a few you might like to look at."

"No, a suitcase," Sadie said. "Nothing too big, but it should be sturdy."

"You're taking a trip?"

"I'm considering it. Do you know when the next train is expected?"

"I think the next one's due through here on Monday."

"Oh, that's longer than I'd hoped. I might need to do something about that. Anyway, the bag?"

"Right," he said. "I don't get a lot of call for luggage, but I know I've got something here. I think . . . Yes." He pulled a barrel of nails away from the wall and reached behind it, pulling out a leather trunk dusted with cobwebs. He made a face. "Sorry. I don't think anyone's asked for a suitcase since my grandfather ran the place."

"Nobody travels much, do they?"

"Not around here."

He found a rag behind the counter. While he wiped down the trunk, Sadie examined a bucket full of umbrellas tucked away in a far corner of the room. She picked out a solid specimen with a brass handle and twirled it about. John held the suitcase up to the lamplight, turning it this way and that.

"A little worn around the corners, but no dents to speak of. Looks like the previous owner might have done some traveling."

"A bit of wear and tear adds character. How much for it?"

"You can have it, Miss Grace. A gift to bring you good luck in your travels."

"Thank you, John. You've always been kind to me."

He set the trunk on the counter and wiped his hands on his apron. "If you'll tell me where you're off to, I can look at the schedule when I go up to the station."

"It doesn't matter where. I'll take the first train out of Riddle, wherever it goes. I feel like kicking some of this Kansas dust off my shoes."

John smiled. "I know the feeling. I hope you're not thinking of a permanent change."

Sadie laid the umbrella on the counter beside the suitcase. "I'd like this, too."

"Oh, that's a fine choice," John said. "It's the best one I've got."

"I thought so." Sadie took a handful of gold coins from her pocket and laid them on the counter. They clinked solidly on the battered wood.

"Is that enough for what I owe?"

"You don't owe that much, even with the umbrella."

"Well, how much is your second best umbrella?"

"There's enough here for three or four umbrellas, if you wanted."

"Good. I'm buying one for you, John. There's a storm coming."

John glanced out the big window at the front of the store and frowned. "There's not a cloud in the sky, Miss Grace."

"Even so. I'd advise you to stay indoors tomorrow."

"I hope you're not expecting trouble."

"Nothing I can't handle. Especially if I have a solid umbrella."

"Give me a minute and I'll wrap your purchases."

"I'll take them as is." Sadie slid the suitcase from the counter and tucked the umbrella under her arm. She glanced at the piano.

"You know, there are pianos all over the country, John."

"But this one is mine, Miss Grace."

He ran his fingers over the keys. The little bell above the door tinkled again and when he turned around he was alone.

CHAPTER 4

The Huntsman was confused.

In his time, he had killed dozens, perhaps hundreds, of men. He had killed women and children. He had killed bears and wolves and mountain lions; he had killed eagles and badgers. He believed he had killed almost every kind of creature there was.

But the girl was something different, and this concerned him.

It wasn't true that she had no scent. He recognized the faint trace of her from the farmhouse outside Monmouth, and from the Quivira Falls rooming house, but it was a strange shifting scent, unfamiliar to him.

When the company made camp again, the Huntsman climbed a tree and watched them. The injured man had improved over the course of the day. He stirred the fire and helped the woman prepare food. He rested often, and the black man checked his dressing more than once, but the Huntsman thought he might live.

He noted this in a peripheral way. He was primarily focused on the child, and he was thinking.

The Huntsman sat in the tree all night and he thought, and he tried to make a decision.

In the morning, the company would break camp and once again roll away in their red coach. They would reach Burden County early the next afternoon, and they would reach Riddle Township well before nightfall.

That is, if they encountered no problems along the way. If the Huntsman didn't stop them.

He had never left a job unfinished.

When the first light of day crept along the horizon like a distant fire, the Huntsman climbed down from his tree and left the woods. The people in the camp had begun to stir, and he walked out across the meadow toward them.

CHAPTER 5

Rose woke early and relieved Benito, who had taken the last watch of the night. He stretched out on his bedroll with Tom's hat over his face and began to snore.

Rose put a pot of coffee on the fire to brew, and checked on Rabbit, who was asleep on a blanket under the coach. When she returned to tend to the fire a man with bright yellow eyes stood watching her.

Rose's breath caught in her throat. She recalled Traveling Horse's song about a hunter with yellow eyes, a creature the Indians feared. Ned's shotgun was propped against a rock fifteen feet from her and she tensed, focused on the short distance and the time it would take to cross it.

"You can get the weapon if it makes you feel safer," the Huntsman said. His voice was deep and halting, as if he were not used to speaking.

"Would it do me any good?" she said.

The Huntsman shook his head.

"Then I'll leave it where it is. If you want some coffee, it should be hot pretty soon."

"Thank you," the Huntsman said.

"It's left over from yesterday, so it's probably not very good."

He shrugged.

"My name is Rose."

He nodded.

"What do people call you?" Rose said.

He thought about it for a minute. He was perfectly still, like a tree. After a while he answered her.

"Some call me Jacob Skinner."

"Is that your name?"

"No."

Rose wiped out a tin cup and used the same cloth to pull the coffeepot out of the fire. She poured and handed the cup to the Huntsman.

"I'll take some bacon, too," he said.

"I haven't cooked any yet. If you want to wait, I'll put some in the pan. I can wake Ned and Moses. They might make biscuits."

"They can sleep. The wounded one needs sleep to heal, and the other one worries too much. He stinks of stomach acid."

"I'll get the pan, then."

"No need, unless you're having some."

"Well, you can't eat raw bacon."

He shrugged again, his shoulders rising a quarter of an inch and settling.

"That child yours?" he said.

He nodded at Rabbit, who was awake now, watching them from beneath the coach. Rose felt a moment of panic, and she glanced at the shotgun again. But it occurred to her that Rabbit had not run when the Huntsman approached the camp. Rabbit always ran when there was danger. Rose felt the tension in her neck and shoulders ease a bit.

"No," she said. "Rabbit isn't mine, but as far as I know she doesn't have anyone else."

The Huntsman nodded, as if that was the answer he had expected. He raised the cup and sipped from it.

"It's not good coffee," he said. "Where did you find her?"

"A man traveling with us said she was living in the woods. He said the Pawnee killed her family and burned their home down."

"Not likely."

"That's what I told him."

"Which man found her?" His yellow eyes flicked toward the coach, where the top of Ned's head was visible in the window.

"The one who found her is dead. We buried him yesterday."

"The old man with spices in his bags."

"Tom Goggins."

"The child killed him?"

"Why would you even think that?"

"The spices he carried were not for food," the Huntsman said. "Why did he have them?"

"He claimed he was a witch-master," Rose said. "You ask a lot of questions."

"You also a witch-master?"

"I'm a schoolteacher. Or I was. Ned and Moses are just travelers, maybe they're looking for work, I'm not sure. And the same goes for Benito, I suppose."

"Then Tom Goggins was the only one of you intending to kill a witch?"

"Well, yes."

He took another sip of bad coffee. Over the rim of the tin cup, he regarded Rose. She found it hard to meet his gaze, and this made her feel angry, but she wasn't sure whether her anger was directed at the Huntsman for intimidating her, or at herself for being intimidated.

"I might let you live," he said.

Rose felt a shiver run up her spine, but she struggled to appear calm. She somehow thought he could smell her fear.

"I wasn't sure when I came into your camp," he said. "But I'm thinking more on it now."

"What are you thinking?"

"Your witch-master is dead. What are your plans now?"

Rose opened her mouth to answer, not sure what she would say, but at that moment Ned swung the door of the coach open and pointed his pistol at the Huntsman. The commotion woke Moses, who kicked Benito awake. Benito pulled a pistol from under his bedroll, and Moses grabbed up the shotgun that leaned against the rocks nearby.

The Huntsman took another sip of coffee. He set the cup on the ground beside him and leaned forward. Then he was on the other side of the fire. He slammed the carriage door shut on Ned's hand, and Ned dropped his pistol. Before it hit the ground, the Huntsman grabbed the revolver from Benito and pointed it at Moses's head.

"Put it on the ground," he said.

Moses set the shotgun down and backed up.

A moment later, the Huntsman was sitting by the fire, his legs folded under him, sipping from the tin cup.

Rose noticed that while the Huntsman was disarming her guardians, Rabbit had fallen back to sleep.

CHAPTER 6

Charlie Gamble hobbled his horse and crawled on his belly to the top of a limestone bluff. He pushed his rifle ahead of him up the hill, and when he came to a place where the slope leveled off, he propped himself on his elbows, opened the rifle's sight, and peered down at the gathering of people below.

In the glow of the morning light he saw a black man, and a white man who wore a mustard-colored hat and moved very slowly around the campfire. Charlie didn't know either of them. A third man had dark curly hair, and Charlie squinted to bring him into focus. He was almost certain it was Benito Cortez. Charlie moved the rifle and sighted down at the fourth man in the group, then he pushed himself back a little way through the grass.

The fourth man, squatting by the fire and talking to a woman, had called himself Jack Starkey. But Charlie knew who he really was.

Charlie thought the situation over for a bit before wiggling forward again and taking up the rifle. At any moment, the Huntsman might jump up and slit the men's throats, and Charlie wanted to see that happen. He especially wanted to see Benito Cortez bleed out in the tall prairie grass.

Charlie made himself comfortable in a patch of clover. He watched the black man fry bacon, and argue with the white man about making biscuits. Charlie could smell the bacon and coffee all the way up the hill, and his mouth began to water.

There was a brown rabbit under the big red wagon, and Charlie took aim at it, thinking he might like a breakfast of fresh rabbit, but thought better of it. Firing the rifle into camp would bring all sorts of unwanted attention.

The woman took up her knitting, a skein of red yarn in her lap, and the white man produced a guitar and strummed it. After a moment, the black man began to sing, and the woman joined in, humming along with the melody. Charlie closed his eyes and listened.

> *Down in the valley, the valley so low,*
> *Hang your head over, hear the wind blow.*
> *Hear the wind blow, dear, hear the wind blow,*
> *Hang your head over, hear the wind blow.*
>
>> *Writing this letter, containing three lines.*
>> *Answer my question, will you be mine?*
>> *Will you be mine, dear, will you be mine?*
>> *Answer my question, will you be mine?*
>
> *Write me a letter, send it by mail.*
> *Send it in care of the Birmingham jail,*
> *Birmingham jail, dear, Birmingham jail,*
> *Send it in care of the Birmingham jail.*
>
>> *Roses love sunshine, violets love dew,*
>> *Angels in Heaven know I love you,*
>> *Know I love you, dear, know I love you,*
>> *Angels in Heaven know I love you.*

The clanging of pots and pans woke Charlie up. The sun was high in the sky and the campfire had died. The prairie was bathed in light, pinpricks of red and yellow wildflowers bright against the green grass. The man with the colorful hat was struggling to pack up the breakfast dishes, and the black man was scolding him.

After a moment of argument, the white man sat down and let the others do the work. Benito Cortez and the woman lashed the pots and pans to the roof of the garish red coach.

There was no sign of the Huntsman. Jack Starkey, or whatever his name was, had left them alive. Benito Cortez was apparently free to continue north, and Charlie knew the US Marshals would eventually give up the search for him. There would be no news of Cortez's death, and Sheriff Jim Gamble would never let Charlie return to Fulton.

Charlie felt a righteous anger growing within him, and he pulled the trigger without aiming. His shot went wide and struck the embers of the cook fire.

The people below him scrambled for cover. The woman pushed the black man toward the coach, and they both went for the horses. Benito Cortez put an arm around the white man and pulled him to the ground.

Charlie's Henry rifle normally held sixteen rounds, but he only had three left. He fired again, and a divot of earth vaporized in front of Cortez. The Mexican crawled on top of the cowboy, shielding him with his body. Now Charlie had two bullets left, but Cortez was showing uncommon bravery by trying to protect the injured man, and making himself an easier target.

The coach was rolling now, the black man trying to bring it around for cover. Charlie took careful aim. As he squeezed the trigger, something yanked him backward, causing the shot to go wild. Charlie dropped the rifle and twisted onto his back. The Huntsman stood over him holding a wicked-looking knife.

"The simpleton," the Huntsman said. "I should have killed you at the ranch."

"You were supposed to kill the Mexican," Charlie said.

"I don't work for you," the Huntsman said.

He leaned forward and reached for the front of Charlie's shirt.

Charlie closed his eyes and windmilled his arms, slapping at the Huntsman and kicking at his legs. The Huntsman grabbed Charlie's right wrist and pulled him up onto his feet. Charlie felt a sharp pain in his belly and turned to run, but his legs didn't obey him. He looked down and saw a bright red flower blooming across the front of his white shirt. He dropped to his knees and whimpered.

"All I wanted was to sit on my porch and fall asleep in the sun," he said.

"Then you should have stayed home," the Huntsman said.

Charlie settled back with his legs under him. He looked at the rifle, so far away, too far to do him any good. And only one bullet left anyway.

The Huntsman picked up the rifle and walked away.

Charlie stared out at the sunlit prairie. A warm wind bent the grass and ruffled his hair. He caught a whiff of rum and heard a child laughing in the distance. He watched his neighbors passing by on the street below his porch. A pretty woman waved at him from across the town square. Charlie smiled and lifted a hand in greeting.

CHAPTER 7

A small black toad wriggled out of Charlie's pocket. It climbed onto his shoulder and hopped onto Charlie's uplifted face. A tear had dried on the dead man's cheek, and the toad stuck out its pink tongue, tasting the salt.

The toad scrambled over Charlie's open lips and slithered into the cooling darkness.

CHAPTER 8

Three men rode into Riddle early in the afternoon. They wore shabby gray uniforms with yellow chevrons, and their horses trembled with fatigue. The men dismounted and tethered their horses outside the Grover Hotel, where a boy offered to feed and water the nags. One of the men cuffed him and chased him off.

Ruth Cookson was at the hotel's front desk. She earned a dollar a week by keeping the guest book, airing the sheets, and making the beds every evening. She was saving to marry Walt Traeger, a young hand at the Paradise Ranch, and after giving half her wages to her mother and buying a fine piece of lace to make a dress, she had already put aside two dollars and sixty cents toward the wedding.

The men wanted the finest room in the house, and Ruth asked them to sign the book.

"How long will you be staying?"

"That all depends," said one of the men. He had a white streak over his temple, and was missing his right earlobe. He winked at her.

The men left and walked up the street toward One-Finger Finlay's saloon.

"I like the look of that girl," said the man with the streak in his hair. "You boys mind if I take her tonight?"

"We could draw straws for her," said another of the men. He had long dark hair, and he combed bison fat into it every morning, to make it shine and to keep it from curling up in humid weather.

He had not bathed in three or four weeks, and the weight of the grease in his hair made his head bow forward like a buzzard's.

They ordered a round of drinks at the saloon, then sat at a table in the corner, ignoring the curious glances of other men in the place. When they ordered another round, One-Finger demanded seventy-five cents, and the man with the white streak laughed.

"Just bring us a bottle," he said. "And run a line of credit."

"Why would I do that? I don't know you, do I?"

"Don't worry," the man said. "We'll pay it when we get that thousand dollars."

"Then you come here for the witch?"

"No such thing as witches, friend. But, yeah, we'll kill that bitch for you, and we'll pay your bill when the time comes."

One-Finger was apprehensive. The men seemed confident they could kill Sadie Grace, but Ubel Crane had been confident, too, and he had failed. If they ended up like Crane, they wouldn't be able to pay their bar bill, and who knew how much whiskey they could drink before they disappeared or were murdered?

"No," he said. "No, I better get that seventy-five cents."

The one whose head bent forward grabbed One-Finger's arm and held it against the table. He pulled a long knife from his belt and laid it next to One-Finger's hand.

"You's missing a finger," he said. His long hair fell like a curtain in front of his face. "That bloody finger on the sign out front must be yours. But what if there was two bloody fingers on that sign? Might double your business."

Two ranch hands who were quietly drinking at the far end of the bar stood up and reached for their pistols.

The man with the streak in his hair laid a hand on his friend's arm and smiled at One-Finger.

"Now, there's no need for gunplay here, nor for chopping parts off nobody."

The third man finally chimed in. He was missing all of his upper teeth, and his yellow hair had receded. He pointed at the ranch hands.

"You put them guns away," he said. "And my friend will let this honest barkeep go."

The boy let go of One-Finger's wrist and returned the knife to his belt. The men at the bar took their hands off their pistols.

"Now, let's be friends," the balding man said. "My name's Albert." He pointed at the kid with the greasy black hair. "This is Caleb, and that's Jeffrey, there."

Jeffrey, the man with the white streak, nodded and holstered his pistol. The ranch hands had not seen him draw it, and they belatedly realized he was quicker on the draw than they.

"Now," Albert said, "we are here to kill a woman named Sadie Grace."

One of the ranch hands gasped. It was bad luck to say the witch's name out loud.

Albert grinned. "You got any others come around here with that intention?"

One-Finger sniffed. He turned his back on the men, went behind the bar, and rested his hand on the shotgun he kept there.

"One did," he said. "That man did not end well."

"Wasn't up to the job, huh?"

"Said he was a full-on witch-master."

"Well, see, it stands to reason that if there's no such thing as a witch, there can't be such a thing as a witch-master."

"What about the county sheriff?" Jeffrey said. "He somewhere about?"

"Earl? He's down in Buckridge."

"How far's that?"

"Couple hours' ride," One-Finger said. "You fellas really don't believe in magic?"

"Oh, now, ain't nobody said that," Albert said. "Sure, there's magic. It's in the air around us, and in the grass underneath of us. Hell, it's probably right there in your little stump of a finger. But that don't mean a lady can waltz around sucking it out of the air and throwing it at us. That's a fairy tale, like mermaids or goblins."

"I seen a goblin once, Albert," Caleb said. "They's all over Kentucky."

"Well, I never been to Kentucky, so I guess I will withdraw my opinion until such time as I see a goblin for myself. Now, how about that bottle of whiskey, friend? I'm parched."

One-Finger took his hand off the shotgun and picked up a bottle from the back bar. The bottle was only half whiskey. One-Finger had a tendency to water his alcohol.

"You really think you can kill the witch?" he said.

"If she bleeds, we can kill her," Albert said. "What did she do to you folks, anyway?"

One-Finger thought it over for a second, then sniffed again and brought the bottle to their table.

"Well, now, there's a story," he said.

CHAPTER 9

Sadie was aware of the three men from the moment they crossed the county line and entered Burden, but she was too busy to deal with them right away. She had a trip to pack for, and her tree needed tending.

She gathered moss from the east side of the tree, and mushrooms from the south side. She pruned a few brown leaves from a low branch, then wrapped her arms around the tall ash and whispered to it. It pleased her to think the enormous ash would outlive everyone in the nearby town. It had absorbed magic from the soil, and from the rain. She thought it possible the tree would live forever.

She had resisted the idea that it was time to move on. She had her house, and her tree; she had the nearby fields and animals. There were still people in town who respected her. Maybe some of them even liked her. She had a life.

But she had gradually begun to realize that she had overstayed her welcome, and that she would eventually lose all the things she loved, whether she stayed or not.

She returned to the house and peered into her scrying cup again. The company to the south was close now, and the red glow among them had become a dark smudge that obscured everything around it. Whatever it was, she worried it might be more powerful than she was. Better, she thought, to leave on her own terms, before her options were cut off by some bit of red magic.

She tended to her potted plants, then took the sheets off her bed and went outside to shake them out. Her new bag wasn't big enough for all the books and maps she wanted to bring, but she rummaged about in the closet and found a steamer trunk that had belonged to the old couple who lived in the house before her. She packed it with her most essential things, and sat on the edge of her bare mattress, looking sadly at the flowers and herbs that lined the baseboards.

"I wish I could take you all with me," she said.

CHAPTER 10

It was Henry Crenshaw's habit on the first Friday of every month to take inventory of his fabric, and he was hard at work, pulling down bolts of gingham and lace and laying them out on the glass-topped counter, where needles and thimbles and scissors were displayed on long felt runners. His wife, Elizabeth, was similarly busy, counting spools of thread and lining them up in narrow racks along the back wall of the shop. Henry looked up at the sound of the little bell over the front door, and stuck his pencil behind his ear.

"How can I help you, gentlemen?" he said.

Three men stood in the doorway. The one with long greasy hair pushed a limp handful of it out of his eyes. "We're just looking around," he said. "Getting a feel for this town of woman haters."

"Excuse me?"

"To be truthful," said a second man with a white streak in his hair. "We appear to have wandered into the wrong place."

"We were looking for guns," said the third man. He was older, and his blond hair was brushed across the top of his head in an unsuccessful attempt to hide his baldness.

"Ah," Henry said. "No, we sell dry goods here. You'll want John Riddle's place, up the street."

"You only sell cloth here?"

"Well, no," Henry said. "We have various items and services available. If you're looking for a new shirt or slacks, my wife's an excellent tailor."

As soon as he said it, he knew he had made a mistake. Their

uniforms were shabby and dirty, but as soon as Henry mentioned his wife, all three men turned to look at Elizabeth, who was rewinding a length of yellow thread that had come unspooled.

"Darling," Henry said. "I'm missing a bolt of muslin. Would you check in the back for me?"

Elizabeth shook her head, about to remind him that the fabric was all right there on the racks, but she saw the three men and caught the look in her husband's eye, and without a word she disappeared through the heavy curtain to the back room.

The man who resembled a buzzard ran his fingers over a machine on display in the front window.

"That's a sewing machine," Henry said. "The only one of its kind in the whole county. I imported it special from—"

"I know what it is," the man said.

"What does it do?" the balding man said.

"It automates the sewing process. See that pedal? You work it and the needle goes up and down, making quick and simple work of almost any mundane sewing task. With that beauty you could sew a whole dress in half a day, and never once prick your thumb."

Elizabeth used the machine to make dresses for the ladies in town, and shirts for the men, but no one had shown the slightest interest in buying it, no matter how often Henry extolled its virtues. He had gone instinctively into his sales patter with the newcomers, but he could see that none of them cared a whit about sewing anything, much less a dress.

"Like I say, you'll want to see John over at the general store. He's got a fine selection of rifles and revolvers. Tell him Henry sent you. Tell him to offer you my discount, friends."

The one with the greasy hair turned away from the sewing machine and tossed his head, causing his hair to swing back and forth so that Henry could intermittently see his eyes.

"Who says we need a discount?" he said.

"Do we look like we don't got money?"

"No," Henry said. "Certainly not."

"And anyway, we already got a line of credit at the saloon. I suppose we can get one at the general store, too, if we want it."

"And I'm sure we can get credit here, too," said the man with the white streak. "If we want it."

"Well, I would need a fixed address. A line of credit would only apply if you lived and worked here in town. If you men are only passing through—"

"We come to rid you of your witch problem," the bald one interrupted. "You ought to be more mindful of how you treat us."

"With that reward money we could come back and buy this store offa you."

"Hell, we could buy this whole damn town."

"Please, gentlemen," Henry said. "Your language. There's a lady present." He belatedly remembered that Elizabeth was no longer in the room, and realized he had accidentally reminded the men of his wife's presence. "The general store is right down the street. I can take you there. You were right, all I have here is fabric and yarn."

"This man seems in a hurry to be rid of us."

"Sure does."

"Not at all," Henry said. He was breathing hard and he could feel sweat breaking out on his forehead.

"I don't much appreciate your attitude, mister."

"But the general store," Henry said.

Elizabeth chose this moment to return from the back room. She had Henry's shotgun and she used it to push the curtain aside.

Caleb immediately drew and fired, knocking Elizabeth back through the curtain. Henry ran to her, and Caleb shot him in the back.

"What did you do, Caleb?" Albert said. "We're supposed to be making friends here."

"I guess I bought us a dry goods store," Caleb said.

"You better hope them wasn't the folks offering the reward," Jeffrey said.

CHAPTER 11

Moses and Benito came back down the hill, Benito carrying the little shovel. Moses had the shotgun cradled under his arm. Rose was surprised to see them return so soon; they hadn't been gone more than ten or fifteen minutes. Ned was sitting in the carriage with the door propped open, making bacon sandwiches from their breakfast leftovers, and Rose was trying to teach Rabbit her figures, using a stick to draw numbers in the dirt. The Huntsman sat well apart from them, out in the field with his legs crossed and his eyes closed.

"There's nobody up there," Moses said.

"No body to bury," Benito clarified. He had kept Tom's old felt hat, after removing the turkey feather, and his big brown eyes were shadowed by the brim. Rose decided the hat made him look older and maybe slightly dangerous.

"Mr Skinner said he killed the man with the rifle," Rose said.

They all regarded the Huntsman, still as a statue in the pasture, long salt grass blowing around him. They knew almost nothing about him, although Moses said he had once heard a nursery rhyme about a hunter with yellow eyes.

"If he did kill that sniper, a coyote must've dragged the body off," Moses said.

"Or perhaps the dead man got up and walked away," Benito said.

"I've seen stranger things this last little while," Ned said. He handed Moses a sandwich and lowered his voice, and the company gathered around the open door of the coach. "I been thinking.

Tom was the one pressing us to go up to Riddle. Now Tom's gone, and I ain't sure there's a reason for it anymore." He took a bite of his biscuit and chewed. "Now, me and Moses was on our way to Nicodemus when we joined up with you all, and that town lays west of here."

"You're all welcome to come with us," Moses said. "My family would put you up."

Benito nodded. "I will go where you go."

"The telegram I sent," Rose said. "When we were in . . . I cabled Philadelphia and gave Riddle as my next stop. If there's a response, it will be waiting for me there."

"Should we consider the bounty?" Benito said. "A thousand dollars is a lot of money."

"We didn't earn that money, son," Moses said. "I don't think I want to claim it."

"And if Tom was wrong about killing that witch—"

"He was," Rose said. "I'm certain he was wrong."

"In that case, them folks might expect us to finish what Tom started," Ned said. "I ain't in no kinda shape for it. Besides, from the look of those clouds a big storm's brewing to the north. We'd be riding straight into it."

"Well, I'm going on north anyway," Rose said. "And Rabbit will come with me."

The Huntsman spoke, startling them all. They were so intent on their conversation that none of them had heard him approach.

"I'm also going north," he said.

"You?"

"Where that child goes, I go."

"I don't think that's necessary," Rose said. She had imagined Jacob Skinner would go his own way. The thought of sharing his company made her uneasy.

He fixed his yellow eyes on her.

"Where the child goes, I go," he said again.

"Then I am going with you, too," Benito said. He puffed out his chest and narrowed his eyes at the Huntsman, trying to appear menacing.

Moses shared a look with Ned. "Well, I guess Nicodemus can wait a few more days," he said. "I've come this far, I might as well see this through."

"Always wanted to visit Burden County," Ned said. "You want a bacon and biscuit sandwich, Jake?"

The Huntsman took the offered sandwich. "Six of us, then," he said. "Seven would be better."

Ned shook his head and pointed at the other side of the fire. They all looked, including the Huntsman, but none of them could see anything but salt grass and dirt.

"We're in luck," Ned said. "I think there are seven of us, after all."

Joe Mullins smiled at Ned. He took the pipe from his mouth and looked at the sky. He saw ugly green clouds rolling in, but he didn't know whether he was looking at the present or the future.

CHAPTER 12

As the three outlaws rode out toward Sadie's house, Albert kept stopping along the dusty trail to sneeze and wipe his nose. The others waited for him.

A tall ash tree stood in the middle of a wide rolling pasture beside the road. Caleb and Jeffrey could smell the sharp scent of evergreen trees, and the soft perfume of flowers. Albert couldn't smell anything. A woman sat under the ash with a gingham blanket spread on the ground in front of her. She had a basket beside her, and a tea service was set out on the blanket. The three men guided their mounts toward the picnic. The pasture was tranquil; as soon as they left the road, the men felt their tension of the long night ease.

The woman wore trousers, her long legs stretched out along one edge of the blanket. Caleb thought she might be some kind of fancy lady from out east. Maybe the women there all wore trousers. Jeffrey had a sudden thought that it must be difficult to ride horses in a dress, and he wondered why women wore dresses at all, when trousers were so much more practical.

They dismounted and sat around the blanket, Jeffrey across from the woman. Lightning flickered around them at the periphery of the field, arcing so quickly it seemed to shoot up from the ground.

"Are you the witch?" Jeffrey said.

"Would you like a sandwich?" the woman said. She reached into the basket.

"No," Caleb said. "We're—"

"I know what you are." The woman unwrapped a watercress

sandwich and nibbled at a corner of it. She looked around at the three of them, and Jeffrey felt suddenly self-conscious about his torn and dirty uniform. Albert wiped his nose again.

"We might not look like much," Jeffrey said. "We're dangerous men."

"Indeed. You killed Henry and Elizabeth Crenshaw. They were good people, but I suppose they were no match for dangerous men."

"We didn't know their names."

"Now you do. Names are important. Would you like some tea, Jeffrey?"

"Lady, we know better than to eat or drink anything you offer us."

"Pity," the witch said. She poured from the pot into her own cup and sipped. "The tea would have been faster and less painful."

Albert sneezed. "Faster than what?" he said.

Caleb reached for his pistol, then stopped and sat back, his eyes invisible behind the curtain of his hair. His mouth opened and a soft green tendril curled out over his chin. It twisted and stretched, and a bright purple iris bloomed at the tip. He fell backward as more flowers sprouted from his nostrils and ears, gently pushing his long greasy hair out of the way.

"You've been breathing my air since you left the road," Sadie said.

Albert tried to rise, but the ground had softened. Mud sucked at him. He smacked his hand against the grass and it stuck.

"This ain't fair," he said. He sneezed again.

"No," Sadie said. "But you killed my friends and that's not fair either."

Albert's chest bulged and his shirt ripped. His rib cage split, and a fine fuzzy web of evergreen roots pushed out into the air.

"I don't suppose it would help if I apologized," Jeffrey said. "We didn't mean nothing. It's just how we are."

"I understand."

Sadie stood and brushed off her slacks. She packed the tea service back into the basket. She shook out the blanket and folded it, placing it at the top of the basket. She picked up her things and headed back toward her house. By morning there would be new growth in the pasture. From the looks of him, Albert would be added to the ranks of stubby evergreens that dotted the meadow.

It pleased Sadie that even the ugliest things could be made beautiful with a little work.

PART SIX

Buckridge

CHAPTER 1

Off in the distance Sheriff Earl Hickman could see an abrupt demarcation where the clear morning sky gave way to something green and poisonous.

Earl had been sheriff of Burden County for nearly five years, and strange sights no longer surprised him. He was a careful man, and not much given to curiosity. He minded his own business whenever possible, and rarely left his office at the county border in Buckridge. He intended to live a long and carefree life, and saw no percentage in going near Riddle unless he had no other choice.

"Looks like a damn bad storm over there," Roy Olin said behind him.

Earl hadn't heard Roy climb the porch steps, and the sound of his deputy's voice startled him so badly he almost fell out of his chair. He glared up at Roy.

"Sorry about that, Earl," Roy said. "I shoulda cleared my throat or something. I was saying that's a bad storm. Looks like it's directly over Riddle."

"Looks that way," Earl said.

"Might be witchcraft, then."

"Could be."

"Yeah," Roy said. "You think we ought to ride up there?"

Earl turned and stared at him for a long moment, then shook his head in disgust and looked back out at the street. Sometimes his deputy's ambition confounded Earl.

"The boys off the Paradise Ranch could be stirring up trouble for her again," Roy said.

Earl frowned, but said nothing.

"Well," Roy said. "I guess you're right. There wouldn't be a whole lot of point to it, would there? If it's them Paradise boys, I guess she can handle them just fine."

"Storms come and go," Earl said.

"Welcome to Kansas," Roy said.

He pulled up another chair. The two men sat and watched the ominous sky north of them.

CHAPTER 2

Black clouds rolled in just after dawn, and Big Bill Cookson's rooster didn't crow. At precisely seven o'clock the sky opened up over Riddle. Sarah Cookson woke late to the sound of thunder, and had to rush to get breakfast ready, while her eldest son, William Jr, pulled a jacket on over his pajamas and ran out in the storm to milk the cows.

Her youngest, Little Willie, fetched water from the well, struggling with the heavy bucket, his new puppy bounding along behind him. Four of his brothers—Matthew, Mark, John, and David—hurried out to get the shutters closed and the horses in the barn.

A leak was discovered in the roof; water sluiced from the ceiling in the twins' bedroom. Bill took a tarp and a ladder around to the side of the house, but the ladder's feet slipped in the mud and Bill fell when he was only halfway up.

One of the dairy cows, normally a gentle old girl, kicked at William Jr and knocked over the bucket of milk. In the light from his lantern, William Jr could see that the milk had already curdled. At the same time, Sarah ladled water into a pitcher from the bucket Willie brought in, and saw it was swarming with maggots. She opened the kitchen window and threw the bucket into the yard. Her eldest daughter, Ruth, cracked an egg full of baby rats into a sizzling pan, and screamed.

"They never should have done it," Big Bill said, limping back into the kitchen, covered with mud. "It's that damn bounty."

"But it's been weeks since they put the word out about that,"

Sarah said. She was holding Ruth, trying to settle the girl's nerves. "That whole business came to nothing."

"Somebody must be coming now," Bill said. "Somebody still aims to collect on that bounty."

"Don't frighten the children," Sarah said.

"I ain't scared," Willie said. He had been rolling on the wet floor, laughing so hard he could barely breathe while the puppy licked his face. Now he sat up and absently rubbed the dog's belly. "Miss Grace won't let nothing bad happen to us."

"Watch your language," Sarah said. Regardless of the boy's intentions, it was bad manners to use the witch's name carelessly.

But Big Bill shot a nervous glance out the window, and nodded. "I hope you're right, son," he said.

Ruth eventually managed to crack eighteen eggs with normal yolks, and Sarah got two pounds of bacon sizzling in a wide pan on the stove. Big Bill put a bucket under the hole in the ceiling, and set out traps for the rats in the kitchen. William Jr brought in a tin pail of rainwater and hung it on a hook in the fireplace to boil. It had been a hectic morning, but when they were all sitting around the table in the kitchen, Sarah smiled and reached out her hands.

"Who wants to lead us in saying grace?" she said.

"I will," Ruth said.

Sarah closed her eyes and listened as her children recited the morning prayer. Behind their voices was the insistent patter of rain on the roof above them, but her family was safe inside. They were warm and dry, and Sarah felt truly grateful for all they had. She thought her youngest son must be right. Whatever was coming to Riddle, Sadie Grace would always take care of her people.

CHAPTER 3

A black bear roamed the streets of Riddle and the wide spaces that surrounded the town. She paused here and there to listen and sniff the air. Rainwater flowed from her fur and pooled in the folds of her skin. She shook herself occasionally to clear her eyes.

She was annoyed by the storm because it had spun out of her control. Sometimes, when she was especially angry or upset, she would forget to pay attention to the sky and it would mirror her temperament. Sometimes that was okay. It could serve as a warning or a deterrent to anyone crossing her territory, but today it was a hindrance. She had a lot of ground to cover and the storm slowed her down.

Piano music drifted out from the general store, muffled by the sound of water dripping off the roof and the low rumble of thunder. She stopped for a moment and listened before continuing her patrol.

Willie Cookson saw the bear late in the morning when he was playing with his puppy in the rain, throwing a stick and then chasing the little dog, who had not yet learned to retrieve things. The puppy growled at the bear, but Willie waved and called out to her.

"I named my dog Sadie," he yelled.

The bear snorted, then turned and disappeared behind the heavy rain.

She moved quietly down the road, a dark shape in the dark air. She rooted in the mud beside the trail and found an old walnut, buried and forgotten by some long-ago squirrel. The nut was partially hollowed out, and a fat white worm squirmed out, dropping into the mud. The bear crunched the walnut between her teeth and spat black splinters across the road. Then she moved on.

She knew the small company traveling north from Monmouth would arrive in Burden County later in the day. The Huntsman had not only failed to stop them, he appeared to be traveling with them. Something else had come riding up ahead of them, too, something familiar but strange. She didn't like the smell of it at all: sulfur, and copper, and toad venom. It wore a human skin, but she wasn't fooled. If the creature had come to kill her, she wasn't sure she could stop it. She felt a twinge of panic and forced herself to focus on the task at hand. *If only,* she thought, *if only I had left this place when the furrows in the fields were still empty of seed, and the people here still loved me.*

She continued working her way around the edges of the town, setting her hexes and wards. She knew nothing would stop the Huntsman, if he had turned against her, and she wasn't sure what could be done about the strange thing with the unpleasant odor.

But she felt she ought to keep busy while she waited for them all to arrive. Her time in Burden County had come to an end, but it wasn't in her nature to go quietly.

The bear stood on her hind legs and roared her displeasure, and lightning split the sky behind her.

CHAPTER 4

At the Burden General Supply, John Riddle stopped playing and swiveled on his piano bench so he could see out the big front window. His music was drowned out by the constant drumbeat of the rain, and the random crack of thunder. The wide road through the center of town had become a muddy river, and John knew as long as the storm kept up he would have no customers. The townsfolk tended to stay inside during inclement weather, unless there was a true emergency. Really, the only reason he had opened the store was to play the piano without interruption. John liked the sound of the piano when nobody else was around; notes echoed and lingered in the big open space, and floated through the air around him. When he was alone, his fingers dancing across the ivory keys, he could imagine he was somewhere else—maybe New York, or San Francisco, or Philadelphia—playing to a packed hall of music lovers.

He glanced at the portrait of his father on the wall behind the counter. John would have quit the town long ago if his father had not died early and left him the store, just as his grandfather, Grover Riddle, had left the store to John's father. The only concession to John's dream of being a musician was the piano. It was an expensive purchase; too expensive for a small-town stationmaster and proprietor of the general store, but John believed it had saved his life. At the very least, it gave him something to look forward to each day.

He covered the piano keys and grabbed his jacket from the coatrack by the door. He couldn't remember whether he had fastened the shutters at the railroad station, and he decided to stop there on his way home.

John opened the door, then jumped back and held his breath as a black bear lumbered past the shop. It stopped for a moment and gazed at John before moving on.

John had seen many strange things over the course of his life in Riddle, but a black bear with blue eyes prowling the main street of town was the strangest sight yet.

He went back inside, closed the door, and locked it. He went to his piano, his foolish, expensive, life-saving piano, and uncovered the keys again. John sat and began to compose a song he couldn't hear over the storm.

CHAPTER 5

One-Finger Finlay ran through the rain and pounded on Andrew King's front door. He had a bottle of rye under one arm, and it was still mostly full. He had taken two slugs from it early in the morning to ease the headache he woke up with.

There was no roof over Andrew's porch. Rainwater ran down the back of One-Finger's collar and into his boots. He wasn't sure Andrew could hear him knocking over the sound of the storm, so he tried the knob just as Andrew swung the door open. One-Finger stumbled inside, nearly dropping the bottle.

"Settle down," Andrew said.

He held a pint bottle of buttermilk and his upper lip was smeared white with milk. One-Finger held the bottle of rye out to him and took off his hat, shaking water all over Andrew's floor. From the state of the place, he didn't think Andrew would mind.

"Missed you down the saloon last night," he said.

It was not in One-Finger's nature to make house calls, but Andrew was one of his best customers and he worried the widower might be drinking at home. As obnoxious as Andrew could be when he was drunk, One-Finger couldn't afford to lose his business.

"Can't touch the stuff no more," Andrew said.

He took a swig of the buttermilk and backed off so One-Finger could close the door behind him.

"You feeling poorly?" One-Finger said.

"The witch did something to me. Gave me a bottle I thought was whiskey, but it wasn't."

"What do you mean?"

"I just said what I mean. I got hold of some potion and now I can't drink no more."

This was the worst news One-Finger had heard in quite some time. Maybe worse than when young Bobby Dwyer got his head stove in, or the fresh news that Duff Duncan had fallen off his horse and broken his neck. Duff had been a good customer, too.

"But I brung you a bottle," he said, and he held it out again, feeling somewhat foolish.

"I told you already," Andrew said. He raised the pint of buttermilk as if he might throw it at One-Finger, but instead he set it on the mantel and grabbed the bottle out of One-Finger's hand. "Here," he said. "Watch!"

He pulled out the cork and took a long swig of rye, the dark liquid mixing with the buttermilk in his whiskers and running down his chin, dripping onto the already damp floor. He handed the bottle back to One-Finger and wiped his lips on the sleeve of his filthy shirt.

"Seems like you can drink it just fine," One-Finger said.

Andrew held up a finger, signaling One-Finger to be patient. A second later, he doubled over and puked buttermilk down the front of his trousers. One-Finger backed away and pinched his nose. The stench of vomit was overwhelming in the small, stuffy room. He belatedly noticed, in the dark corner opposite him, a congealed puddle of old sick.

"You been throwing up all night, Andy?"

Andrew suddenly vomited again, this time spattering the hems of One-Finger's trousers. He heaved until there was nothing left to bring up, then wiped his mouth again and stood up straight.

"I told you," he said. "I can't drink no more."

"Well, don't that beat all."

"Didn't say I was happy about it. It's a damn curse is what it is."

"What are you gonna do now?"

"What the hell can I do?"

"I heard Old Man Paradis is putting together another posse. Maybe if they killed that witch, it'd break the curse and you could drink again." He didn't know if there was any logic in this, but he was hopeful.

Andrew seemed to take the suggestion seriously. He nodded, and picked up the bottle of buttermilk from the mantel. He held it out to One-Finger, but the saloonkeeper shook his head. There were traces of yellow puke swirling about in the white liquid.

"You're on to something there," Andrew said. "You think if she died that'd bring back Mary and Olivia, too?"

One-Finger shrugged.

"Or maybe if I catch her," Andrew said, "I can make her give me another potion that'd take this curse off, so I can drink."

"That's a good idea," One-Finger said. "I bet she has another potion that'd do that very thing. I bet she's got potions that'd make it so you never got sick again."

"Never mind that. She'd never give me such a thing. She likes seeing good folks suffer. I guess I ought to hope she gets herself killed pretty soon though."

"I heard about a place once, had a witch. One day, the town strung her up in the middle of the square, and the minute her neck snapped everything she done came undone, just like that." He snapped the fingers of his good hand.

"That a true story?"

One-Finger shrugged. "I heard about it, is all."

Andrew stared away at the wall and nodded slowly, as he mulled over the idea of the witch being dead. He continued to nod while his jaw clenched and unclenched. He appeared to have forgotten the saloonkeeper was there.

One-Finger glanced out the window at the roiling green sky. It looked to him like the storm might last all day. He took a swig from the bottle of rye and went to get a cloth from Andrew's kitchen to wipe off his boots.

CHAPTER 6

Sheriff Earl Hickman and Deputy Roy Olin were standing on the office porch, passing a cigarette back and forth when a stranger rode into Buckridge. The man waved to them and steered his horse toward the sheriff's office. Roy noticed the Wells Fargo satchel tied to the stranger's saddle and thought he might be a representative of the bank.

"Hullo," the man said. "One of you the sheriff?"

"That'd be me," Earl said. "Earl Hickman. This here's my deputy, Roy."

"Good day to you both," the man said. He looked up the road toward Riddle, where the ugly green clouds swirled.

"That storm don't seem natural," he said. "Looks like you folks might have a witch problem."

"Wouldn't call it a problem." Earl glanced at the sky. "She mostly keeps to herself. Roy and me try not to bother her, and she don't bother us in return."

"That sounds like a good arrangement," the man said.

"If you're after the bounty, I'd advise you to turn back around," Earl said.

"First I've heard of a bounty." The stranger glanced again at the sky to the north, then flashed his teeth at Earl. "Say, I'm being rude," he said. "My name's Gamble. Call me Charlie. I'm in need of some new clothes."

He pulled open his vest and showed them the bloodstained shirt underneath.

"Mister, that looks bad," Roy said. "We got a doctor right

outside Buckridge who could take a look at that wound." He was inordinately proud of the fact that the county had recently recruited a doctor.

"Oh, this isn't my blood," Charlie said. "But you should see the other fella." He chuckled and winked at Roy.

"You with Wells Fargo?" Earl said.

Charlie seemed confused for a moment, then he noticed Roy eyeing the satchel.

"Right," he said. "I guess I'm new to the job. I've been guarding this payroll cash, which is how I got in a little scrape." He looked down again at his bloody shirt. "Up until recently I was a deputy down in Fulton, Texas. Done some marshaling, too, in my day."

"If you're not here about the bounty, what brings you to Buckridge?" Earl said.

"Well, I'm after a Mexican killer name of Cortez," Charlie said. "He's traveling with a band of outlaws in a stolen Wells Fargo coach."

"You're looking for 'em around here?"

"I have good reason to believe they're headed up this stretch of road. I guess you haven't seen 'em?"

"No, sir. You're the first suspicious character we've seen in a while."

Charlie chuckled again. "Well, I'd appreciate it if you'd keep an eye out. It'll be hard to miss 'em. They painted my coach bright red."

"Interesting," Earl said.

"What's that?"

"I say it's interesting that these bandits stole your coach, but left you with a satchel full of money. Not much good at being bandits, are they?"

"No," Charlie said. "I guess not. My business is catching them, not figuring them out. Fellas, this shirt has gone all stiff and uncomfortable on me."

"If you head down this road a bit farther," Earl said, "you'll find Mrs Porterhouse's place. She's good with a needle and thread. Ought to be able to whip you up a new wardrobe pretty quick."

"Much obliged. I'm in kind of a hurry. I'd like to put a posse together to go after that Mexican."

"Mostly farmers around here," Roy said.

"But if you're serious about it," Earl said, "you might talk to Teddy Paradis. His ranch employs about half the men in Burden County."

"I'll do that. Where would I find that ranch?"

"Can't miss it," Roy said. "Straight up this road, past Mrs Porterhouse's place. There's a big fancy sign out at the entrance."

"You might want to wait until that storm passes," Earl said. "You're likely to ride right up on it. Mrs Porterhouse usually has a room to let, if you're inclined to stay on a bit. She serves a decent meal, too."

"Thanks for the advice, Sheriff, but I don't mind getting a little wet."

Charlie winked again, then tipped his hat and spurred his mount on up the street. Earl and Roy watched him go. Roy struck a match and lit another cigarette.

"That fella seems a mite soft to be a Marshal," Earl said. "Or even a deputy, for that matter."

"Well, he works for the bank now, don't he?" said Roy.

"I guess so."

"He does seem odd, though."

Earl accepted the cigarette from Roy and took a drag. He handed it back.

"Yeah," he said. "Seem coincidental to you we got a storm

brewing up in Riddle when this fella rides in determined to go up that way, come rain or shine?"

"You think he's lying about coming for the bounty?"

"Hard to say," Earl said. "But it might be good if you kept an eye on Mr Gamble."

CHAPTER 7

They stopped the bright red coach on the road a mile south of Buckridge. After their experience in Quivira Falls, they were all nervous about entering a new town. The Huntsman had ranged ahead, then waited by the side of the road for the wagon to catch up. When they reined in the horses, he squatted beside the open door of the coach and watched the landscape around them.

"The sheriff will see this thing before you get into town," he said.

"Is the sheriff expecting us?" Moses said. The Huntsman shrugged.

"The witch might still be alive," Rose said.

"She is," the Huntsman said.

"If that's so, she may already know we've reached Burden County."

"She does," the Huntsman said.

"How do you know?"

He pointed and they all looked ahead at the dark green patch in the northern sky.

"So we're headed into more danger," Moses said. "I'm sick and tired of heading into danger."

"Ought to be used to it," Ned said. "Happens every damn day." Despite the blanket on his lap, he was shivering.

"Could you talk to the witch for us?" Benito said to the Huntsman. "Tell her it was Old Tom who wanted to kill her, not us?"

"She won't be happy with me," the Huntsman said. "I was supposed to stop you coming here."

"Then why didn't you?" Ned said. "These last few miles I been waiting for you to turn on us. Why haven't you?"

"Maybe you'd shoot me with that pistol you've got."

The Huntsman smiled, the tiniest twitch of his lips. Ned pulled the blanket aside, revealing his revolver, which he laid on the seat beside him.

"Would it stop you?" he said. "If I did shoot you?"

The Huntsman shook his head.

"Then why *did* you let us get this far?"

The Huntsman shrugged again.

Rose was watching the distant storm clouds curl around themselves, bright lightning arcing toward the ground. "You know," she said, "this whole time, I don't think I actually believed there was a witch at the end of the road. I thought we were only humoring Mr Goggins. But now that we're here . . . Well, now that we're here, I'm afraid."

The Huntsman stood and stretched. "You could turn back."

"I can't do that," Rose said.

"Suit yourself. I'm going to scout ahead some more. The man who shot at you is ahead of us on the trail, but his stink is different now."

"I thought you killed him," Ned said.

"I did. He has become something else. A being lives inside him. There's a word for it, but I forget."

"Possessed," Rose said. "You mean he's possessed."

The Huntsman nodded.

"Like the man at the ranch," Rose said. "He wasn't really a person anymore."

"He was the devil," Moses said. He shuddered, remembering

how he had dangled helplessly above the ground, struggling to breathe.

"If I don't return by nightfall, turn this wagon around and take the child somewhere safe. I'll find you when I can."

With that, the Huntsman loped away across the prairie, and was quickly lost from sight in the tall grass.

"We're supposed to wait here all day?" Moses said.

"You said you were tired of the constant obstacles we've encountered," Rose said. "Perhaps Jacob can help us avoid further danger."

"Why are we doing what he says, anyway?" Ned said. "He says he's coming along with us and we let him, he says to wait here and we sit. Seems like he took charge without anybody batting an eye."

"Because he knows what he's doing, and we don't," Rose said. "I think it's as simple as that. And I don't think we could have stopped him from coming with us if we wanted to."

"He said we could turn back," Benito said. "Maybe we should. I have a bad feeling."

"I need to find out if my mother got my telegram," Rose said. "As far as I'm concerned, we can leave after that. I will be happy to go somewhere far away from witches and devils."

She was grateful the others had come with her, and she worried they might still abandon her. Somewhere along the road, she had begun to trust and depend on the three men who had been strangers to her only days before. She watched their faces and opened her tobacco pouch to fill her pipe.

Moses smiled at her. "Well, if that witch knows we're here, maybe she also knows we don't mean her any harm."

"We're gonna get wet," Ned said. "That storm looks bad."

"We should hurry, then," Benito said. "We could get back here by nightfall, if we hurry. Or maybe even farther away."

"Jacob said to stay here," Rose said.

"Ned, if there's trouble you're in no shape to deal with it."

"Moses, in your whole life, have you ever known me to stay put?" Ned said.

"I've only known you about five years," Moses said.

"The only time I stay put is when I'm dealt a good hand at the table. Right now, all we got is a choice of bad hands. I say we move, and move fast, like Benito says. Just so long as I don't gotta get up and run."

"Then we should go now," Benito said. "Let Jacob catch up to us."

"He can do it," Moses said. "That fellow is quick."

"Well," Rose said. "Let's hope he's able to find the man who tried to shoot us. Let's hope he can take care of that problem for us."

"Lord knows we got enough problems," Ned said.

None of them saw Rabbit's expression change. She was staring out across the field in the direction the Huntsman had gone; as quick as a flash of lightning her brow creased and her eyes narrowed.

But by the time Rose turned to find her, Rabbit's face was once again a blank mask.

CHAPTER 8

Teddy Paradis was dozing on the porch when Jim Garber hollered that someone was coming up the road. Teddy opened his eyes. Jim, of course, meant that someone had left the main road and was coming up the trail under the big sign out front. The sign was solid, with two poles holding up a giant slab of oak with the word PARADISE burned into it. Even in the pouring rain, there was no missing it, or mistaking the trail for a branch of the main road.

Teddy watched the stranger ride up toward the house. He wasn't much to look at, a small fellow with rashy skin and a sopping wet purple cloak. Teddy recognized the heavy purple fabric from the window of Mrs Porterhouse's home down in Buckridge, but the tailoring didn't look like her usual fine work.

When he reached the house the stranger stayed on his horse, but tipped his hat.

"I'm looking for somebody name of Teddy Paradis," he said.

"State your business." Teddy's afternoon nap had not been especially restful, and he felt crankier than usual. He didn't invite the man up onto the porch to dry off.

"My name's Charlie Gamble," the man said. "Heard you might lend me some men."

"Nope," Teddy said. "You can ride on back the way you came."

"Now, wait a minute," Charlie said. "I can pay cash money for your trouble. Surely we can talk."

Teddy nodded thoughtfully. Cash money entitled the man to a few minutes.

"My boys are busy, son."

"I'm only looking to borrow them for a few hours."

Some of the ranch hands had gathered around despite the rain, and were listening to the conversation. Johnny Barth was right up at the front of the small crowd of Paradise men, no doubt gathering gossip to take back to the boys in the mess hall.

Teddy blinked slowly, and let his eyes drift shut. He considered trying to improve on his earlier nap, but then changed his mind and opened his eyes back up. "I don't much care for games or haggling, Mr . . . What'd you say your name was?"

"It's Charlie. I love games and haggling, but we can be direct."

"What kind of work you need done? Not much around here except farming and ranching. You don't look like a farmer or a rancher to me."

"No, I ain't a rancher," Charlie said. "Nor a farmer, neither."

"Then you come for the bounty," Teddy said. "Putting up that reward was a damn mistake, and it got one of my best boys killed already. You ought to ride back down that road and forget all about it."

Charlie Gamble took off his hat and wiped the rain out of his eyes. "I'm not here for no reward, sir. If I was, I wouldn't be talking to you. I'd just kill that witch of yours, take my money, and leave."

Teddy scoffed and closed his eyes again. "That little girl'd kill you as soon as look at you. Or worse."

Charlie giggled, a high-pitched sound that reminded Teddy of a squealing pig. "She might try. Truth is I'll probably play with her a bit and take her body for myself. This one was already dead when I got it. It's a mite stiff and itchy."

"You have my answer, mister. I ain't gonna risk my boys on whatever you got in mind. Now scat before I have them run you off."

Charlie looked around at the gathered men.

"You boys really gonna run me off?"

A couple of the newer hands stepped closer, as if they might be thinking of pulling the stranger down off his horse and hauling him back out to the main road. Teddy liked the fact that he had so many strong boys ready to do whatever he told them to. It took some of the sting out of getting old.

"Well, now, this is a mistake on your part," Charlie said. "I'm starting to feel like I shouldn't be nice to you no more."

Teddy had the peculiar sensation that he was floating upward, toward the roof of his porch. He looked down and saw his chair below him, still gently rocking. Teddy's breath left him and he couldn't get it back. He struggled, clutching his throat and swinging his atrophied legs about. The yard out front of his house began to blur, but he could still see his men moving toward the stranger, some of them drawing their revolvers.

"Tut tut," Charlie said. "Guns are dangerous."

Johnny Barth, who was closest to Charlie and already had his pistol out, spun on his heels and fired at Bill Cassidy. Bill fell against Matt Hawke and they both went down in a heap. Several of the others rushed to untangle them; a few stood where they were, looking back and forth, uncertain whether to help their friends or try to deal with the stranger.

"I didn't do that!" Johnny shouted. "My arm moved by itself. I didn't mean it, fellas!"

Teddy's vision went dark then, punctuated by swirling pinpricks of light, but just before he lost consciousness he was abruptly dropped back into his chair. He fell forward and landed on his hands and knees, gasping for air as his vision slowly returned.

"Mr Paradis, would you kindly ask your men to lay down their weapons?" Charlie said.

Teddy nodded. His voice came out as a croak, and the frightened ranch hands dropped their pistols in the mud.

"Good," Charlie said. "That's very good of you. Now, I've changed my mind. I would have gladly paid you for your help, but you've been rude to me, so I believe I'll just take what I want."

"Can't," Teddy managed to say.

"I surely can, sir."

"You're a witch," Johnny Barth said. "You made me shoot Bill. You're a damn witch, ain't you?"

"What do you know about witches, boy?"

"I know regular folks can't make a man shoot against his will."

Charlie looked at the sky. "No, I ain't a witch, nor a ghoul, nor nothing like you've seen before in your miserable lives. I'm something else entirely, and I'm here because this county has power in the soil and in the air. I've spent centuries crisscrossing the globe, looking for places like this."

He turned back to Teddy Paradis, who sat on the porch with his back against his rocking chair, trying to figure out how to rid himself of the stranger.

"I'll be here until I decide to leave," Charlie said. "Meanwhile, I still require some of your men. There's a red coach coming up that main road. They're not far behind me. The driver's a negro, and there's a white cowboy inside the wagon. Neither of them should give your boys too much trouble. Nor should the Mexican who's riding with them. I'd like a few of you fellas to intercept that coach and kill those men."

"My boys don't answer to you," Teddy said. He felt his throat closing again, and his right leg moved of its own accord, bending upward at the knee. There was a loud crack, and Teddy screamed.

Charlie turned and addressed the gathered ranch hands. "Your boss finds himself indisposed all of a sudden." He pointed at young Wayne Traeger, who was trying to back away without being noticed. "You there, pick two or three good men and head down toward Buckridge. You'll encounter that coach before you get too far."

"You could maybe pick somebody else for it, mister," Wayne said. "I got a lot of chores to finish up around here."

He felt himself blush. His skin prickled and itched. He looked at the ground, hoping his face wasn't so red that the other men would notice, but the burning sensation increased. His cheeks felt like they were on fire and he rubbed them with the palms of his hands, then clawed at his skin. The heat was coming from his skull, and he dug into the soft flesh under his eyes, trying to get at the source of the pain.

Then it stopped. The heat subsided as quickly as it had come, and the only pain he felt came from the fresh wounds he had made with his fingernails.

"You sure you don't want to go looking for that red coach?" Charlie said.

Wayne nodded. "I'll do it."

"Good," Charlie said. "One more thing . . . those men who are coming up the road have a woman and child traveling with them. Do whatever you want with the woman, but bring the child to me."

CHAPTER 9

Roy Olin rode out from Buckridge late in the morning and came back with news.

"The Wells Fargo coach that fella warned us about? It's headed this way. Big as life, and red as a barn."

"Well, I'll be," Earl said. "So that peculiar sonofabitch was telling the truth, after all."

"There's a Mexican kid riding alongside the coach."

"I did some checking on that while you was out scouting. Turns out there really is a Mexican by the name of Cortez who's wanted down in Fulton, Texas, for killing a deputy's wife."

"Don't mean it's the same Mexican riding this way."

"Nope."

"I been thinking," Roy said. He lit a cigarette and took a drag before passing it over to Earl. "Our friend Mr Gamble didn't seem all that broken up about getting bushwhacked. And he said those bandits painted his coach red, but how could he know about that unless he stood around and watched them do it?"

"It's peculiar, all right."

"What're you thinking?"

The sheriff sighed. "I guess I better stop them folks here. I ought to at least ask them some questions."

The sheriff's office was at the south end of the unnamed road that ran through Buckridge. The town was a sprawling maze of hastily constructed one-room structures, but the main road curved up through the east side of town, then northwest across rolling pastureland. The air was hazy and yellow, the storm near Riddle growing in fury as the day wore on.

Roy left Sheriff Hickman standing on the porch and went inside the office to trade his rifle for a shotgun. When he came back out, carrying the shotgun and a leather strap with buckles at both ends, the great red coach was rolling up the street toward them. Up close it was an impressive sight. Roy had once seen a traveling circus in Salina, and the painted Wells Fargo wagon looked like something that might have been left behind when the circus pulled up stakes and moved on.

In the driver's seat was a black man, his brown derby tilted at a rakish angle, and the Mexican boy rode behind the coach. Earl stepped off the porch and raised his hand. The driver reined in the team and climbed down.

"Sheriff?" he said.

Earl glanced down at the star pinned to his chest. "Earl Hickman," he said. "And over there's my deputy, Roy."

The black man tipped his hat to each of them in turn. "I'm Moses Burke, and that's Ben back there on the horse."

The Mexican waved, and Earl nodded at him. Roy held the shotgun down at his side, but kept a tight grip on it, waiting to see what Earl would do.

"We could sure use a doctor if you've got one," Moses said. "We've got a man in the wagon with a gunshot wound."

"We got a doctor," Roy said. "How bad is he?"

"The bullet passed through, but he's lost some blood."

"How'd it happen?" Earl said.

"We ran into a little trouble south of here."

"That trouble happen to go by the name Charlie Gamble?"

The Mexican jumped in his saddle, but Moses Burke was unperturbed.

"Don't know that name," he said.

"Where you folks out of?"

Moses was frowning now. "Nowhere in particular, I guess," he said. "Most recently Monmouth."

"That's down by the Oklahoma border?"

"That's right. We're headed up to Riddle now, but it looks like a pretty bad storm ahead of us."

"Kansas weather," Earl said. He kept his eyes on the Mexican, who so far had not spoken or moved to get down off his horse, but was fidgeting in the saddle. "Rain usually dies down pretty quick. You gentlemen are welcome to stick it out here while our doctor patches up your friend. Couple places you can get a hot meal and a bath."

"I could sure use a bath, but I suppose we ought to keep moving."

"I'll send Roy to fetch that doctor in a minute, but if your friend ain't in too dire a situation I wonder if you'd answer where you got this wagon? I'd say it's every bit as big as a Wells Fargo coach."

Moses stared at the coach as if seeing it for the first time. He took off his hat and scratched his head.

"Tell you the truth," he said, "I believe it might have been a Wells Fargo coach at one time. We found it sitting by the side of the road. Figured there was no sense letting it rot there when we could put it to use."

"You found it sitting empty, huh? That's a lucky break."

"Could be some bandits got there before us and chased off the driver."

"Well, that makes sense." Earl motioned to Roy. "Why don't you go ahead and hobble these horses, Deputy, in case more bandits come along to finish the job."

Roy stepped off the porch and kneeled in the road, setting

his shotgun down within easy reach. He buckled the ends of the leather strap around the lead horse's legs, a big spotted roan.

"Is that necessary?" Moses said.

"I like to be cautious," Earl said. "Saves me time later." He narrowed his eyes at the Mexican. "Mister, you say your name's Ben? That wouldn't be short for Benito, would it?"

Benito finally dismounted, landing lightly on the balls of his feet. Earl put his hand on the grip of his revolver, but left it in the holster. Roy reached for his shotgun and stood back up, circling around to stand beside Earl.

"There's no need for gunplay," Moses said. "We've got nothing to hide."

"I never said you did," Earl said. "But we're on the lookout for a fugitive. Or I should say he may or may not be a fugitive, depending on the facts as they come to light. He'd be a Mexican fellow, goes by Benito Cortez."

"Oh," Moses said. "Well, that's a relief. No, this young man is named Benjamin Smith. I can vouch for him personally."

"Smith? That's a Mexican name?"

The door of the coach swung open and a man with a yellow hat put his legs out and pushed himself upright in the road. His waistcoat was open and his shirt was soaked with fresh blood. The man held his right arm stiff against his side, as if trying to hold his internal organs in place. He was sweating and shivering, but he grinned at the two lawmen and touched the brim of his yellow hat.

"Howdy," he said. "I guess I must have dozed off in there. Name's Ned Smith. Ben here is my brother. He takes to the sun a little better than I do. Always getting mistook for a Mexican."

"You're saying he's not a Mexican," Earl said.

"No more a Mexican than I am, mister."

Ned took a step away from the coach and his legs buckled. Roy dropped his shotgun and rushed forward, but was too late to catch Ned, who pitched face-first into the dirt. At the same time a woman scrambled out of the coach and hurried to Ned's side. Together, she and Roy rolled the injured cowboy onto his back. Roy pulled the man's vest aside to examine the wound, but drew back in surprise.

"Earl, this man's got a star pinned to to the inside of his vest," Roy said. He frowned at Ned. "Why didn't you tell us you were the law?"

Ned turned his head and spat blood into the dirt. "I took this star off a fella who was acting unkindly towards my friend. Been a year or two back. I keep it to remind me I should never trust a lawman."

"Then you are a criminal, sir," Earl said.

"Naw," Ned said. "That fella was plenty dead when I took his star. He wasn't using it no more."

"This wound's festering," Roy said. "I think I better fetch the doc."

"Go on," Earl said. "I got the situation in hand here."

Roy grabbed his shotgun and leaped up onto the porch. He ran into the office, and a moment later reappeared around the far side of the building riding a black-and-white mare. He whipped her into a full gallop and rode up the street out of sight.

"He'll be back presently," Earl said. He squinted at Rose. "Ma'am, are there any more people in that coach?"

Rose was using a handkerchief to wipe Ned's forehead. She looked up and frowned at the sheriff.

"None of us has committed a crime, sir. I don't care for your tone of voice or your insinuations."

Earl almost smiled. "Well, ma'am, I don't mean nothing by my tone of voice. But this road runs through my town, so I suppose I got a duty to ask questions when folks come riding in with a man that's been shot up and admits to taking a badge. Not to mention you're in a stolen coach, and I'm pretty sure the bank would like to get that back from you."

Benito had thought it wise to keep his mouth shut and let the other men talk, but now Ned was unconscious and the sheriff was disrespectful toward Rose.

"You should mind your manners around the lady," he said.

"Hush, Ben," Rose said.

"Mr Smith," Earl said to Benito. "How about you and your brother Moses pick up your other brother and carry him into the office. You can lay him in one of the cells back there, since we got no occupants at the moment."

"Then we are under arrest?" Benito said.

"We can leave that decision for later. I'll revisit the question when Roy comes back with the doc and we've all had a chance to get to know each other. For now, I'd feel better if you were all in one place so I can keep an eye on you."

CHAPTER 10

I say we keep riding," Matt Hawke said. "We ought to ride straight down to Mexico."

"He'll find us," said Johnny Barth. "You saw what he did to Mr Paradis. That was powerful magic."

"Probably more powerful than the witch," Wayne Traeger said.

Jim Garber, the oldest of the four cowboys, kept his eye on the terrain ahead of them and said nothing. Charlie Gamble had scared him badly, and he was still trying to figure out what he had seen back on the Paradise Ranch. He was inclined to agree with Matt Hawke. He didn't think he ever wanted to return to that ranch.

The trail they were on wound around clusters of red cedar and crab apple trees, sometimes dwindling to little more than a dirt path with patches of stubborn weeds. Limestone formations jutted from the gently sloping pastureland in the near distance. The sun was hot, south of the storm, and their damp clothing had dried stiff against their skin.

"I don't know why you didn't pick your brother to come with us," Jim said to Wayne. "Why am I here and Walt ain't?"

"I did pick him," Wayne said. "I didn't wanna leave him behind like that, but he wouldn't come along. Said he had something else he had to do."

His face stung where he'd scratched it. He kept rubbing his eyes and cheeks, which only made them burn more.

"Maybe Charlie Gamble's more bark than bite," Matt said,

trying to bring the conversation back around. "Could be he'd never find us down in Mexico."

"He made me shoot Bill," Johnny said. "That ain't just barking."

"You wanted to shoot Bill anyway."

"Why, I'd never shoot Bill. Sometimes we go at it a little, but that don't mean I'd shoot him."

Matt shook his head at Jim, who shrugged. Bill Cassidy had accused Johnny Barth of stealing his best knife, an ivory-handled beauty that had passed down from his father. When the knife turned up in an outhouse, Bill recollected that it might have fallen out of his pocket when he was relieving himself. Johnny still seemed sore about the entire incident long after Bill had apologized.

"No," Johnny said, "that crazy son of a bitch made me shoot Bill, and if he can do that, he can surely find us, no matter where we hide out."

"Well," Matt said. "I don't much wanna kill some folks on the say-so of that scary son of a bitch. I ain't a killer, and they didn't do nothing to us. If we're not gonna go to Mexico, maybe we ought to turn around and head back to the ranch. We could say we never found them folks."

"That idea don't appeal to me," Jim said. He had begun to feel a tremendous sense of dread, and the closer they got to Buckridge the more the feeling grew in him. But as frightened as he was of what lay ahead of them, his fear of Charlie Gamble was greater.

"I ain't a killer, neither," Johnny said. "But I don't think we got a choice in the matter. You were there when the witch made Duff fall off his horse and die. Same could happen to any of us, if Gamble gets it in his head to do it."

"Well, it's true Duff fell off his horse," Wayne said, "but that might've been bad luck on his part. It might not have been the witch's doing."

"We all know she did it," Jim said. An idea had just come to him. "Maybe if we asked her, she could take on this fella for us."

"You forget we were there riding against her with Duff?" Johnny said. "She's likely to kill us instead of Charlie Gamble. Maybe they're even friends. Witches know each other."

"Dammit, Johnny, you keep shooting down every idea we got."

"Well, I do have an idea of my own, but I don't know as it's an especially good one."

"Tell it."

"As I see our choices . . ." Johnny held up a finger, even though none of the others was looking at him; they were all busy watching the ground for holes and rattlesnakes. "If we bypass them folks and ride down to Mexico, Gamble's probably gonna come find us someday, maybe when we least expect him, maybe when we're all settled in with pretty Mexican wives, and a bunch of half-Mexican brats underfoot."

"So you say." Matt thought he might be able to find a Mexican wife, but Johnny had a large wart on the side of his nose with thick white hairs growing from it. Matt didn't think most women, Mexican or not, could overlook that wart long enough to marry Johnny Barth.

Johnny ignored him. He held up another finger. "If we do as he says, and we kill them folks for him, he's liable to kill us anyway. He seemed damn vicious to me. I bet he already killed half our friends while we're out here running his errand for him."

Jim shivered. "So you're saying we're damned if we do, and we're damned if we don't."

"I'm trying to say there's a third option," Johnny said. "What if we go on ahead and kill these people, but then we take the woman and the child with us, and *then* we ride down to Mexico? Gamble's got some kind of interest in them."

"He don't care about the woman."

"Just the child then, but if he does come looking for us we got something to bargain with. Anyway, it wouldn't hurt to take the woman, too, in case we don't find no Mexican brides."

"You're talking about hostages?"

"If you wanna call it that. I call it an ace up our sleeve."

This made some sense to Matt Hawke, who had already secretly given up and was starting to wonder what would happen to his few possessions back at the Paradise Ranch when Charlie Gamble killed them. Jim could also see the logic in what Johnny was saying. He nodded slowly and steered his horse around a suspicious clump of dirt.

"We might be doing that woman and child a favor," he said. "For all we know, them men they're with took them from their family. We'd probably be a lot nicer to them."

"That could very well be," Johnny said. "Yeah, we might be doing them a favor. That woman might even be grateful towards us."

Matt didn't think the woman would be that grateful, especially when she got a look at Johnny, but he bit his tongue. Johnny was sensitive on the subject of his wart. Still, the more Matt thought about it, the more he liked the idea.

They rode on quietly, each of them thinking about warm Mexican beaches.

"Say," Wayne said after a while. "Maybe these folks have some money. We could have a nice stake for ourselves by the time we get to Mexico."

This idea brightened their mood even more, so that when they rounded a bend in the trail and saw Buckridge up ahead, and a big red coach sitting in the middle of the street, they were in decidedly better spirits.

CHAPTER 11

One minute Joe was walking along a path that cut through fields of green corn, the next he was standing in front of a sign.

YOU ARE NOW LEAVING BUCKRIDGE. SEE YOU ON THE WAY BACK THROUGH.

Joe wasn't a strong reader, not like Rose. He stood for a moment, sounding out the words, then turned and saw the big red wagon far behind him, stopped in front of a building with a wide porch. Ned Hemingway was lying in the street, and the others were gathered round him.

Joe kept telling himself he would get used to the way time jumped around on him, but it was still mystifying. He had somehow traveled forward along the road without seeing the others, and had got ahead of them. He set off back toward them and passed through a few confusing seconds of nighttime, the moon orange and full above him. He was sitting in the farmhouse, and Rose sat across from him at the little pine table, reading aloud from one of her books. He was standing under the sycamore tree, looking out at the uneven rows in his field. He was in Buckridge, Kansas, looking down at Ned, who bled freely from the wound he had received in Quivira Falls.

"Well, this ain't good," Joe said to himself.

He knelt and put his hand against Ned's abdomen, and the blood stopped flowing. Ned gasped and his eyes opened. Joe tried not to dip his fingers too far inside Ned, but he wasn't solid enough to feel what he was touching and when Ned tried to sit up

Joe's hand went right through him. For a dizzying moment Joe was in a dark saloon, holding a royal flush. He pulled his hand back.

"The bleeding's stopped," said a nearby man. "Ought to move him before it starts up again."

The man had a sheriff's star pinned to his vest, and his hand rested on the butt of a revolver. Joe ignored the man and concentrated on keeping his hand near Ned's body, keeping the flow of blood to a minimum. The sheriff stepped up onto the porch and opened the door. He held it open and stood behind it, as if he had extended a cordial invitation and was willing to wait all day for a response.

"Sir," Benito said. "There is no reason to arrest the others. It's me you are interested in. I will stay with you if you'll let them go."

"I'd like to keep you all around until I hear back from the bank you stole that coach from, and from the sheriff in Texas where the bank fella says he was deputy. I guess I need to figure out what questions to ask before I can ask 'em."

The buzzing in Joe's head had grown louder, so loud he couldn't think. He only knew that Rose must be in trouble. He left Ned's side and stepped up onto the porch. The stairs rotted under his feet, then turned to green wood. The sun moved from afternoon to morning, and a bird's nest appeared in the porch rafters above him. Joe stuck his hand out and poked his fingers through the sheriff's chest. The man's eyes went dull, and he stopped breathing. Joe took a step closer and leaned forward, overlapping the sheriff's skull with his own.

It was a strange sensation, being two people at once. Joe saw the sheriff as a young boy, sitting by a green river with a net, saw the present moment, and saw his skin wrinkle and his hair go gray. He saw the sheriff lying dead in the street, still bleeding from his throat. Joe wondered what would happen if he pushed himself farther into the sheriff, layered his entire body over that of the other man. He pulled his head away and the sheriff staggered back against the wall.

"You okay, Sheriff?" Moses said.

"I guess I lost my train of thought," the sheriff said. He found his chair, sat down hard, and massaged his temples. He glared at the assemblage in the street and shook his head.

"I just had a vision I was on a farm," he said. He pointed at Rose. "You were there, miss, reading me a story."

"You're overheated," Rose said.

"No," the sheriff said. His speech was slurred and he spoke slowly. "Whatever that was, it wasn't natural."

"It could be a sign," Ned said. He had pushed himself up onto one elbow and was watching Joe with wide eyes. "Maybe we're supposed to keep going up that road, and you're supposed to let us."

The sheriff nodded slowly and looked up the road to where the sky swirled black and yellow, a thin stripe of sunlight visible beneath the clouds at the horizon. "If it was a sign, I sure wish I knew who sent it."

"Does it matter?"

The sheriff took a deep breath and nodded. "I guess I don't really have much to hold you on," he said. "All of a sudden I feel tuckered out. Between you folks and that strange fella come through earlier I feel pretty sure I'm getting lied to, but I don't know what side to land on." He paused, then slumped farther down in his chair. "I think you folks better move on along before I change my mind. But I got to keep that red wagon. It don't rightly belong to you."

"Yes, sir," Benito said.

"You can forget we were ever here," Moses said.

"Don't come back to Buckridge. If you do, I'm gonna throw you all in a cell, purely on principle."

They picked Ned up and maneuvered him onto the friendly gray sorrel Benito had been riding. Moses grabbed the reins and waited for the others to gather what they could carry, but Rose was standing frozen in the road. She had followed Ned's gaze and was now staring past the sheriff at the shadows of the porch.

"Joe?" she said. "Is that you?"

CHAPTER 12

H e's been following us," Ned said.

"You see him, too?" Rose said.

"Who's following us?" Moses said.

Before Ned could respond, the porch railing beside Benito popped and splintered. At the same time, they all heard a rifle shot echo down the shop fronts. Moses didn't hesitate. He picked up the slack in Betty's reins with one hand and grabbed Rose's elbow. He ran, pulling them around the corner of the building, Ned bouncing awkwardly on the horse's back.

"Rabbit," Rose said. "She's still in the coach!"

The team, still hobbled and hitched to the wagon, neighed and snorted as the crack of another rifle shot accompanied the thud of a round smacking into the dirt road.

"Ben!" Moses shouted. "Come on, boy!"

But Benito stood motionless in the street, staring at the splintered porch railing beside him. For a moment he thought he was back in his lover's bed before her husband had burst into the room. Marie whispered in his ear, her dark hair tickling his cheek. At the sound of a third rifle shot he finally looked around, confused, trying to find Charlie Gamble and thinking somewhere in the back of his mind that if he stood up to the deputy this time, he might save poor Marie's life. The great red coach sagged forward as one of its front wheels shattered, and the team of horses panicked, the lead horses rearing back and slamming into each other, frantic to escape the leather strap binding their legs.

"Take cover!" the sheriff hollered. He was still moving slowly as he rose from his chair and drew his revolver. He stumbled down the porch steps and pushed Benito into the dirt. There was another loud crack and Sheriff Hickman spun on his heels. He dropped the pistol and fell on his face without trying to catch himself. Benito crawled to him and rolled him over. The left side of the sheriff's throat was gone; his blood pumped out onto the packed dirt.

"Ben, get out of there," Moses yelled again from around the side of the building.

Benito came awake. He grabbed the sheriff's pistol from its holster, then jumped to his feet and ran toward the sound of Moses's voice. Another bullet whizzed past him and thunked into the road as Benito dove past the end of the porch. When he was close enough, Moses grabbed him and pulled him around the corner.

"You hit?"

Benito shook his head.

"Who's that shooting at us now?" Ned said.

"I don't know," Moses said.

The shooting had stopped. They heard distant hoofbeats, then silence.

"Give me my pistol," Ned said.

"It's on your hip, Ned."

"Oh, so it is."

"Mr Hemingway, you look about as yellow as your hat," Benito said.

"I'm good," Ned said. "Help me down off this nag so I can shoot."

Benito steadied Ned while Moses poked his head around the corner of the sheriff's office. Townsfolk peered out from behind curtains up and down the street. The barbershop door opened an inch or two and a man peeked out, then slammed it shut again. Earl Hickman lay still and silent in the road. The dark pool under his head had already begun to lose its bright sheen. At the north end of town, Moses could hear the whinnying of nervous horses. He didn't know the layout of Buckridge, but the shooters had evidently taken cover farther up the road. He pulled his head back and got Benito's attention.

"Lay down some fire for me," he said. "I'm gonna try to sneak around behind them."

"I'll do it," Ned said. "No sense you getting shot up, too."

Rose grabbed Benito's arm. "You have two revolvers. Give me one of them."

He hesitated a moment, then handed the sheriff's pistol to Rose.

Moses shook his head. "If they think we're stuck here they'll come along this way sooner or later. I'm hoping there isn't more than a man or two out there. If that's all it is I think I can take them, long as I get behind them and they don't see me coming."

Benito nodded. "What if they are already sneaking up on us?"

"Then I guess I'll meet them halfway," Moses said. "Wait five minutes and start making some noise."

"Please be careful, Mr Burke," Rose said. "Mr Hemingway and I have seen a portent of death."

"Portents don't scare me, Mrs Nettles. They don't hurt as much as a bullet."

CHAPTER 13

Moses crouched low and moved quickly across a footpath and into the shadows behind a leather goods shop that had clearly started as a tent, but now had a wooden walkway and a canvas overhang propped up with long poles.

A man with a white beard and deep creases in his brown face grabbed Moses's arm and tried to pull him inside the shop. Moses pulled away and shook his head, then sidled along the opposite wall, keeping his back to the line of buildings. He reached a side street and could see the main road at the far end, where a man with a rifle crouched behind a rain barrel with his back to Moses.

"Hey!" the man shouted, and Moses jumped back, thinking the man had seen him. "Hey, you fellas! We just want the kid."

"And the woman," came a second voice from somewhere on the other side of the main thoroughfare.

"We got no beef with you boys," the first man shouted. "Give us the woman and the youngster and we'll head on down the road."

Moses flattened himself against the wall of a woodshed and tried to think. The two men knew about Rose and Rabbit, and had planned their attack. They might have followed the big red coach to Buckridge and circled around, but Moses felt sure he and Ned would have spotted them out on the open road. Even if they had somehow missed two horsemen following them, he thought Jacob Skinner would have noticed.

The men had to have come from the opposite direction, from Riddle. The only person who could possibly know about them was the witch of Burden County. Moses didn't understand why she would be interested in Rose and Rabbit, but he decided he would ask the men after he captured them.

He ducked past the mouth of an alley and moved farther down, then took a diagonal side street angling north and west. He knew where the first man was, but he wanted to locate the second man and determine whether there were more shooters spread out across the town. He was edging around the side of a saloon when Ned's voice came echoing up the street.

"We don't got a woman or a little girl with us!" His voice was loud and clear.

Moses peered around the corner and saw his friend standing in the middle of the street. Ned was making himself a target, giving Moses the time and opportunity to get the drop on the shooters, but it wasn't the distraction Moses had intended, and concern for his friend muddled his thinking.

"We didn't specify it was a little girl!" the first man shouted. He was barely five yards from Moses, in the next alley over.

"Neither did I," Ned said.

"Yes, you did," the second gunman yelled out. "You said you didn't have a woman or a little girl with you."

"Well, we don't," Ned said.

"What we're trying to say here," the second man said. "It might've been a boy we was talking about."

"We don't got one of those, neither," Ned said. "So take your pick."

A pebble hit the ground near Moses's foot and bounced onto the toe of his boot. He looked up and saw Benito waving at him from the mouth of the alleyway opposite. Moses scowled at him. They'd had a plan, rough but solid, and yet nobody was following it. He shook his head and pounded the air with his fist, but Benito misunderstood. He grinned and gave Moses a thumbs-up.

"We got you boys surrounded," Ned said. "You might as well come on out so we can talk about this."

Moses pointed ahead to where the first shooter was hidden, then pointed across the street and held up two fingers, indicating there was a second man somewhere in Benito's vicinity. Benito nodded and faded back into the shadows.

"We don't believe you," the first gunman shouted. "You gonna give us them girls?"

"Told you we don't got no girls," Ned said.

"Mister, I'm gonna shoot you where you stand!"

Moses took a deep breath and holstered his pistol. He ran around the corner into the street and back into the next alley, barreling full speed into the first gunman, who was in the process of reloading his rifle. Moses slammed the man's face against the wall, and the rifle flew from his hands, skittering across the alley floor.

Moses took a step back and drew his pistol. With one arm pinning the gunman to the wall and his pistol held tight in his other hand, he took a second to catch his breath. The shooter was wearing spurs and a big straw hat with a hole in the crown. Moses glanced at the rifle on the ground and saw it was an ancient single-shot.

"Well, you're no kind of assassin I've ever seen," Moses said.

"My mouth's bleeding," the gunman said.

"I got one of them, Ned," Moses hollered.

"How many men they got?" Ned called out.

"How many of you are there?" Moses said to the gunman.

"You didn't gotta hurt me. We was just gonna take the woman and the girl and head out to Mexico. We coulda left you out of it, but now my lip's split."

"I asked how many of you!"

He grabbed a handful of the gunman's hair, and wheeled at the sound of Benito's voice.

"There were two of them," Benito said. "I got the other."

He was crossing the street, pushing the second gunman ahead of him. The man Benito had captured was wearing chaps and had a big wart on his nose. To Moses's eye both men looked like cowboys or ranch hands. Mercenaries traveled alone or in pairs; cowboys banded together.

"This isn't right," Moses said. "Benito, get back. Take cover."

A divot of clay exploded at Benito's feet. He let go of the gunman's arm and dove to the side. The gunman jumped the other way and fell hard on his back with a loud grunt. A second divot popped up, accompanied by the sound of gunfire.

"Dammit, Matt, you almost hit me!" the gunman shouted.

"Who's shooting?" Ned hollered down the street.

"All you fellas stay where you are, and let Jim come on out of that alley," came a voice from above. Moses looked up to see a man peering down at him from the rooftop of the saloon across the street. Benito flattened himself against the wall behind Moses, then slid to the ground. Moses lowered his pistol, and the man with the bleeding mouth glared at him before slinking out into the street.

"I had him," he yelled up at the man on the roof. "You didn't have to shoot at Johnny."

"I wasn't shooting at Johnny."

"Well, anyway, you almost hit me," Johnny said. He stood up and brushed himself off.

"You boys come on out of that alleyway with your hands where we can see 'em," came another voice.

Moses looked and saw a fourth man on the rooftop opposite the saloon. He and Benito had been so focused on the men on the ground, they had left themselves open to ambush from above.

Moses helped Benito up, and they stepped out with their arms raised.

"We really was gonna let you menfolk go your own way," the fourth man said.

"Hell with that, Wayne," Johnny said. "If you don't shoot 'em, I will."

CHAPTER 14

The red coach rocked back and forth as the frightened horses jostled one another. The coach was too wide to allow for more than a single man on a horse to pass it in the road. Across from the sheriff's office was a blacksmith's forge, and beyond that was open farmland. The town was surrounded by open space, but had grown inward, cramming new buildings so close to existing structures that there was barely room between them.

Sheriff Earl Hickman remained on his side in the street, and Ned stood over him, making a target of himself. Rose hoped there wouldn't be two bodies to bury at the end of the day.

"Told you we don't got no girls," Ned yelled. He glanced at Rose and winked.

Rose moved quickly across the narrow gap between the sheriff's office and the coach, then checked to make sure her new pistol was loaded. So far no one had fired on Ned, but Rose was prepared to shoot back and buy Ned time to take cover again. It wasn't much of a plan, but they were counting on Moses and Benito to stop the gunmen at the far end of the street.

Rose lightly rapped on the back of the coach with her knuckles. "Rabbit?"

There was no answer.

Rose peeked around the side of the carriage to make sure Ned hadn't collapsed or changed position, then edged around to the far side and cracked open the door. The coach was empty.

Rose wasn't surprised. At every sign of danger they had encountered, the child had run. Rose wasn't even surprised that Rabbit had managed to get out of the coach and away without anyone seeing her.

With the wagon door open and blocking the view from the road, Rose felt momentarily free from scrutiny. She turned and scanned the opposite side of the street, where Rabbit must have gone. Between the blacksmith and the livery, she could see open sky and the swaying tassels of corn husks.

"I'll whistle when it's safe," she said, though she knew Rabbit must be too far away to hear her voice.

The horses pulled against their harness, rocking the coach, and another stomach spasm doubled Rose over. She gasped and bit her lip to keep from crying out. Her vision doubled and she grabbed the edge of the wagon's long bench to steady herself. A moment later the pain eased, and she was able to stand up straight again.

She heard a note of alarm in Ned's voice and men's voices shouting, then Ned was limping past on the other side of the coach.

"They got Moses and Ben," he yelled as he passed out of sight at the front of the coach. "Sounds like there's at least four of 'em. Take cover and stay down, Rose!"

As Rose turned, ready to join him in a last stand from the high porch of the sheriff's office, her copy of *Dombey and Son* fell out at her feet. She bent and picked it up as if in a trance, momentarily forgetting the chaos around her: the panicked horses, the distant yelling, the gnawing pain in her stomach. The book fell open to the page where she had saved the letter from her mother. She took it out, but didn't unfold it.

She felt darkness pushing at her from the periphery of her vision. She believed Joe had tried to warn her that she would die in Buckridge, Kansas, and she felt certain she would never make it all the way to Riddle, never see Rabbit to safety, never see her own mother again.

Rose reached into the pocket of her dress and found Joe's pipe and the box of matches. She stuck the pipe in her mouth and puffed on it while it took the fire. When the tiny flame touched her fingertips, she held it to the corner of her mother's letter. The paper caught fire and Rose dropped the match. She stuck her singed fingers in her mouth and stood watching the letter blacken and curl, a thin tendril of smoke wafting away in the breeze, then she put the letter back in the book with the burning edge sticking out at the top, and put the book on top of Old Tom's saddlebags on the floor of the coach. She picked up her valise and slung it over her shoulder, then closed the door and went around to the front where the horses were snorting and pawing, their eyes wide with fear.

She knew she was in full view of the shooters, but she didn't care. She accepted that every moment might now be her last. She put her hand on the neck of a lead horse, a lovely brown-and-white roan, stroking his mane and feeling the taut muscles under his skin, then she kneeled in the dirt and unbuckled the leather strap around his front legs. She had barely freed the roan's left leg when he kicked out, knocking her down. Rose pulled her knees up to her chest in time to keep from being trampled as the horses leaped forward, pulling the lopsided coach along on its three good wheels.

A bullet plonked into the road beside Rose. The roan reared back and plunged forward again, but the damaged corner of the coach dug into the dirt and created a pivot point that slowed the team. Rose heard something snap in the rig.

"Rose, get out of there," Ned shouted. He was leaning against the wall of the sheriff's office and Rose could see he was too weak to move.

"I'm giving Mr Burke the distraction he asked for," Rose said.

"And now I'm going to go look for Rabbit." She didn't know if he heard her.

A plume of smoke billowed from a window of the coach, and within seconds its entire back end was aflame. The horses pulled harder and yanked the coach free, plowing ahead down the street.

Rose crossed the road toward the gap between shops. She heard distant shouting and then another rifle round was suddenly hanging in the air beside her head, vibrating slightly as if held in a strong breeze. Joe flickered into sight, and was gone. She kept moving and the shell whizzed past, stirring her hair. It smacked into the corner of the sheriff's office behind her, an inch from Ned's face. A shower of splinters exploded outward, and Ned slumped to the floor of the porch.

Rose walked through cool shadows that bordered the east end of Buckridge, until she was standing in the middle of a narrow field of grass with tall corn in front of her. The field stretched away to her left and to her right as far as she could see. She turned and saw smoke over the rooftops behind her. She heard men screaming, and gunshots, and she hoped her friends were alive. She hoped they would have better luck without her.

She turned and plunged between the rows of corn.

CHAPTER 15

The Huntsman emerged from a cornfield north of Buckridge and saw smoke. He heard the sounds of war: men yelling and guns firing. He sighed. He had been gone perhaps two hours, and the foolish people he traveled with had already found more trouble for themselves. He had told them to wait for him. Buckridge itself was unremarkable, but he would have advised them to go around it. There was a grassy path that bypassed the town, bordering a cornfield, and the trail past it to Riddle was wide and clear.

Closer to Riddle, he had found the road littered with hexes and traps, and the Huntsman had turned back to help the little company in their stupid red wagon survive the remainder of their journey.

The wind blew from the south, and the Huntsman sniffed the air. He sifted through the scents that came to him and organized them in his mind. The black cowboy and the Mexican boy were nearby, perhaps only a hundred yards away, but hidden from view by the low structures at the edge of town. The white cowboy was farther away, still at the south end of Buckridge, and the woman was far to the east, moving at a steady pace away from the town.

There were hundreds of other human smells in the area, as well as the mingled scents of cows, horses, dogs, sheep, birds, and rodents.

There was also the lingering toad-odor of the man he had killed on the ridge. The Huntsman had smelled him on the road, too, and knew that whatever the dead man had become, he was waiting somewhere near Riddle.

What puzzled the Huntsman was that he could not smell the child. If she were dead, he would still smell her; her scent would be sharper in the first hour after death, but there was no sign of Rabbit in the breeze that came to him. The only possibility he could think of was that Rabbit had somehow circled around to the north and was upwind of him, headed toward Riddle. There were many dangers on the prairie for a small girl traveling alone and the Huntsman considered doubling back, but if he had guessed wrong, he would not find her to the north, and time would be wasted. Time was one thing the Huntsman couldn't control.

He had no interest in the two cowboys, the Mexican boy, nor the woman with arsenic in her veins. He had accompanied them because the child was with them, and the child was a mystery to him. He had not encountered a mystery in a very long time. Without the child, the little band of people in the red coach were insignificant.

And yet one of those people might be able to tell him where Rabbit was.

He sighed and set his bag down under a half-dead elm whose roots had pulled up from the ground, then he rolled his head from side to side, loosening his stiff neck. He had begun to feel old lately.

He readied his bow and nocked a fresh arrow, then set off toward town again, passing the sign that read YOU ARE NOW LEAVING BUCKRIDGE. SEE YOU ON THE WAY BACK THROUGH.

CHAPTER 16

Jim Garber knelt on a rooftop across from Wayne Traeger. Between them, they had a good view down into a sort of canyon made from the haphazard arrangement of little shops and one-family homes. Johnny Barth and Matt Hawke were below, corralling the negro and the Mexican. There had been some debate about whether to kill the men or tie them up and leave them. Jim was in favor of tying them up, but was ultimately overruled by the others.

There was smoke and a lot of noise coming from the direction of the road, but Jim couldn't see much past the tall chimney in front of him. He watched Matt and Johnny discuss things for a moment, then Johnny ran to the end of the alley and peered around the corner. He made a funny little dancing motion and jumped back just as a team of horses passed in the street dragging a fiery red coach with flames billowing behind it.

In his excitement, Jim forgot to hunker down behind the chimney, and he stood up on tiptoe so he could see better. Across from him, he heard Wayne make a gurgling noise, barely audible above the whinnying of the horses and the scraping of the three-wheeled wagon along the street. Wayne staggered into view with an arrow through his neck. He dropped his rifle and grabbed his throat with both hands, but the arrow was lodged in his jawbone and when he tugged at it fresh blood gushed down his chin and pooled above his collarbone. He tumbled off the roof and smacked into the ground below.

Jim dropped to his hands and knees just as an arrow zinged

through the space he had occupied half a second before. The arrow plunked into the chimney and vibrated angrily.

Jim crawled on his belly to the edge of the roof and cupped his hands on either side of his mouth.

"Ambush!"

But nobody heard him. Matt was herding the negro and the Mexican against the wall, getting ready to shoot them, and Johnny was kneeling beside Wayne's body, as if he could still help him.

In the street, the wagon tipped over and the rig snapped, pulling one of the horses down. Its leg broke and it began to scream. The other three horses tore loose and galloped away together. Something in the wagon exploded with a thud that puffed out its walls, then sucked them back in. The entire thing collapsed in on itself in a cloud of noxious yellow smoke, and Jim—who knew he ought to be paying attention to the fact that someone was shooting arrows at him—watched the poor horse still attached to the rig as it tried to stand. Its tail caught fire and flames leaped over its hide as it pulled itself in small circles, helplessly tangling itself in the trace while its skin sizzled.

Jim felt somehow distant from himself. The things happening in the street and in the alley below him were terrifying, but he was above them. They were happening without his involvement, and the chimney was a solid thing that anchored him to a place of relative stability. He crawled forward on his elbows and knees so he could see down into the alley again.

"He's dead!" Johnny shouted the obvious. "Wayne's dead, fellas!"

Matt lowered his pistol from where it was pressed against the negro's head and turned toward Johnny. From his high vantage point Jim saw a shadow move across the alley floor behind them. Seconds later, Matt collapsed. His pistol skittered across the ground and smacked into a wall. Johnny Barth grabbed his shoulder and screamed. Everyone was moving too fast and the light was too dim for Jim to see what was happening, but it was clear they were under attack.

In the alleyway, a tall man with a long gray beard moved into a ray of sunlight and looked up at Jim, then casually swept a blade across Johnny's throat. Johnny fell as Matt staggered to his feet, but the gray-haired man turned and stabbed him in the temple with the same blade he had used to kill Johnny. The old man moved deliberately, seemingly in no hurry, and yet the ranch hands had no chance to react. Within seconds, Jim was the only one of the four ranch hands left alive.

He scrambled away from the edge of the roof and crawled to the other side where barrels were stacked against the wall. In his panic he misjudged his footing, dropped the rifle, and tumbled to the ground. The barrels bounced out into the street and rolled to a stop against the smoldering ruins of the red coach.

Jim got to his feet, and stumbled forward, a searing pain shooting from his ankle to his hip. His saw his rifle on the ground ten feet away and hobbled toward it. With each careful step, he could feel bones grinding in his ankle and he gritted his teeth to keep from yelling. He stopped long enough to grab the rifle, nearly losing his balance again, then hopped past the ruined coach and between the buildings on the far side of the road. He was exposed when he reached the strip of grass that separated the town from the cornfields, but he ignored the pain in his ankle and kept moving. He didn't look back in case the tall man was at his heels.

Once he entered the rows of corn, he took a moment to breathe. He pulled up the hem of his trouser leg and saw his ankle was already swollen and turning purple. He knew he should remove his boot before he had to cut it off, but the corn husks underfoot were rough. He would have to get through the field before he could attend to his injury. He mopped the sweat from his neck and pushed on, moving more slowly now, confident that he was safe and out of sight.

He had lost Johnny, Matt, and Wayne. He didn't have the hostages they had set out to get, and he felt certain if he returned to the ranch Charlie Gamble would kill him. His ankle was broken and he didn't have a horse. He couldn't remember which direction Mexico lay in, and he had nowhere else to go.

But he wasn't dead yet, and that was some small comfort.

CHAPTER 17

Charlie Gamble spent an hour making Teddy Paradis dance around the yard on his broken leg. Every time Paradis fell, Charlie would cause him to get back up and stagger around in a slow circle until he fell again. Teddy screamed and cursed at Charlie, and eventually he began to cry. At last Charlie grew tired of watching the old rancher twist in the dirt, and cut off Teddy's head with a butcher's knife. He made the old man's body continue to dance about, but he no longer found it amusing.

In the second hour, he shut all but four of the remaining ranch hands in the mess hall and sealed it with wards at the door and at each of the windows. He set the building on fire and stood at the edge of the flames listening to the shrieks of the burning men.

He made the four remaining men stand at attention and watch the fire. When the screams subsided, and the smell of charred man-flesh had wafted away on the breeze, Charlie looked about for something else to help him while away the afternoon.

Teddy Paradis's twitching headless body stumbled against him and he pushed it away, annoyed. His stomach was bothering him. Charlie burped and pulled a toad from his mouth, but it was dead.

This had never happened before, and Charlie cast a suspicious glare at the rolling green clouds above the town, two miles up the main road.

He let the dancing body fall down and lie still, then he went into the house and checked the big grandfather clock in the front hall. It had not even been three hours since he sent the cowboys south to intercept the group coming to Riddle. He didn't know how long it would take them to stop the great red coach, but he thought he might have to wait at least four or five more hours to hear back from them.

He growled. He had been stuck in the middle of nowhere for longer than he cared to remember, and he wasn't having fun anymore.

He considered removing the wards from the mess hall and raising up the corpses of the ranch hands inside. He could pit them against the four remaining Paradise men, who were still rooted to their spots outside, or he could send them marching up the road to Riddle or down the road to Buckridge. An army of dead cowboys might stir up some amusement. If he sent them to Riddle, they might even vex the witch a bit, but he knew it would be a minor inconvenience for her, at best, and it would certainly make her aware of him, if she wasn't already. He wasn't sure of his potency now that he was on her land. The dead toad was a bad sign.

He wondered about the child. He wondered if the men he had sent to fetch her would succeed. He wondered if it might have been a good idea to send more men.

He slit his horse's throat and examined the arterial spray across the grass of the paddock, surprised to see that the child was already moving toward him, and more quickly than a man on horseback could travel. As he watched the signs in the blood, he fretted.

"Never send someone else to do what's best done yourself," he said aloud.

"Sage advice, Mr Rigby," he answered. "Oh, now, I meant to say 'Mr Gamble.' My mistake."

"Think nothing of it," he said.

He counted the cowboys standing outside the mess hall and saw there were only three.

"I thought there were four of you," he said to the nearest man. "Where'd the other one go?"

"Walt left," Bill Cassidy said. "He tore off outta here when you was killing your horse." The gunshot wound Johnny Barth had inflicted was dark and leaking pus.

"Well, how did that happen?" Charlie said. "I didn't say any of you could leave."

"He stuck a penny under his tongue as soon as he saw you coming." A tear rolled down Bill's cheek. "I guess he was lucky he wasn't in the mess hall."

"Well, well, well," Charlie said. "Somebody's taught you folks a trick or two."

"Why can't you leave us be?" Bill said.

"It's not in my nature to leave people be."

"Then go somewhere else, mister. Bother somebody else."

"I will, once I've concluded my business here. Maybe I'll take you with me, Bill Cassidy. You can take Mr McDaniel's place at my side. I'll introduce you to pleasures you've never dreamt of."

"I wish you wouldn't."

"Bah, I miss Mr McDaniel. I never had to make him do anything."

Charlie tapped his feet and twirled about on the dirt path. Behind him the dead horse rose on trembling legs and stood waiting, its throat still dripping.

"The child is coming," Charlie said. "And I think the witch must know I'm here, but I feel a strange reluctance to move on. Perhaps I'm tired. There's so little to engage me anymore, Mr Cassidy."

Charlie bent and picked up Teddy Paradis's ruined head. He turned it this way and that, examining it in the wan sunlight.

"This is all so boring," he said. "Did you know I was born in a fire, Mr Cassidy?"

Bill was thinking about his mother and the way she squinted

when she smiled, how she had stroked his hair when he was young until he fell asleep, and how she had made him learn to read and write, even when he complained that those were useless skills for a cowboy, which he knew he would someday be. Now he wondered how long it had been since he had written his mother a letter, and he wondered who would tell her the news that he was dead.

"This is my hundredth body," Charlie said. "Or maybe it's the thousandth. I lose track. I wasn't always called Charlie Gamble. You wouldn't be able to pronounce my original name, the name I had when the fire died and I rose as a swarm from the pit, my skin crusted with blood and ashes."

He sighed.

"I had worshippers then, and I did many terrible deeds, Mr Cassidy. I laid with beautiful women and they gave birth to horrors. I laid with beautiful men and planted the seeds of war. A king displeased me, and I marched against him. I conjured a plague of insects that consumed his army. I took his harem for myself, and I ate the children of his courtiers. There are still statues of me, you know, buried under stones deep in the sand, put there to ward off death and bad luck. Oh, I miss those days, Mr Cassidy. So few people pay me the proper respect now."

He grabbed Teddy Paradis's hair and lifted the head high. Rainwater dripped from its bloody scalp. He swung the head like a lantern.

"Look around us," he said. "Nothing in that direction, nothing in the other direction, everywhere there's nothing, but still you people come. You hope to find something in the midst of all this nothingness, and that's where I thrive, Mr Cassidy. I live in the hope."

He stuck the severed head on the horn of his saddle and pressed it down hard to keep it from wobbling.

"We'd better get moving, Mr Cassidy. There's a family reunion underway, and I'm afraid I'm going to be late."

Charlie mounted the dead horse and left the Paradise Ranch, a plume of smoke in the sky behind him to mark where he had been. Bill Cassidy followed him on foot and the last two ranch hands trailed after.

As they passed under the PARADISE sign at the main road, it fell to the ground and splintered into a hundred pieces.

CHAPTER 18

The cowboy with the knife in his skull staggered around the alley, firing blindly, and Jacob Skinner nocked an arrow. Moses grabbed the Huntsman's arm, ruining the shot.

"He's out of ammo," Moses said. "You don't have to kill him."

It seemed to Benito that Jacob had already killed the man. His skin had turned gray around the head wound, and he was grunting, as if trying, and failing, to form words. Benito had to look away. He saw a flash of movement from the corner of his eye and turned in time to see another of the gunmen limping into the cornfield, past where the red coach quietly smoldered.

"There's one left," Benito said. "I will get him."

"No," Moses said. "Wait!"

But Benito was already gone, chasing after the last of their attackers. The body of the dead horse twitched as its muscles cooled; its hide smelled like burned hair and steak. Benito ran on through the narrow space between buildings to a flat grassy path beyond.

The man had already disappeared into the corn ahead, and Benito didn't pause before plunging in after him. Green husks rasped against his skin and tore at his clothing, and he felt like he was running very fast, pushing the stalks down and leaping ahead before they could whip back at him. He knew he wasn't as smart as Moses, nor as skilled as Jacob, nor as handsome as Ned, but he was younger than any of them. He could run quickly, and he was strong. He would catch the gunman who had pinned them down in the alley. He would show them all how capable he was, and the others would be proud of him.

The rows of corn went on and on, and some of the stalks reached high above his head. Benito could hear faint sounds behind him that made him think Moses and Jacob had followed, but he was sure he would catch the gunman first. The broken stalks and trampled rows ahead made Benito feel he was close and perhaps even gaining ground. The man had been limping, and Benito had all the energy in the world after escaping death in the narrow alley.

And then he crashed through a row and the gunman was sitting on the ground in front of him, tugging at his boot. Benito stopped, surprised. The gunman dropped his boot and scooped up his rifle. He didn't bother to aim; he raised the weapon and fired. There was a deafening explosion and Benito fell, snapping the springy stalks behind him. He landed with a thud that raised a cloud of chaff and dust around him.

It seemed there was something heavy sitting on his chest, and he couldn't breathe. But above him the sky looked very blue. He was glad the storm was still miles away so he could see how pretty the sky was. He watched a bird glide in tight circles above him. He heard corn rustling nearby, and the gunman hobbled into view, his rifle gripped tight in both hands.

"Dammit," the man said. "All I wanted was to go to Mexico. I never wanted to kill nobody."

A man with a droopy mustache appeared in the space between the rows. He knelt beside Benito and rested his hand on the boy's chest. He smiled at Benito and nodded, and Benito smiled back. He understood that this was the husband of Rose Nettles, and he was glad to finally meet him.

"I think I am going to see Marie," Benito said to the man.

Behind Rose's husband, the gunman raised his rifle again and

Benito tried to put a hand up. He didn't think he could stop the round, but the man was standing too close and Benito couldn't see the sky. There was a sudden flurry of movement and Jacob Skinner burst into sight. He slammed into the gunman, who fell to one side and dropped the rifle. There was a snapping sound, sharp and distinct above all the sounds of the cornstalks and the insects, and the man grunted in surprise. Benito could see that his foot was bent at an odd angle. He fell to the ground beside Benito, and turned his head to look at him, his eyes wide. He opened his mouth, but before he could speak Jacob hauled him up by his hair and slit his throat. A gusher of blood spilled out onto the dirt. Jacob dropped the body; the gunman's eyes were still open.

The Huntsman knelt beside Benito and frowned.

"I am dead," Benito said.

"Not yet," Jacob said. "I can finish you, if you like. It would be a mercy."

"No," Benito said. "Thank you, but I believe I will lie here and look at the sky. It's very clear and bright today."

But Jacob had already risen and stepped out of Benito's line of sight. Benito tried to move his head, to see where the Huntsman had gone, but his muscles didn't respond. He decided that was fine. He didn't need to look at the ugly old man. Instead, he watched the hawk flying far above him, circling the field, and he wondered what it could see from up there.

CHAPTER 19

Rose imagined the pain in her stomach as a beast she was carrying across the fields of corn. She had left her friends behind, and her books, too, but she no longer cared. She had become accustomed to leaving things behind.

She wanted to call out to Rabbit, or whistle for her again, but she kept her jaw clamped shut. She was afraid that if she opened her mouth she would scream.

She could accept her own death, and the deaths of the men in her party, but not Rabbit's. She needed to make sure the girl had escaped Buckridge—yet another of the murderous little towns arranged like beads on a string. Maybe they could even make it the last few miles into Riddle, where Rose still hoped to find an answering telegram from her mother. It would be good to feel that final connection to her past before she died.

Cornstalks slashed at Rose's legs and forearms, but she ignored the pain. Her valise smacked against her hip and one of her knitting needles poked her. She stepped in a rut and fell, and heard herself finally scream, but it was as if the sound had come from somewhere far away.

A curtain of cornstalks parted and Rabbit stepped into the row beside her.

The child approached Rose, crunching on dead husks, and leaned over her. Rabbit's expression was a mix of curiosity and concern, but there was something else in the darkness of her eyes, something cold. In a sudden burst of clarity before she passed out, Rose knew that she had been deluding herself throughout the journey north. She had meant to help care for the little girl, but a new certainty settled in her as deep and painful as the agony in her stomach: her decisions had never been her own.

"Why did you bring us here?" she said to Rabbit.

The girl cocked her head to one side and opened her mouth as if to speak, but the sky opened up and blackness poured out, and Rose felt relief wash over her as she was swallowed up and destroyed.

CHAPTER 20

Roy Olin saw a column of smoke above Buckridge and spurred his horse faster, leaving Doc Priddy behind. A mile outside town he had to move off the road as a team of three horses tethered to a broken rig trotted past. When they had gone, Roy whipped his horse into a full gallop.

Townsfolk milled about in the street, some of them watching a wagon burn itself out, others carrying bodies. Roy dismounted so he could talk to Luke Radkins, who stood on the porch of the milliner's store, surveying the chaos as if it were an ordinary Saturday evening.

"That one there is Johnny Barth," Luke said, pointing to one of the bodies. "You know him from off the Paradise spread. Rode in with a couple other fellas and shot poor Earl."

"Shot Earl?"

"Killed him dead."

"What do you mean, they killed Earl? Nobody killed Earl. Hell, I ain't been gone more'n an hour or two."

"Earl's dead as can be, Roy, and them Paradise boys done it."

Roy left Luke and ran up the street toward the sheriff's office. He saw Earl's hat before he saw Earl. It was rolling on its brim, carried along by the breeze. Roy picked it up and dusted it off. Someone had moved Earl out of the road, and the body lay on the porch of the sheriff's office. Roy took the steps slowly. He stood and stared at the body, fiddling with Earl's hat. He didn't hear

Luke come up behind him, and when the old man poked his arm he jumped.

"What you want us to do with the stranger?" Luke said. "I don't figure you'll want to arrest him, since it was the Paradise boys done most of this. The only thing I don't know is how the coach caught afire. That one's a mystery to me."

"What stranger?"

"The negro Earl was talking to when he got shot. He's right over there with his friend. Won't leave his side."

Roy finally noticed Moses Burke sitting in the alley beside the sheriff's office with his back against the porch. There was another man on the ground with his head in Moses's lap. Moses was holding a yellow hat.

"Get a couple men and put Earl in a cell," Roy said to Luke.

"You want us to put him in a cell?"

"I don't . . . I swear, Luke, I was scarcely gone an hour. I don't understand how this could happen."

"I told you how it happened, Roy. Them Paradise boys—"

"Put Earl inside," Roy said. "Put him on a bunk in there."

He stepped off the porch and approached Moses. The man on the ground wasn't dead yet, but Ned Hemingway was nearly unrecognizable. Half his head was a pulpy mess that reminded Roy of beef stew. Moses was busy picking big splinters of wood out of his friend's face, and Roy turned to scan the building behind them. It looked like a rifle round had blown out the corner of the sheriff's office, and it wasn't hard to figure out that Ned had been standing in the wrong place and caught a face full of wood.

Moses opened Ned's vest. His fancy shirt, with metal tips on the collars and fringe along the pockets, was slick with blood.

"Howdy, Deputy," Ned said. His voice was a low croak. "I guess we brung some trouble to your town."

"I guess you did."

"I hope you won't hold it against my friends."

"I can't say yet," Roy said. "But I heard it was the Paradise boys done all this."

"It was somebody's boys," Ned said. "But it wasn't us. We was just traveling through. We didn't mean no harm."

"I hear you."

"Would you give me and my friend a minute?"

Roy nodded and turned away. Luke was leading two teenage boys up the porch steps. They stooped and picked up Earl's body, one boy at each end. Staggering under Earl's weight, they carried him into the building. Roy followed.

"I sure didn't see it going this way," Ned said.

"Who could have seen such a thing," Moses said.

"Maybe a witch could've."

Ned's chuckle turned into a coughing fit. When he could breathe again, he turned his head and spat bile into the dirt.

"Last time I was tore up like this you patched me up pretty good. That's the only reason I let you hang around me all these years. Just in case it happened again."

"Hush up now," Moses said. "We can talk when you're rested up."

"Sure," Ned said. "Sure we can. Something else I never told you. You're a lousy poker player. You got a tell."

"I don't have a tell."

"Then why do I beat you at cards every damn time?"

"You're lucky is all. And you're not gonna make me mad."

"Mad's not such a bad thing," Ned said. "I sure don't want you getting any sadder."

"I'm not sad."

"Would you give my hat to Benito? It's a good hat and it shouldn't go to waste. Would you do that?"

"You're going to need that hat," Moses said.

"Just do that one thing for me."

Moses nodded.

"Good," Ned said. "Kid needs a decent hat."

CHAPTER 21

Moses was still sitting with Ned's head in his lap when the Huntsman walked out of the cornfield carrying Benito in his arms.

"Not him, too," Moses said.

"My fault," the Huntsman said. "Getting old and slow."

"I was supposed to give him Ned's hat."

"He won't be needing it."

"Well, damn." Moses stared out at the cornfield as the Huntsman laid Benito down in the patchy grass beside the sheriff's office.

"Mrs Nettles?" Moses said.

"She's out there," the Huntsman said. "The poison's about run its course in her."

"Poison?"

"Arsenic builds up in the blood. She reeks of it."

"You left her?"

"I can only carry one body at a time. Do you know where the child is?"

"Rabbit?" Moses said. "She probably ran. She always runs when there's trouble. I hope she keeps running until she's far away from this place."

"It's strange," the Huntsman said. "I can't smell her out there."

He turned and walked back the way he had come, between the buildings and out across the grass. Moses could see sunshine to the south, beyond the shadows of Buckridge. He watched the Huntsman disappear once again into the corn, and watched the plants spring back into place behind him as if he had never passed that way.

Roy came out of the office and took off his hat. He ran his fingers through his thinning hair and sighed.

"I guess we can put that Mexican's body in there with Earl," he said. "We got more cots."

He looked down at Ned's body. The fringe on the gambler's shirt fluttered as a gentle wind blew across the dirt and moved the weeds that grew up through the planks in the sidewalk.

"I'll get the boys to carry your friend in there, too. Not much of a sheriff's office anymore. More like a morgue."

The teenage boys came and lifted Ned's body from Moses's lap. He could see they were trying to be gentle and respectful, but he stopped them for a moment so he could button Ned's vest. He didn't like it flapping open.

"We weren't supposed to be here," he said to Roy, when the boys had taken Ned inside and Roy had helped Moses to his feet. "Ned and I never meant to come up this way at all."

As he said it he wondered what had compelled them to fall in with an old witch-master, a little girl, a widow, and a Mexican boy. He wondered why they had driven a bright red coach in the wrong direction from Nicodemus where Moses's family was waiting for them.

"It doesn't make a damn bit of sense," he said aloud.

Roy understood. When he had rolled out of bed that morning, it had seemed much like any other day in recent memory. Now Earl was dead, half the town was shot up, and there was a Wells Fargo coach smoldering in the street.

He looked up the road to where the bodies of the three Paradise boys had been laid out. Bessie Mangrove was covering them with clean sheets she had brought from her house. Some of the local boys had braved the smoking remains of the coach and freed the burned horse from its harness. They dragged it a little ways off and stood arguing over whether horse meat was better than goat meat.

Bessie stopped what she was doing and shaded her face with her hand when Doc Priddy rode past her. Roy started laughing when he saw the doctor coming. He couldn't help it. In the time it had taken him to fetch Doc Priddy, six men had died, and there was no longer anyone for the doctor to treat.

Moses stared at him.

"No, sir," Roy said. "It don't make a lick of sense."

PART SEVEN

The Old Tree

CHAPTER 1

Rabbit ran barefoot through the corn until she broke out of the rows and saw the dark sky ahead. She was pleased to be so close to her goal after what had often seemed a meandering and treacherous journey.

She had been raised by an old couple, childless and alone, who treated her as if she were their own, and she repaid their kindness when she could. The man was a hunter, but his eyesight was no longer keen. Rabbit made sure there was always game on the hunter's land, animals that were slow or distracted when he came across them. Sometimes the old man would bring her things— mushrooms from the woods, or moss from the side of a tree, or a tattered squirrel tail—and she would use them to perform small magics for the couple. She kept the house in the woods free of mice in the wintertime, and free of mosquitoes in the summertime. Bad weather tended to pass to one side of them or the other. The hunter's wife always found what she needed in the pantry, and the fire was never difficult to light.

The old man died first. He tripped over a root and fell on an arrow he had nocked. Rabbit was unhappy with herself. She had thought the path was clear enough, and had failed to take into account his failing eyesight. She found him and brought his body back to the house. The old woman stopped eating and drinking when she saw her husband's corpse, and she died five days later, despite Rabbit's efforts to keep her alive.

The following morning Rabbit burned the house with the old

couple's bodies in it. She had to move on, and she wanted no trace of herself left behind. There were people who would try to kill her if they knew what she could do.

In the warm ashes of her former home, she performed a minor scrying spell. She needed to find two things: a new home and a teacher. She was powerful, but there was much she could learn.

When she had settled on a destination she set out along a bank of the Arkansas River, heading north and west, up through Oklahoma. She traveled during the day and slept in tall trees at night. She ate nuts and wild berries, and caught frogs and craw-dads in the shallow water near the riverbank. She was barefoot and hatless, but sharp rocks and rough bark didn't bother her, and the warm sun didn't burn her skin.

On the third day after leaving the old couple's house, she came upon the body of a man in a field of holly and wild onions. The man's skull was smashed and his face was so severely beaten that Rabbit couldn't see his eyes. He had been cut open from his throat to his groin and his liver was missing, as was his heart and one of his kidneys. Strips of meat had been carved from his thighs and back, and he had been scalped.

The dead man's possessions were strewn about the field: a pick and shovel, an iron pan, and a tinderbox. She thought the man might have been a failed miner, searching for gold and silver lost by travelers on the plains. Whomever had killed him, they hadn't bothered to steal his meager belongings.

Rabbit grabbed a handful of grass and twisted it into a simple sigil that would draw coyotes and cats, so the body wouldn't spoil and go to waste, then she turned in a slow circle, looking for smoke. Far away to the north she saw a wispy gray column. She sniffed the air and smelled meat cooking.

She backtracked to the river and crossed it, then continued on her journey, keeping the water between her and the ghoul.

She woke the next morning in a black walnut tree and saw a man standing beneath it. He stared up at her with his hands on his hips.

"About time you woke up," he said. "I was about to come up there and fetch you down."

Rabbit said nothing.

"I got breakfast frying over by the rocks. If you're hungry, I'm happy to share."

He giggled and Rabbit felt a chill run up her spine.

"You're not very polite," he said. "Don't you ever say nothing?"

Rabbit reached up and found the branch above and pulled herself higher in the tree. She could smell the strange man; his toad scent wafted up to her. Grease oozed from his pores. She knew he had murdered the poor miner and eaten his flesh.

"No need to be afraid," the man said. "Name's Rigby, and I might be of some use to you. Lotta bandits and Indians roaming up and down along here. You ought not be traveling alone." He glanced around him. "Unless you got people somewhere nearby."

When she didn't respond he smiled. His teeth were yellow and sharp.

"No, I don't think you got any people, do you? You're all alone in the world, ain't you, little one?"

She didn't answer. She didn't even blink. She kept her gaze steady and thought about the various ways she might protect herself if he decided to climb the tree. But he didn't.

"I can wait," he said. "You got to come down sooner or later."

He sat and rested his back against the tree trunk and pulled a tin of chewing tobacco from his pocket. He stuffed a wad of it behind his lower lip and began to hum. Rabbit climbed up even higher in the tree, until the branches were nearly too thin to support her weight. She found a comfortable fork and settled in.

They waited all that day, he beneath the tree and her high

up in it. The sun moved across the river and the shadow of the tree traveled in a wide arc across the prairie, and neither of them spoke again or shifted position. When the sun set and Rabbit was no longer able to see Rigby below her, she set a snare below the fork, using four nuts and a whip-thin branch, then she slept.

When she woke the sky was pale in the east and dew coated the leaves around her. Rigby was gone from his post beneath the tree.

She waited another day and another night before she climbed down from the walnut. After her encounter with Rigby, she decided it was dangerous to travel alone. She found a beaten trail and changed her aspect to that of a rabbit, following the scent of men and magic into a scrubby acre of woodland.

Her first meeting with the witch-master went badly. Tom Goggins caught her with a binding spell and prepared to shoot her for his supper. She was forced to change her aspect again in front of him. In her panic she presented herself to Old Tom as a boy. She didn't understand why, only that it seemed to her to be a good idea. She had learned to trust her instincts.

Tom Goggins turned out to be a poor guardian, but he had a large quantity of powders and metals in his bag, and she helped herself to his supplies whenever he slept or passed out drunk, teaching herself new spells and potions.

She arranged for Tom to learn about the bounty on the witch in Burden County. She knew his avarice would spur him northward, where Rabbit wanted to go. She sensed a kindly soul lingering near a sycamore tree, so she snuck a quantity of *origanum dictamnus* from Tom's saddlebag and severed the bond between Joe Mullins's spirit and his body. At the same time, she compelled him to follow her.

The hex Tom made was clumsy and useless, and when he hammered it into the sycamore she had to push him out of the way of a falling branch. The branch landed on her head and dislocated her shoulder, and Tom carried her into Monmouth.

When she met Ned Hemingway and Moses Burke, she decided it would be good for them to accompany her, too. Mr Burke seemed to know a great deal about science and medicine. Rabbit had little knowledge of either subject. She thought Mr Hemingway might be generally useful, and it was clear he would go wherever Mr Burke went.

Rose Nettles didn't need to be compelled to join them. She made up her own mind to go along, and she had the makings of a fine guardian. Rabbit was quietly pleased.

As they made their way north toward Burden County, Rabbit saw that the witch was trying to slow them down. All along the path were traps and hazards that Rabbit found herself unable to predict. She felt a cloud of influence around the little company that she wasn't able to pierce, but she was determined to plow forward. The witch might know they were coming, and might try to stop them, but Rabbit had nowhere else to go. She would not be dissuaded.

Rabbit heard strange music long before they reached the crooked woods. It would have been wiser to go around, but the others decided to go straight through. Rabbit used her small magics to keep them all together and did what she could to mute the influence of the trees. They made it through unscathed, but Rabbit assumed the witch was watching and would throw more obstacles in their way.

The creature calling itself Rigby was ahead of them on the road. The moment Rabbit set foot on his ranch, she smelled the toad thing under his skin. If he caught her, Rabbit knew he would eat her flesh, and burn her bones, and crumble them to make his bread. Her magics would flow into him and make him stronger.

That night she fled. By then, the company she had formed had brought her nearly halfway to Riddle. She didn't want to leave them, but they were no match for Rigby and she decided she would have to go the rest of the way on her own.

She was mildly surprised when Rose came after her, and even more surprised when she recognized the girl under the skin of the hare. At that moment Rabbit knew Rose had a little bit of magic in her, too, though she was unaware of it.

After that morning, there were two members of the company who knew that Rabbit wasn't all she seemed to be and accepted her. Rabbit began to wonder whether she needed to go to Riddle, after all. It was possible she had already found what she was looking for in her little band of misfits.

But they couldn't stay at the ranch, and they couldn't return to the crooked woods, so they pressed on northward.

There were six of them, but seven was a better number. There was a young man hiding in the barn. He was a good man, but without any prospects, friends, or family, so Rabbit gave him the idea that he should hide in the Wells Fargo coach before they left the ranch.

As they approached Quivira Falls, Rabbit sensed a danger that reminded her of the trees with their strange music. Elvira Bender used her own kind of magic to influence the new arrivals, making them feel drowsy and complacent. Rabbit fled again, but this time she sought out Joe Mullins and hurried him up the road.

Even with Joe's help, they barely escaped Quivira Falls. And they lost Old Tom along the way. Rabbit hadn't much liked Tom, but she missed him anyway.

Now they were six again.

Rabbit was particularly worried about Rose. She had consumed a quantity of arsenic over time, and arsenic didn't leave the body. Rabbit could smell it on her. Rose was slowly dying.

Ned was dying, too. Despite Joe's interference, Elvira Bender's bullet had nicked his liver. Rabbit didn't know how to save him. The herbs in Tom's saddlebag were meant for scratches and burns, and she had never learned healing magic.

Rabbit felt certain she would lose them all, one by one, on the road to Burden County.

Until she sensed someone watching them from the trees, someone who had followed them through Quivira Falls, and maybe through the cursed ranch and the haunted woods, too. The newcomer was unlike anything she had encountered before, and yet she immediately understood who and what he was.

That first night after she noticed the stranger, she watched Benito march away to his doom, carrying nothing but a hatchet. She followed and observed the Huntsman while he was still unaware of her. She watched him stalk Benito, and she thrilled at the economy of his movements, the efficiency of his pursuit.

She would never need to worry about his safety, and with him along she would worry less about the others.

When the Huntsman closed on Benito, Rabbit finally stepped in. She made herself known to the ancient creature, and he backed away. And, as she had hoped he would, he joined her makeshift family.

And now she had nearly reached her goal. She had arrived in Burden County and Riddle was only a few short miles away.

She left the fields of corn behind. She stayed close to the creek, back in the trees, climbing up into them when the underbrush proved impassable. She stopped at the edge of Riddle. Rain fell like a dark curtain at the town's border, and Rabbit sensed snares everywhere around her and ahead of her, though she could not see them.

She crossed the empty road and followed a familiar scent through a pasture. The Huntsman stood like a scarecrow in a sea of grass. He didn't move when she approached, but Rabbit knew he was aware of her presence. She waited beside him until he finally looked down at her.

"Hello, Grandfather," she said. "Will you take me the rest of the way now?"

CHAPTER 2

They buried Benito Cortez and Earl Hickman in a tiny graveyard outside Buckridge. Only a handful of people attended the funeral. Roy Olin read a passage from the bible, and spoke a few words about his friend Earl.

When it was Moses's turn to speak, he hesitated. He knew almost nothing about Benito, and didn't think it was his place to eulogize him. But he was the only one who could, so he cleared his throat and rolled the brim of Ned's hat as he spoke.

"Young Benito had a good spirit," he said. "He was helpful when he could be, and he tried his best. I wish he would have . . . Well, anyway, I was proud to know him." Moses's throat closed up and he found he couldn't continue. He turned to Roy, who nodded and shoveled dirt onto the plain pine caskets.

Some of the townsfolk pitched in, covering the graves and tamping down the dirt. An old man pounded a wooden cross at the head of each grave, and Bessie Mangrove came along with a bunch of flowers that she divided. She laid half the flowers on Sheriff Hickman's grave, and half on Benito's. Moses thought it was a kind gesture. Benito was a stranger to her.

Three of the markers in the cemetery bore the name Olin, and when the service ended Moses asked Roy about them.

"My family," Roy said. "Wife and two boys. The pox took 'em last year. I looked high and low for a doctor willing to come out here and help, but by the time I found Doc Priddy it was too late.

I was bringing him here to Buckridge when they expired. I never got to say goodbye."

"I'm sorry," Moses said.

"The doc's saved more than a few lives since he came," Roy said. "There's people here who would've surely died if I hadn't got him to come here and talked him into settling down. I figure my wife and boys ended up helping this whole county, even if they never knew that's what they were doing."

Moses admired the man's ability to see the positive side of his family's death. He wished he could feel the same about his own losses.

"Your doctor came too late to save my friends, too," he said. "Must be a habit with him."

Moses could see by the look on Roy's face that he had said the wrong thing. He hung the yellow hat from the crossbar of the marker on Benito's grave.

"Ned wanted the boy to have this."

Moses talked to Doc Priddy before he left.

"I was wondering," he said. "Maybe you'd hold on to my friend Ned for a couple days. I'll be back for him."

"Why, there's room to bury him here, if you wanted to," Doc Priddy said. "We can lay him next to your other friend there."

"Well, Ned and I were headed to Nicodemus before we got sidetracked. I believe he'd want us to finish that trip together. My family's got a little plot where I could bury him amongst people who aren't so much strangers. I don't think they'd mind."

"I'll keep him for you," Doc Priddy said. "Mind if I ask where you're off to?"

"In all the confusion, I've lost track of a couple members of my party. I'd like to see they're all right before I move on. Or I'll bury them if I have to."

He tipped his hat to the doctor and mounted his horse, turning her nose toward Riddle.

"Good luck to you, mister," Doc Priddy said.

"Thank you," Moses said. "Way things have been going, I'm sure I'll need it."

CHAPTER 3

John Riddle locked the front door of the Burden General Supply and ran to the porch overhang of the barber shop next door. From there, he cut through Quaid Gentry's blacksmith forge, then the livery stables, and emerged five minutes later a few yards from the train station. He could see that he had indeed left the shutters open. One of them had come loose and was banging against the side of the building.

He dashed across the street and inside, where he dried his hair with a horse blanket left over from the previous autumn, when a Tennessee woman had given birth on the floor of the station. He had been unprepared at the time, but now John made sure to have clean blankets and towels on hand.

There was a puddle of rainwater under the window, and he used the blanket to mop the floor before grabbing the swinging shutter and latching it.

Edward, a boy he employed to clean up, had left a telegram on John's desk, weighted down with a horseshoe. John read the telegram over twice.

PRIVATE CAR TO ARRIVE LATE MORNING OR
EARLY PM STOP ONE PASSENGER STOP

This was news to John. There were no trains expected before Monday. The private car was unscheduled and sudden, which might mean it carried a dignitary or an entertainer. Three years earlier, the governor of Kansas had used a private car to travel through the parts of his state he hadn't yet seen, but that train hadn't stopped in Riddle. It had merely slowed, so the governor could lean out and wave at the dozen or so people gathered on the platform to see him go by.

John checked the clock, then took a look around the station. Edward had done a decent job cleaning the place. John got a fire going in the stove to warm the room up. He was tidying his desk when he heard a train whistle over the sounds of the storm. He picked his favorite umbrella from the stand near the door—big and sturdy with a wooden handle carved in the shape of a duck's head.

The locomotive rounded a bend in the track, pulling two cars and belching smoke into the dark clouds behind it. It ground to a halt and John hurried out onto the narrow platform to greet it. A few minutes passed, and the umbrella kept his damp hair from getting any wetter, but he could feel his boots filling up. At last, the door of the first car opened and a porter helped an old woman step out. John nodded at the porter and held out his elbow, positioning the umbrella over the woman. She took John's elbow and he led her into the dry station.

"Oh, my, but it's vicious out there," the woman said when John had shaken out the umbrella and propped it against the wall near the stove. "That's some storm."

"Yes, ma'am," John said. "It seems to be hovering right over the town."

"How strange."

"We're used to strange things here in Riddle." He pulled out a chair and took her handbag from her, setting it on his desk. "What brings you to our town?"

"Thank you, sir," the woman said. She sat and arranged her skirts. "That was quite a journey, and it was undertaken in a rush. I feel positively overwhelmed."

"Let me get you a cup of tea," John said. "Or would you like something stronger?"

"I'd take a whiskey, if you've got it."

John got a bottle from his desk drawer and showed it to her for her approval. She nodded, and he poured three fingers into a clean glass from the shelf above the stove. She took it in both hands, sipped, and smiled.

"That hits the spot. Now, I hope you can help me. I've come to take my daughter home. Her name is Rose Mullins."

CHAPTER 4

Rose drifted in and out of consciousness. She felt insects creeping along her skin, and a scattering of raindrops on her face. She heard the rustle of leaves, and smelled smoke wafting on a cool breeze. She dreamed that a black bear found her in the field of corn and sniffed at her, its wet nose raising goosebumps on her throat.

When she woke she was lying on a daybed in a cozy room. Rain lashed at the shutters, and wind whistled beneath the eaves. The pain in her stomach was tolerable. She raised her head and saw a woman sitting across from her on a cushioned chair, reading a book and sipping from a mug. The woman looked up at Rose, and used a ribbon to mark her place before setting the book on a low table beside her.

"Rabbit," Rose said. "Where's Rabbit?"

"Are you hungry? I've got a mushroom stew on the stove."

"No, Rabbit is . . . there was a child traveling with me. A little girl." Rose sat up and swung her legs over the edge of the bed. Her boots were gone, and the floor was cool against her bare feet. "Where am I?"

The woman stood and left the room. She wore a billowing shawl, and her red hair hung loose around her shoulders. She returned a moment later carrying a tray with a teapot and tongs, a porcelain mug, and a variety of little pots with lids. She set it down at the end of the daybed.

"You're a guest in my home," she said. "Call me Sadie."

"You're her," Rose said. "The witch of Burden County."

"No," Sadie said. "I'm not 'of' anywhere, and I'm moving on from here anyway. I wanted to meet you first, Rose." She picked up the tongs. "Would you like one lump or two?"

"Meet me? Why me?"

"I'm curious about all of you in that strange group from Monmouth. But you were the only one I found conveniently asleep in a cornfield, so I'll talk to you first. You didn't say how many lumps you'd like."

"Thank you, I don't take sugar."

"This isn't sugar. I'll give you two."

Sadie opened one of the little pots and fished out two dripping brown globs, which she dropped into one of the mugs. She stirred the contents and handed it to Rose.

"What is this?"

"Drink it. Why were you sleeping in a field?"

"I was looking for Rabbit."

Sadie narrowed her eyes. "You say there was a girl traveling with you, but I watched you and I'm not aware of any child."

"You watched me?"

"Of course. You came to kill me, didn't you?"

"Tom was the one who wanted to kill you. The others . . . we had our own reasons for making the journey, but I don't think any of us wants to hurt you."

"Which one of you is Tom?"

"He's gone now. There were ghouls. They used a cleaver on him."

"Oh, yes," Sadie said. "You met the Benders. I'm surprised they only got one of you."

Rose glanced at the shuttered windows, and at the door on the far side of the room. To get to the door, she would have to pass the witch. While she considered her options Sadie quietly watched her, a smile playing at the corners of her lips. Even in the dim glow of the lantern, Rose could see that the witch was lovely. Her nose was slightly crooked and her eyes a bit too large for her face, but the faint lines that bracketed her mouth and the corners of her eyes lent her an air of kindness and intelligence.

Sudden pain arced through Rose's body like lightning and doubled her over. It passed quickly, leaving a tingle in her fingers. When she sat back up the witch was standing beside the bed. Sadie put a hand on Rose's back and took the mug from her, lifting it to Rose's lips.

"Drink," she said. "I promise it's not poison."

She tipped the mug and Rose let the warm liquid trickle down her throat. It tasted like honey and lavender.

"What is it?"

Sadie was already back in her chair, one leg curled under her. She brushed a strand of hair behind her left ear. "I can smell arsenic on you," she said. "Keep drinking. That tea will leach the poison from your body."

"Why would you want to help me?"

Sadie shrugged. "Why wouldn't I? Didn't you say you wish me no harm?"

Rose took another sip. Over the rim of the cup, she gazed around at the potted plants, the shelves of books, the weather-beaten table in the corner that was cluttered with bottles and jars.

"You live here by yourself?" Rose said. "Without anyone?"

"It suits me."

It had never occurred to Rose that she could choose to live alone.

"What are you reading?" she said.

Sadie glanced at the book next to her. *"Malleus Maleficarum,"* she said. *"The Hammer of Witches*. It's not got much of a plot. Do you read?"

"I love books."

"This one's filled with recipes for killing witches," Sadie said.

"Why would you want to read that?"

"Know thine enemy." Sadie shrugged. "I took it from a man who came to kill me. He probably wasn't much different from your friend Tom. I'm curious, would you have shared in the bounty if your friend Tom had piled rocks on my chest until I couldn't breathe?"

"I wanted no part of that bounty."

"You're a bit of a mystery, Rose. You say you love books and you don't want money. You don't intend anyone harm, and yet someone has slowly poisoned you over the course of many years. Why is that?"

There was the sound of a distant explosion and the house shook. The jars on the table clinked together, and a sprinkle of plaster dust drifted from the ceiling.

"What was that?" Rose said.

"Someone else is coming to kill me, and they've tripped one of my alarms. People have been coming from all over."

"We weren't the first?"

"Hardly," Sadie said. "Some have come from much farther than Monmouth."

"I'm from Philadelphia. Originally, I mean."

"Why did you leave?"

"I wasn't wanted there," Rose said.

"But someone wanted you here? Was it Tom?"

"No!"

"I didn't think so. You don't strike me as a witch-master's apprentice. I take you for either a farmer's wife or a schoolteacher."

Rose blushed. "Must I be one or the other?"

"There aren't many prospects for a woman around here. It's mostly whores, wives, and schoolteachers. You're no whore."

"I was a schoolteacher, then I was a farmer's wife."

"And what are you now?"

"You make it all sound so . . ."

"I don't mean to be cruel," Sadie said. "Like I say, there aren't many prospects."

"Oh, I don't know what I am, or what I'm doing. My husband died and I went with the others to safeguard the child, but now I've lost her. She's out there somewhere."

"Whose child is she?"

"I'm not sure it's my place to say," Rose said.

Sadie stirred the liquid in her mug and laid the wet spoon atop *The Hammer of Witches*. She stared into the mug, deep in thought. Rose looked around for her boots, but didn't see them. After a moment, Sadie looked up again and frowned at Rose.

"Your husband," she said. "What was his name?"

"Joe Mullins. I saw him when we reached Burden County. I know what it means to see a spirit."

"What does it mean?"

"That I'm dying."

"Do you see his spirit now?"

Rose shook her head.

"Did you bring Joe's body with you?"

"Why would I do a thing like that?"

"Spirits remain with their bodies unless someone frees them, and I don't think your witch-master Tom was powerful enough to do that. I saw something following you that might have been a spirit, but I don't understand how that could be. There's a red cloud obscuring things. Is it possible—"

She was interrupted by a knock at her front door. Sadie set her cup down and crossed the room.

"Who's there?"

Rose heard a muffled voice from the other side of the door. Sadie hesitated before turning the knob and swinging the door open. A young man hurtled headlong into the room. He was soaking wet and his eyes were wide with panic.

"Umbunnies umming."

"Hello, Walt," Sadie said. "Try saying that again." She held out her hand and the young man spat a penny into it.

"Somebody's coming," he said. "There's somebody at the ranch, but he's not a real man."

"What is he?" Rose said.

The boy looked at her, startled. He evidently hadn't expected Sadie to have company. He realized he was wearing his hat inside the house, and removed it.

"It's a devil," he said. "A devil's on its way here, Miss Grace."

"I know," Sadie said. "I've got traps all around, but they haven't slowed him down." She pointed to the back of the house. "Go dry yourself off, Walt. You'll catch your death."

Walt nodded before rushing off through a narrow doorway.

"He's a good boy," Sadie said. "Plans to marry Ruth Cookson."

"What he said . . . A devil's coming here?"

"A minor devil, and we have some time yet before he arrives."

"But Rabbit's still out there," Rose said. "You have to help me find her."

"You still haven't told me whose child she is, Rose Nettles, or why you brought her here."

Rose swallowed the dregs in her mug. The liquid had grown cold and taken on a musty flavor. Her eyelids grew heavy and she fought to stay awake.

"I think it's the other way around," she said. "I think Rabbit brought me here."

CHAPTER 5

The road to Riddle curved around a deep gully that added an hour to Moses's journey. He kept his Appaloosa trotting along at a good pace, and let his mind wander. He had no desire to continue up that particular road, but he needed to see the journey to its end. There had been five of them at the start of their expedition—six, if Ned was to be believed about the ghost of Rose Nettles's husband—and they had gained and lost people along the way. But now there was only Moses, and his feeling was that all the hardship and loss had to mean something. If he turned back or took another path, none of it would have mattered, least of all Ned's death.

Moses would find Rose and Rabbit. He would see that they were safe or he would bury them, then he would ride up to the witch's house and he would say hello. Maybe he would tell her why he had come, if he could figure that out for himself. Maybe he would tell her about Ned and the others, and everything that had happened. Or maybe he would just introduce himself and ask her name.

When his curiosity was satisfied, he would ride away from Burden County, and he would do his best to forget he had ever heard of such a place.

The road ended south of Riddle in a jumble of rock and sod, as if the earth had shifted, creating sheer bluffs and basins. Moses led the Appaloosa around and down into a crater. He found a natural path back up the other side and dismounted, leading his horse by her reins up the narrow trail. Coming up out of the ground, he heard crackling flames before he saw them.

The pastureland around Riddle was an inferno, the grass burned black, threaded with veins of red and orange fire; trees and bushes blazed. He could feel the heat of it wicking away the sweat on his face, drying his eyeballs in their sockets. He picked a path through the flames, leading the nervous horse.

At the other side of the burning grassland, he mounted the Appaloosa and spurred her on. The road resumed after a few yards, and Moses looked back at the ruined landscape.

"Be glad we weren't here when this happened," he said to the horse.

Rain hung like a curtain at the outskirts of the town, and he pushed the horse into it. The storm came so hard that it stung his cheeks and flattened the crown of his hat. He dug in his heels, struggling to keep the Appaloosa moving forward, wind threatening to tear him out of the saddle.

The street through town was deserted, the dark shapes of squat square buildings looming up on every side, with only an occasional candle in a window to prove that people still lived there.

When he drew even with the town's general store, he saw a man standing under the overhang, out of the rain. Moses waved at him and the man waved back. An old woman stood in the open door behind him. Moses dismounted and tethered the Appaloosa to a post, then ascended the steps and introduced himself. The man was John Riddle and the woman was Mrs Giles Bradshaw.

"What happened to your town?" Moses said.

John shook his head. "I'd advise you to turn back, friend. This is a dangerous place to be right now."

"I'm looking for a woman who might be traveling with a girl. Her name's Rose."

"Rose?" Mrs Bradshaw said. "It wouldn't be Rose Mullins, would it?"

"She calls herself Nettles now."

"That's my daughter."

"I don't know about her," John said. "But an old man and a girl came through here a short while before you. There were two strange men following them. Then all hell broke loose."

"The old man . . . he have a long gray beard?"

"You know him?"

"Not really," Moses said. "Calls himself Jacob."

"I guess Sadie set some traps, but they didn't stop him."

"Do you know where they went?"

John pointed north and Moses sighed. "Of course they went north. It's always north."

"Like I say, you'd be wise to turn back," John said.

"Do you think Rose is here?" Mrs Bradshaw said.

"I hope not, ma'am."

Moses nodded at John Riddle, and tipped his hat to Mrs Bradshaw. Her dress was so new and clean he thought she must have come from someplace fine. She was used to better things, and he wondered how she must feel to be standing in the rain in Burden County.

"I guess I'll keep going," he said.

"If you find Rose, tell her I'm here," Mrs Bradshaw said. "Tell her I came for her."

Moses left the Appaloosa where she was tethered and walked on up the road. Mud sucked at his boots, and the hems of his trousers grew heavy; his wet clothing stuck to his skin.

The buildings in Riddle were as cramped and crowded as those in most other towns Moses had seen. The saloon had a sign depicting the bloody stump of a finger.

Moses thought about Ned's body laying in a coffin down in

Buckridge. He thought about getting out of the rain, stopping in at the saloon and having a drink, but he pressed on.

If he ever met up with Ned again, his friend would want to hear the end of the story.

Moses reached the edge of Riddle without seeing any sign of Jacob Skinner, Rose Nettles, or Rabbit. He kept walking.

Rainwater soaked his eyebrows and ran into his eyes. Dead cornfields huddled around him, brown and stumpy against the gray-green horizon.

As the road left town it became a narrow path through the prairie. He saw a single tall tree in the middle of a wide field, like a signpost. Beneath the tree a man in a purple coat stood with his arms out. The Huntsman hovered in the air above him, the old man's legs kicking uselessly, his fingers clutching at his throat. Rabbit was perched on a high branch of the tree above them, and she raised her eyes to watch Moses as he approached.

Moses didn't recognize the man in the purple coat, but he recognized his laughter, barely audible over the sounds of the storm. Moses remembered dangling in the air while the life was choked out of him. He remembered Rigby's high-pitched cackle.

Moses drew his revolver and took aim.

CHAPTER 6

When Bill Cassidy was four years old he wandered into a rattlesnake nest. It was his first memory. He remembered the snakes coiling and hissing at him, their tails vibrating so fast they were a blur. He remembered his father and his older brother yelling at him from the other side of a dry creek bed, and he remembered his mother crying and making the sign of the cross.

It was the most terrifying thing Bill had experienced, until the day he followed Charlie Gamble up from the Paradise Ranch and into Riddle.

Bill didn't want to follow Charlie. His legs moved of their own accord, no matter how he tried to stop or turn the other way. Charlie rode on, and Bill had no choice but to follow. His arm throbbed with pain where Johnny Bart had shot him, but the bleeding had already stopped.

He supposed that didn't matter, though. He was certain Charlie would kill him, as he had killed all of Bill's friends at the ranch. He hoped it would be less painful than burning up in a sealed mess hall. He hoped his severed head wouldn't decorate Charlie's saddle alongside Teddy Paradis's.

They stopped outside town, where there was a chasm surrounded by craters and massive slabs of rock. The landscape was on fire, and beyond it raged the fiercest weather Bill had ever seen. He thought maybe he was already dead and had gone to hell. He began to cry.

"Oh, stop," Charlie said. "It looks like someone's been here before us and got the worst of it. The witch spun a wicked web around her territory, but someone walked right on through, didn't they? Still, we ought to take precautions. Do you know what insurance is?"

He put his hand up to his face and belched, and a shiny black toad tumbled out onto his palm. He held the toad out to Bill.

"Put it in your breast pocket."

"What will it do?"

"Not to worry. It'll know what to do when the time comes."

Bill tried not to take the toad, but he raised his arm and the toad hopped into his hand. It crawled up his arm and into his pocket. He felt it turn around and settle its gentle weight against his chest.

"Will it kill me?" he said.

Charlie laughed. He spurred his dead horse and led Bill down into the crater, across and up the other side. It felt like he was tethered to the demon. He stumbled and was yanked to his feet by something he couldn't see. Charlie rode straight through the wall of fire as if it weren't there. Or as if he came from someplace where everything was always on fire.

The flames burned, and Bill thought for a moment he was going to suffer the same fate as the other ranch hands who had been burned alive by Charlie Gamble. But then he was through, and his skin was beet red, but it didn't hurt as much as he'd expected. While he was puzzling that out, they plunged directly into the storm. Bill's hot clothes steamed and crackled. The toad squirmed in his pocket and Bill retched, but nothing came up.

He trudged behind Charlie's horse, slipping and stumbling in the mud. The town was eerily quiet and empty. Charlie stopped outside the general store. There was a light on, and faint piano music wafted out at them under the sound of pounding rain. Charlie leaned back in the saddle, spread his arms wide, and shouted at the storm.

"This place is mine now! You all belong to me! I'm going to kill your witch and take your bounty and take the power in your soil! Wait for me! I'll be back!"

The piano music stopped. Charlie laughed again and the horse lurched ahead as if he had snapped the reins. Bill followed.

Beyond Riddle they came upon a wide field. A big ash tree was visible through the gray sheet of rain. Charlie stopped again and sniffed the air.

"That's your tree, isn't it, witch? Are you up there or are you in your house? Why can't I tell?"

He led the way across the pasture. The footing was difficult and uneven. Bill stepped in a hole and fell. Before he could get back on his feet he was dragged across the grass at the same pace as the horse.

An old man stood under the tree, and a little girl sat on a branch above him.

"You're looking for her, too," Charlie said to the old man. "The witch."

"Not like you're looking for her," the man said. "I know what you are."

"I know what you are, too," Charlie said. "But I'm older and stronger than you."

The old man suddenly had a long knife in his hand and was already in mid-leap, a leap so long and so high that Bill didn't think a human being could manage it. But Charlie gestured and the man stopped in midair. Charlie raised an arm and the old man rose up into the branches of the tree. The man's legs kicked and he grabbed his throat, but Charlie only laughed. He kept his arm in the air while he swung one leg over the saddle and slid down from the horse. The old man spat and struggled, and hung on to his knife, but it was clear to Bill that his efforts were useless.

Bill heard a crack of thunder, but it didn't build the way thunder usually did. Charlie jerked forward. Black blood spattered out across the grass and was pounded away by the rain. Bill turned and saw a black man wearing a derby. The man fired again and Charlie's head exploded in a fountain of gore. The old man fell to the ground, and Bill realized he could move on his own. He turned to run, and slipped, falling face-first in the wet grass. He rolled over, relieved to finally be free.

The black toad was perched on his chin. Bill watched, wide-eyed and frozen, as the toad crawled up and into his mouth.

He heard a rattling sound in his skull, and his last thought was of his mother crying.

CHAPTER 7

Rose was sleeping again on the daybed, with another cup of strong tea on the table beside her. The farmer's widow was snoring and Sadie no longer smelled arsenic on her breath. Walt Traeger offered to look after the sick woman, and Sadie left him there. She quietly latched the door behind her before opening her umbrella. The sky was the exact color of the dead cornfields to the south and to the east, the rain coming harder, smudging the horizon.

At least, Sadie thought, the storm would help douse the fires south of town. Her traps and alarms had failed to stop a single creature from crossing the county line. Once she dealt with the intruders she would have to heal the ruined pastureland.

The one bright spot she could see to the bounty on her head was the collateral damage that had been done. Many of the ghouls in Quivira Falls had been dispatched; the cursed forest had burned; Teddy Paradis was dead, and so was the lazy sheriff in Buckridge; and all these changes had required very little nudging from her. She could leave Kansas without a single pang of guilt. The people of Burden County no longer needed her quite so much.

She would not miss many of them. She thought she could list on the fingers of one hand the people still loyal to her: John Riddle, Walt Traeger, Sarah Cookson and her family. Sadie smiled. She didn't have enough fingers after all to count the Cookson family. She was trying to remember all the boys' names when she found one of them beside the trail ahead of her, scooping up mud.

Willie Cookson looked up at her as she approached, and dropped the stick he was using to dig. He was covered in mud up to his elbows. His pup ran to greet her, tripping over her own out-sized paws and rolling over to let Sadie scratch her belly.

"I'm searching for buried treasure," Willie said. He stood and held out his hand so she could admire the spent bullet casing he had dug up.

"You're getting wet out here," Sadie said.

He shrugged. "I don't mind."

"You could catch your death."

"I have my dog Sadie to protect me." He knelt again and scratched the dog's ears. Her hind legs kicked reflexively and she lapped at his muddy arm.

"Here," Sadie said. She handed him the big umbrella with its heavy brass handle. He almost dropped it, and she had a sudden realization that he would use it to dig in the mud as soon as she had passed out of sight.

He handed the umbrella back to her and shook his head. "I'm already soaked," he said. "And Mama would be mad if I took your umbrella from you."

"Then go home, Willie. Go home out of the rain and take your family inside with you. Tell your mother to lock the doors and windows. This is not a good day to seek treasure."

"This is the best day for it because everything's soft and runny," he said. "It's easier to dig."

"Willie, there are dangerous people about, and I don't want to have to worry about you. Promise me you'll go home?"

He hesitated, but finally nodded. "I'll go home."

"Good." She stood and ran her fingers through his sopping hair. "You're a good boy."

She left him there, struggling to hang on to his wet wriggling dog. She had gone only a few steps before she turned around and hollered over the storm.

"Find a different name for that dog!"

CHAPTER 8

The devil's head was split open. Blood rippled down his shirtfront and spattered the strange purple cloak he wore. The Huntsman dropped to the ground and took a moment to catch his breath. He saw Moses Burke standing thirty yards away, gripping a Colt revolver. They nodded to each other and the Huntsman turned his attention to the devil's companion, his familiar. He looked like a cowboy, and his arm hung limp at his side, the sleeve of his shirt bloody and torn. The man tripped and fell, and something shiny and black crawled into his mouth.

The Huntsman didn't pause to think. He clenched his knife between his teeth and ran on all fours across the pasture. He leaped on the cowboy, felt his skin tingle, and knew the man with the toad in his belly was a devil now.

The Huntsman slid his sharp knife under the cowboy's jawbone, twisted the blade, and pulled his arm down in one swift motion. The man's eyes opened wide as his guts spilled out onto the grass. The Huntsman pulled out the cowboy's stomach and sliced through the warm membrane. He scooped out a handful of half-digested bacon and cheese. The dying cowboy clawed at him, but his fingers slipped off the Huntsman's wet skin. The Huntsman held the cowboy's stomach like a bag. He reached in again and found the wriggling toad, pulled it out and dropped it, then crushed it under his boot.

The cowboy curled up in a ball. His flesh tightened and his bones cracked as he shrank into himself, then he grew still and silent.

The Huntsman turned and watched the devil's corpse rise, his spirit forced back into Charlie Gamble's broken body.

Moses fired the revolver again, but this time Charlie was prepared. The bullet whipped around him and plunked into the trunk of the tree. Above him, Rabbit climbed to a higher branch. As the devil's head began to knit itself together he looked up into the tree and his face split in a wide grin.

"Rabbit!" Moses yelled, but the Huntsman was already running.

CHAPTER 9

The buzzing in Joe's head grew louder and more insistent as he walked. He had lost track of Rose in the field of corn, but was compelled by the hornet's buzz to keep moving. He walked through the rows—watched the corn go through its harvest, grow again, die, and rot—and he walked across a flat plain, covered with purple clover.

At last he reached a pasture with an ash tree that was tall and wide. It stood unchanged in Joe's eyes as the grass around it turned brown, then green again. A fierce storm blew around him, and that, too, remained, as if it were not a natural phenomenon of the changing seasons. He saw people in the field, and recognized Moses Burke and Jacob Skinner. He saw little Rabbit sitting on a branch high in the tree. But he didn't recognize the dead man on the ground, or the woman walking toward the tree, or the man with the purple robe and blood on his face who pointed up at Rabbit.

It was plain that the man in the purple robe posed a danger to Rabbit. Joe concentrated and everything grew still around him. The rain stopped in midair, the man in purple froze in place, the bullet stopped in the barrel of Moses's revolver. Even Jacob was motionless, caught mid-leap above the tall grass.

But Rabbit moved in the tree. She stood, holding on to the broad trunk, and smiled down at Joe. In his peripheral vision, Joe saw other movement, and he looked past the tree, across the field, to the road. The woman was still walking toward the tableau under the tree. She was carrying a sturdy umbrella with a brass handle, and she was astonishingly beautiful, he thought. She looked directly at Joe, and a curious expression played across her features.

He watched as she left the road and walked across the grass. She stopped in front of him and stuck out her hand, testing the air, then she lowered the umbrella and closed it.

"You must be Joe Mullins," she said.

Joe nodded.

"You can talk if you like," the woman said. "I can hear you."

It had been a long time since Joe had spoken to the living, and it took him a moment to find his voice.

"You'd be the witch of Burden County," he said.

"People keep calling me that," she said. "My name is Sadie."

"Who is he?" Joe said. He pointed at the man in purple.

"I don't know *who* he is," Sadie said. "But I know what he is, and I'm afraid he might have enough power to destroy a ghost."

Surprised, Joe stared at the man, and saw him move. He turned very slowly on his heels, and his expression was changing, his smile growing wider, his eyes rolling in Joe's direction. Joe could sense that he was losing control over the man.

"What should I do?" he said.

"I can think of two options," Sadie said. "Stand here and wait until he breaks free of your influence, or stop him."

"How?"

"I'm no spirit, but I know that once you're unstuck from the flow of time, there are things you can do to affect it. You're doing it now, but I think you can do more."

Joe remembered how he had entered the body of the sheriff in Buckridge, how he had changed the man's mind by sharing his life. Sadie put her hand on Joe's arm, and he was surprised that he could feel her touch.

"If you do this," she said, "it could be the end of you."

He smiled. "I'm already dead."

"He might take you with him to the infernal place he comes from."

Joe looked up at Rabbit. Sadie followed his gaze, and frowned.

"I didn't see you there," Sadie said. "How is it possible I didn't see you?"

Joe steeled himself and walked away from Sadie toward the tree. The man in the purple cloak had managed to turn completely around and was glaring at Joe. Joe could not remember when he had felt more afraid, but he had been heard and touched, and he decided that ought to be enough for a dead man.

The man in purple pointed at him and Joe floated up off the ground. He kept moving forward. The ground, he thought, was no more important to him than the air. He didn't need it in order to walk. He let everything else go, and focused on closing the gap between himself and the devil.

From the corner of Joe's eye, he saw the Huntsman resume his forward rush, and he saw a bullet exit the barrel of Moses's gun. But Joe reached Charlie Gamble first, and he kept going.

CHAPTER 10

Willie's pup sniffed the dead cowboy's body and squatted to pee on it. The man's eyes were open, staring up at the sickly sky. His guts were spread across the grass. Willie picked his puppy up and let her lick his chin. He had seen a dead man once before, lying in the road outside the saloon, but that was from a distance; his father had rushed him past and told him not to look. As far as Willie could recall, the dead man in front of the saloon had had his guts inside his body.

A black horse stood untethered a few feet away, and Willie could see that its throat was gaping open. Willie tightened his grip on the wriggling puppy and approached the horse. If it would let him get near, maybe he could lead it home. His mother might be able to stitch the wound, the way she had sewn up his brother David's thumb when he hit it with an axe. David still didn't have any feeling in that thumb, but it had healed so you could hardly see the scar.

The horse didn't move as Willie drew near. He touched its shoulder and its eyes rolled to look at him. Up close, Willie could see that the gash in its neck was much too deep for his mother to help. He could see bones beneath the skin and muscle.

There was a dark shape high on the saddle, and Willie stood on his tiptoes to get a better look. When he saw what it was he screamed and dropped the pup. She ran around his ankles and yipped at him until he picked her back up. He patted the horse's neck, though it hadn't moved when he screamed. He took another look at the thing on the saddle horn and verified that it was a human head. He touched it. It was firm and cold, like leftover porridge. When he pulled his hand away, the head came loose and fell. It thunked into the mud, face up, rainwater pouring into its open mouth.

Willie recognized the head as belonging to Mr Paradis, an old rancher his father didn't like. Willie clutched the puppy tight in his arms and looked around, half expecting a headless body to come staggering out of the mist.

He knelt and poked at Teddy Paradis's head again. It rolled on its side, and Willie jumped back up. He took a step back and bumped into the horse, shifting its blanket and saddle. He had been so interested in the head that he hadn't noticed the satchel tied to the saddlebag. He could read the words stenciled on its side: WELLS FARGO. He transferred the puppy to his other arm and worked at the clasp with wet fingers, thinking maybe there was another part of Mr Paradis inside the bag. Or maybe another head. He already had a good tale to tell his brothers, but two heads on a dead horse would make the story even better. The clasp came loose and he opened the flap. Inside were stacks of money banded together with paper strips. He took one of the bundles and stuffed it in his pocket, excited that he now had evidence to show his brothers.

When he turned around a girl was standing in the grass next to the dead horse.

The girl blinked at him and wiped a hank of wet hair out of her face. She was barefoot and he thought she wasn't much older than he was. He recognized the look on her face. It was the same look his sisters gave him when they thought he was being especially annoying. There was something familiar about her, in the set of her jaw and the way she stood.

"Who are you?" Willie said.

"Go home," the girl said. "It's not safe for you here."

The witch had said the same thing when she found him digging by the side of the road, and Willie realized who the girl reminded him of.

"How come I never saw you before?" he said.

The girl shook her head impatiently and held out her hand. A strong gust of wind whooshed across the grass and pushed Willie toward the narrow road behind him.

"Go home," the girl said again. Then she turned away and was gone, swallowed up by the storm.

Out across the field, lightning arced again and again, slashing across the sky and slamming into the ground. With each bolt came a rumble of thunder, louder than any Willie had heard before. His ears felt like they might burst, but in the brief interval between thunderclaps, he heard screams that carried over the sounds of the storm.

He knew the girl was right, that he should go home, but at home he would be pressed to complete his chores, and his brothers would tease him. Willie couldn't bring himself to leave the witch's pasture, where he had found a severed head, an undead horse, and a bag full of money. He was certain there was more intrigue and adventure to be had. He wrapped his arms firmly around his puppy and walked toward the lightning.

CHAPTER 11

Charlie Gamble felt another bullet smack against his skull. An instant later the wild man was on him, stabbing and slashing. The Huntsman drove him back against the ash tree, moving too swiftly for Charlie to react.

Dark clouds closed above him and a blue-white bolt of lightning shot through the top of his head and down through his body, pinning him to the spot. He smelled his own flesh burning.

There was a *thing* inside his head, a thing feeding him false memories of a mortal life on a little farm. His glorious birth in fire and blood was being replaced by fragmentary echoes of tilling fields and harvesting wheat, puffing on a pipe while he listened to a woman read to him. The thing in his head was erasing him, and his body was failing him.

He flung the wild man far across the pasture and out of sight, hoping for a few seconds to heal and think. The effort took more out of him than it should have. He belched, and felt his mouth fill, and spat a black shape into his hand. It was mangled and lifeless, and he threw it away in the grass.

Another bullet hit him in the thigh and he stumbled. The black cowboy was circling him at a distance, methodically firing at Charlie, wearing him down. The black man's body was strong, but Charlie wasn't close enough to take it over. He considered his options. The wild man and the witch had fierce protective magics. He might kill them, but he would never own their bodies. The girl they were protecting was another matter. Her body was young and strong, and she was still unskilled with magic.

But when he looked for her again in the tree she was gone.

Charlie scanned the terrain for the girl, and was surprised by another bolt of lightning that brought him to his knees. Green tendrils poked up through the soil, wrapping around his limbs, exploring his dead flesh for openings.

The witch stretched her arms wide to the storm and the air crackled with electricity. Charlie gestured and she burst into flames, liquid fire flowing across her limbs.

The rain extinguished the fire before it could harm her, but the witch was dazed. Charlie got to his feet and staggered forward. The wild man was returning already, a vague shape moving quickly through the storm. Charlie wasn't sure he was a man anymore; he looked like a dog.

He finally spotted the girl standing in the grass twenty yards from him. Charlie hadn't noticed her approach. He grinned and took another difficult step forward. Each of his legs felt like it weighed a thousand pounds; the thing inside him was still eating his memories. The girl held out her hand and the Huntsman stopped in his tracks. She lifted her other hand, and Charlie heard a train rumbling toward him.

He experienced a confusing moment as the horizon disappeared and the sky split apart. A bank of clouds twisted and dipped, then dipped again and a black funnel spiraled toward the ground.

Charlie lost his focus for a moment and the farmer-thing inside him took over. In that instant, Charlie understood what a tornado was and that he needed to look for a ditch or a gully in the field, but the farmer wouldn't let him. Charlie stood motionless, unable to run or even fall to the ground.

The tornado whirled and hopped above the prairie, following a twisted route. Moses was the first to react, backing toward the road. The Huntsman tried to pull Rabbit to safety, but she waved him away. He stood behind her, unwilling to leave, sheltering her in his arms. Sadie took a step toward her tree, then changed her mind and followed Moses. They both took cover in the gully beside the road as the tornado passed overhead. It jumped over them and hit the field, churning up soil and flinging stones.

The twister was charcoal against the smooth gray-green sky, and the noise it made drowned out every other sound. Charlie fought for control of his body and tried to alter the tornado's course, but it came on. He caused the air to catch fire around it, but it siphoned the flames into itself, whooshing and wheeling and crackling. The grass beneath it turned black as it came.

It reached the great ash tree in the middle of the field and hovered in place for a split second, the mass of the tree like an anchor. Then, with a horrible rending sound, the tree was pulled out of the ground, flinging mud the length and breadth of the pasture. It spun, its branches bending and breaking.

A twisted root skewered Charlie as the tree toppled and rolled beneath him. The sky opened again and lightning branched down, striking the tree. The massive ash groaned and shivered, then split in two down its length. Charlie was thrown free and he felt the spirit of the farmer leave him. He stood and laughed, and the air around him rippled with energy.

"Enough!" Rabbit shouted. She pointed at him and a spark flew from her finger.

Charlie Gamble exploded in a shower of gristle and shimmering black toads. Nobody there knew his name, but if Benito Cortez had finished the trip to Riddle, Kansas, he might have told them a little about Charlie. So might Sheriff Earl Hickman, though his knowledge had come secondhand.

The echoes of thunder faded, and as suddenly as it had appeared, the tornado retreated into the clouds. The rainfall became a gentle spring drizzle. Rabbit breathed a sigh of relief and turned her face to the sky, letting the rain cool her skin. Moses dragged himself out of the gulley and rolled over on his back, half certain that he was dead after all. He grinned at the Huntsman, who stared in wonder at the ruined pasture.

Sadie crawled over Moses and stood. Then she ran toward the charred crater where her tree had stood.

"The toads," she yelled. "You have to kill the toads!"

CHAPTER 12

Killing the demon was the hardest thing Rabbit had ever done. She wanted to lie down in the grass and sleep, but the witch was shouting about toads.

She looked and saw a puppy, fat and playful, snapping at tiny black shapes in the grass a few yards from her. The boy she had met at the edge of the field caught up to the little dog and dropped to his knees. Scooping the pup into his arms, he poked his finger into her mouth and flicked out a toad.

She watched as the wet black toad hopped up the boy's arm, over his chin, and into his mouth.

An instant later the Huntsman was there. He lifted the boy by his hair, dangling him over the wet ground, and pulled a knife from his belt. The boy dropped his puppy. He windmilled his legs and slapped at the Huntsman's arm. Rabbit turned her head and saw the witch running across the field. She shouted, but the Huntsman ignored her. He sliced through the air and the boy went limp. The Huntsman pulled the toad from the boy's mouth and crushed it in his fist.

The witch screamed and clapped her hands. The pasture shook, grass bent around her in a wide circle, and a bolt of lightning flew from the sky, striking the Huntsman between the eyes.

Rabbit's vision went white.

CHAPTER 13

The rain stopped as suddenly as it had begun. Sadie carried the boy's body, and Rabbit followed with the puppy in her arms. The little dog trembled, and Rabbit stroked her soft fur and whispered to her.

Before they reached the Cookson farm, they encountered Big Bill, out searching for his missing child. He took Willie's body without a word, and turned toward home. Sadie and Rabbit stood in the road and watched him go, then Sadie turned her face to the sky and spoke without looking at the girl next to her.

"I never knew I had a daughter," she said.

Rabbit scratched the puppy behind her ears and said nothing.

"No," Sadie said. "That's not entirely true. I don't remember anything from before. I woke up on the riverbank and a doctor told me I had carried a child. I just never . . ." She trailed off and was silent for a long moment.

"I guess I wasn't much older than you are," she finally said.

"I told that boy to go home," Rabbit said.

"I told him, too," Sadie said. "He made his choice."

"You didn't have to kill him," Rabbit said.

Sadie understood she wasn't talking about Willie Cookson. "I didn't kill him," she said. "When the lightning passed I looked for the Huntsman's body, but it was gone."

She thought it was possible he had dragged himself away to die, but she doubted it. Jacob Skinner, or whatever name he went by, was very hard to kill.

"I don't know your real name," she said to Rabbit.

"The man and his wife called me Girl. And Old Tom called me Rabbit because I was a Rabbit when he found me."

"Those are labels, not names."

Rabbit shrugged.

"Anyway, I'm glad to finally meet you," Sadie said.

"Can I stay?" Rabbit said.

"No," Sadie said. "At least, not here. But when I move on I won't stop you from following if you want. It's a free world for some."

Rabbit put her nose in the puppy's fur. When Sadie turned and headed for home Rabbit went with her.

CHAPTER 14

The little house with green shutters was busy all the next day. People came and went, and Sadie grew frustrated at times because she wanted to rest and think, and she wanted to talk to the girl who had come so far to find her.

Walt Traeger busied himself in Sadie's kitchen, making watercress sandwiches and lemonade. He set out a platter of cheese and bread and tiny sausages, but few of Sadie's visitors ate anything.

Rose woke with a sour taste in her mouth and a mild headache, but the pain in her abdomen had gone. She was delighted to see Rabbit, and she hugged the girl so hard that Rabbit could scarcely breathe. Rabbit's puppy squirmed in the small space between them. When it nipped at her arm, Rose released Rabbit and took a step back.

"Where are the others?" Rose said.

Rabbit shook her head. She had rarely spoken more than a dozen words at a time, not even when she had lived with the old man and his wife by the banks of the Arkansas River. There was too much to tell Rose, and she didn't know how to tell it.

"They're dead," she said at last.

"All of them? Ned, Moses, Benito? Even Jacob?"

"Not Moses," Rabbit said. "He's alive."

Roy Olin came to the house an hour after dawn, driving a wagon. In the back were four bodies, covered with blankets. Roy sat outside and waited until Sadie came out onto the porch.

"Deputy," she said. "What can I do for you?"

He tipped his hat. "I guess I'm not a deputy anymore, miss," he said. "Earl's dead . . ." He rubbed a hand over his face and sighed. "He's dead, so I guess that probably makes me sheriff."

"I see," Sadie said.

"Seems like the whole county had one hell of a time last night." He hooked a thumb over his shoulder at the four bundles in the back of the wagon. "I was trying to bring these boys back up to their ranch. Thought old Mr Paradis might bury 'em there, or at least tell their families where to find them. But, darn, Miss Grace, the ranch ain't hardly there no more. Most of the buildings are burnt to the ground."

"Was anyone left alive?"

Roy shook his head. "I never seen anything like it. I suppose I'll take these boys over to the cemetery. Gonna be a lot of fresh graves out there pretty soon."

"Do you have Wayne Traeger there?" Sadie pointed to the back of the wagon, and Roy nodded.

"Oh, poor Walt," she said. "He's lost his brother."

"Walt's alive?"

"He's in the house."

"He might be the only one left alive from that ranch."

"You'll find the body of Bill Cassidy in the pasture," Sadie said. "Would you see he gets a decent burial alongside his friends?"

Roy took off his hat and wiped his forehead. "What in Sam Hill happened, Miss Grace? Pardon my language."

"I stayed here too long, Mr Olin. I liked it here, but I should have moved on sooner. Bad things follow me."

Roy took a handkerchief from his vest pocket and blew his nose. He opened it and inspected the contents, then folded it back up and put it away. "I don't intend to be mean-spirited toward you," he said without looking up, "but Earl and me, we're different sorts of men. He could look the other way about things.

Me, I have trouble settling my mind. It might be good if there was less to worry about."

"I understand, Mr Olin."

"Thank you, miss."

He turned the wagon around on the narrow path, and Sadie went back inside. She broke the news to Walt Traeger that his brother had died in Buckridge.

"Wayne was always the sort to follow along with the other boys," he said. "He never listened much to me." Walt sat on the floor and the puppy climbed into his lap. "We always thought we might go out on our own and run some cattle or maybe some sheep. I don't know what I'm gonna do, now he's gone."

"I have a thought or two," Sadie said. But she decided to wait to discuss Wayne's future prospects. Later, perhaps, he might think about taking over the Paradise Ranch. And it occurred to her that Roy Olin would be looking for a new deputy. If Walt Traeger chose to remain in Burden County, he would have a fine future ahead of him.

When Sadie opened the door later in the morning, she found John Riddle standing on her porch with his hat in his hands. Next to him was a well-dressed woman whom he introduced as Mrs Giles Bradshaw.

Rose was overwhelmed to see her mother after so long a time. The two women rushed into each others' arms and wept. Sadie gave them a moment to themselves and escorted John Riddle out to his carriage. Rabbit followed. When they were alone, watching the carriage bounce away on the graded path, Rabbit asked, "Where will we go now?"

"We?" Sadie shook her head. "Sorry, it's going to take me some time to get used to this."

Rabbit shrugged.

"I don't know where we should go next," Sadie said. "Maybe we need a little help deciding."

She plucked a hair from her head and pulled it taut. It glowed red in the sunlight.

"Go ahead," she said to Rabbit.

Rabbit pulled out a brown hair. When she held it up between her hands, it flickered green and yellow.

"Now think about your question and let it go."

"That's all?"

"That's all," Sadie said. "The magic is in us and all around us, and if you ask the right question it will always provide an answer."

They released their grip at the same time and the two strands of hair floated away, intertwining as they rose into the air.

"East," Sadie said. "They're drifting east."

"And north," Rabbit said.

"True. I guess northeast is as good a direction as any."

"But that wasn't magic," Rabbit said. "That was the wind."

"What do you think magic is?"

When they rejoined Rose and her mother, Rose was almost vibrating with excitement.

"She's asked me to return home with her," Rose said. "To Philadelphia."

"My house is large and empty," her mother said. "And it echoes when I speak. I would very much like to have my daughter back."

Rose knelt in front of Rabbit and took her hands. "She said you can come with us. You could live in a big house, and go to a proper school, and take baths, and wear shoes. Would you like that?"

Rabbit bit her lower lip and looked up at Sadie, then shook her head.

"You should go," Sadie said. She tickled the puppy's ears. "Mrs Nettles knows about children. She can give you a better life than I could."

"Oh, no," Rose said. "We wouldn't dream of separating you now that you've found each other. And besides, I think I owe you my life. Would you let me return the favor?"

"You're both welcome to come with us," Mrs Bradshaw said. "There's more than enough room."

Sadie looked around at her plain but comfortable home, at her books and plants. She looked at the others, three people she had just met and knew little about. She had always made her own way in the world, and the idea of going away with Rose Nettles and her mother felt uncomfortable and frightening. But Rabbit was smiling up at her, and Sadie felt something she hadn't experienced before and didn't entirely understand. All she knew was that her life of solitude and independence was gone. It almost made her angry.

"Philadelphia," she muttered. "North and east."

"What was that, dear?" Mrs Bradshaw said.

Sadie cleared her throat. "Thank you," she said, with all the grace she could muster.

CHAPTER 15

Neither Rose nor Rabbit owned much of anything, and Sadie had already packed most of her things. Mrs Bradshaw had left her own bags at the train station, unsure of where she might be staying or when she might be leaving.

Sadie gave Walt Traeger her key to the front door.

"While you decide what to do with yourself, please water my plants," she said.

But there was one piece of unfinished business to deal with before the day was done.

"Rose," Sadie said. "Tell me something. Do you see your dead husband?"

"Your dead husband?" Mrs Bradshaw said. "Oh, dear."

"No," Rose said. "Do you see him?"

Sadie pointed to where Joe stood. He had positioned himself in a shadowy corner of the parlor and he held his pipe in his hands, clearly uncertain whether he ought to smoke it in the presence of so many women.

"I think you're fooling with me," Rose said. "Is he really here?"

"I suppose my tea did the trick," Sadie said. "Only the dying can see the dead."

"Ned saw him, too," Rose said.

"Ned died," Rabbit said.

Sadie pointed again at Joe. "This is a problem. He ought to be with his body."

"I made him follow me," Rabbit said. "I'm sorry."

"We need to send him back," Sadie said. "You should thank

him for his help before you release him. He nearly went to pieces when the demon did."

She frowned at Sadie. "If he goes home to his body, won't he be lonely? No one's there at his farm anymore."

"I don't know if spirits get lonely," Sadie said.

"Could he come with us?"

Mrs Bradshaw shuddered, and Sadie shook her head. "No," she said. "He should be with his body."

"I'll release him," Rabbit said.

"Wait," Sadie said. "I think we ought to give him something for his journey back."

She went to a table under the window and chose a dusty brown potted plant. She brought it out and set it on the floor.

"Dittany," Rabbit said.

"*Origanum dictamnus,*" Sadie said. "I assume it's what you used to sever the bond with his body?"

"But this plant is dead."

"So is Joe," Sadie said. "He ought to be able to carry a little of it with him."

Rabbit smiled. "Then let's show him how to use it."

CHAPTER 16

A small crowd had gathered at the station to see for themselves that the witch was leaving. Sadie looked for Sarah Cookson with a mixture of eagerness and dread, but Willie's mother had stayed home. Sadie wasn't sure what she might have said to Sarah if she'd had the chance. She couldn't think of anything that would help either of them feel better about what had happened. She had overstayed her welcome, and Willie had paid the price.

John Riddle saw the look on her face and misinterpreted it.

"You can always come back and visit the place," he said. "I'll still be here."

Sadie offered him a sad smile. "I hope you won't be, John," she said. "I hope someday you'll go someplace where there are lots of pianos and people line up for blocks to hear you play."

"Maybe I'll come visit you in Philadelphia," he said. "I'll bet they have a piano or two there."

"I'm sure they do."

Moses Burke had come to say goodbye to Rose and Rabbit.

"I have a puppy now," Rabbit told him. "She has to ride in a cage with the bags."

"What's her name?" Moses said.

"I don't know yet," she said. "It's a large decision to make."

"I'm not used to hearing your voice," he said. "I like it."

He tipped his hat to Rose. "Mrs Nettles," he said. "It was a pleasure making your acquaintance."

"I almost forgot," Rose said. She rummaged in her bag and

pulled out a long red scarf. "I knitted this for you, for when the cold weather comes."

He took it from her and wrapped it around his neck. "I'll cut a dashing figure with this," he said.

"I was knitting one for Mr Hemingway, too, but I never . . ." She broke off and Moses nodded.

Rabbit interrupted their awkward silence. "What's in that bag?"

Moses glanced at the Wells Fargo satchel tied to his saddle. "Found it in the field next to a dead horse. I don't figure it belongs to anybody at this point."

"You could return it to the bank," Rose said.

"I could," Moses said. "Or I could give my friend the fanciest damn funeral anybody's ever seen. I'll make up my mind about it pretty soon."

Mrs Bradshaw came to the edge of the platform and beckoned to them. "It's time to go," she said.

An excited murmur ran through the crowd and people began to move to one side or another. The hairs stood up on Moses's forearms, and Rabbit disappeared. Sadie heard a loud report and something whizzed past, slamming into the locomotive behind her. Andrew King, the aggrieved widower who had put a bounty on her head, pushed his way through the throng, aimed his revolver at Sadie's head, and pulled the trigger.

A bullet could be seen to freeze in midair. It trembled, then fell in a slow arc, thunking uselessly into the dirt at Sadie's feet. A split second later, there was another gunshot and a hole appeared in Andrew King's forehead. He dropped his gun and fell lifeless on the tracks.

Moses holstered his Colt.

"You shot him," Rose said.

"Thank you," Sadie said.

Rabbit was there again. She came to Moses and took his hand. "You have to go," she said.

"Someone's going to fetch Roy Olin pretty soon," Sadie said.

"All of you get on the train right now," Mrs Bradshaw said. "You too, Mr Burke."

"Thank you," he said. "But Ned Hemingway's waiting for me down in Buckridge, and neither of us has failed the other yet."

"Be safe, Mr Burke," Rose said. She kissed his cheek and he turned away.

"Always was."

Moses mounted his Appaloosa and turned her around. Without another look back, he rode through the crowd and out of Riddle. Nobody tried to stop him, and nobody moved to pick up the body of Andrew King.

He had not been well liked.

The two widows, the witch, and Rabbit Grace boarded the train. The crowd broke up in twos and threes, and left the station. There were chores to be done.

The locomotive built up steam and chugged away down the track, billowing smoke and cinders behind it.

Joe Mullins's body was wrapped in a yellow curtain under the roots of a sycamore tree down near the Oklahoma border, and it called to him. He could feel it in his nose, like a sneeze building. He walked away from the train station and headed south.

He met Willie Cookson sitting on a stone by the cemetery gate.

"You're a young'un," Joe said. "That's a shame."

"They told me to go home," Willie said. "The witch and the girl."

"They told me the same. I'm going home now."

There were many spirits milling about in the cemetery. They didn't look like fit company for a young boy, and Joe guessed the stone Willie sat on was as far from his body as he could get.

"I have a farmhouse down south," he said. "It's not much, but I like it pretty well."

Willie grinned at him and hopped up. Joe found the essence of dittany in his pocket and said the words Sadie Grace had taught him, then Willie left his body behind and they walked away together. The road was repaired, the fires extinguished, the blackened sod replaced with fresh green grass. The sky turned gray and snow fell, then the sun came up and butterflies fluttered by them.

They passed through Buckridge, and Joe said hello to Earl Hickman.

"I thought I might find Benito Cortez or Ned Hemingway here," Joe said.

"Oh, Ned was around for a while, but his friend come and took his body away. Ned went along with it."

Benito had not been seen since his burial.

"I guess he must've went on," Joe said. "You going to go on?"

"So far as I know, I got nobody waiting for me," Earl said. "Now that Roy's sheriff, I don't have a whole lot to do in a day except sit on the porch and watch people go by. I always have enjoyed that, and I believe I'll stick here awhile and enjoy it some more."

Joe and Willie left him there, and continued south. Day turned to night, and then to day again. Winter followed spring, and autumn led directly to summer, but Joe had grown used to the strange passage of time. He didn't feel the heat of summer or the cold of winter. He didn't get hungry or tired, or even bored. He just walked, and Willie was content to walk with him.

After some time, they came across Tom Goggins sitting on the stump of a dead tree.

"Well, hello," Tom said. "I swear you just left me here."

"It's been a little while," Joe said. He put his hand in his pocket and pressed the dead stems of dittany between his fingers, but he didn't say the words Sadie had taught him. After a moment he withdrew his hand from his pocket.

"Willie and me have got a long walk ahead of us," he said. "I hope you'll excuse us, Tom."

"Oh, that's fine," Tom said. "I've got plenty to do here. It's a big land, and someone's got to watch out for toads."

"There's no better man for the job," Joe said.

He tipped his hat and walked on. Willie followed. Soon it was night again, and almost instantly it was the following day, and they came across the remains of a child in the tall grass. A small pair of red shoes had been set neatly beside what was left of the body. Joe shuddered and took Willie's hand, and they moved on.

They encountered Madelyne Russell a mile on, standing beside the train tracks north of Quivira Falls. Joe counted four children standing with her. Winter had come again and the sky was gray.

"Hello, Miss Russell," he hollered when he was close enough to be heard.

"It's good to see you, Mr Mullins," she said.

"Have you lost some children?"

Madelyne pursed her lips and looked down at the boy next to her. He tucked his bible under his arm and took her hand. He stared at Willie, and Willie stared back at him.

"When they heard the train wasn't coming for them, they began to fade away, one at a time," Madelyne said. "These four are all that's left."

"But you didn't fade away with 'em," Joe said.

"As long as some of the children remain, I feel I must stay. I'm responsible for them, after all."

Joe nodded and sucked on his pipe. "I don't mean to be forward, Miss Russell, but I have a hundred-sixty acres down south from here. There's grass and trees, and bugs and critters. There's a nice little house I built myself. It seems to me it might be a better place for children than these rusty old train tracks."

Madelyne smiled, her neckline turning vivid pink in the sudden afternoon sunlight.

"That sounds very pleasant, Mr Mullins."

"You're welcome to come along with me and Willie. We're headed there now."

"I don't think we can."

"I might know a way."

"Would you like that, children?" Madelyne said.

Four heads bobbed, and four voices shouted, "Yes!"

"Then thank you very much, Mr Mullins," Madelyne said. "We would be glad to take you up on your kind offer."

"Please call me Joe," he said. He crushed a little of the dead dittany in his fingers and said the words he now knew by heart.

He offered his arm and she put her hand in the crook of his elbow, and they walked south, away from the train tracks. Willie fell in with the boy who still clutched his bible under his arm. The afternoon sunshine held.

They had been walking for some time, the children breaking away to chase one another, or to look at dead things by the side of the road, when Madelyne cleared her throat.

"I don't mean to be forward, Mr Mullins," she said, "but I wondered what became of your wife."

"She's gone ahead with her own life," he said, after a moment.

"I'm sorry."

"No need," Joe said. "I never did make her happy. I wanted a family, and I guess she didn't want my children, or to be with me. One night when she thought I was asleep I saw her put poison in her tea. I thought she was so unhappy that she was . . ."

"Oh, Mr Mullins. How awful."

"Well, that made me feel pretty sad, so the next morning I put some of that poison in a glass of milk and drank it down. I put a lot of that poison in there, to tell the truth. Later on, when I was under the sycamore tree, I got to figuring I made a mistake. I was so mixed up about losing her that I went and left her with nobody. I was glad when I got to follow her up north. Anyway, she seems happier now, and I don't guess she'll miss me now, if she ever did."

Madelyne reached out and touched his arm.

"None of that matters anymore," she said. "It's all in the past."

They soon came to the ranch, where dead men stood outside the bunkhouse, watching as living men tore the building down.

More men rode through the pasture, rounding up cattle and wild horses. Isaiah Foster sat watching the men at work. When he saw Joe coming, he waved.

"Hello, Joe," he said. "How long has it been?"

"I got no idea," Joe said. "Isaiah, this is Miss Madelyne Russell, and these are some children. I don't know all their names yet."

Isaiah introduced himself, and Joe listened carefully to the children's names as Madelyne called them, one by one, to shake the man's hand.

"Some men showed up this morning," Isaiah said, when he had greeted the children. "Might have been yesterday or last year. They're tearing down the bunkhouse, and airing out the main house, getting the horses all rounded up in the barn. They fixed the fence down yonder, and I expect they'll build another bunkhouse soon enough. Turn this into a working ranch again. Pretty soon it'll be like nothing bad ever happened here."

"It could be a good place," Joe said.

Isaiah sighed. "Maybe, but it's not where I'd choose to be."

Joe offered him the pipe. "Miss Russell and the kids and me are all headed down to my farm. We'd sure enjoy your company."

"Come with us, Mr Foster," Madelyne said.

Joe liked the way she said *us*.

Isaiah agreed, and so they all walked across the pasture together, Joe and Isaiah and Madelyne Russell, telling one another stories from their lives, and the children following at their own pace, taking time to spook the horses and hide behind cows.

An Indian stood at the tree line on the far side of the pasture, watching two red-winged blackbirds build a nest in a tall spruce. Joe recognized the man as a White Mountain Apache.

"Well, shoot," he said. "I didn't know Traveling Horse died."

Traveling Horse seemed pleased to see them, and nodded politely as Joe introduced him to Madelyne and Isaiah. Joe handed his pipe to the Apache.

"How did you come to be here?" Joe said.

"It was very strange," Traveling Horse said. "I crossed the great river into Texas and met two white men. I had ridden with one of them before, so I joined them for a time. But then they fell upon me and slaughtered me. They cooked and ate me as my spirit looked on. I could do nothing to stop them."

"That's horrifying," Madelyne said. Joe knew she had met a similar fate in Quivira Falls.

"It sounds like a disagreeable end, that's for sure," Joe said.

"After it happened, I journeyed, from here to there, and back, but I am unable to go farther north and I don't understand why."

Remembering that McDaniel had died at the ranch, and that Rigby's body had been destroyed there, Joe had a notion about why Traveling Horse was able to travel up through Texas and Oklahoma, but only halfway through Kansas, the route taken by the two villains. His idea was of an indelicate nature, though, and he decided not to share it. He had a great deal of respect for Traveling Horse and didn't care to insult him.

"We're all headed down to my farm," Joe said.

"I remember where it is," Traveling Horse said. He blew a plume of smoke and took another puff from Joe's pipe.

"Would you care to come along?"

"Thank you. I believe I will watch these birds finish their nest and lay their eggs. Then I will watch the white men catch their horses. Perhaps after that I will visit your farm."

"You're welcome anytime," Joe said.

They said goodbye, and Traveling Horse returned Joe's pipe. They left him there, watching the blackbirds flutter back and forth with twigs and bits of straw. Joe hoped he would see the

Apache again. Traveling Horse had met a great number of famous people and was an excellent storyteller.

Across a field of blue and yellow flowers they encountered a fence that stretched high overhead, and far in both directions. A jagged hole had been chopped through the center of the fence, and Isaiah stopped there.

"Maybe we should go around," he said. "This ain't a good place for children."

"This ain't a good place for nobody," Joe said. "But I can't think how it could hurt them now. They're already passed on."

"Most of these children have seen the worst the world has to offer," Madelyne said.

That settled the matter, and they walked on through the hole in the fence. The air was gray, and trees that had once stood tall were now blunt black poles jutting from the ashy soil. Men, women, and children wandered about, shrieking and moaning.

"Their bodies came down from the branches," a voice said.

Joe turned and saw the little girl he had met in the woods on his journey north.

"Hannah," he said. "What happened here?"

"Hello, Mr Mullins," the girl said. "The bodies that were on the ground burnt up, and some of the spirits faded away. Now everyone's confused and scared."

"Is there anything we can do to help?" Madelyne said.

"Thank you, ma'am, but I don't think so. Oh, Isaiah, you've come back!"

"Hi there, Miss Hannah. I believe I'm just passing through. My body ain't here no more."

"But how did it happen?" Joe said.

Mr James peeked around the scorched trunk of a pine and removed his hat.

"It was the Huntsman, Mr Mullins," he said.

"Hello, Mr James. I'm surprised the Huntsman would do this. He seems very particular in his actions."

"You know him then?" Mr James straightened up a bit, impressed, and fastened the top button of his shiny suit coat. "He's a frightening creature."

"He set us on fire for no reason," Hannah said. "I think he's a bad man."

"Well," Joe said, unwilling to commit one way or the other about the Huntsman's virtue. "Why don't you come with us?"

"Oh, yes," said one of the orphan girls, whose name Joe had been trying to remember since Madelyne mentioned it. "Do come with us."

"The more, the merrier," said a boy. He thumped the cover of his bible like a drum.

"I wish I could," Hannah said. "But I'm stuck in this old place."

"I don't think you are," Joe said. "I know a spell that frees spirits."

"Do you mean it?" Hannah said. "Wouldn't it be wonderful if we could leave, Mr James? How I hate these nasty old woods."

Mr James shook his head. "I believe I should stay. What I done to end up here was dreadful, and this is my penance. But what you did was noble in its way, Hannah, and well-intentioned, though not to be encouraged. You go on with these nice people."

They spent some time trying to persuade Mr James to leave the evil woods and travel south with them, but in the end he sat down on a smoking log and refused to listen to them anymore.

The little party moved reluctantly on, leaving the woods and passing through the second fence to another sunny field of flowers. Hannah's eyes were wide with wonder, staring around her at every butterfly, bee, and blooming dandelion she saw.

"I thought I would never leave there," she said.

Eventually—though it was hard to tell quite how long it took, since they passed through three winters, but only a single summer—they reached the crossroads outside Monmouth where the sycamore grew. Beyond it was the little farmhouse, just as Joe had left it.

A living family had moved into the house during his absence. Joe thought he recognized the man as Friendly Turtle, an Osage Indian from the Big Hill band. Friendly Turtle had found the old plow and was working to straighten out the rows in the field. He stopped working when his wife brought him food. She was carrying a baby in a sling, and Friendly Turtle kissed it on the forehead.

Joe was happy the house had found new people to live in it, and he discovered that if he didn't want to see the Indian family they simply weren't there for him, in the same way spirits were generally invisible to the living.

The two families lived side by side for more than a year, and neither paid much attention to the other until Friendly Turtle's youngest boy, who had just begun to walk, left the house one autumn afternoon and wandered out to the road. A hungry coyote had been circling the farmhouse for several days and nights, emboldened after stealing a chicken from Friendly Turtle's coop. Isaiah found the child's spirit at dusk. He gathered the boy up and whispered to him in a calming tone, though he knew the boy didn't understand his words.

Isaiah brought him to Joe and Madelyne. Joe sighed heavily and turned away to light his pipe, while Madelyne stroked the boy's soft hair.

"Poor Mr Turtle," Joe said. "And his wife, too."

They introduced the boy to the other children, who were delighted to have a new playmate, particularly someone so small they could hide him from one another in the roots of trees and beneath the chicken coop.

Friendly Turtle buried his son near the sycamore tree, unaware that Joe's body lay only a few feet away.

"It's a good spot for it," Joe said, watching as Friendly Turtle scooped dirt into the small grave.

Joe and Madelyne and Isaiah stayed for the short ceremony Friendly Turtle and his wife performed, then they walked up the hill and watched the children play.

"It's getting crowded here," Isaiah said.

"Seven kids to look after now," Joe said.

"There's plenty of room," Madelyne said. "And they aren't hard to look after."

"I always did want a big family."

Candlelight flickered in the windows of the farmhouse as the living went about their business. The ghostly laughter of children rolled across the gentle hills. Joe puffed on his pipe and blew a smoke ring. He watched it waft away, glowing orange in the light of the setting sun.

"I heard seven's a pretty lucky number," he said.

"It'll do for now," Madelyne said.

ACKNOWLEDGMENTS

I am, as always, indebted to my literary agent, Seth Fishman, and to everyone at The Gernert Company. And I am grateful to my editor, Kelly Lonesome, for her insightful suggestions and boundless enthusiasm, to Kristin Temple, to Michael Dudding and Valeria Castorena, to Alexis Saarela and Sarah Weeks, to Sarah Walker for her meticulous copyedits (if there's still a typo in this, it's because I accidentally added one at the last minute), and to everyone at Tor/Nightfire. To my early readers: Philip Grecian, Roxane White, Alison Clayton, Kacy Meinecke, Laura Lorson, Paul Fricke, Jeremy Lott, Lori Haun, and Dan and Kate Malmon.

And, of course, I am grateful to Christy and Graham for all the magic they bring to my life.